THE
BOOK
OF THE
UNWINDING

ALSO BY J.D. HORN

Witches of New Orleans

The King of Bones and Ashes
The Book of the Unwinding
The Final Days of Magic (forthcoming)

Witching Savannah

The Line
The Source
The Void
Jilo

Shivaree
Pretty Enough to Catch Her: A Short Story
A Peculiar Paradise: A Short Story
One Bad Apple: A Short Story
Pitch: A Short Story
Phantasma: Stories (contributor)

THE
BOOK
OF THE
UNWINDING

A WITCHES OF
NEW ORLEANS
NOVEL

J.D. HORN

Published by 47North, Seattle

www.apub.com

Amazon, the Amazon logo, and 47North are trademarks of Amazon.com, Inc., or its affiliates.

ISBN-13: 9781503901100 (hardcover)
ISBN-10: 1503901106 (hardcover)
ISBN-13: 9781503901094 (paperback)
ISBN-10: 1503901092 (paperback)

Cover design by Rex Bonomelli

Printed in the United States of America
First edition

For my darling Quincy, whose dedication comes years too soon.
Daddy loves you, little man.

CHARACTER LIST

THE MARIN FAMILY

Celestin Marin—Patriarch of the Marin family and deposed head of the Chanticleer Coven, once New Orleans's most powerful and influential coven. Celestin, intent on commanding the power promised in *The Book of the Unwinding*—a legendary grimoire that reveals the secrets of how to survive and prosper in the final days of magic—murdered his own son and grandson, and slaughtered many of the region's witches at the ball intended to memorialize him.

Laure Marin—Celestin's deceased wife. Obsessed with another woman's husband, Laure encouraged her rival to work a risky spell outside the auspices of the coven, claiming it would protect their children by suspending the dangerous *The Book of the Unwinding* between realities. The spell led to Laure's commitment to a psychiatric facility for witches and her rival's death. Laure is the mother of Nicholas, Vincent, and Fleur.

Nicholas Marin—Celestin and Laure's elder son. Nicholas challenged Celestin to become the head of the Chanticleer Coven, but he has now lost the coven and the one woman with whom he may have found love. Nicholas is the father of two sons: Luc and Hugo.

Astrid Andersen Marin—Nicholas's missing wife. Though Astrid is generally regarded as a fragile, artistic witch who used her magic to escape the Marin family intrigues, her surviving children have come to learn she may be working with Celestin to further his plot.

Luc Marin—Astrid and Nicholas's eldest child, and failed challenger to his father's position as head of the Chanticleers. Celestin murdered Luc as part of his plan to access the magic held in *The Book of the Unwinding*.

Hugo Marin—Astrid and Nicholas's younger son. Hugo has long relied on drink and drugs to mask his own sensitive nature.

Alice Marin—Raised to believe herself to be Astrid and Nicholas's daughter, Alice has learned that she's the product of an affair between Astrid and Celestin. Only recently released from a sanitarium for witches, Alice has once again been confined, this time on the Dreaming Road.

Vincent Marin—Celestin and Laure's middle child. Murdered by Celestin, who then assumed his identity. Vincent was blessed with a lack of magic that for a while allowed him to lead an independent life of his own choosing. Unmarried and childless, he long tried to act as a father figure for Nicholas's neglected children.

Fleur Marin Endicott—Celestin and Laure's youngest child. Celestin forced her into a marriage of convenience with a Washington up-and-comer, Warren Endicott. As that marriage comes to its dissolution, Fleur is determined to become her own woman. But after the slaughter of witches, she finds herself facing much greater challenges than building a new life.

Lucy Endicott—Like a millennial Mephistopheles, Fleur's outwardly superficial and undeniably spoiled teenage daughter feigns indifference, but always finds ways to improve the lives of those around her.

THE SIMEON—PERRAULT FAMILY

Soulange Simeon—The spell that led to Laure Marin's commitment also caused the death of this once great Voodoo practitioner. Bad blood has run between the families ever since Soulange was found dead and Laure wandering mad out on New Orleans's haunted Grunch Road. With her daughter Lisette's help, Soulange's spirit derailed Celestin's scheme at the slaughter of witches. Soulange was the original proprietor of the famous French Quarter Voodoo supply store, Vèvè.

Alcide Simeon—Soulange's husband, musician. Blames the Marin family for his wife's death.

Lisette Simeon Perrault—Soulange and Alcide's daughter, Lisette has run Vèvè since her mother's death. Following the slaughter of witches, Lisette has renewed her commitment to her mother's faith. Lisette doesn't realize that she may be the one person standing between New Orleans and those who would sacrifice the city.

Isadore Perrault—Lisette's husband and owner of one of New Orleans's premier landscaping companies. Although Isadore takes pride in having a true partnership with Lisette, he defers to her in matters of religion.

Manon Perrault—Lisette and Isadore's elder child, Manon is a no-nonsense self-starter who has recently completed her undergraduate degree in business.

Remy Perrault—Lisette and Isadore's teenage son. A visual artist, Remy has recently begun to attend college. Remy is involved with Lucy Endicott, a relationship both families tolerate, but neither celebrates.

The Witches of New Orleans

Evangeline Caissy—Stereotypes would imply that the solitary witch, a red-headed Cajun, is more temper than heart, but her past has taught her both patience and compassion. A former exotic dancer, Evangeline now runs her own Bourbon Street club, Bonnes Nouvelles. She finds herself at the center of machinations put in play centuries before her birth.

Mathilde, Margot, Marceline, and Mireille—The sister witches. Having arrived on the banks of the Mississippi before New Orleans became an American city, the four sister witches are New Orleans's first and oldest sorceresses. They are heartless, ruthless, and capable of changing form to meet their needs. Mireille, the youngest of the sister witches and Evangeline's mother, died after falling for a storefront church preacher and turning against magic. The surviving three acted as Celestin's accomplices at the slaughter of witches.

Delphine Brodeur—The sister witches' former servant, Delphine was brought to New Orleans at the age of thirteen, over two centuries ago. Her attempts to exact revenge on her former mistresses ended in her own gruesome death.

Frank Demagnan—The slight, though preternaturally strong, funeral director whose family has met the mortuary needs of the witches of New Orleans for as long as there have been witches in the Crescent City.

The Chanticleer Coven—Once dozens strong, at the time of the slaughter of witches, the moribund coven had dwindled to the Marin family and eight degraded witches: second in command, covetous **Gabriel Prosper** and his sister **Julia**, the vain and punctilious **Monsieur Jacques**, the steadfast and sturdy sergeant-at-arms **Jeanette**, the elderly and addled **Rose Gramont**, Rose's much younger self-appointed caretaker **Guillaume (Guy) Brunet**, and a brother and sister duo known as **"les Jumeaux"** or **"the Twins,"** who strive to function as a single, indivisible entity. Fleur Marin Endicott, who is attempting to rebuild the coven, believes the Twins to have been the sole survivors of the slaughter.

Nathalie Boudreau—Part-time chauffeur, full-time psychic, Nathalie has a sixth sense that lands her in situations her good sense would tell her to avoid.

Lincoln Boudreau—Nathalie's cousin. Charming and flirtatious, Lincoln is a street musician who has Evangeline Caissy in his sights. He also has a secret.

Washington (Wiley) Boudreau—Lincoln's younger brother and fellow performer. Hardheaded and passionate, Wiley shares his brother's secret.

Babau Jean—Also known as "John the Bogey," Babau Jean is New Orleans's own born and bred bogeyman. Go on. Turn out the lights. Face the mirror. Call his name three times. He'll see you.

ONE

Nathalie Boudreau knew better than to open that damned door.

Still, here she stood in the service entrance of Demagnan Mortuary, and the knob was turning.

She'd known better than to take the job as Frank Demagnan's assistant, too. She'd had a bad feeling about it from the second she'd arrived at the mortuary for the interview. That feeling had only sharpened when she shook hands with the slight man, her eyes fixating on the horseshoe mustache riding his upper lip, its lusterless blackness in sharp contrast to the pallor of his skin. Frank had handed her a man's black single-breasted suit coat with matching flat-front trousers and sent her off to the restroom to try them on. When she returned to his office, he had nodded with approval of the fit and offered her the job on the spot.

She should've said no. She should've thanked Frank for his time, given him back his suit, and called Isadore Perrault about the job he'd offered her with his landscaping company.

After all, the Perraults—Isadore and Lisette—seemed like nice people. Good people. But odd things had been happening around Nathalie, and to her, too, ever since the night she'd offered herself up as a *chwal* to the spirit of once renowned Voodoo queen Soulange Simeon, Lisette's mother. Having Soulange ride her, having all that power zip around inside her . . . well, it had kicked something loose in Nathalie.

Something Nathalie's own mama had always spoken of as "the shame." Something others called magic.

Nathalie hoped it was only a phase she was going through. She thought if she steered clear of Lisette and Vèvè, Lisette's Voodoo supply shop off Jackson Square, she might go back to the way she'd been before, that the switch Soulange flipped on might flip itself back off.

And so she'd accepted Frank's job offer. Oh, sure, she'd heard that little voice in the back of her mind chattering away and clanging cymbals like a windup toy monkey, but that hadn't stopped her. That little voice wasn't the one who had to pay rent and make groceries. The wages were the best she could find, almost as good as the security position she'd been let go from, and the bodies she handled were already bagged, if coming from the coroner, or boxed in a coffin, if headed to the cemetery.

Nathalie had been working for Frank for going on eight weeks now, but she still found herself waiting to exhale, her stomach knotting up whenever the man drew near. There were bits and pieces about Frank Demagnan that didn't fit. Like her eyes were hiding the truth about him instead of revealing it. She'd tried to pinpoint the source of her unease at least a hundred times, but she couldn't. It felt like there was something that caused her to gloss over inconsistencies, and the harder she tried to get a grasp on what was bothering her, the slipperier her grip became.

Still, a few odd things about him had begun to sink in.

For starters, his grip was too firm for his delicate hand. He was way too strong for his size. Nathalie stood a good six inches taller than him and outweighed him, she estimated, by maybe twenty pounds, but she doubted she could lift and shift two hundred pounds, give or take twenty, of could-not-be-deader weight. Still, Frank managed to wash and dress the embalmed bodies on his lonesome, and he alone lifted them into their caskets. She knew looks could be deceiving. She had a passel of male cousins, guys she used to wrestle until her mama made her stop, who didn't look like much dressed, but showed nothing but wiry muscle when stripped to the waist. Still, Nathalie couldn't shake the feeling that if Frank's shirt popped a button, he'd bleed out sawdust.

She never had to spend too much time around him, though. Almost like he sensed and maybe even sympathized with her discomfort, Frank tended to make himself scarce after giving her a to-do list. Nathalie mostly just drove bodies—and occasionally the bereaved—to and fro, so the work wasn't all that different from her part-time gig shuttling live passengers around town. The Demagnan clients were quieter, especially the dead ones, though she'd picked up one little old lady at the coroner's office who'd cajoled Nathalie into taking her on a tour of childhood memories. Nathalie had watched out of the corner of her eye as the old lady's spirit transformed into a vision of a young girl, dressed in a blue pinafore, with ribbons in her hair. The spirit placed a spiderweb kiss on Nathalie's cheek and flitted off to wherever she was bound. Most people would've lost it, but the nostalgic passenger was far from Nathalie's first ghost. She'd been seeing spirits since before she could understand there was any difference between them and regular folk.

Nathalie had always been able to see things, to know things that she shouldn't. That was how she knew something wrong—real wrong—had happened since she'd left the mortuary last night. But that wasn't the only thing worrying her. Her hand still hovered an inch over the knob when it twisted open, turned not by her fingers but by sparks of light that had shot from her fingertips and spun around the doorknob. Now *that* was something new.

Nathalie heard a soft click and the door eased open, its swing soundless.

"Well, damn," she said, feeling the dank air-conditioned coolness waft out and clutch her like a clammy hand.

The service entrance opened into the embalming room, an unlovely gray cell tacked onto the back side of the redbrick colonial. No doubt the embalming room had been state of the art when built, but Nathalie found herself eying the asbestos ceiling tiles every time she set foot in the place.

Nathalie poked her head in the room. "Mr. Demagnan?" There was silence except for the buzz of an overhead fluorescent fixture that bathed the room in cold white light. Nathalie dragged the heels of her wing tips as she stepped over the doorsill. "Frank?" she called out to her employer. She reached back to close the door behind her, but then thought better of it. Though she'd been in this room dozens of times, something told her she shouldn't venture too far inside without a ready exit. It was the kind of *something* she knew better than to ignore.

She'd been sweating outside on the ramp leading to the entrance; while it wasn't a record high, mideighties was still damn hot for gaining on Halloween. Still, not more than two steps into the room, the sweat between her shoulder blades turned into an icy trickle. Her first thought was that Frank must have turned the air-conditioning on full blast, but there was something different about this chill. Nathalie felt it slithering over her, caressing—no, tasting—her.

Nathalie crossed herself, an unconscious gesture, a catchall ward borrowed from the only kind of magic her mother could abide.

Her eyes scanned the room, darting from the empty embalming table to the aluminum mortuary cooler, the embalming room's sole contemporary piece of equipment, stationed in the far corner. All three of its doors hung open. The now empty center tray jutted out like a mocking tongue. Frank wouldn't have left it hanging open. He tended to be easygoing enough but was a stickler when it came to order.

Nathalie sidled up to the cooler, taking a quick peek into the upper—empty—and lower—also empty—compartments. While she'd dealt with spirits all her life, she'd never really dealt with the dead until she started here. She still hadn't moved past being creeped out by the work Frank did. Using the back of her hand, she pushed the center tray back into the cooler, then eased the compartment door closed until she heard its latch catch. She closed the bottom door next, casting a quick glance over her shoulder as she did so, certain she felt the weight of someone's stare.

The room was empty.

She reached back without looking to close the cooler's top drawer, then startled as she felt a finger trace down her hand and wrist.

At the same moment, as if by sympathetic magic, the embalming room's exterior door slammed shut. Nathalie jumped and faced the door, then advanced on it, ready to pry it off its hinges if the damned thing didn't open back up with a tug.

Music, a scratchy ragtime tune, began playing in the front part of the house. She stopped in her tracks and exhaled, laughing at herself. Frank was here. Probably upstairs in his private quarters. It was only the magic, the odd sparks and light, that had her spooked.

A heavy double-hinged door on the embalming room's northern wall separated it from the older, but nicer, part of the mortuary. On the door's reverse side was an "Employees Only" sign, its oversize, bold font intended to save mourners from any trauma they might experience if they were to discover the clinical horrors hidden within. Nathalie crossed the room and pressed the button beside the door, using the automated function more out of habit than necessity. Most times she passed through this door, she was either wheeling a body to the viewing room or heading in the opposite direction, back through the embalming room, to load one into the Demagnan hearse. A single click as it swung open and held itself in place, gaping before the dark hall that led deeper into the mortuary.

The cold fluorescent light of the embalming room stretched her shadow out long and thin before her, like a finger pointing toward the mortuary's heart. Nathalie patted the wall, feeling around for the hall's light switch. Her fingers brushed it, and the hall lit up. No spooks. No goblins. Only a hall she'd walked twenty times or so. Still, she hesitated at its mouth, once again struck by a sense of wrongness.

The music had been turned up even louder, and she could hear Frank shuffling about on the floor above, his footsteps heavier than she would've expected. She nodded, a confirmation to herself that she was going in, and—affecting confidence—took a few strides up to the open door of the viewing room. The overhead light was off, but the dim light filtering through the room's sole window, an oval bull's-eye window over the dais, showed it was empty.

The music stopped. The shuffling continued.

Nathalie advanced to the foot of the stairs. "Mr. Demagnan?" she called. "It's me. Nathalie."

No response.

The music started over. The same tinny piano playing the same plunky tune. She couldn't think of the song's name, or even pull a single lyric to mind, but the old bit of ragtime sounded familiar. A fuzzy recollection surfaced from her early childhood, a point where all her memories were golden, if blurry. This was a tune she'd heard played on a fiddle by someone from the shunned side of the Boudreau family—the relatives who made no objection to working magic.

"You all right up there?" she said. "I don't want to disturb you if you are." A thousand images of what Nathalie might confront if she surprised Frank when he thought himself to be alone flooded her mind, most of them involving the ghastly sight of his naked, too-pale flesh.

No answer. The music started over.

Maybe he had the recording on repeat. Maybe the heavy shuffling she'd heard was Frank up there, sick or injured, crawling across the floor rather than walking. Nathalie squared her shoulders and mounted the first few steps. "I'm coming up, Mr. Demagnan. I just want to check in on you." With no one around to witness it, she decided to let her extra sense scout ahead and prepare her for what her eyes might soon discover. She focused on a spot in front of her, envisioning a quarter-sized orb, silver and undulating like a ball of mercury. She blew on the orb and watched as it rose toward the landing.

A quick sharp sound, like the pop of frying bacon, and her head began reeling. She rocked back, dizzy, but somehow managed to catch hold of the railing and resist the urge to hurl. The music ended and the same song started up again. Another flash of memory, a bit sharper this time, of a smiling gray-haired man with wild eyes, working the bow across his fiddle till the bow's hairs smoked. She shook off the image and decided to turn back. Get out of here and find her cell phone, which she'd been charging with the hearse's cigarette lighter. Incongruous to the moment, the realization struck her that a person would have to be a hard-core smoker to light up in a hearse. She pushed the thought away. *Get out. Get the phone. Call emergency services and report a gas leak. Let the firemen find what they find.*

Something brushed up against her leg, and she nearly fell backward down the stairs she'd climbed.

A flash of gray fur passed her, then stopped at the topmost stair and turned back to look at her. A small cat with saucer-like green eyes. Nathalie realized it must have crept in while the outside door was open, and followed on her heels through the automatic doors. The cat yowled at her, and she had the strangest sense it was trying to communicate with her.

"You come on back down here," Nathalie said, keeping her voice low. The cat tilted its head and stared at her like she was an idiot. "Come on," she tried again, this time with a beckoning wave. The cat corkscrewed around on the step and advanced to the landing, disappearing from Nathalie's view.

Get out of here. Get to the hearse. Get to your phone. Call the fire department.

A chilling cry. The cat, afraid or maybe in pain. Nathalie cast a glance down the stairs, toward the hall that would lead her out of this place.

Another cry, this one heartrending. "Well damn," Nathalie said, and climbed the remaining steps to the landing.

Get the cat. Get out of here. Get to the hearse. Get to your phone. The music stopped, then started up again.

A fresh bowl of the lavender potpourri Frank had peppered all over the house rested on a walnut demilune table beneath the landing's window, but the cat was nowhere in sight. "Kitty?" Nathalie said, feeling foolish. If she were watching herself on screen, she'd be the first to scream, "Get out!" A mewling, weaker but more desperate, sounded from one of the rooms near the end of the long hall that bisected the upper floor. The next-to-last door on the left creaked open. Nathalie half expected to see a disgruntled Frank exiting the room, carrying the stray by its scruff, but the hall remained empty.

A pathetic keening pulled her down the hall to the open door. She bounded through the doorway, planning to throw herself on whomever— or whatever—was harming the poor cat, but other than the cat itself, the room stood empty. Nathalie scanned the space, trying to sense if there was something her eyes couldn't register. Being invisible, Nathalie had learned, did not equate with being absent.

The cat sat on a dark wood credenza, surrounded by framed photos, and contemplated her with a look of triumph in its eyes. Opposite the credenza, to Nathalie's right, sat a gray metal tanker desk like the one she remembered her first-grade teacher having. The two pieces of furniture seemed at odds with each other. A clicking sound coming from the direction of the facing windows caught her attention. An old-fashioned record player, housed in a wooden cabinet stained the same color as the cat's perch, stood between the windows. The record player's arm lifted and moved outward, dropping its needle back onto the black disc spinning on the turntable. Nathalie crossed to the player and snatched the needle off the record.

By instinct if not from memory, she knew to twist the volume knob to the left. The turntable slowed. She reached out and touched the record to stop it from spinning. Most of the label had peeled away from the disc, and what remained had faded, leaving only the words "Don't Scare Me Papa" legible. She noticed a switch on the record player offered three options: 78, 33, and 45 rpm. The first had been selected. The extra speeds told her that even though the player looked old, it was newer than the record. A reproduction.

A commanding chattering drew her eyes back to the tiny cat. Not much bigger than a kitten, really, but in possession of a lion's regal mien. Nathalie felt the feline will her forward, the animal's continued vocalizations so close to a spoken language, she found herself saying, "Pardon?"

Nathalie reached out to touch the cat, but it sidled backward, knocking over one of the frames as it did. The action appeared deliberate, so she kept her eyes on the cat as she picked up the frame. "Don't think you're not in trouble for tricking me into following you."

The cat responded with a flat and unimpressed-sounding meow. Nathalie looked down at the picture she held, expecting to see the pale, pinched face of a member of Frank's family, but it was instead the familiar portrait of a woman with a strong nose and high forehead, her dark hair parted down the center. Nathalie recognized the face in an instant, the Vieux Carré's infamous Madame LaLaurie. When the fire brigade had come to put out a kitchen fire in the LaLaurie mansion, they discovered a nightmare scenario of murder and twisted medical experiments. Stories about Madame's fate differed, but Nathalie had always hoped the woman had found herself a fitting one. The photo looked like one of the old postcards you used to be able to find anywhere in the Quarter. She returned the frame to its place on the credenza. Behind it sat a color newsprint photo that depicted an even more familiar face—a good-looking guy with a radiant smile and dimpled chin.

She'd actually met this guy, not long after Katrina, when she'd drifted back home to New Orleans from Natchitoches. Bars weren't as stringent about checking IDs in the months following the storm, so she'd had a few shots with him, even though she hadn't quite hit drinking age. He was a fixture in the French Quarter right up until the day he jumped to his death from the roof of his North Rampart Street apartment. After the police scooped him up, they discovered he'd killed and cooked his girlfriend before taking his deep dive.

Beside his photo sat an old daguerreotype showing two men sitting side by side. Their heads lay at unfeasible angles on their shoulders, the crowns touching. Nathalie caught herself tilting her own head, trying to touch her ear to her shoulder like the men in the photo. A neck didn't bend that far unless it had been broken. The men's eyes were open but—she leaned in to get a better look—held the glassy blankness of death. The inscription on the bottom of the picture's silver frame read "John and Wayne Carter." She'd always figured these guys were part of the city's folklore, like the fictitious sultan of the LaPrete mansion, but if her eyes were to be believed, the blood-drinking brothers had indeed lived, and they'd died just like the story claimed—at the end of a rope. Her eyes darted around the other photos collected there, picking out the black-and-white image of Lee Harvey Oswald.

She took a step back. There were twenty or so other photos crowded onto the credenza's top. The one thing the people portrayed in them shared was murder.

Front and center on the credenza was the collection's sole double frame, an ornate silver thing with a nymph holding a flower branch at its center. Scrollwork ran down each side and met at the bottom to create a platform beneath the nymph's feet. The image on the left was what appeared to be a somewhat recent photo of an older man with a thick mane of gray hair and piercing black eyes. She didn't recognize him, but she found herself wondering what he could've done to earn himself pride of place in Frank's murderers' row. The man exuded confidence and charisma. She found it hard to pull her eyes away, but when she did, she felt her heart flutter. The right side of the frame held a picture of the most beautiful woman Nathalie had ever seen. Any fear Nathalie had felt coming into Frank's quarters evaporated.

This woman's features struck Nathalie as familiar, too, but her memory was blurred, like they had met in a dream, or, far more likely, when Nathalie was two shots past tipsy. The photo seemed to be a candid shot, the woman's light brown eyes turned down and away from the camera. She'd been photographed running her fingers through her pixie-cut chestnut hair. Her eyes showed a vulnerability that made Nathalie eager to protect her, but she seemed to glow with a power that made her doubt the woman could need protection. The inclusion of her image in this gallery of monsters angered Nathalie—a powerful gut reaction she knew better than to doubt. Nathalie might have met this woman, or she hadn't, but she knew with absolute certainty her face didn't belong here among these murderers.

The cat wound its way through the maze of frames until it arrived beside the woman's photo. It rubbed its cheek against the frame's edge, then gazed up with a look of expectation in its eyes.

Nathalie brushed her fingers over the cat's head in acknowledgment. Unable to help herself, she lifted the frame and focused on the woman, the man to her left now forgotten. She began examining the picture in detail, trying to find any clues to the woman's identity. The lighting was poor, so she removed the photo from the frame and carried it to the window. A sliver of blue sky showed on the photo's upper left, a white stone wall in the background. No. It wasn't a wall. It was a tomb. An open tomb. She squinted to make out the name carved into the lintel: Marin.

And then it hit her. The night of the massacre, the night she'd offered herself up as *chwal* to Soulange Simeon. Her memories of that night, from the second Soulange had entered her until Nathalie came to outside the old church, her pant legs soaked to the knee with blood, were confused, fuzzy. Nathalie *had* seen the woman in the photo, only she'd seen her while Soulange was in the driver's seat. She picked through the jangled pieces where Soulange's thoughts had once intertwined with her own, surprised when she turned up a name. *Alice*. In the photo, this Alice looked like an innocent, but during the slaughter, she'd been standing on a stage, above the gore that had pooled all around.

Standing beside Babau Jean.

Nathalie had a flash from her childhood—the pale bogey with the bottomless black eyes, watching her from her closet mirror while she lay in bed, her sheet pulled up over her head, and dragging his sharp nails *rtch-rtch-rtch* down the glass.

The cat hissed like a hot pan doused with ice water.

Nathalie startled and dropped the photo to the floor. Something compelled her to snatch it up and slip it into the inner pocket of her suit coat. She turned her attention to the cat, then scanned the room, trying to figure out what had set it off.

She couldn't see anything, but she sure as hell felt something.

The cat stood and arched its back, fixing its own gaze on the hall. The shuffling sound Nathalie had heard from downstairs began again, this time punctuated by a click. The cat hissed and jumped, disappearing in midair. Nathalie staggered backward and then spun around, sure that it had been a trick of the light, and the cat was somewhere nearby.

In the hall, the sound of scraping followed by another thump, like something heavy being dragged and dropped. *Click.*

Scrape. Thump. Click. The sounds chased each other, gaining speed. *Scrape. Thump. Click.* The sounds grew louder, closer.

Nathalie's heart mimicked the accelerating rhythm, her eyes fixed on the doorway. A pale hand near floor level reached around the frame.

She started to advance, certain Frank must have fallen ill, then stopped in her tracks as her brain registered what her eyes were seeing.

It was Frank all right. She watched, horrified and sickened, as he dragged himself into the room.

First she saw the rough stitches around his wrist. Thick black yarn tied together an angry red gash, reconnecting his hand to his wrist, but the hand had been sewn onto the wrong wrist, the thumb pointing outward. His head and torso pulled into view, the same cruel stitching around his neck. His head pointed upward toward the ceiling, but so did his shoulder blades. Nathalie's rational mind insisted that he had to be dead, that nobody could survive such a gruesome alteration. *Scrape.* His right hand, attached to his left wrist, dragged a revolver along the wooden floor. He pushed into the room and then collapsed. *Thump.* The hand fumbled with the pistol, struggling to point its muzzle at his temple. *Click.* He strained to raise himself back up. Nathalie realized that his left and right legs had also been switched. Not only switched, but reattached at the thigh backward so that his feet pointed in the same direction as his chalky buttocks.

He pushed back again, this time falling to his side. His eyes met hers and widened—despite her shouting, he mustn't have realized he was no longer alone. His lips began working, but no sound came out. His chest pushed up, his right arm flailing out in a wide, wild circling gesture before he collapsed again. One by one, the fingers of the hand nearest the desk folded in toward the palm, leaving his index finger to point in the general direction of the desk. The hand rose and slapped against the floor, beating a desperate tattoo.

Nathalie reached out to try to read his thoughts, something she didn't often do, but whether blocked by his trauma or her own fear, she couldn't glean anything.

"The desk?" she said, surprised by her own restraint in not trampling over the sad body on her way to the door. The hand banged against the floor with even greater vehemence. She crossed to the desk, positioning herself so she could keep one eye on both Frank and the exit. The desk's surface was empty except for a red stapler and a dish of the horehound candy he was always sucking on whenever guests weren't present. Rejecting both as possibilities, she started tugging open the desk's top drawer.

Click. Click. Click.

She looked up over the desk at him. His hand had once again found the pistol and was pulling its trigger over and over. She knew then what he wanted. She riffled through the remaining drawers until she uncovered a box of .38-caliber bullets. She pulled out the handkerchief Frank had insisted she carry so she could offer it to any mourner in need and retrieved the box. Her DNA was bound to be all over the damned place, but that much she might be able to explain away. Her fingerprints on the bullet box would without a doubt be a bit harder to dance around. She may want to help him, but she sure didn't want to get caught up in the aftermath of his actions. She set the box on the desktop, closed the drawer, and then carried the wrapped box to his side. Kneeling beside him, she held the box up so he could see it. The relief in his eyes confirmed she'd understood correctly. He pushed up once more, grasping for the box and knocking it from her hand. The box tumbled to the floor and fell open, letting a handful of bullets slip out and roll toward the desk.

"It's all right," she said, trying to keep her voice calm. "I got this." Nathalie knew how to shoot. Hell, after learning from her grandmother, she'd turned around and taught the neighborhood boys. She used the handkerchief to take the gun from his hand, then aimed the muzzle at the floor and rested the butt of the gun on her knee. She could do this blindfolded. In the pitch dark. Still, her hands started shaking, and the layer of cloth between her fingers and the pistol almost allowed the gun to slip from her grasp. She bit her lip and concentrated, tightening her grip, then lifted a bullet. Not with her hand, but by looking at it and wanting it to move. The bullet jumped up and landed right in the cylinder.

In spite of everything, she'd managed to amaze Frank. She could see it in his widened eyes. In the way his hand, which had continued slapping the floor like a metronome, hurrying her movements along, fell silent. She closed the cylinder and placed the revolver in Frank's hand. His fingers grasped it like they were thirsty for it and his index found the trigger. His eyes met hers. Without a word, he asked one final favor. He raised the gun, and Nathalie took his hand between hers, helping him steady it as he aimed at his temple.

His finger squeezed the trigger.

TWO

Alice Marin's skin tingled. The air around her felt charged, electric. The sharp scent of City Park's freshly cut lawns permeated Popp Bandstand, where she sat, her back resting against one of the dome's pillars. Beneath the green note an air of ozone lingered.

She set the book she'd been reading, a novel she'd read a dozen times before, down beside her. Her eyes, following her instincts, drifted upward to the dome's ceiling—a pale aqua wheel within a wheel, split by spokes that divided the outer wheel into twelve equal segments, like the twelve houses of a blank astrological birth chart. Or like a clock, cataloging the endless march of time in this place.

She saw a spark, overhead at first, then drifting to eye level. It seemed like nothing more than a pinprick of light, but it began to grow or, more precisely, the space around it seemed to fold back. A window to the world she'd left was opening in the world she now knew. Soon that window would become a door—temporary and, for her, impassable.

"I knew I would find you here," Sabine's French-accented voice called to her. Alice glanced back to see her coming down the path, the sight of Sabine's smile driving away any thought of the spark and the world from which it came.

"Come on, you. Get a move on," Sabine said. "We're already late."

Alice paused, trying to remember what plans they had made, and how they could possibly be late. She came up empty. Where, really, was there for them to go? Still, she liked the thought that she'd gone off to read and lost track of the time. That she and Sabine had made plans together.

"Alice," Sabine called again, still smiling, but with a growing impatience in her voice. Alice pushed herself up and reached for her dog-eared paperback copy of *Frankenstein*.

A hand grabbed her shoulder. She turned, startled at first, but then remembered the scintillation that had caught but failed to hold her attention.

"Daniel," she said, taking in his broad smile and wholesome face. His red hair had grown a bit since she'd last seen him and was now a mass of unruly curls.

"How's my girl?" he said, pulling her into a tight bear hug. He smelled of petrichor and vanilla, of verbena and old books. The first scent came to him naturally. The vanilla, likely from some baking project. The verbena from the soap he favored. The old books, no doubt, from the time he'd been spending poring over arcane tomes, trying to find a way to release her from this world.

"How's my girl?" Alice heard the words echoed in Sabine's voice. She broke free of Daniel's embrace to look for Sabine, but she was gone.

Daniel didn't seem to have noticed her.

"The pewter terror sends her love," he said, speaking of her childhood pet. The first time Daniel had come to her, it had been Sugar who'd led him here. Daniel could pass between worlds because, as a servitor spirit who had been created primarily to care for Alice and her older brothers, he was made of magic itself, and that magic was bound to her. Sugar could cross the barrier because, well, she was a cat. It was no accident that witches and cats had come to associate with each other. "She wanted to come, but I wouldn't let her," he said. "The poor thing is slowing down, and it's too hard on her."

"Poor thing?" Alice said. "If I didn't know better, I'd say you were growing fond of her."

"Suffice it to say a good nemesis is hard to come by. I'm doing my best to keep the wretched beast alive and happy for as long as I can. Besides, I can't help but feel a bit of sympathy for her." He cocked an eyebrow and leaned in like he was about to share a delicious tidbit of gossip. "Evangeline seems to have come undone. She gave the cat up. After all these years. Turned the creature, litter box and all, over to Hugo. Sugar's back in the house with me, right where she . . ."

A group of children rushed by the bandstand, running, laughing, only to vanish into thin air.

"Oh, my," Daniel said, reaching out to take her hand. He seemed determined, desperate even, to maintain physical contact with her.

This is all illusion, she remembered as the truth reasserted itself. There was no true physical contact for her anymore. Not here on the Dreaming Road, where her biological father, Celestin Marin, had deposited her.

Celestin's ambition was to unlock the power of *The Book of the Unwinding* and become the witch who would capture the last breath of magic, the one who would recreate it in his image. That role would only be bestowed on a witch who lacked progeny, but Celestin was willing to sacrifice his entire line to ensure that he be the one. He'd already murdered her older brother Luc and her uncle Vincent—Alice still thought of Vincent that way despite having discovered Celestin, not Nicholas, was her biological father. At least Celestin had done the others the kindness of a clean kill, but she was his favorite child. He didn't have the heart—or was it the courage?—to murder her outright. Instead, he'd turned her own power in on her, creating an artificial world—a prison—on the astral plane for her psyche to inhabit. One day that prison would do what he couldn't. It would kill her, exhausting first her magic and then her life force.

And though it went unsaid, Alice knew Celestin still walked free in the common world, unpunished and unrepentant. The old spider was spinning a tightening web, fangs dripping the poison that sprang from his heart. Daniel wouldn't have held back news of Celestin's capture.

Alice's corporeal body, Daniel had told her on a previous visit, was back in New Orleans. Before absconding for parts unknown, Nicholas had signed his power of attorney over to Alice's aunt—no, she corrected herself, her sister—Fleur. Fleur had thought she might be better off in the care of professionals, but Daniel had put his foot down, insisting no clinic could provide more diligent care for her than he could, having been created to do so. After what Alice felt sure had been much cajoling, Fleur consented to return Alice to her old room in Nicholas's house, but only on the condition that Daniel agree to daily visits from a nurse. Alice loved Daniel all the more for wanting to care for her empty shell, but it really didn't matter where her physical form slept. She'd lost faith in ever returning to it.

The world in which she found herself wasn't completely cut off. Celestin had left an opening, something he could use to siphon power from her should he need to supplement his own, though she doubted he'd need to after feeding from the dozens of witches he slaughtered the night of his memorial ball.

Alice believed she wasn't the first Celestin had caught in such a trap. She suspected he might have drawn from dozens, maybe even hundreds, of witches over the years. Rumor had it that witches around New Orleans were taking to the Dreaming Road in greater numbers, preferring a life spent in dreams to reality. The decaying state of magic was widely held to be the reason, but Alice no longer believed the theory. Celestin, Alice suspected, had been behind many, if not most, of those disappearances. He wasn't the type to handle his own housekeeping;

though. He probably had a partner helping him dispose of the vacated bodies.

"How many?" Daniel said, giving her hand a light squeeze. "How many are here with you?"

"I don't know," Alice said, her claim both true and false at the same moment. She hoped he'd interpret her words to mean she hadn't played a conscious role in their creation. The truth was, she'd simply lost count.

His mouth pulled into a frown, and his head tilted back. He looked down his nose at her. Daniel had been created to see through her and her older brothers' dissimulations. Even here, even now, he could still sniff out a lie. "How long has this been going on?" His disappointed tone transported her back to her early childhood, to a time when Daniel towered over her, asking her why she'd thought it would be a good idea to glue Hugo's shoes to an antique Mohtashem Kashan rug.

"Not long," she said, rushing to add, "only since your last visit." Another hybrid of truth and lie.

"I see," he said, casting a glance at the bandstand's concrete steps. He crossed to them and sat down, then leaned over and wrapped his arms around his knees.

She reached down to retrieve her book before following him. As she drew near, he looked up at her. He straightened up and patted the open part of the step beside him. She joined him there.

He took the book from her hand and examined it. "I can identify with the monster," he said. "Abhorred and deserted by his maker. Driven to desperation by the primal loneliness of being separated from one's source." Daniel wrapped his arm around her shoulders and pulled her toward him. "Some people really stink at parenting, huh?" He gave her a quick hug, then released her.

"It's weird," she said, giving voice to a thought that might be better kept to herself, "but I believe in his own warped way, Celestin does love me." She looked for a reaction from Daniel, but his expression remained neutral. "He could've," she pressed on, "put me in a hell where my terror would've burned through my magic and drained my life force in one hot minute on the natural world's timescale." Daniel bit his lip. His gaze was fixed on his shoes. "Here on the Dreaming Road," she continued, intent, for reasons she herself couldn't grasp, on defending Celestin's actions, "he could've made sixty seconds seem like an eternity. Instead, he designed this realm for me—or at least for the child I was when he first attempted to draw me here—as a place where I'd be happy. So happy, in fact, that I'd never want to leave." She felt something click in her mind, and then she realized there it was, the reason she'd been looking for.

She knew this world, hanging somewhere in the astral plane, was a trap. It was slowly draining the life from her, just as Celestin intended it to, but there was no denying the appeal of a world that molded itself to her heart's desires. It was, without question, a better place to live than anywhere she'd spent her earthly days. Alice opened her mouth to speak, to tell Daniel that to some degree Celestin had succeeded in reaching his goal, but he spoke before she did.

"It'll be a moot point soon anyway. This," he said, clapping his hands, "isn't a mere social visit. I came bringing news." He paused and smiled at her, waiting, it seemed, for her to react as the child she'd been and beg him to share. After a few moments his face fell, reflecting his disappointment, it seemed, that she hadn't. Still, that gleam persisted in his eyes. "I believe we've made some progress."

"What kind of progress?"

"I've discovered gravity," he said, and winked.

"Gravity?"

"Yes, the gravity of rightful destiny." He held up his finger, a signal for her to have patience. "Like a river flowing between its banks, every person has a path they're born to follow. Celestin's repeated interference has pulled you from yours, but the whole universe is tugging on you, trying to pull you back in line."

"I don't believe in destiny."

"Okay, then," he said, brushing off her protest. "Don't think of it as destiny. Think of it as a natural trajectory." He glanced away. "Although," he muttered under his breath with every intent that she should hear him, "it's still destiny whether you want to believe in it or not." He shifted on the step, angling his body toward her. "I've uncovered your rightful trajectory," he said, crossing his arms and leaning back a bit. "Would you care to hear about it?"

"How?" she said, rising and turning on him, impatient with this fairy tale he was spinning. She suspected it was no more than another story, like the comforting ones he once used to lull her back to sleep after a nightmare. "How exactly did you do that?"

"I know a system," he said, sounding defensive.

"And what is this system?"

"It's one I created myself." He rose and rested his fists on his hips, a defiant posture. "It's a bit of a hybrid. It involves casting spells and rolling dice. A bit *I Ching*, a bit gut instinct . . ."

"With a pinch of Dungeons & Dragons." Alice regretted the sarcasm in her tone.

His shoulders slumped, and he reached toward her. "Maybe so, but it worked. I'm sure of it." He stepped forward and grasped her shoulder, gazing down at her with such intensity, such infectious hope, that she could almost feel herself giving in to it. He seemed to sense her wariness slipping away, so he struck. "We've found her, my love," he said. "We've found your rightful destiny. She's been circling those closest to you, spiraling in toward you from the moment your plane touched down in New Orleans."

"Okay, then. What comes next?" she said, this time taking care to speak her mind without worrying about his feelings. "Princess Charming will wake me with true love's kiss?"

"Well, no," he said, releasing her and taking a step back. "I'm sure it won't be easy as all that." His face scrunched up, and he tilted his head as he considered her question with far greater sincerity than it had been asked.

"Who is this 'we' you're talking about anyway?" she asked, breaking into his thoughts. She couldn't believe he'd caught Fleur or Hugo up in his well-intentioned farce.

"Well," he said, his chin lowering toward his chest, a glint of guilt in his eyes. "The feline and I."

"You and Sugar." She stood and descended the steps, planting her feet on the ground in a wide stance and resting her hands on her hips to signal her rekindled incredulity.

"Yes. She's quite devoted to you. Even after all these years." A sad smile rose to his lips. "As am I."

She couldn't say if it was the twitch of his eyelid or the quiver in his voice, but something told her that this conjured man and an aged cat counted as the only two on the other side who hadn't given up on her. Who hadn't decided her situation was hopeless.

Alice opened her mouth with the intention of going along, of pretending she believed the scheme he'd dreamed up was anything more than wishful thinking. Instead, she surprised herself. "I love you, Daniel," she said, drawing closer and placing her hand on his cheek. "I've always loved you." Her hand dropped, resting on the point on his chest beneath which any real man's heart would lie beating. "But you have to leave now." Sabine appeared before them, thirty yards or so away, standing in the shade of an ancient oak. "And you can't come back. It's too painful."

"Ah, now there, my girl," he said, his Irish brogue resurrecting itself. "You have to show some patience. I know it's been difficult waiting for a solution, but we've only been at it three months . . ."

"It's been," she said, stepping back from him, "going on seven years here. And almost five months have passed since I last saw you."

He opened his mouth, ready to protest, but she held up her hand to stop him. "Please. If you love me, you'll go." She lowered her hand

and started walking away. She stopped and looked back at him, and her heart broke. He looked stricken, his green eyes wide and his mouth hanging open. "I'm sorry," she said, "but this is my home now. We both have to get used to that fact." This time she made it two steps before she stopped once more. "I love you," she said, not daring to look at him again. "Goodbye." She strode away from him, keeping her focus on Sabine, who held out a hand to her, love in her eyes, her face lit up with a warm smile.

The group of children coalesced from nothing and ran past her. A blond, curly-haired boy looked back at her as he followed the rest, his face the picture of delight. A pair of bikers whizzed past, aimed in the direction of the peristyle. Alice looked down to see a young mother lying on a blanket with a book in her hand, her baby shaded in a portable bassinet.

"Oh. No. You. Don't." Daniel caught up to her. He grabbed her by the arm. "You don't walk away from me." It shocked Alice to hear hot anger in his voice. She hadn't thought him capable of it. "The more of them," he said, his eyes narrowing as he pointed at Sabine, "you let into this world, the quicker your own end will come."

"I know. They're my creations, but without them . . ." Her voice caught. "The loneliness, Daniel. It's unbearable."

"Ah, my love. I know. I know, but it's a lie that they're your creations. I know you believe it, but you've been deceived." He glared at the simulation of Sabine. "Look at her. Really look at her. See her for what she is, and not what you need her to be."

Alice shook her head, not wanting to risk losing all that she'd managed to find in this world, but after a moment, she gave in to the distress she heard in Daniel's voice. She focused on Sabine, and although Alice noticed nothing untoward at first, she began to pick up a thin black aura outlining her.

"The entity you're looking at isn't your creation," Daniel said. "It's a former dreamer who lost herself on the Dreaming Road. She's donned a mask, assumed the identity you provided her, but she's nothing more than a demon now. A vampire of sorts." He paused. "It started with her, didn't it? She came first, and then the others . . ."

"We were the only two people in the world for a while. She seemed happy at first, but then she started to grow restless. She said it was unhealthy for the two of us to be so dependent on each other," Alice said. "That we needed to get out. Meet new people. Make friends." Alice wondered at herself. How had she never noticed Sabine's aura? "She said we'd be stronger from it."

"I've studied these beings," Daniel said, his voice calmer now that he sensed she'd accepted what he was telling her. "Watched their comings and goings as they pass through the astral, always seeking out the brightest lights to siphon." He moved forward to stand beside her. "They were all once dreamers. Dreamers exactly like you. I've seen the lights of others go out . . . and I've seen them rise again in darkness." He took her chin in his hand and turned her face toward him. "Celestin doesn't truly love you, or he would have never imprisoned you on the Dreaming Road. Yes, the world he's engineered is pleasant. It feels, I'm sure, like home, but this world is growing smaller and darker every day. Harder for me to find, and increasingly difficult for me to enter. It's burning out. *You're* burning out. Partly because of them." He released her with a slight nudge that turned her gaze back to Sabine. "When that happens, you'll become like these creatures." His chest heaved like he might cry. "A hungry ghost, full of predatory cunning, but driven only by hunger, every shred of your humanity gone. Devouring any light you find, until all light has been extinguished and there's nothing but eternal darkness."

For an instant, all guises fell away, and Alice caught a glimpse of the creature she'd invited into her world. The one she'd allowed herself to love. A gray corpse with sunken black eyes stood beneath the oak's canopy. The corpse's mouth gaped open in imitation of a smile. A withered hand waved her forward. The next moment, it was once again Sabine. Alice recoiled at the memory of this creature's tender touch.

Daniel must have realized what she was, at last, witnessing. "It's no coincidence that Babau Jean built his paradise here."

Babau Jean, the bogeyman that did indeed exist. The entity had started off as a servitor spirit, not so different in essence from her own beloved Daniel. His creator had used him to feed off the life force of bereaved wives and mothers who'd lost loved ones in the Civil War, but Babau had somehow survived his creator's death and become something more.

"How long," she said, "have you known about these things?"

"Not long. Only since my last visit," he said, turning her own words back on her. "Let's try an experiment, shall we?"

Alice glanced over at him. "What type of experiment?"

"Starve them. Let's see if ignoring them makes them go away."

"Alice," Sabine said, her voice bright. "Aren't you going to introduce me to your friend?"

"That one," Daniel said, "is going to be the toughest. She's more invested in you. She's had her hooks in you the longest."

"Alice," Sabine called again, now sounding a bit peeved.

"Don't look at her." Daniel turned her toward him. "Look at me."

"Alice." Sabine's temper seemed to be heating up. "I will not let you treat me this way."

"She's already worried." Daniel cast a hard glance over Alice's shoulder. "I think we may be onto something. Can you be strong? Strong enough to let go of what you know isn't good for you, even if it feels right? Even if it feels comforting?" He smiled and took her by the chin once more, this time making her nod. "Yes, you are," he said.

She hoped it was true.

He dropped his hand and leaned in to plant a kiss on her forehead. "Now, I need one more thing from you. I need your permission."

"Permission to do what?"

"Permission to throw a bit of force behind gravity. To help it bring you back in line with your rightful destiny."

"I told you," she said, hugging him, resting her head on his chest. "I don't believe in destiny."

He slipped from her embrace, then placed his hands on her shoulders. "But you do believe in me?"

She nodded.

"And you grant me your permission?"

She nodded again.

"I won't let you down," he said, already drifting away, slipping backward into the same light that had announced his arrival.

"I know you won't," she said, shielding her eyes from the bright flash. He was gone. "At least not on purpose."

"I knew I would find you here," Sabine called to her, and Alice glanced back to see her coming down the path. It seemed that, unable to process what had occurred, the demon had hit reset, an attempt to start again at the point it had last felt in control. It reached out for Alice, trying to catch her hand, but Alice pulled away. "Come on, you. Get a move on," it said. "We're already late."

"You go ahead without me," Alice said. "I think I need some me time."

THREE

Lisette Perrault held a small, square-edged bottle of black enamel paint in her left hand, and a brush she'd borrowed from her son, Remy, in her right. She stepped back and focused on the storefront window's centermost pane, the frenetic parade of late-morning tourists making their way to and from Jackson Square nothing more than a kaleidoscope of color behind her own dim reflection. Between her ghost and the maelstrom stood Papa Legba's vèvè, perfectly rendered, the product of her own work and intention.

The Voodoo supply shop Lisette had taken over from her mother, the Vieux Carré's illustrious mambo, Soulange Simeon, got its name from the symbols her mother had painted on the multipaned window that faced onto Chartres Street. The vèvès were pictographs representing individual loa, the spirits who acted as intercessors between humans and Bondye—the good, though transcendent, god. Three, going on four, months ago, the shop had been vandalized. A hoodlum had shattered all the window's panes save one, destroying most of her mother's painstaking work. Lisette now understood that what her mother had created there—a marriage of her art and devotion—was as precious as any of St. Louis Cathedral's murals. She regretted that she'd never really appreciated her mother's work for what it was until it was too late.

One restoration down, and a slew more to go. Still, her mama would've been proud to see the first. Lisette retrieved the paint bottle's lid. She twisted it closed and dropped the brush into a jar of paint thinner Remy had provided her.

Her son had volunteered to recreate the vèvès. He would've done a beautiful job, she had no doubt about it, and likely could have finished in no more than a few hours, but she needed to do this herself.

For years, Lisette's honoring of the loa had been perfunctory, performed not out of reverence, but half out of guilt and half out of a desire to keep up appearances for the business's sake. Her faith had been severely shaken by her mother's death. No. Her mother's murder at the hands of Laure Marin. If the loa hadn't protected her mother, a dedicated mambo, how powerful could they be?

Then came Katrina. The day the levees broke, what was left of Lisette's beliefs went with them. She and Isadore had packed up the kids and headed out of the storm's path, but her father had stubbornly insisted on hanging on, riding out the storm. Right here in Vèvè, where he felt closest to her mother. When they returned to New Orleans, they found him holed up here, hiding out to avoid evacuation, safe but a bit screwy from loneliness and hunger. This store, in the very spot her mother had felt guided by the loa to open it, still stood strong. Upon discovering that the roof of their own house had been ripped off by the winds, they joined him here, the whole family sharing shelter until they could get back on their feet. Now Lisette had to wonder how she hadn't seen this shop itself as a gift of the loa.

It had taken more than a simple sign to rekindle her faith. It had required a night spent with her mother's spirit and a visit from an emissary of Papa Legba, the guardian of the crossroads between the living and the dead, to convince her to drop her false pride and let herself believe again. She'd made a vow, both to her mother and to the loa themselves, to honor them. To herself, she'd made the promise that she wouldn't link her continued devotion to the loa to world events turning out the way she felt they should.

She'd thrown herself into a contemplation of the loa, choosing to make the recreation of the vèvès a chance to reconnect with them, a penance and an act of devotion. Such an intention required preparation.

Marie Laveau, New Orleans's nearly sainted Voodoo queen, had once conducted Saint John's Eve ceremonies on the banks of Lake Pontchartrain near the mouth of the Bayou St. John. For three moons Lisette had purified herself, bathing her head with water from the nexus where Pontchartrain spills into the Bayou St. John. There was no easy land access to that spot, so Lisette had paid her daughter's friend, the young gay fellow who sold Manon five-dollar coffees, to paddle his kayak up Bayou St. John to the spill gate to fetch the water.

Then she fasted, feasted, and anointed herself with the water. She lit candles and danced and drank rum until her head spun—until she sensed someone else join her in her body and look out through her eyes. That was when she knew the door she had slammed shut was once again open. She was finally ready to recreate her mother's vèvès, and, as practice dictated, the first would be that of Papa Legba.

She'd practiced drawing, then painting, his vèvè over and over again, until she could do it backward from memory, until the movements came to her as natural, so that she could recreate it, as her mother had painted the window's original vèvès, in reverse. Lisette had always believed her mother had done so to allow passersby to see them from the correct vantage point. Now she realized this assumption was, at least partly, wrong.

"They're going to want to see out," her mother had said, turning back from her work to smile at Lisette, at the time a spindly preschooler. Lisette had all but forgotten that moment until a comment from an unlikely source—Nathalie, the driver who'd picked up her and her mother's spirit out by Grunch Road. The younger white woman, who didn't know a damned thing about Voodoo, said that as a girl she'd been afraid to pass by the shop because of the faces staring out from it. Nathalie's words had offered Lisette a long-overdue revelation—the vèvès not only symbolized the loa; they summoned them.

Their restoration would be the work of her hand alone, but she'd enlisted her husband Isadore to build a new altar, a solid oak one to withstand the years, and her son to decorate it. She'd expected Remy to work directly on the wood, but he returned two days later with a white linen altar cloth, the image of her mother embroidered at its center. The image was surrounded by a blood-red circle, from which six- to nine-inch strands of silk thread radiated out like veins, their edges intertwining. He'd chosen to honor his ancestor in a flash of brilliance that made Lisette begin to see her own mother as one of the loa, a personal connection to the spirits that would make any lapse of veneration impossible. It was a damned masterpiece, and she'd told Remy as much.

"You think everything I do is a masterpiece," he'd said, trying to sound cool. "It's all done by computer now. I did the drawing and specified the colors, but the computer did the needlework." His words were full of modesty, but she could see the delight in his eyes.

She cast another look at her own masterpiece—Remy's talent hadn't just dropped out of the air—only to witness another now all-too-familiar sight, her father, Alcide, weaving his way down Chartres Street toward the shop. A wide and foolish smile stretched his lips as he waved a brown-paper-bagged bottle around before him like he was captain of a one-man krewe, intent on making his very own Mardi Gras parade.

Ever since the burial of Celestin Marin's physical body, Lisette's father's visits were like thunderstorms—they caused little lasting damage, but they were loud and sometimes frightening. With a sigh, she backed away from the window and crossed the room to step behind the counter. Using it as a fortress, she folded her arms across her chest, bracing herself.

The bell over the door clanged, announcing her father's arrival. He stumbled over the threshold and barreled toward one of the shelves. He managed to catch himself, but dropped the bottle in the process.

Lisette heard a pop as the glass shattered inside the paper bag. The shelf hid her view, but she could smell the alcohol seep out. Sour mash whiskey, she guessed from the scent. Her father's face clouded over as he stepped back and stared down at the waste. He began to stoop.

"Leave it," Lisette said. The two sharp words betrayed her anger. The last thing she needed was for him to cut himself.

He looked at her with wide, confused eyes, then his jaw tightened. "You watch your tone, missy. I am still your father."

"Really?" Lisette said, grabbing the sturdy gray metal garbage can her mother had bought, and stomping up to him. "'Cause you sure don't act like him. My father is a stand-up man, not some stumbling drunk." She knelt beside him, incapable of looking at his face, and focused instead on his left shoe, now an island in the growing puddle of alcohol. She lifted the dampened paper bag by its corners, shifting it with care and dropping it and the bottle it still held into the can.

"I came here," he said in a stentorian voice, his volume prompting Lisette to glare up at him. "I came here to talk to you. And you, you're gonna listen."

She snatched up the can and stepped wide around him, holding up one hand behind her to signal she didn't want to hear a thing he had to say. He lunged at her, his movements far sprier than his age and intoxication should allow. He grabbed her hand and spun her back around, the movement tugging and twisting her shoulder.

She cried out, shocking him sober. He released her.

She lowered the garbage can to the floor by her feet, though she never took her eyes off him. He must have seen a reflection of himself in them, because his complexion turned gray. "I'm sorry," he said, his hand now trembling as he reached out to her. "I'm sorry, baby. It was an accident. *Popa* would never hurt you on purpose."

"And still," she said, reaching up and rubbing her tender left shoulder, "I'm hurt." She worked it around, deciding the injury wasn't serious, but she was hurt and angry enough to play it up all the same.

He took a step toward her. "I'm sorry . . ."

"Why," she said, cutting him off, "don't you go on and speak your piece? Or"—she swatted away his hand—"do you think you've done enough damage for one day?"

His eye twitched, and a line formed between his brows. She could tell he was feeling good and guilty. He started to turn away, but then his temper flared up again. "I'm not the one doing damage," he said, pointing at her. "I'm not the one letting Remy see that Lucy girl."

"So that's what this is about," she said, retrieving the can and walking away from him. "Remy is eighteen now." She reached the counter and dropped the can for effect. The rocking bang followed by the crash of shifting shards of glass was everything she'd hoped it would be. She moved behind the counter, placing her hands on it and leaning forward. "He's a grown man. Maybe he isn't old enough to drink"—she paused on the word—"but he's sure old enough to date anyone he damned well pleases." She straightened. "You of all people should know the best way to drive young lovers together is by trying to pry them apart."

"Oh, I know all right. I remember you running after Celestin's son, Vincent. You're the one who got us tangled up with that family in the first place."

His meaning began to dawn on her, and she shook her head. "Oh, no, Daddy, that is not fair."

"Not fair?" he said, drawing nearer. She could see tiny veins on his temples popping out. "What's not fair is that your mama is dead. Dead because of Laure Marin."

A loss of life. A loss of mind. A loss of love. A loss of fertility. The fourfold sacrifice Laure had convinced Lisette's mother it had been necessary to make to protect their children from the dark and seductive magic contained in *The Book of the Unwinding*.

The Book, hidden away for centuries and fettered by a force that held back its darkness, had passed into folklore. But then something—and as far as Lisette could ascertain, no one seemed sure what—changed, and the Book began to call out once more. It had, Laure claimed, begun grooming her daughter-in-law, Astrid, to help manifest its evil in this world.

Laure's professed goal had been to place the Book beyond the reach not only of Astrid, but of any other the Book might seek to beguile. She succeeded in painting a dire enough future that Lisette's mother believed it was worth laying down her own life to constrain the Book once more by locking it between dimensions. Securing it so that even if the ward were broken, only someone capable of existing on the two planes at once could ever lay claim to it.

While Laure's concerns about Astrid and the Book may have, in fact, been true, Lisette remained convinced Laure had turned these developments to her own selfish end. If the woman had held any true concern for her children, it had come secondary to her desire for Lisette's father. Laure's obsession was, Lisette privately thought, what had set all of this mess into motion. The woman had believed she would be strong enough to withstand the madness she was courting. That she would find a way to capture Alcide Simeon's grieving heart and make it her own once she'd eliminated the woman she saw as her rival. Still, in the end, neither family had been left untouched by the matriarchs' spell. Laure was found wandering around Grunch Road, lost in a nightmare from which she'd never awaken.

"Yes, Mama's dead because of Laure Marin. Because Laure Marin wanted you for herself."

Lisette's father barked out a laugh. "Gossip from the devil's own lips passed secondhand by the bitch's bitch daughter to your ears. Oh, yes," he said nodding, "I know you've been cozying up to Fleur Marin whatever-the-hell-name-she-married-into." He glowered at her, as if he were daring her to defend Fleur. Lisette refused to take the bait. "Even if it were true," he continued, though he seemed deflated by her silence, "I never led that woman on." He slapped his hand down on the counter. "Never." A cruel glint, the spark of a long-nurtured resentment, formed in his eye. "And she could've never gotten to your mama if it weren't for the little passade between you and her boy. I hadn't given her a thought in years."

"What we shared wasn't a passing fancy. Vincent and I were going to marry," Lisette said, surprised to find herself defending a relationship that had ended more than two decades ago.

"I don't care. You were the one who opened your mother to Laure Marin's influence. All that making nice. Family getting to know family. Building trust." He turned his head and spat, like the words had tasted bitter in his mouth. "Though I can see you haven't learned a damned thing, 'cause it isn't only your son who's been blinded. I thought it would be over once the river washed away Vincent's ashes. That you'd be done with the Marins. But I was wrong. You're nursing that viper Fleur in your bosom, and it won't be long before you feel her fangs."

Lisette couldn't deny that she had been seeing a lot of Fleur since Vincent's memorial. It seemed natural, if only because Fleur's father was a common enemy, one who would no doubt return and need to be vanquished. They shared knowledge with each other—Fleur about her type of magic, and, although Lisette still felt strange acknowledging it, she was teaching Fleur about her kind of magic, too. Fleur had even joked that they should form a coven, though she acknowledged it would be like trying to pair alternating current with direct. "Fleur isn't her mother."

"And you," her father said, his eyes narrowing, his jaw jutting forward, "aren't yours."

In spite of her newfound devotion, his words hit her hard. She caved in on herself, her shoulders slumping forward, a bite of pain in the left one as they did. "No, Daddy, I am not." A sense of resignation outweighed her anger.

He turned away from her and crossed to the altar, contemplating, Lisette knew, the image Remy had created of her mother. His shoulders heaved once, then again. A loud sob escaped him. He looked back over his shoulder at her, his eyes red and wet. Lisette now understood what her mother had meant when she'd said she was the only woman who could've saved Alcide Simeon from himself. He was lost and determined to self-destruct without her.

Lisette had hoped that she would help him find peace by telling him what had happened the night of the witches' ball. How even though Lisette had at first resisted the idea, letting that Nathalie girl offer herself, she and her mother had joined together, Lisette serving as her mother's *chwal*, to prevent Celestin from achieving his goal of acquiring *The Book of the Unwinding*. How she'd later watched Soulange step into a beam that shone like light but felt like pure bliss.

"What isn't fair," he said, returning to an earlier theme, "is that your mama lived for these spirits. Maybe if she'd lived just a little more for me, she wouldn't have been so willing to lay down her life." He turned away with a loud cry. "They took her from me. Now they're gonna take you, too." His hands shot out and grasped the edge of the altar cloth. He yanked it back, ripping it off the table, sending the candles and figurines, flowers and herbs and incense, Florida water and rum flying into the air, where they seemed to hover a moment longer than gravity should allow. Then everything came crashing down.

He seemed as shocked by his actions as Lisette felt. Their eyes locked as each struggled to find words.

"So," Lisette said, unlucky enough to win the race, "you intend to keep on then, till you drink yourself to death."

He dropped the altar cloth to the floor, melted candle wax seeping into the fabric.

"That seems to be the plan," he said, his voice quiet, his eyes cold.

Lisette turned away, her own eyes brimming with tears.

The bell over the door clanged, and her father was gone.

FOUR

Evangeline Caissy stumbled through her bedroom's open French doors to the bijoux garden, tumbling forward onto the patio's rough brickwork. The fall skinned her hands and knees, an irritation to gild an already breathtaking agony. Every bone in her was bending, cracking, breaking at once. The pressure squeezed in from every direction, as if she were sinking deeper and deeper beneath the sea. Her body was growing smaller, denser, even as it was being reshaped. A detached witness in her mind, a part of herself that had somehow managed to take shelter behind a breakwater, wondered whether knowing to expect the agony made the transition easier or even more hellish. But no seawall could resist the crashing waves. Soon the detached witness would be washed away, too.

Dark of the moon.

Ever since the slaughter at the witches' ball, on the nights between the waning and waxing crescents, Evangeline's will was no longer her own. They had taken to playing with her, her mother's sister witches and Celestin, twisting and mangling her body into the bastardized form of a crow. But it was more than a game, she was sure of that. They'd set out to teach her. Teach her who she was, what she was capable of.

Celestin had waded through the blood of family and friends to claim *The Book of the Unwinding*, but Marceline had made it clear that she believed she and her sister witches were the rightful inheritors of its magic. Neither party had any real intention of sharing. The only way Evangeline could fathom the alliance was to imagine that the sisters saw Celestin as a useful, though ultimately disposable, tool—and without a doubt, vice versa. For now, they shared a common goal. And a common need.

They all needed the darkness Evangeline carried in her. This she sensed in the pit of her stomach, though she had yet to discern the role they intended her to play. Perhaps nothing more than to walk in her mother's footsteps, thereby increasing, or perhaps balancing, their power. They couldn't force her to act. But they could try torturing her until she acted willingly, if only to stop the pain.

She'd been horrified the first time Marceline had called this form forth, a meshing of crow with a raptor's sharp beak and claws. Repulsed to realize this *thing* had been lurking inside her, hidden within her all along, tangible proof that the evil her mother had sought to leave behind had been passed on to her by blood.

That night, the night of the slaughter, Marceline had enticed Evangeline to join her and her sister witches Margot and Mathilde, all in their shifted forms, in the carnage. She'd almost given in to the staggering urge to rip apart Hugo Marin. Though she'd devoted the last several years to keeping Hugo alive, in that moment, it had seemed to her that piercing him with beak and claw was the sole remedy for her suffering. Only her own shock at the sudden transformation had allowed her to resist. To ignore the voice shrieking *Murder, Murder* in her mind, and instead carry Hugo to safety, dropping him outside the cursed ballroom to his feet from six feet in the air before she tore off in search of . . .

A rush of jumbled half memories, the vague impressions of her human psyche peeking out from behind a wall of avian instinct. The two sides, the human and the animal, were at odds, her avian mind filled with impulses her human mind refused to process.

She felt—or was it feared?—the memories would return if she let them.

If she allowed herself, she might even relish them.

That last thought hadn't been born in her own mind. It had crept in from beyond, seeking to sink its tendrils into her soul and bring her down, like Japanese honeysuckle—pretty and sweet-smelling, but capable of toppling even a deep-rooted tree.

She'd expected the transformation to occur again tonight, even tried to prevent it by knocking herself out with a cocktail of booze and sleeping pills that might've killed an ordinary woman, but there seemed to be no way to resist. The pain ripped her from a near coma to wide awake. The first time, the change had taken place in mere moments. Over these last three months, the process had slowed down, growing even more agonizing with each iteration. Celestin and the sisters wanted to make a point.

Excruciating. Maddening. Warping.

A sound met her ears, her own scream, but she didn't recognize it. The cry was not a noise a human voice would make.

Struggle begets pain, a cool, inhuman voice whispered in her burning mind, the words like velvet wrapped around barbed wire. In life, Celestin's voice had a rich, polished timbre, a condescending tone, and an accent he'd cultivated as a student at the Sorbonne. Those qualities were all lost now. The voice she heard in her mind sounded of dry branches clacking together in the night breeze.

I am the balm to ease your suffering. The very source of her torture presented himself as her salvation.

She might go mad. She might die. But she would never turn to Celestin as savior. Nor, despite the similarities in their magic, would she accept the sisters as kin of any kind.

Her eyes locked on her hands before her, each digit snapping, but the dim light spilling from her bedroom onto the patio grew blinding. Dazzling violet hues confused her as her field of vision stretched, her eyes seeming to work independently of one another.

Dizzying. Disorienting. She began retching, but there was nothing in her stomach to come up but dissolving benzos and vodka.

A hot sting like a flaying whip as her skin began to shred. The last shards of consciousness began to slip away, and a merciful darkness reached out to embrace her.

But he stopped it from touching her. He held her there, awake, aware, and in pain.

Give yourself to me. Your agony will be nothing more than a forgotten dream.

But it was too late. Words no longer held meaning.

When Evangeline surfaced, she came to in human form. Naked. The skin of her arm sticking to her side. Walking. The frenetic pounding of drums sounded somewhere in the distance. She followed it blindly. Her eyelids seemed gummed together. It took some effort to separate them. A fire burned in the distance, a raging inferno that seemed to further chill rather than warm her skin, and that gave but little light. It burned in a clearing at the center of a thick clump of cypresses.

It promised her absolute indulgence, if not pardon.

Murder was the first act of magic. An old witch's saw she'd heard a million times sent a shiver down her spine. She realized she could no longer tell where Celestin's thoughts ended and her own began.

Her eyes adapted to the darkness, and she realized that she was making her way along a land bridge, a thin stretch of earth bisecting a bayou's waters. Red lights shone everywhere around her. They floated on the water's surface, tiny paired *fifolets* leading her deeper, deeper into the inky stand of cypress. A pair of the lights dashed toward her, proximity revealing them to be an alligator's gleaming eyes.

Her heart pounded, certain it would soon be on her, but the creature stopped a yard or two before her, lowering its head as if in greeting. It turned away and strode across the thin strip of land, its scaly body dripping water, before slipping back beneath the bayou's surface. Maybe it was magic that had protected her, or perhaps the temperature had dropped enough that the crawling terrors had stopped feeding.

Come, ma chère, the thought projected into her mind. She recognized its source as Margot. *They're curious, but they won't harm you. Think of it as a professional courtesy. They recognize a fellow predator when they see one.*

Evangeline looked back over her shoulder, considering turning around, running away, but the land she'd crossed by foot was now lost beneath a rising tide. All that remained was a sea of glowing red eyes. A mad thought hit her, and she tried to will herself to change, to sprout the wings that might carry her away.

"Oh, no." Margot's voice blew over her like an icy wind, causing goose bumps to rise on her sticky skin. "You haven't paid the price for the ability to transform at will . . . yet. Though eventually you will. Sooner or later we're all his children. The wise witch knows to bargain for something in return."

The water behind her continued to rise, an unnatural tide spilling up over her feet. She caught her breath and pushed forward, not exhaling till she once again touched dry ground. As she did, a high-pitched whining sound added itself to the thumping of the drums. Three discordant notes, repeating themselves in a rhythm that shared nothing with the drumbeats.

A crow swept down just inches from her face, near enough that Evangeline could feel the wind its wing beat back as it climbed once more. The wing fanned the reek of charred flesh into her nostrils.

Sacrifice. Mathilde's feverish mind shouted out a single-word explanation, the thought dipped in bloodlust, trimmed with a sick glee.

Still, she moved forward.

The dark fire at the center of the clearing exerted its own bewitching gravity.

The dark fire was alive.

Evangeline passed through the cypress curtain, catching hold of the innermost tree to keep from being pulled into the flames.

The din of a thousand drums assaulted her ears. She scanned the surroundings, but there were no drummers. The frenzied pounding was the beating of the pyre's heart.

The flames held on to their light with a miser's grip, but gave off what seemed a scorching cold in abundance. Evangeline felt her skin reddening.

Her dark-adapted eyes discerned movement. Pale figures, seemingly locked in orbit, circled the conflagration with raw, thrashing motions that could have been either a kind of dance or a desperate attempt at escape. As they jerked and squirmed in passing, Evangeline saw their pallor was limited to the sides facing away from the fire. The sides facing the conflagration were grotesque: features melting, charring, burning away to blackened bone. The icy blaze was consuming them. Varying degrees of devastation indicated some had joined the dance later than others. A skeletal dancer fell away to ash, and a fresh new figure, this one a young man, his skin as snowy as if he'd never seen the sun, his movements graceful, his limbs lithe, drifted toward the circle and was caught in the pyre's gravity. Steam began to rise from his body, then smoke, and he drifted away from Evangeline's field of vision, circling to the distant, darkest side of the fire.

The sharp, whining notes crept back into her consciousness, making her aware that they had never been silenced. They were enchanting her, weakening her, even now. She startled as she realized their source sat beside her. Glowing the cold silver blue of moonlight, a male—a naked, bald mound of luminous fat that looked less like a man than a massive, eyeless baby—sat cross-legged at her side, a red stone flute pressed to his lips.

Carnelian, the name of the stone came to her, as if that fact held some importance.

The three notes repeated, each one sonorous with meaning. *Oblivion. Sweet. Eternal.* She felt a tug, a hunger, willing her forward.

Her hand fell away from the tree. *Oblivion. Sweet. Eternal.* She took a step forward.

"No, *ma chère fille,*" Margot said, her now-human form materializing between Evangeline and the dim, searing flames. "That fate is not for you." She pressed a blue stone flask to Evangeline's lips. "It will never be for you," she said, tilting the flask.

Sweet, honeyed wine poured past Evangeline's lips. She tasted a trace of licorice. The scent of mothballs reached her nose. Her throat constricted, and she tried to spit the liquid out. Margot caught her by the chin, her clammy touch forcing Evangeline's mouth to close.

"You must swallow," Margot said. "It's nothing that will harm you. A taste of Le Mort's elixir, that's all. It will help you resist the temptation." Evangeline struggled, but Margot's will proved stronger. Evangeline surrendered, allowing the sweet, foul tincture to trickle down her throat.

In an instant, Evangeline's senses both sharpened and dulled, leaving the sound of the stone flute now muted, as if it were being played a world away, but augmenting her night vision so that she could discern the entity that hung at the center of the dancers' orbit. She perceived the entity as masculine, though it seemed nonsensical to hang a gender on such a being. It was older than time ever would or could be, a dark star feeding on light. "Where are we? What is that thing?" she said, her words hushed, even though she sensed the creature heard all. Saw all.

"We," Margot said, "are at the center of all madness. Madness may not be the source of magic, but it is a gateway." Margot plugged the lapis lazuli flask with a stopper made of the same carnelian as the man-baby's flute, then knelt on the ground, prostrating herself and kissing the earth that lay between her and the being of darkness in the blaze. She pushed herself into a squatting position, then held up a hand, a wordless request for Evangeline's assistance.

Evangeline hesitated, despising Margot's touch, but the older witch, impatient and entitled, flapped her hand, the wordless request turning into a silent command. Evangeline took Margot's hand and helped her rise, releasing her grip as soon as Margot had found her footing. Evangeline despised her mother's sister witch—a feeling that was per-haps returned, judging from the look of contempt in Margot's eyes. "*That thing*," she said, her acerbic parroting of Evangeline's words con-veying a greater sense of disapproval than outright censure ever could have, "has been known by many names, though the one that has always resonated with me is 'the Dark Man.'"

Mathilde spiraled in from overhead, a writhing rodent caught in her claws. She seemed unaware of Evangeline's presence, one eye fixed on her prey, the other missing. The night of the ball, Margot had pecked the eye out in an attempt to keep Mathilde's bloodlust from claiming Marceline as victim.

Still in flight, Mathilde finished the rat off with three vicious jabs of her sharp beak. She dropped the bloodied corpse at Margot's feet. An offering of fealty, or perhaps a gift given in affection.

Mathilde touched down and turned toward the dark fire. She began bobbing, lowering herself to the earth and rising back up—bowing, it seemed, as best as her feathered form would allow. For a heartbeat, Evangeline could almost feel the presence of Mathilde's human mind, but then it slipped away again, the bowing motion turned into a pecking search for insects. Margot kicked the dead rodent away, sending Mathilde hopping backward to reclaim it.

"She's mostly lost," Margot said, focused on Mathilde. "One sister trapped in animal form, another in animal mind." Mathilde feasted on her prey, undisturbed by Margot's words. "Each change, *ma chère*, will make you less of what you were and more of what you will be. You may writhe and struggle with the determination of that poor rodent, but you are looking at your own future. We both are."

"None of you are sisters, not really," Evangeline said, less out of spite than to draw her own attention away from Mathilde's shredding and swallowing of fur and flesh.

Margot didn't rise to her challenge. Instead, she fell as silent as stone, appearing to contemplate the great darkness before them.

Evangeline advanced on her. "Why are you doing this to me? Why did you bring me here?"

Margot's laughter rang out, and Mathilde added her own rough caws, though Evangeline sensed the elder witch was reacting to sound rather than meaning. "But my dear, we didn't. You were drawn here by your own darkness."

"I don't believe you."

"Believe me, don't believe me. It's of no consequence," Margot said, managing to sound offended nonetheless. "I didn't come here to quibble with you. Time will tell." Then she paused, seeming to reconsider her words. "*Blood* will tell." Three pointed words wrapped in cotton to hide their sharp edges. Evangeline knew better than to touch them.

"She doesn't blame you, you know," Margot said, lifting her hand to point at the night sky. A gargantuan bird circled overhead, a black bird in an onyx sky. Evangeline couldn't make out the form directly, but she perceived it through the starlight it blocked, and the sound its black wings made as they beat against the night air. She knew it was Marceline, still trapped in the form she'd taken to assist Celestin Marin in slaughtering the witches at the ball. The necklace Hugo had put around the shifter's neck would keep her in that form until death—unless Marceline found a loophole in the magic. "Marceline's always been fond of you. She is paying the price for that affection now."

"I'm not to blame. What happened to her was of her own doing."

Marceline's caw rang down like a contradiction descending from the sky.

Margot rocked back a bit, lifting her head and looking down her nose at Evangeline. Her eyes flashed and she opened her mouth to speak, but then seemed to think better of it. She shrugged her shoulders. "We are who we are," she said, her tone conciliatory. "You'll come to understand that. Accept it. Then perhaps you will judge us more kindly." Once again, her eyes turned skyward. "Watch her." Evangeline heard something akin to pride in the witch's voice. Marceline climbed higher and higher, her flight a tightening spiral. She reached the spiral's apex, then hung there, unmoving. With a sudden cry, she turned toward the earth and plummeted. "Like a shooting star," Margot said, raising her clasped hands, shaking them in excitement, cheering Marceline on.

Evangeline's eyes struggled to follow Marceline's meteoric descent through darkness, until a blinding flare shot up from the dark form, and the quaking earth knocked her to her knees.

It took some time for her vision to clear. "I don't understand." She forced herself up on unsteady legs. "What just happened? What did she do?"

Evangeline sensed Margot was wrestling with herself. "She freed herself in the only way she could."

"She's gone?"

"She may very well be," Margot replied. Evangeline thought she could see a tear tracing its way down the witch's cheek. "Or the dark fire may renew her. Return her to this world, a true phoenix." Margot seemed to remember herself. She straightened her shoulders and lifted her chin. "It was a calculated risk," she said, her voice turning cool.

"When will we know?" Evangeline turned back to the dim conflagration.

The being's heart beat louder, faster. The sound of the flute grew louder.

"Careful, young one. I'm beginning to think you've come to care what happens to her." Margot reached out and placed a finger on Evangeline's forehead, touching the spot mystics speak of as the "third eye." She seemed to be searching for something buried deep in Evangeline, though Evangeline couldn't imagine what she might expect to find there.

"You were wrong, you know," Margot said. Evangeline could sense that the older witch was struggling with herself. "When you said we weren't real sisters. We were sisters, we four. Driven by hunger, by shame, by stifled rage, we went together into the shadowy wood to pledge our troths to Lucifer. The Devil." She spat out the words contemptuously, then chuckled. "We knew nothing of magic at the time, but we believed what we'd been taught, so we went off together to seek a shared damnation. That act alone bound us as sisters," she said, her speech slowing, a hesitation before crossing some unseen barrier. "But Mireille and Marceline," she said, "they were sisters before our encounter with the font of our powers. They were sisters by blood. Marceline is your aunt."

FIVE

St. Ann Street, just off Dauphine. The arch of Armstrong Park in plain view. Fleur mentally ticked off Hugo's directions till she stood before the *you-can't-possibly-miss-it* Creole cottage that belonged to Evangeline Caissy. The cottage, painted a shade too deep to be called salmon, too bright for coral, winked at her with its dazzling citron right door that peered out from between open sky-blue shutters. Like many of the neighboring houses, the cottage had two front entrances separated by two windows. The cottage's left door and center double windows were all hidden behind closed shutters—the shutters all identical in length and painted the same brilliant blue. Only the citron steps leading up to the shuttered door betrayed its purpose.

The Caribbean color palette suited the house. Brilliant. Welcoming. The sight of it made Fleur smile. In spite of the Garden District mansion Fleur had inherited from her parents, she felt a twinge of envy for Evangeline's sweet little cottage. No, she realized, if she envied the solitary Cajun witch anything, it was the independence she'd always enjoyed. Unlike Evangeline, Fleur had been passed, hand to hand, from father to husband, a tool to help both fulfill their ambitions.

But those days were good and done.

Fleur mounted the right-hand steps and prepared to rap on the door, but it swung open before she could act.

"What?" Evangeline said, though the word was more of a challenge than a question. Evangeline pulled back from the bright light of day. She looked like a ghost, pale, drawn. She'd lost a good ten, maybe fifteen pounds since Fleur had last seen her. Back in July. At Vincent's memorial, when they had poured his ashes into the Mississippi River, only a few blocks south of where they now stood.

"How," Fleur began, distracted by the deep purple circles beneath Evangeline's red-rimmed eyes. Those eyes squinted against the sun, and Evangeline raised her hand to shield them. "I was going to ask how you're doing," Fleur said, "but I don't have to. You look like hell." She moved to push past Evangeline.

"I don't remember inviting you in," Evangeline said, stepping forward to block Fleur's way.

"I've come to help." Fleur caught a whiff of alcohol seeping through the woman's pores. If anyone struck a match, she and Evangeline both might light up like torches.

"Help?" Evangeline said with a laugh that felt like a slap. "I don't need help, especially not from my bastard ex's prissy little sister." Evangeline stepped back, one hand on the door, preparing to close it in Fleur's face.

"No?" Fleur said. "Well, then I ask you to consider the most salient point from among the many reasons I think you do."

Evangeline froze, and Fleur knew the color rising to the woman's cheeks was not the flush of health—it was a sign of her red-hot temper. "And what in the hell might that be?" she said, grinding each word between her teeth.

"Hugo asked me to come. He thinks you need an intervention. Stop and think about it. *Hugo* thinks *you* need an intervention."

Evangeline's eyes opened wide. She slipped back from the doorway and retreated into the shadowy interior of the house. Not quite an invitation, but it would do.

Fleur entered the house and closed the door behind her. With all of the other shutters closed, the darkened, airless room felt too close. From across the room, she heard a click, and a lamp came on.

"I've always respected you," Fleur said. An odd place to begin, perhaps, but she sensed it was something Evangeline needed to hear, and moreover, it was something she needed to say. From what Hugo had passed on to her, Nicholas had been carrying Evangeline around like old chewing gum on the bottom of his shoe for years. He'd misled her about many things in general, but about Fleur in particular, projecting his own prejudices against Evangeline's background and occupation onto his sister.

She glanced around the cluttered room. "May I?" she said, nodding at a sofa swallowed up in a sea of empty bottles and dirty clothes.

"I don't live this way," Evangeline said, tossing a guilty glance at the dirty laundry and the empties swaddled in it. "This isn't me. Not normally." Beneath the shame rode an anger that might blaze at the tiniest spark. She rushed around Fleur to clear a space on the sofa, snatching at the items there like they had insulted her, and dumping them on top of another mound that rested on a moss-green eyesore of a club chair.

"I know it isn't," Fleur said, moving toward the sofa. "Hugo tells me you've long been the glue that's held his life together. That is why your current state has him shaken." She sat, crossing her ankles and smoothing her skirt, growing self-conscious beneath the weight of Evangeline's leaden stare.

"I'm sorry," Evangeline said, perching herself on the edge of the club chair's cushion.

Fleur raised her eyebrows and shook her head to signal she didn't understand.

Evangeline leaned forward a bit. "For calling you prissy." Her apology was sincere, earnest even, but the word still sounded silly.

"Prissy," Fleur said with a laugh. "Were I you, I would've gone with 'presumptuous bitch.'" Evangeline's eyes widened and her lips parted—ready, Fleur intuited, to protest the harshness of words she'd not even said. Fleur held up her hands. "Among my circle of friends, that's considered a compliment."

"You need better friends."

"I've heard you clean up nicely. Maybe you could be the first."

Fleur spotted a flicker of a smile on Evangeline's lips, but then the other woman looked her up and down, her gaze hardening. She was suspicious of her overture, and Fleur couldn't blame her. Not after the dozens, if not more, of her brother Nicholas's subtle betrayals.

Fleur felt a wispy tingle at the edges of her senses. Evangeline was an empath, and Fleur could sense that the other witch was casting some type of psychic net over her, intent on divining her true intentions. It wasn't worth trying to hide anything from her. Good thing Fleur had come to share all. "I would've come anyway," she said, intent on revealing the truth before Evangeline could uncover it on her own. "Even if Hugo hadn't asked me to. I have my own selfish motives to see you straighten yourself out."

"Imagine that," Evangeline said, then ran a hand through her tangled mess of red hair, "Honesty from a Marin." Fleur suspected Evangeline was reacting more to Fleur's aura than to her words.

"I'll always speak the truth to you," Fleur said. "That's the 'bitch' part. I'll earn the 'presumptuous' by assuming you'll always want to hear it." She fixed Evangeline with her gaze, trying to shake off the woman's magic. It surprised Fleur to find she couldn't. It pleased her, too. She needed a strong witch like Evangeline. "Listen. My father and mother. Your mother and her 'sisters.' They've all committed abhorrent, unforgivable acts. We are both decent, caring women, and we cannot help but feel ashamed. But we can't let that shame pull us out of the world, keep us from attempting to work good in it. And you do bring a lot of good . . ."

"I can't help you with Alice, you know," Evangeline said, "if that's what you're after."

Fleur had been prepared to discuss Celestin. Her best hope for drawing Evangeline out of her spiral of self-contempt and shame, she thought, was to engage her in a discussion of their common enemy, and how best to defeat him. She hadn't anticipated Evangeline would bring up Alice, at least not first thing, but empaths are led by strong emotion, and while on the topic of shame, Evangeline had easily tapped into Fleur's greatest regret. Fleur turned the image of Alice around again and again her mind, still trying to fathom that the girl she'd believed to be her niece was in fact her half sister. It was even harder to accept that her brother Nicholas, knowing that he couldn't be Alice's father, had purposefully painted the child as unstable and left her to rot in a psychiatric care facility.

Once Fleur had been able to project her psyche to a distant point, up to hundreds of miles if need be, but even if her power had been running at full force, the wards placed over the institution would have precluded her little magic trick. All the same, she could have made the trek the common way. It would've been simple enough to travel to the island: hop on a direct flight from Reagan to the Portland International, then charter a sea plane to carry her from there. Still, Fleur had never once visited Alice. She'd acquiesced to Warren's wishes. "No need to draw attention to the situation," her husband would always say whenever Fleur mentioned Alice. If she'd made even a single trip to Sinclair and spent an hour or two with Alice, maybe she would've ascertained the truth. Maybe all of this suffering could have been avoided. But no matter how convenient, she couldn't blame her soon-to-be ex for keeping her away. The fault lay with her. She should've told Warren to stick it. The desertion seemed a gross enough betrayal coming from an aunt, but somehow it struck Fleur as an even worse offense for a sister. Now it was too late to ever make it up to Alice. She had been lost to them once again, and this time for good.

Once a witch's magic turned in on itself, it created a closed and almost unbreakable circuit. It didn't matter whether they'd done so willingly or, like Alice, had been forced. There were legends, but no one in living memory had ever come across a witch who'd taken to the Dreaming Road and then returned. "No. I'm aware you can't," Fleur said. "None of us can help Alice. We missed our chance to do that when she was here with us."

"But you're still lying to Hugo and Daniel," Evangeline said, reading her guilt if not her thoughts, "telling them that you'll find a way to save her."

"Yes, I am. Hugo needs the lie. As far as Daniel is concerned, I'm half convinced he senses Hugo's need and is only playing along for his sake. Each time Daniel manages to enter Alice's world, he comes back seeming more discouraged. Sooner or later I'm going to have to tell Hugo there is no Santa Claus, and that's only the first reason I need you to pull it together."

"I am together," Evangeline said, with a lot of defiance but not much conviction.

"You're a mess," Fleur replied. "A disaster." Evangeline didn't even flinch. Fleur suspected she hadn't yet said anything to her that she hadn't already been telling herself. "You smell like a brewery—a filthy brewery, at that." Nothing. "You're throwing everything you love away. You've turned your lovely home into a tomb." Evangeline's eyes drifted over the room, but she remained silent. "You're letting your club go to seed. You're letting your employees down. I mean, for God's sake, Hugo's been running the place . . . yes, Hugo . . . trying to make sure you still have a business to return to when you snap out of this little pity party you've been throwing yourself. Oh," she added, deciding to hit where she knew it would hurt, "I should tell you that you've broken your cat's heart. Daniel says Sugar is pining for you."

There it was. Evangeline trembled. "I couldn't keep her. I couldn't."

"Why? Are you trying to make those who love you feel the way Nicholas made you feel?"

"It has nothing to do with Nicholas." Evangeline spoke his name as if her tongue were made of barbed wire.

"Then what is it?" Fleur pressed. "Why are you doing this to yourself?"

Evangeline's eyes narrowed. Fleur didn't have to be an empath to know Evangeline was considering tossing her out. She might have pushed too hard, but she'd gone in knowing her attempt at tough love might backfire. "Maybe," Evangeline said, steam rising off the word, "you should get to telling me what it is you're wanting from me."

Fleur decided a direct approach was best. "I'm rebuilding the Chanticleer Coven . . ."

Evangeline's eyes turned to flint. "Why? Is your father planning another massacre?"

Fleur felt the twined strands of shame and rage she'd been carrying inside her tighten once more in her stomach. She'd returned to New Orleans—in part—to bury Celestin, but the cunning bastard had managed to do the impossible and outwit death. He'd sacrificed nearly every witch between Texas and Mississippi to lay claim to their power.

Fleur knew she'd been pushing Evangeline. Still, the woman's callous sarcasm struck a nerve. "I'm sure if he were, your fine feathered aunties would have let you know," she snapped.

Evangeline jerked back, like Fleur had slapped her. Her eyes went wide as if she were reliving the horror of that night.

Fleur reminded herself that she owed Evangeline a debt of gratitude. Without her, Hugo would have been one of the fallen. Fleur's own eyes moistened. "I'm sorry," she said, forcing herself to regain composure. She wiped away her tears with two quick swipes. This wasn't like her. Years as a politician's wife had taught her how to function above her emotions, but here she was striking out at someone whose help she needed—worse, crying over it. "Really, I am."

A silence fell over them. Fleur felt the psychic net Evangeline had woven around her wither away.

"We've both drawn blood," Evangeline replied. Not a formal armistice, but the best Fleur could hope for. Evangeline's shoulders relaxed; her gaze seemed fixed on an invisible point floating somewhere between them. "Any sign of Celestin?" Evangeline shuddered at her own use of the name, then crossed her arms and rubbed at the gooseflesh.

Evangeline was clearly horrified by the thought of Celestin, but the question still struck Fleur as casual, as if she'd asked only because she could tell it was expected. Fleur envied the younger witch her ability to see behind false fronts with such ease.

"No," Fleur said, focusing on the facts she knew, trying to keep this new apprehension from shading her aura. "He's been lying low since the massacre." Those who remained had been left to piece together an explanation for Celestin's murderous activities from the bits of information they'd gleaned from a ghost, a servitor spirit, and a cat. Incomplete evidence, no doubt, but at least the sources were trustworthy. "Don't take this the wrong way," Fleur said, "I'm happy Lisette and Soulange succeeded in checking Celestin that night, but it seems he burned through a lot of lives for nothing, and we can't assume he's done."

Evangeline's eyes darted to hers. "Whatever Celestin and Astrid are up to, it's related to that damned book. Marceline and her sister witches, my 'aunties' as you call them," she added, a fine coat of resentment varnishing her words, "are all about getting hold of it."

"Yes, I know." Until a few months ago, Fleur had always believed *The Book of the Unwinding* to be nothing more than witch folklore. Then, mixed in with Astrid's belongings, Daniel had uncovered a copy of *The Lesser Key of Darkness*. The mad monk Theodosius was credited as the author of both. *The Lesser Key*, Fleur now understood, was a primer or even a catechism for those who would make use of Theodosius's greater work. Fleur had scoured every reference she could find to *The Book of the Unwinding* with the fervor of a new convert. There were a thousand conflicting accounts of what the book actually contained, but each agreed on a single point. If Celestin's goal was to become the King of Bones and Ashes, the master of magic described in *The Lesser Key*, he'd have to sacrifice his entire line. He was well on his way. He'd murdered Vincent, taking over his identity and performing a flawless impersonation. And her nephew Luc. They'd long believed he'd taken his own life, but he, too, had died at Celestin's hand. Then there was Alice, wiling away in a closed-off, artificial world . . .

Celestin would have killed Fleur, too, maybe even kicked off the carnage the night of the ball by spilling her blood, had she not surprised him with an act of defiance. She'd spat in the face of Gabriel Prosper, the man who'd tried to wrest control of the Chanticleer Coven from Marin hands. She couldn't have suspected that her own father was masquerading behind Gabriel's features. Even so, she knew the stay of execution he'd granted was a reprieve, not a pardon. He would come for her again when it suited him. Fleur could never let it come to that. She was all that stood between him and her daughter, Lucy. And Hugo, too.

"I'm rebuilding the coven." She repeated herself to give her time to regain her nerve. "I want you to join us."

"Never," Evangeline said, shaking her head, rising to her feet. "I will never join Nicholas's coven."

Fleur scooted forward, realizing only after she moved that her subconscious was readying her to give chase if necessary. "But it isn't Nicholas's coven anymore." She steadied herself, trying to quash the desperation pushing her to irrationality. Cool heads, not rash actions, win the day. "It isn't even Nicholas's city anymore." Fleur dangled the sentence like bait, hoping Evangeline might be interested in news of him. But the woman didn't bite. "He's gone off, out west. Maybe he's trying to find new ways to access magic like he claims to be doing, or maybe he's looking to find himself." Fleur hoped it was the former. She was counting on it.

"It doesn't matter," Evangeline said, and Fleur witnessed the last glint of feeling for Nicholas fade from Evangeline's eyes. "It's a fool's errand either way."

"You're right." Fleur had a flash of Nicholas as the fool of the tarot, a bindle and stick on his shoulder, one foot perched on the edge of a precipice. If he did fail . . . No, she couldn't let herself go there. She needed to focus on her own efforts. She needed Evangeline to see her as an ally. If that meant besmirching Nicholas, so be it. In her shoes, Nicholas wouldn't hesitate to do the same. "The peregrinations of a self-absorbed man are of no importance."

Fleur searched her heart for a flicker of affection for her brother. She found gratitude with ease, but what little love she uncovered had nearly been starved to death. She suspected that Vincent was the only one of the three of them who'd ever really been worth a damn. "What does matter is we witches, real witches, seem to be a dying breed. You're one of the few witches left in New Orleans who's retained any kind of real power. I need you . . ."

"To help you keep Celestin from picking the rest of you off like beer cans on a fence."

Fleur didn't understand Evangeline's simile, but she decided to let it pass. "Yes, in part to combat Celestin, but I have other . . . concerns." She paused, debating the best tack to take. She decided to start by revisiting familiar territory. "Magic is fading—"

"Magic is fading. Magic is dying." Evangeline sang the words as if she were composing an extemporaneous lullaby. "Do you think I could've been with your brother as long as I was without learning that tune?"

Fleur nodded. "Fair enough. I know witches first raised the alarm long ago, and frankly, I'm pretty damned tired of thinking about it, too, but that doesn't mean the problem isn't real. Some witches are saying the waning of magic is natural. That it has happened in the past, and the pendulum will swing back. I find the slim evidence they offer unconvincing. More wishful thinking and blind faith than fact. No, I don't believe this decline is temporary, and I have no faith in magic's anticipated resurgence. However, I do believe that together, we can make the decline easier for one another . . ."

"Then your selfish motives come in an altruistic wrapper."

"In this circumstance, I believe the greater good aligns with my own desires. Perhaps, together, we can stave off the end. Perhaps we might even discover a method to reverse the course. Push the damned pendulum back."

"Maybe," Evangeline said, "it's good that we're going extinct. Maybe magic should die with us."

"Oh, but to you, death seems theoretical. You're still young and healthy, but there are some out there whose continued existence hangs on magic."

"I'm sorry for them, but too many of us have held on to life long past the ordinary—"

"My Lucy died in utero. She stopped moving at around six and a half months. The doctors wanted to induce early labor . . ." Fleur's voice faltered, but she'd waded halfway into the Rubicon. She had to press on. "You hear such horror stories about resurrection spells backfiring, but I couldn't let her go. I restarted her heart, and my magic has regulated its every beat since. But my power is falling away. More and more quickly each day. I told you I'd be honest with you, and I warned you my motives were selfish. I want you to join the Chanticleers—my coven—because I need your power, and I need to be able to control it."

SIX

Lisette regretted her decision to pick up a newspaper when she stopped at the gas station for a coffee.

Forget Celestin Marin. Forget forbidden magic books and the mad monks who write them. There was enough going on in the everyday world to scare a body to death.

She sat behind the counter at Vèvè, perusing the journal, wondering what in the hell was wrong with people.

People with guns in their hands. People without love in their hearts. People who still—honest to God—thought their damned race made them innately superior to others. People who cared more about winning than even their own best interests, happy to follow red-faced religious hypocrites and fat, lying politicians through the gates of hell itself, if it meant they got to brag about beating everyone else there.

She folded the paper and set it aside.

Yeah, there were a hell of a lot of things in the world to be afraid of, but today, she wasn't going to focus on that.

Today, Lisette would be grateful.

Grateful for Isadore, her husband, her rock.

Grateful for his landscaping company and her shop. Grateful for the sufficient income the businesses generated.

Grateful for their children, Manon and Remy, both good, responsible young adults, though neither of them had made it home last night, and neither of them had been considerate enough to check in to say where they'd be.

Lisette felt her lips pursing and realized she was veering off course. She forced her thoughts back to her list.

Grateful for the Tremé neighborhood galleried cottage her family shared. Grateful for its beautiful Eastlake trim and its graceful, rounded steps. Grateful for Isadore's roofer-friend's estimate that its composite roof with overlapping tile joints should last another ten years, Bondye and both named and unnamed storms permitting.

Grateful that her father would soon catch hold of himself and get back to being the man she knew, loved, and respected.

Well, okay, that last one might be more wishful thinking than gratitude, but maybe the universe wouldn't be paying close attention, and she could slip in a suggestion while it was otherwise occupied.

The damnedest thing was that even though she hated his behavior and despised what he was doing to himself, she couldn't say her father was wrong. After his visit yesterday, she couldn't shake the feeling that he might have a point about history trying to repeat itself. It wasn't only Fleur Marin showing up on her doorstep all the time, going on about *The Book of the Unwinding* and the past, trying to be her best friend, it was also Remy getting all caught up with Fleur's daughter.

A rapping sound startled Lisette out of her thoughts.

A bent old man in a worn straw hat stood outside Vèvè, tapping one windowpane with his cane and holding a garish cartoon tourist map up against another. He held a pipe clenched between his teeth. There was something familiar about him, and even though she couldn't place his face among her father's friends, she felt certain she'd encountered him wandering around the Quarter. Then again, maybe she was wrong about that. It'd be odd for someone who lived here to carry around a map of the area.

Their eyes met, and in that moment she knew him. *Oh, of course.* She grasped the hem of a slippery epiphany. The vèvès not only symbolized the loa, they summoned them . . . which meant this was Papa Legba incarnate, not a mere spectral impression. Before she could finish processing the realization—at the same time completely logical and, to her stubbornly skeptical nature, utterly absurd—he was gone.

She rushed to the window, then out the door, looking up and down the street to see if she could spot him. The old man, though deep down she knew he wasn't a man at all, had vanished. The map he'd been holding lay on the sidewalk like a silent witness to his visit. Lisette bent over and picked the map up, flipping it from side to side, looking for . . . what? A scrawled line of communication? An X to reveal a treasure or to lead her to a rendezvous? She saw nothing of the sort.

Still, Lisette couldn't shake the feeling that the map itself had been the message—or at least part of it—even if it looked like nothing special. It was the kind of map hotels handed out at check-in: the French Quarter front and center, the rest of the city be damned, with numbered dots denoting points of interest, the whole thing bordered by coupons promising BOGO drinks and free desserts with the purchase of any entree. She'd encountered various iterations of it a million or two times over the years, sweat-dampened copies clutched in tourists' hands, others tossed into the trash or blowing down Chartres Street.

She tried to fold the map, but it didn't seem to want to follow its creases. She managed to quarter the page, leaving Armstrong Park and Congo Square at the top and Jackson Square beneath her thumb, the crosshairs of the bull's-eye pattern of its paths lined up with the center of her own thumbprint. Still, the layout was deceiving—Congo Square wasn't true north, and Jackson Square, the oldest public grounds in the city, lay much more southeast than south in relation to Armstrong Park.

She was shaking her head, half thinking the man had been a hallucination, when the vèvè in the window caught her eye. She focused her full attention on it, certain it was the key to the spark of insight that was struggling to life inside her. Her eyes traced the lines in the order she had painted them: the bold vertical line at the exact center of the pane, the horizontal line that crossed it at a perfect ninety-degree angle to form the center cross, then bisected Legba's hooked cane—his *poteau-mitan*—that connected worlds together, and the freer curving lines beyond.

Suddenly, she saw it. The crossroads of Legba's vèvè matched the crossing of the paths in the park where the statue of Jackson stood.

This time the map cooperated as she folded it into a tight square. She held the page up to the window, positioning it with St. Ann Street running a perfect horizontal across the top, so that the park's crosshairs were in line with those on the symbol. The bells of the cathedral began to chime, and she glanced up Chartres Street toward the church, deep in thought. As the bells tolled, she turned back to the map, rotating it one hundred eighty degrees so that the Cabildo, the cathedral, and the Presbytère were shown on the right.

"That's it. That's it," she heard herself saying. The three buildings now lined up with the triplet five-pointed stars arrayed on the vèvè's right-hand side. The pedestrian walkway before the three buildings even suggested Legba's cane, the curve of where Chartres Street met St. Peter Street an allusion to the cane's hooked handle.

St. Peter, indeed.

Over the years, the loa had come to be syncretized with the Catholic saints. Some claimed it had been done so the loa could be venerated right under the eyes of those who would have otherwise forbidden it. Others held that the connection went deeper than that. That on some level the different personalities were the same—one spirit wearing different masks. The various aspects of Papa Legba had been equated to St. Peter, St. Lazarus, and St. Anthony. It struck her there was another geographical correspondence—St. Anthony's Garden sat behind the cathedral. She gazed at the map and vèvè side by side, trying to call the Lazarus connection forth. The beep of a car horn caused her to look up. She lowered the map and turned to face the square. A part of her protested leaving the shop unattended, but she still found herself walking down Chartres toward Jackson Square.

She felt a tiny spark go off in her mind. A correspondence to St. Lazarus seemed at first to be unaccounted for in her theory, but St. Ann Street, once the home of Marie Laveau herself, ran along the opposite side of the square. If Lisette remembered the legend correctly, it was St. Lazarus who'd carried St. Ann's bones to their final resting place.

She followed along the pedestrian stretch of the street and took note of the Pontalba Buildings flanking the square on either side, their position echoing the placement of identical leaves on the top and bottom of Legba's vèvè—further proof that the connection was real. Quick steps carried her into the center of the square dominated by the statue of Jackson, his horse forever rearing up like Pegasus about to take to the sky. An intentional insinuation or not, the image of a literal rider and horse sure called to mind the metaphorical relationship of loa to *chwal*.

She carried on toward the river until the path spilled her onto Decatur Street. She stopped on the sidewalk that lay beyond the gates, noticing that even the layout of Washington Artillery Park and the steps leading up to it seemed to mimic the curve of the bow and serpent that separated a single five-pointed star from the rest of the symbol. Glancing at the map, Lisette decided the solo star's position would match the rough coordinates of the park's cannon.

She turned a full circle, taking it all in as if through new eyes, this ancient field of execution where she'd played when she was a small girl, this former military drilling ground where she'd taken her own babies to play.

Her mama had always told her that a person didn't need to scratch too deep into New Orleans's surface to uncover hidden magic, but spotting vèvès woven into the borders of the rugs of the Hotel Monteleone's lobby or making half-joking conjectures about the location of the seven Gates of Guinee was one thing. This was another. The symbols that matched up with Papa Legba's vèvè spanned commerce, religion, government, military, and judicial power. It made sense that in the early New Orleans, these institutions would find themselves located cheek to jowl with each other, but it was a real awakening to realize that the very layout of the original city corresponded to the symbol of the guardian of gates and crossroads.

Either New Orleans had been built to serve as a crossroads or the land itself had demanded it, influencing the powers that be to cast the city in a mold that would leave it as such.

She heard a whistle and turned toward its source. A small black dog, the same wiry-haired mutt she'd encountered the night she and her mother had walked into the middle of Celestin Marin's massacre of witches, shot through the square, catching up to its master. The old man doffed his straw hat, and in a blink the two were gone.

SEVEN

"There are seven gates," Daniel said, then slapped Fleur's hand away from the thin red volume on the table before her. "No, no, that is not for you." His gloved hand snatched back the book he called *The Lesser Key*. "Sorry, but you are a Marin, and I shouldn't have to point out that it doesn't seem to take much to turn you people."

Fleur couldn't see the life Daniel claimed existed within the book— the cilia-like sensors reaching out, testing, perhaps even tasting the reader to determine if their spirit could be seduced, corrupted. She flushed, a bit angry at being treated like a child—and at his lack of trust—but Daniel didn't seem to notice. His attention was focused on the book as he flipped through its pages.

"Seven," he said, glancing up, his eyes glowing with goodwill and enthusiasm.

She swallowed her anger and her pride. After all, Daniel had been created to nurture and protect children. Maybe what Daniel had implied about Marin blood was true. Maybe it would be best if she didn't touch *The Lesser Key*.

"Just another clichéd mystical number," he continued, rolling his eyes in a none-too-subtle imitation of Lucy. "Seven seals. Seven days to create the earth," he began reciting, assuming the teenager's patented blend of affected irritation and apathy. Fleur couldn't help but smile—partially in appreciation of his humor, partially from a sense of relief. Daniel hadn't noticed that there was anything wrong with Lucy, or he wouldn't be mimicking her. "Seven Mithraic mysteries. Seven rungs of the ladder of virtue. Seven chakras." He reached up with his free hand to tap the top of his head, moving down progressively to touch his forehead, his throat, his chest, and stomach. His hand hesitated, then he blushed like a schoolboy and shrugged. "Well, you get the point."

Fleur nodded and focused again on the book he held. When he'd told her to look at it through a witch's eyes, she could have laughed. She counted as less and less of a witch each day. She reserved every ounce of her magic for one purpose—keeping her spoiled, impossible, loving, generous girl alive. It had felt good to confess this to Evangeline, to share the truth with another human being, even if the fiery witch had told her to go to hell. It was okay. Evangeline would come around. She would. She had to. A tear brimmed in Fleur's eye, and she brushed it away.

"Allergies," she said in response to Daniel's inquisitive look.

"Oh," he said, wrapping the book up in the special blessed terry-cloth towel he reserved for that purpose. "I've got some raw local honey in the pantry . . ."

She held up her hand. "No. No. I'm fine." It was too late—she'd triggered his caregiver mode. She could sense him scanning her. His forehead creased as his brows lowered, an impressive simulacrum of true human concern. She did have to hand it to Nicholas and Astrid. When it came to servitor spirits, they did excellent work. They might not have been caring parents, but they'd made one.

"I do care." Daniel slipped the swaddled book into a clear plastic bag, pinching the zipper closed. "Maybe my feelings aren't 'real' enough for you, but I do have them, and they seem plenty real to me."

Fleur jolted, her mouth gaping open in surprise. He'd read her thoughts. Daniel, she remembered, had been gifted with rudimentary telepathic abilities, although his talent couldn't begin to match Evangeline's power to discern emotions. Surprise boiled over into anger. "I need you out of here." She tapped her temple with her finger. "Understand?"

"Certainly." Daniel's calm, one-word agreement caused the temperature in the room to drop twenty degrees. At least it felt that way.

Great. Fleur had managed to alienate one of the two beings, human or otherwise, who hadn't slammed the door in her face. Like quiltwork, she was trying to sew together a coven from tattered scraps. She hadn't approached the Twins yet. She knew that they would be offended if she *didn't* take it for granted that she could count on them. But Hugo, the Twins, and she did not a coven make.

The only other witch who'd taken her seriously, Eli Landry, had sought *her* out. She wouldn't have had either the heart or the nerve to approach him, but he'd caught wind of her efforts from the other witches. Eli had been her first love, and she his. They'd reconnected the morning of Celestin's memorial ball, bumping into each other by chance outside a coffee shop on Prytania. He'd asked to be her escort at the ball, and she'd agreed, if only for old times' sake.

That he would issue such an invitation after all this time, despite the callous way she'd broken things off with him, spoke to his kindness and loyalty. To think, he'd only escaped Celestin's murder spree because he'd left the ball early to check on her after her intentionally dramatic exit. But then, Eli was a singular man.

Still, she couldn't much blame the others for shooing her away. Most of the surviving witches in New Orleans were solitary, and as far as Fleur could see, there was a good reason for that. Independent, strong-willed, odd, and surly, these were the kids who'd gotten report cards marked "does not play well with others" and considered it a badge of honor. They seemed content to keep things that way, especially since the best pitch she'd come up with sounded something like, *Hello. My dead father recently slaughtered a half dozen or so different covens. Would you care to join the new one I'm convening? He'll likely come after us.*

She sighed, almost giving in to a sense of defeat. *No.* She caught hold of herself. Self-pity was a luxury she couldn't afford.

"I'm sorry," she said. Daniel's cool, passive expression melted into a moue—a sign, Fleur decided, that she should be a touch more effusive in her apology. Ah, what the hell. She *was* sorry. "I shouldn't have . . . discounted your feelings. It was insensitive of me, and I've exposed my own ignorance in doing so."

He raised his chin. "Well, perhaps I am a touch sensitive."

Fleur couldn't help but smile. This fellow, she decided, was good at conveying layered messages. He'd managed to take partial responsibility for the unpleasantness, all while impressing on her that his emotions were both real and calibrated with precision.

Daniel hadn't always known he was a servitor spirit. Nicholas and Astrid had led him to believe he was the ghost of an Irish worker who'd died during the construction of the New Basin Canal. Fleur had thought it a cruel ruse, but—count it as yet another moral failing on her part—never spoke up about it. After Katrina, he had disappeared. Years came and went, and she never gave the dissolved servitor a thought. Then, every bit as unexpectedly, he returned in full and solid form. Fleur didn't know how Daniel came to learn that he'd never lived as a man, that he'd been created to watch over Nicholas's children. She supposed it had been left to Hugo to expose his parents' lie after Daniel returned. Her nephew had been the only one left to tell him. They had—they *all* had, including her—abandoned Alice in an institution, and Luc had long since been reduced to ash and bone.

"I know you were acting out of concern . . . genuine concern. It's only . . . ," she began, trailing into silence. She felt the same trepidation she always felt when in the confessional, pretending to confide in the attending priest. She required neither the good father's benediction nor heaven's absolution, but her husband had always maintained attendance was important for the sake of appearances. Warren knew more about appearances than any other person Fleur had ever met, so she'd made a habit of going once, sometimes twice a week. Every time the father's smooth, pale hand pulled back the curtain, Fleur rattled off a list of half-truths and imagined venial sins invented as misdirection to draw the priest's attention away from heavier, veiled truths. Well, today she didn't have it in her.

Today she didn't want to have it in her.

Daniel might be sweet. He might be helpful. His concern might be the most genuine Fleur had ever encountered. Still, she owed him no accounting. He wasn't entitled to an explanation of situations that counted as none of his business. She closed her eyes and drew a breath. "Could we . . ." She opened her eyes and plastered her most diplomatic smile on her face. "Seven?"

"Seven?" he looked at her with wide, confused eyes. "Oh," he said, nodding as her meaning hit him. "Yes, indeed. Seven." He pulled out a stool from the counter and perched himself on it. His mien reminded Fleur of her old freshman English lit professor, well versed and eager to impart knowledge to fertile minds. "*The Lesser Key*," he began the lecture, "alludes to the seven gates of the underworld, a single line, which doesn't provide much insight if taken out of context, but when you consider the concept in light of the illustrations on the book's center pages, its heart, if you will . . ." He reached behind him for the plastic-enveloped book.

"That's okay," Fleur said, prompting him to face her. "I know. The King of Bones and Ashes and the Queen of Heaven." Every detail of the primitive portraits of the two personages had been burned into her memory. She didn't need to see the images again.

"Yes, both aspects of Inanna and her consort Damuzi. If you remember, the night of the ball honoring your father, I understand that Julia and Gabriel—that is, your father impersonating Gabriel—arrived dressed . . . or, in Ms. Prosper's case, undressed except for a rather impressive emerald necklace . . . as these gods."

Fleur flashed back to the sight of Julia Prosper walking into the hall, her head held high, her regard proud, withering even, a necklace of diamonds and teardrop-cut emeralds fit for royalty cascading onto her breasts. In that moment, Fleur felt certain, Julia had seen herself as royalty. In the next, she was dead, her exquisite necklace dripping blood. Fleur felt her own blood drain from her face as she considered how close she had come to sharing Julia's fate.

Yes. She remembered. "I was there. I don't think I'll ever forget."

"Well, no. I can see how you wouldn't," Daniel said. Then, seeming to realize his faux pas, he rushed on. "I believe there's a reason why *The Lesser Key* presents Inanna as nude, except for that final bit of jewelry."

Fleur leaned forward and raised her eyebrows, a silent cue for Daniel to continue.

"Inanna attempted to annex her sister's kingdom, the underworld, but to reach the underworld she had to pass through"—he held up a finger—"seven gates."

"Okay," Fleur said. "So?"

His eyes caught fire with enthusiasm. "Each gate had a guard, and each guard commanded her to remove one item of her attire. But it was a trap, a trick played on her by her sister. With each item she removed, she grew weaker. The last adornment she relinquished was the necklace. Inanna found herself powerless before her sister after passing through the final gate."

"I take it her sister didn't welcome her with open arms."

"Oh, my goodness, no." He shook his head. "Theirs was a magic without mercy. She turned Inanna over to—as you might guess—seven judges, who tried and then executed her."

"A happy ending then?"

"Well, no. Not quite happy for the Queen of Heaven, but not the ending of her story either. She was brought back to life via some kind of pixie dust or the like, and negotiated her way out of the underworld by promising to send another to take her place." Daniel leaned back, his lips pursing as he stared at some point between them.

"What is it?" she said, jarring him from his reverie. "Whom did she send?"

"Her husband Damuzi . . ." His head tilted to the side and his jaw jutted out. She could sense he was weighing a decision of some sort. "There's a detail of the story I've overlooked . . . until now. It strikes me that it may be important."

"What might that be?"

"Inanna also sent Damuzi's sister."

"I see," Fleur said. "You suspect Astrid might have roles for Nicholas and me to play in her scheme."

"I found the book among her belongings. On the bright side, at least from your perspective, Damuzi's sister volunteered to take his place six months of the year. Unless you're inclined to take Nicholas's place . . ."

"I assure you, I am not."

Daniel shrugged. "Then you should be free and clear."

"Why then? Why everything but the necklace?"

"I think it's a sign that our Inanna hasn't taken the final step. She hasn't yet sacrificed the last of her power. Everything in there," he pointed his thumb back over his shoulder to the counter where *The Lesser Key* lay, "appears to be about self-sacrifice, not your good old Buddha-like denial of the illusion of self, but about erasing one's presence from this world."

"For what purpose?"

"Dunno. To become worthy of *The Book of the Unwinding*? To conquer the underworld?" He chuckled at what he seemed to think a joke, but something about the notion struck a chord.

"Or maybe," Fleur said, "to bring something back from the underworld." She had trouble swallowing the idea of shades wandering through a down-below for all eternity. She wondered if this "underworld" might be an actual place, a hidden dimension, or a state of mind.

Daniel ran his fingers through his curly mop of ginger hair. "Murder was the first act of magic," he said, his tone confirming that he felt she might be on to something. He fell silent, seeming to play with the idea in his mind. He did, it dawned on her, have a mind. Being manufactured did not mean he was unreal. She'd be more careful, more considerate toward him going forward.

He tapped his finger on his temple. "There's one aspect of all this that has been nettling me."

"Yes?"

"I believe we know the 'why' of what we've been seeing. Magic is fading away, and most witches aren't willing to let it go without a fight. Celestin," he said, using his given name—an intentional choice, she was sure, to absolve her of her relationship to him—"was willing to give up his own life, take the lives of his family members." He held his hands out before him, palms up. "Become a mass murderer even. But," he said, flipping his hands over and slapping his knees, "magic isn't only disappearing from New Orleans. It's disappearing from the entire planet."

Fleur nodded in agreement.

"Then why does New Orleans seem to be the epicenter of the madness? On the surface, it seems like a confluence of chance, but if you think about it, it's almost like it was planned all along. That this city was chosen to be where magic would make its last stand. *The Book of the Unwinding*, the manual for surviving the final days of magic, was brought here back when the Vieux Carré was still kind of new."

Fleur shrugged. This wasn't news. "Evangeline has told us her mother and her mother's sister witches were charged with carrying it here, to what was then a godforsaken outpost at the end of the world."

"Yes, I know, purportedly to move it beyond the reach of those who might be seduced by it. I'm thinking that could have been a cover story. That this city was built here, and the Book brought here, for a very specific reason." He tilted his forehead forward and gave her a knowing look.

"All right. I'll bite," she said. "What is that reason?"

He smiled, his face taking on the smug, satisfied look of a paper-back mystery detective standing in a drawing room, preparing to reveal the identity of the murderer to his captivated—and captive—audience. "Seven," he said and winked at her.

"Seven?"

"Yes. The seven gates. To the underworld. As your new best friend Lisette Perrault could tell you, tradition holds they're all located right here in New Orleans. The seven Gates of Guinee."

Lisette Perrault. The daughter of the woman her own mother had murdered. The mother of the young man Lucy loved. Fleur felt the ground tremble, then realized that the earth hadn't moved. It was she who was shaking. The pieces had begun to fall together, and she hated to see Lucy's face on even the far edge of the picture they formed. "I, I," she stammered, "I need to go."

Daniel jumped to his feet. "I know I should hasten the parting guest out the door," he said, holding up a hand signaling her to wait. "But before you go, there's one more item we need to discuss." She stood there silently, feeling the pulse pound in her neck. "Alice," he said, when she failed to respond. "We need to talk about Alice. I know you've given up on her, but I think I've found a way to bring her back."

Fleur grasped the edge of the table, both anxious to hear his idea and dreading it.

EIGHT

Fleur's aura had been the black-purple of a physical bruise, with pin-pricks of red sparking out. Anguish with a desperation shooter.

No wonder the witch was desperate. Evangeline sensed Fleur's magic tank was nearing empty. She was running on fumes. Soon she was going to watch her daughter die, and she'd not even made it halfway to realizing there wasn't a damned thing she could do.

There wasn't a damned thing Evangeline could do either.

If she could help, she would, but how the hell was she supposed to help anyone when she couldn't even help herself? Evangeline hadn't found the strength to speak to Fleur of the torture Celestin and the sister witches had been inflicting on her. She'd tried to convince herself that she'd kept quiet so as not to add to Fleur's burden, but deep down, she knew Fleur had it right: Evangeline was ashamed. Ashamed of her own powerlessness.

No. She was in no shape to help Fleur with her troubles.

Nicholas might be able to buy his niece some time. If he would. Given his track record with his own children—and Evangeline still saw Alice as his, regardless—he sure as hell couldn't be counted on. There was the possibility that he might swoop in at the last minute. Play the great hero. Nicholas was good at that. Grand gestures that made him look like a bigger man than he'd ever be.

Much more likely that Hugo would step up. That boy—that crazy, self-centered, irresponsible, good-time boy—he'd give it all up, every last drop of his power, to give Lucy even one more day. And he'd do it without a thought. Because, in spite of his many exasperating faults, half of which she suspected him of affecting to serve as armor, that's who he was, what he did. He took care of the people he loved. Even when they didn't want him to. The son of a bitch.

He was the reason Evangeline was standing in front of her mirror, attacking her hair with her new rotating round brush dryer. Hugo had made it clear that he wasn't letting up, so today she'd go in to Bonnes Nouvelles, if only to kick his ass.

At first, Hugo had just come around himself to nag her.

Then he'd risked sending a couple of the dancers by. Evangeline had stopped them at the door.

"Girl, you need to let it out," Samantha had counseled her. "Have a good cry."

"Girl," Brie had said, mimicking Samantha's inflection, "you need to get right back in the saddle and find yourself a new man. Your old one, well, honey, he was *too* old for you anyway. He sure wasn't worth all of . . ." She craned her neck and looked around Evangeline's shoulder at the already deteriorating condition of the house. ". . . all of this."

"Right," Evangeline responded through gritted teeth, "just when I thought we'd pass the Bechdel test."

Her visitors stared at each other blankly. Brie shrugged. Samantha took her hand. "Oh, honey. I'm sorry, but I'm sure your doctor can give you something to clear that up."

Evangeline had promised to come into the club the next day, lying to get them to leave her front steps without hurting their feelings. That was going on two months ago.

A parade of casual acquaintances had joined the assault next.

A trickle, then a stream, of regulars from Bonnes Nouvelles. "Not the same without you around, E. C. You get better, and you get on back to us."

Andrea from her book club, bearing a copy of the month's selection, now last month's.

Even Miss LaLaurie Mansheon, the formidable drag queen bouncer who'd once chastised her for not teaching Hugo better manners—hello, irony—had shown up in full regalia at her door. The fancy new dryer Evangeline now held had come as part of the care package LaLaurie had pulled together at Hugo's—Evangeline felt sure—persuasive behest.

"A little pick-me-up," LaLaurie had said, setting the basket down at her feet and backing away like she was making an offering to an angry god, or trying to earn the trust of a wounded animal.

That second one rang a bit too true.

Evangeline finished with the dryer. Her hair was still nothing but a knotted mass of split ends. "Can your conditioner hold up to therianthropy?" She spoke the words aloud in her best commercial model voice. *Therianthropy.* The ability to change into animal form. A new word for her vocabulary. A new word she'd rather not have learned.

She sat the dryer down and riffled through the gift basket, the pink—yes, pink—cellophane it'd come wrapped in now on her bathroom floor, joining a week's worth of towels and washcloths. A week's worth that had been lying there for nearly two months.

Cruelty-free makeup. At least Hugo paid attention. Still, it was a good thing LaLaurie, with her knowledge of cosmetics, had pulled the gift together. Hugo may have picked up on her horror of animal testing, but he wasn't the kind of gay to know how to choose a quality brand. Her luck to be saddled with the only gay in three states who couldn't even help pick out an outfit. Hugo always delivered the same bored "as good as the last three" type comments you'd expect from a straight guy.

When unannounced visits from acquaintances hadn't helped Hugo meet his desired end, he'd started sending around absolute strangers to annoy her. To make it less painful to come out than to stay in.

Canvassers. Pollsters.

Magazine sellers bearing clipboards that held both order forms and reference letters from some unknown agency guaranteeing the salespeople were neither identity thieves nor murderers.

Two realtors. *We heard you were considering selling. Market's hot.*

A well-groomed couple wearing modest, boxy, pastel apparel and offering copies of *The Watchtower*.

Girl Scouts. She'd ordered three boxes of each flavor like Hugo had promised them she would. Son of a bitch.

Innocuous, sweet-faced teenage boys wearing matching sweat-dampened short-sleeved white shirts and long black pants.

An admittedly hot UPS guy who delivered empty boxes three days in a row.

And the assault had continued this morning with Fleur's visit.

Drift. Associate. Enumerate. Drift.

Evangeline's mind kept on chattering. Jumping from one item on the list to another. Making as much noise as it could.

It wasn't loud enough.

There in her own reflection, she saw a dark speck in her right eye, the creature in her looking out, watching her.

Evangeline slammed her balled fists into the mirror over and over again, cracking the glass, not caring if she cut herself, hoping she would, wanting to feel anything other than the cold, gnawing certainty that the world was coming to an end. That good and evil had duked it out, and she'd been on the losing side. Darkness was now creeping around, swallowing each and every glimmer of light.

She'd lost control of everything. Even of what happened to her own body.

She slid down to the cold, hard tile, wrapping her arms around her legs and rocking back and forth. Just as she started to call out for Sugar, she remembered she'd sent her poor old baby girl away. She couldn't have kept her. The first time Evangeline had transformed in her presence, the animal mind quickly gained the upper hand, and she found herself wondering how the cat might taste.

She went up on her knees and flipped open the toilet seat, sending the gift basket sailing into the tub. She clutched the porcelain bowl and leaned over it, retching and heartbroken at the memory. *Mama's sorry. Mama's sorry.* The words repeated in her head until her stomach settled, until her breathing slowed.

Get up, get up.

She took a deep breath and forced herself up on wobbly legs. She pressed the flush and let the seat slam closed.

Evangeline bent over the tub, fishing through the basket's spilled contents for eyeliner and mascara. She found them and turned back to the cracked mirror, only then thinking to check her hands for cuts. Not even a tiny one, as though some force in the universe was taking care of her. Or, a more likely scenario, flexing its muscles to prove its total control over her. She went up on her toes, leaning in to view her reflection in one of the larger islands of cracked glass, and started applying the makeup by rote. Her body carried her through the well-practiced actions.

She took one more look in the mirror, then turned her eyes down to inspect her outfit, the only clothes she had that could even pass for clean. She grimaced at the cutoff shorts she'd found wadded up at the back of her closet's top shelf and the Baker-Miller pink tank top emblazoned with the words "Maid of Honor." She'd gotten the shirt at a former employee's second—no, third—wedding, when she'd been asked to step in at the last minute for the real maid of honor, whose car had broken down outside Montgomery, Alabama. The shorts, she used to dance in, way back in the day. About the only thing going right was that her thirty-something ass still managed to fit into her twenty-something pants. She used that thought as fuel to carry her through her silent house and out the door.

Evangeline stepped over the threshold of the house and pulled the door closed behind her. Two steps down, she froze. The light was dazzling. She realized she hadn't been outside—not in daylight, not as herself—for months. She held her hand up to her eyes to block the light, stumbling down the last couple of steps. Sweat beaded all over her body and her heart started trying to beat its way out of her chest. She heard a pounding in her ears, irregular, frenetic. Alien and familiar in the same instance. It was her own pulse. And it was also the pulse of the darkness that had swallowed Marceline whole. She spun around, readying herself to run back up her steps. To fling open her door and dive into the cool safety of her house.

A horn blared behind her, and she realized she was standing in the dead center of St. Ann Street. She turned toward the sound. A heavy-duty pickup revved its engine behind her. There was something familiar about the truck. The name Perrault in white on the green hood almost triggered a connection, but her head was throbbing, her vision blurring on the edges.

The guy on the passenger side leaned out the window. "Wake up, you damn bitch," he said and took off his green ball cap to wave it at her.

"Hey, baby doll," the driver shouted out. "When I said I would hit that, this isn't what I meant."

Both men started laughing, but when Evangeline didn't clear out of the way, the passenger called out. "Maybe you need a little encouragement?" He looked over at the driver, grinning. Evangeline picked up on his feelings more than his words. They were dark and ugly.

Then the driver pounded on his horn. Again. And again. Each sounding a bit longer, a tad angrier.

The noise hurt Evangeline's ears.

Enough.

Her head tilted to the side, and every window in the truck shattered. There was a moment of silence, then the glass fell like a gentle rain into the truck's cab, covering but not harming either man. Evangeline smiled. Both men had chalky faces and eyes as big as silver dollars. "Gentlemen," she said, and laughed. If she hadn't heard the sound coming from her own lips, she would never have recognized it. A high-pitched cackle that made the group of onlookers scatter.

That felt good, didn't it?

She carried on down the center of St. Ann Street till she reached Bourbon. For the first time in a long time she felt normal. "Yes," she spoke aloud. "That felt very good."

NINE

Nathalie jolted wide awake. A horn was blaring, and she grabbed the wheel and stomped the brake. Only then did she remember that she was sitting parked on the block of St. Ann Street between Burgundy and Dauphine. Right on the heels of that recollection came another memory, that of helping Frank Demagnan put a pistol to his temple and pull the trigger. She'd helped the man kill himself.

No, that couldn't be right. He must have been dead already. His head had been taken clean off and stuck on backward. The thing that had dragged itself into his study might have been moving, aware even, but it sure wasn't alive. Not in any regular sense.

Just like her mama had always warned her would happen, she'd opened herself up to magic, and dark magic had found her. There was no denying what she'd witnessed was the worst kind, the kind her daddy's family used to say could get a witch "put down," things like resurrection spells or stealing the vital force of children to extend your own life. She couldn't imagine what Frank had gotten up to that would make someone want to do what had been done to him. She couldn't imagine any crime that he could've committed to justify it. Frank's killer was a monster, no doubt, but Nathalie took it as cold comfort that it clearly wasn't *her* monster. Had the killer been Babau Jean, she didn't harbor a single doubt that she would've been flopping on the floor right beside Frank.

Still, Nathalie hadn't gone home last night. She'd been too freaked out to be alone, half certain the police would show up at her door, and dead-on certain that if they did, she'd end up in the criminal ward at East Louisiana State Hospital, wrapped up in a straitjacket and wearing one of those masks that kept inmates from biting staff.

Yes, detective, I was there. No. I don't usually go into his private quarters, but a strange cat led me . . . No, I know there was no cat. It disappeared right before zombie Frank crab-walked into the room.

Nathalie hated lying. She tried not to, and when she caught herself in the middle of a lie, she always fessed up. Well, almost always. But, dammit, there were times . . . and this was sure one of them. She'd have to face the law sooner or later, and it might just take a gargantuan whopper to land her clear of this one.

The horn blared again, pulling her out of the interrogation scenario she'd imagined at least six times now, about five seconds before the bad cop made his appearance. She turned the key in the ignition and rolled down the window. The radio news channel came on—she'd been listening to it all night while she drove around, wishing she knew where she could get her hands on one of those police scanner radios. Pick up on whether anyone—anyone else, that is—had discovered Frank's body. Maybe there was an app she could get? She glanced at her phone lying dead on top of the folded Demagnan Mortuary suit jacket that rested on the seat beside her. She'd left her charger in the Demagnan hearse. She'd have to stop by a store to buy a new one, as soon as she felt sure her photo hadn't been shared on every channel and on the front page of the *Picayune*.

She flicked the radio off and stuck her head out the window to get a better view of what was going on. About half a block down, she spotted a white commercial pickup with an attached trailer sitting right at the intersection, in the middle of the street. The driver must've been having some kind of meltdown, because he banged on the horn again, playing it like he was Gabriel warming up his chops for Judgment Day.

Then the noise stopped.

She could sense a dark energy rising, feel that something wrong was about to happen. She caught herself holding her breath and wishing the badness away, reaching, she realized, for the photograph she'd taken from Demagnan's like it was a good luck piece. Was it her talent for reading people's natures or just wishful thinking that made her take this as another sign of Alice's innocence?

A shower of falling glass.

Nathalie startled, then rubbed her tired eyes, because from this distance it looked like every single window in the truck had caved in all at once. Then came a sound that imitated laughter, but held no joy. The cackle—that was the word—sent shivers down her spine badly enough that if the one-way street hadn't been blocked by the truck, she would've fired up the engine and gotten the heck out of there.

For now, she was stuck, so she waited, watching as a group of pedestrians took off in every direction away from the truck. They were following, it seemed, her own instinct for flight.

Everything fell still for a good sixty or so seconds, then the doors on the truck's cab flung open. First the passenger, then the driver piled out, dancing around, brushing themselves off, examining their arms and legs.

Her first thought was to go to the guys and see if they needed any help, but she could already hear the scream of sirens approaching. Anywhere else in the city, it might've taken at least fifteen minutes, maybe even half an hour, for the police presence to show up, but the French Quarter was how this town ate. The serving and protecting got done with a much greater sense of urgency around here. When the police got here, they'd most likely be looking around for potential witnesses. But she wasn't a witness. Not really. She couldn't offer up even the slightest insight. She rolled up the window and slipped down in her seat, ducking low, hoping to go unnoticed.

In a bizarre incident today, the still unexplained, simultaneous shattering of a commercial truck's windows led to the discovery of the city's most gruesome murder scene since the infamous Axeman's spree.

Wait, a realization broke into her imagined news bulletin. *That was it.*

The song playing on Frank's turntable was "The Axman's Jazz." Its composer had been inspired enough by the mass murderer's activity to write the sick ditty, but not enough to learn the correct spelling of the murderer's alias.

"Don't Scare Me Papa." That was the other name for the tune.

She had a flash of her father's great-uncle, the one who told fortunes, saying he was going to play a tune just for little Nat. His eyes had gone glassy and his lips had twisted up into a maniacal smile as he sawed the tune on his fiddle. She'd been terrified by the old man and his music. She remembered sobbing into her father's arms as he carried her from the parlor out to the porch.

Nathalie shuddered and sat up straight. At that very moment, a patrol car crept past her. The officer on the passenger side was watching out his window. His sharp eyes met hers, but the white Crown Victoria continued past.

Down the street, the truck's passenger was making himself busy, sweeping glass out of the truck cab into a large gray garbage can. She strained her eyes to make out the name stenciled on its side.

Perrault.

Well, damn.

All of a sudden being right here, right now, felt a lot less like random chance.

The can looked pretty full by the way the man strained as he dragged it behind the truck and hefted it up onto the trailer. One of the patrolmen was talking to the truck's driver, but the other officer, the one who'd spotted her, stepped around him and started coming her way, his walk the confident mosey of authority.

Well, double damn.

Nathalie plastered a blank-eyed and innocent expression on her face. *Why no, officer. Didn't see a thing. Only pulled in a moment before you. Some kind of disturbance?*

The policeman had come close enough that she could hear the sudden squawk of his radio. The officer stopped, his gaze fixed on Nathalie, even as he bent his head to speak into the mic that rode his shoulder like a flat, black, plastic parrot. "Yeah." She half heard him, half read his lips. "We're on that code fifty-five. St. Ann and Burgundy." Squawk. His eyes widened. "Okay, we're on our way."

He turned back. Curious, Nathalie opened her SUV's door so she could better make out what was going on. "Multiple thirty Uptown," she heard him call out to his partner. "You guys," he addressed the truck's driver and passenger as he walked back toward them, "need to take this thing up to Rampart Street and call yourselves a tow. Don't you be trying to drive it any farther than that."

"You heard him," his partner said to the driver, who was still circling the truck, red-faced and shouting that he'd get the bitch who did this if they didn't get her first. It was his buddy who followed the officer's orders. He climbed in behind the wheel and started the truck's engine. The original driver kept on shouting they were both going to get fired, but still he opened the passenger door and climbed in. The truck headed right on Dauphine. If its occupants intended to follow the officer's orders, another right would point them back to Rampart Street.

The blue lights on top of the police cruiser began flashing, and the siren screamed to life. The car shot forward, paused briefly at the intersection, then tore out of sight. Five seconds later, Nathalie sat alone in the relative midafternoon quiet.

She didn't know what a police code thirty was—a quick prayer in case it meant victims—but if there were multiple ones, it couldn't have anything to do with her and Frank. The only incident Nathalie had been a party to had involved exactly one victim. She reached over and picked up her phone, the contemporary pacifier, even though she knew full well it was out of juice.

A white glow formed around her hand, and the phone sprang back to life with a full charge. She stared down in surprise at its glowing screen, at her own glowing hand, pleased that for the first darned time since this crazy stuff had started happening around her, it had finally worked to her benefit.

Her pleasant sense of warmth fell straight away when her driver app opened itself, unbidden, and announced that her next passenger was waiting in Bayou St. John. She canceled the ride and closed the app. It fired right back up and told her once again she had a passenger at a residence near the Magnolia Bridge, wanting to go to an address on Prytania. She hit cancel again, but when she tried to close the app, it kept firing the same message at her. She tried to turn the phone off, but instead it started to ring the waiting passenger.

Maybe that's what happened when you used magic to charge your phone?

"Hello, then," the voice on the other end said. In those three clipped syllables Nathalie thought she heard the ghost of an Irish accent. "Is this the driver?" he said. When she didn't respond, he called into the phone, "Hello, is anyone there?"

She held the phone up to her ear. "Yes, this is Nathalie, your driver. Well, not your driver. I'm afraid there's been a bit of a mistake . . ."

"You're a driver, and I need a ride. No mistake in that, is there, love?"

"Uh, no, sir," she said, wondering if she should come down on him for the love bit, or if maybe he was just foreign. "There isn't. It's only that I'm not on duty right now. By the way, no offense, but I'd appreciate it if you didn't call me 'love.'" She sandwiched that in. "For some reason"—she lowered the phone to cast a guilty glance at it, then lifted it back to her ear—"the system has me locked in on you, even though I didn't accept your request. I've tried to cancel, so someone else can pick you up, but . . ."

"I've tried to cancel, too," the man cut her off, like he was trying to cover his hurt at being rejected. "Three times, as a matter of fact, but each time you keep accepting."

"No, sir. I really haven't been. I'm so sorry for the inconvenience, but believe me, I'm not in any shape—"

"It's an emergency," he said, though his sudden panic sounded a bit put on.

"Then maybe you should call 911?" *How is that,* she asked herself, *for irony?*

There was a pause, and Nathalie was sure she heard a hiss in the background.

"It's my pet," the man said. "A . . . dog. I have a dog," he added, even though she hadn't considered pressing for clarification as to his pet's species. It was true enough, though, that after the disappearance of Good-bye Kitty, she'd had enough of cats to last her a good while. "Oh, please, the poor little fellow's gotten ahold of something . . ." Another pause. "Toxic. Yes, poisonous," he said, almost like he was being coached. "I can't reach anyone else. My car won't start, and your app won't let me connect to another driver." Another pause, this time followed by a rather sincere sounding, "Please, you're our last hope."

"All right," she said, capitulating. "All right. I'm on my way."

"Yes," the man said. "Thank you, love." Then, as a seeming after-thought, he added, "Please leg it, won't you?"

"Um . . . sure," she said, but the man had already hung up. "And don't call me 'love.'"

She took a left on Bourbon. Always a bit of traffic there, though more distracted pedestrian tourists than vehicles. It would let up in a couple of blocks, past Lafitte's. That part of the Vieux Carré was nothing but one-way streets and dead ends, so she carried on to Esplanade Avenue, the first street that would lead her straight up to Moss. As she was about to cross over Burgundy, she noticed an emergency vet, and made a mental note to offer to drive her fare and his ailing pup there as a quicker alternative to the Prytania Street address he'd requested.

Her phone alerted her that she'd arrived as she pulled up in front of a large, well-kept Creole-style country house. A slim-waisted guy with red curly hair and broad shoulders stood under the house's gallery, waving at her with the same hand holding his phone. She rolled down the passenger window and leaned down to announce the obvious—that she'd arrived—but he was already making his way down the walk toward her.

He stopped about halfway across the yard. "Please," he said, waving her forward even as he stepped back. "Can you come in and help me with . . ."

"We're not supposed to . . ."

"Oh, please," he said again, turning around and dashing through the still-open door.

Nathalie thought it over. It might not be a good idea to go in after him. He was well built, athletic even. In a fair fight, though, she figured she could take him. Problem was, few fights were ever fair. Still, she'd trained in hand-to-hand combat and knew how to disarm an assailant. Most likely it would never come to that. She'd just go in and help the guy carry his pooch out to her car. The worst that was likely to happen was that the dog would end up releasing from both ends all over her back seat. Even so, she'd still drive the poor thing to a vet, because . . . Well, because dog.

Her would-be passenger popped his head back out the door and waved her forward again. "Come along," he called out to her, then disappeared back into the house. She focused on the feelings she was picking up from him. She had tried to take a peek inside his head, but her ability seemed to go on the fritz with this guy. All her life, she'd been able to read people without meaning to, picking up on their emotions and sometimes even their thoughts. Maybe she was still in shock, or maybe it was just lack of sleep, but with this guy, it was almost like the feelers she sent out like psychic radar passed right through him rather than bouncing back. That might have been enough to send her scurrying, but what she *could* pick up from him felt a bit like cuddling a warm, fuzzy blanket.

She got out of her car and headed down the walk. She stuck her head through the open door, the situation feeling a tad too familiar as she did. "Hello," she called.

"Yes," a response came from down the hall. "Back this way, love. Do come through."

"Uh, please stop calling me 'love,'" she said, though her voice came out weak as she crossed the threshold, taking care to leave the door wide open, warm fuzzies or no.

"What was that, my dear?"

"Nothing," Nathalie said with a sigh. She shook her head and carried on down the hall. Her eyes grazed the grand staircase and then followed the polished dark wood banister snaking its way up to the second floor.

A too-bright light spilled in through the landing window. In the center of the radiance, a figure coalesced. A young girl, it seemed—six or maybe seven years old—standing on her tiptoes to peer out the window. Most folk who caught a glimpse of this apparition would think it was a ghost, but Nathalie had seen more than her fair share of ghosts. This girl was no spirit. She seemed more like a memory, or a character from a story the house itself wanted to share with her.

The bright light dimmed, and the vision faded, so Nathalie braced herself and carried on toward the end of the hall where she could hear movement. But then she heard the door close behind her. She looked back to find the tiny gray cat that had led her to Frank's quarters stalking toward her, readying itself to pounce.

"Oh, for the sake of grateful glory, you dreadful beast," the man called out. Rather than turning, Nathalie moved back until she had them both in her field of vision. "Will you please," he said, pushing along a rolling serving cart that held a fancy, three-tier serving rack heavy with crustless finger sandwiches and cakes, "stop terrorizing our guest?"

The cat winked one eye, then gave a short, low, almost threatening purr.

"I am not afraid of you, you toothless old thing. No one is," the man said, releasing the cart and straightening.

Another purr, this one piqued and aggrieved at the same time. Nathalie had the oddest feeling that even she could understand its meaning.

"Well, I assure you that you will be," the man said, continuing to scold the cat, "if you keep this behavior up."

A silent glare passed between the two.

"You have to sleep sometime." He growled out each word and stared the cat down. Unless Nathalie was mistaken, the cat blinked first. The man smiled and turned to Nathalie, his sunny disposition recovered. "I do apologize, Miss Boudreau, for her terrible manners. Oh, and for our little subterfuge as well, but I'm sure you'll understand it was a matter of expediency."

Crazy world or not, Nathalie wasn't going to let that one pass. "Ms. Boudreau."

"As you like," the man said, pressing his hand over his heart, she sensed, as a form of apology. Suddenly, it hit her.

"Wait. What subterfuge and how do you know my last name?"

"Which answer would you prefer first?" He seemed genuinely concerned with providing her the requested information in the order she desired.

"Either." Maybe it was the cat. Maybe it was running on two hours of sleep. Maybe it was helping her boss blow his own dead brains out, but Nathalie had almost reached her limit. For the first time in a long time, she felt ready to boil over.

"To begin with," he said with a boyish smile and shrug, "there is no sick dog, which is bad in the sense that I did lie to you, but also good if you stop and think about it. I mean, you strike me as being a kind person who wouldn't want a dog to suffer."

A flat, perhaps even sardonic meow.

"Oh, no you wouldn't either," he said, grousing at the cat.

Nathalie got the sense these two enjoyed each other. That not knowing how to share their affection otherwise, they showed it through petty squabbles. Not all that different from her paternal grandparents, really.

"So, no sick dog," he continued. "No stop sign–running rush to the vet."

"How about my name?"

"Oh, we know much more than that about you." Coming from anyone else, the words would have sounded totally creeper, but this guy said them with the innocent pride of a fourth-grade bookworm giving the year's first book report. "Do come join us for tea, and we'll discuss all that." He grabbed the handle of the cart and began pushing it down the hall, back toward the entrance. He turned left into the room directly off the foyer and paused, looking back at her. "Such a treat to have a proper guest for a change. Gives us the chance to use the formal sitting room." The cat padded ahead of both of them over the threshold.

Nathalie considered the situation and weighed her options. The guy seemed sweet. A bit weird, but sweet. Probably not the person behind what was done to Frank, but this tea party he was throwing for her might arsenic and old lace her down a permanent rabbit hole. The most logical response would be to get the hell out of there. Occam's razor and farewell. "Uh, thanks, but no thanks."

The man pulled a pout and stared at her. "But I've made scones. Sweet *and* savory." He put special emphasis on the conjunction. "Sandwiches, too, though the tuna is for the pewter terror."

A demanding meow echoed from the sitting room into the hall.

She tried to smile. Tried to find a polite string of words. The best she could muster was a simple "No." Right now she was kind of over trying to please people—and their cats. She started toward the door.

"Oh," he said, sounding surprised, "I'd assumed you would want to hear about our Alice."

She stopped, shocked to hear the name spoken aloud. "Alice?"

"Yes," he said, his voice bright. "The young woman in the photo you stole from your . . . defunct employer's quarters. No need," he said, taking on the tone of a kindergarten teacher, "to dissimulate. Sugar watched you take it herself. Not to worry. It's all right that you did. It should belong to you anyway." He turned, pushing the cart forward with his right hand, and reaching up over his head to wave her forward with his left. "Come join us, and we'll tell you about Alice and a little something occultists speak of as 'the gravity of rightful destiny.'"

TEN

Alice held out no hope for the tangled skein of magic Daniel was attempting to weave into a rescue plan, but she knew he was out there trying. She would hold on for as long as she could, if only so when it was all over, he might come across some strand of evidence that would let him know she had tried. That she had shown faith in him.

She had constricted her world to a tight circle, its radius the equivalent of not much more than a single city block. The circle centered on the right triangle where Esplanade Avenue meets Ponce de Leon, then joins with Grand Rte. Saint John and Mystery streets to form Fortier Park. It pleased her, seeming both poetic and symmetrical, that in both worlds the park lay at the point where the search for eternal life ended and the mystery of what was to come next began.

All points beyond the circle's periphery blurred and were lost in a shimmer like that of a heat haze.

It didn't surprise her that this tiny green space would be the final landmark at the end of her existence. When she was a young girl, still living in Nicholas's house, this park, or rather the actual park in the common world, was the farthest she'd been allowed to wander on her own. For young Alice, this park had meant adventure and independence, as well as the limit of her freedom. Alice now spent all her daylight hours here. Alone.

She no longer had the luxury of companionship, but she still allowed herself sunlight. A few hours each day.

She shook her head as she parsed that last thought. *Sunlight.* An artificial brightness that burned away her magic, fed from her life force. *Hours.* She no longer even had a feel for what the word meant. Alice was losing any sense of time. Each "day" lasted only a few "hours," and each moonless night an eternity.

At dusk, every dusk, she rose and headed home. Not to a replica of her father's house, but across Esplanade Avenue to the loft she'd once shared with Sabine. The apartment took up the entire upper floor of a red, two-story shotgun-style house with orange and yellow trim and an apple-green door. Muddied Waters, the coffee shop she and Sabine had run together, monopolized the house's lower floor.

They'd picked the house's exterior colors almost as a joke, each pushing the other to the most garish possible combinations, each too stubborn to admit she'd prefer a more traditional palette. Alice had thought she would hate the scheme, but then she'd seen the colors together. They were perfect, revealing a beauty she would've never imagined on her own.

She froze as the truth, so easily forgotten, crashed in on her once again.

She had done exactly that—imagined the colors on her own. And her partner had not been Sabine, but something that looked and acted like her.

She stood stock-still in the center of her living room, her mind drifting as her eyes followed the swinging tail of the preposterous cat clock that "something" had wanted for her birthday. A momentary burst of voices—happy customers who didn't exist outside the Dreaming Road, reveling in the illusory café below—reminded her that she had imagined it all. That she was *still* imagining it. Even the concept of "below" was a pretense.

The café. The fulfillment of a wish built upon the image of a real café, one she'd hoped to visit, maybe with Hugo or Lucy, the two members of her family that she'd held the most hope of growing close to.

The sounds from below gave way to total silence.

Je pense, donc je mens. I think, therefore I lie. She heard the words in Sabine's voice, but the thought was her own. Perhaps the only thing she truly owned in this counterfeit world.

It made sense that Sabine was the last of the shades to linger here.

They'd been happy together, Sabine and she. Every adventure they'd experienced together had formed a zigzagging path that had led them both to being better people than either could've been on her own. Even their disagreements had always resolved themselves in ways that led to a greater closeness.

But none of it was real. Perhaps it never had been, even in the common world.

Alice and Sabine were no more than girls when they formed a friendship on Sinclair, though Alice had imagined she might one day love Sabine as more than a friend. The other girl hadn't voiced any romantic interest in her until the day before she left the island and disappeared from Alice's life. Now, Alice couldn't help but wonder if she'd imagined it. Perhaps Alice had projected the qualities she'd hoped to find in Sabine onto her, much as she'd done here on the Dreaming Road.

Sabine. A ready-made disguise she'd crafted for the hungriest of the shadows, the demon—no, she reminded herself, the twisted spirit—that had sunk its teeth deepest into her. It had been the first to come and remained as the last yet to depart. Alice feared this spirit, newly aware that it was her own mirror. In its insatiable darkness, she saw her own future.

The spirit still circled her home without fail every night, until the first rays of Alice's determined sun forced it to retreat. It could no longer abide the light, now that Alice had seen through its disguise. Even now, it was calling out to her, wailing a piteous cry with one feigned breath and hurling the basest obscenities with the next. As she did every night, Alice pretended to ignore the creature's cries and curses, the scratching sounds it made clawing at the house's siding. Until their other nightly routine happened—she broke.

Alice flung the window open and leaned out. "Go," she said, her voice low and quavering.

It looked up at her, a palpable shadow in the darkness, no longer capable of assuming, or maybe no longer caring enough to don, Sabine's appearance. "Go," Alice said again with growing vehemence, even though she knew her anger only excited the spirit more. "Go." This time the word came out in a high-pitched and furious scream. Instead, the ravenous shadow drew closer, emboldened, strengthened, nourished by her rage.

"Let me in," it keened. Its voice, its accent, its intonation, all perfect imitations of Sabine's. It lifted its claw and began scratching the siding again. "I love you, baby."

Alice closed her eyes and let a wave of hot anger pass, saddened to recognize the wrath she felt was aimed not at the creature below, but at Daniel. Her former nanny, who loved her. Who missed her. He seemed to be one of the few beings in the common world who did. Though he assured her that the entire family and beyond, a world of witches, was assisting him, she understood his efforts were in fact single-handed. He was trying to save her with his mad talk of rightful destinies, trying to bring her home to him. She would always love him, no matter what—but she hated him, too. He had forced her to see the ugly truth, and a dreamer will always hate the one who woke her.

She tried to keep a tally of the days since she'd last seen Daniel, using the method Sabine—the common world Sabine—had taught her, the first four marks forming a box, the fifth a diagonal strike through. The sheet now held seven tiny boxes, a single strike crossing each of their hearts. Thirty-five days for her. Maybe a day for Daniel? She couldn't be sure. The more lies she excised from her perceived reality, the longer time seemed to stretch out. Perhaps this was good. Perhaps she'd slowed the rate at which her power burned away, giving Daniel's attempts to save her more time to succeed. That, or she'd discovered the secret to making hell eternal.

She closed the window and took a step back, preparing to settle in for another unrelenting night.

A handful of lights twinkled in the darkness, but Alice suspected the only stars left to shine in her artificial sky were the seven she could spot from her current vantage point. Together they formed a facsimile of the Big Dipper, an asterism that belonged to the Ursa Major constellation. Ursa Major, the Great Bear, seen as a plow by some, a wagon or chariot by others. *Constellations.* Another set of stories built upon vague impressions.

Unlike in the common world, the asterism didn't seem to sail across the night sky. Each night, it glowed to life and then faded out, never changing position in the sky. In the common world, the Big Dipper seemed to revolve around Polaris, the North Star, the star at the tip of the Little Dipper's handle. Polaris was hidden in her world, but if there was any way to orient the Dreaming Road to the common world, this could be a clue. Maybe the tip of the dipper's cup still pointed toward true north?

Alice wondered if she should mark each star's position relative to her window pane to see if the seven visible stars rotated around an unseen Polaris. If they did, she'd have a chronometer, perhaps not a true measure of time in the common world, but at least something to help her catalog the passing of the year here.

As above, so below. She decided against blackening the glass. By the logic of magic, and the reason of the Dreaming Road, blacking out their position on the window might well extinguish their light from the sky. Still wrapped up in the attenuated logic of dreaming, she suddenly found herself, brush in hand, daubing paint on the glass. The image she was painting—a pair of crossed lines festooned with curly braces and tipped with six eight-petaled flowers—had no relation to the positions of the stars. Alice felt as if another hand, one more familiar with and practiced at making the sign, guided hers.

She felt she should recognize the symbol, like it was something she should remember from childhood, but it held little to no meaning for her. She deduced that the plus sign dominating its center had to do with a crossroads of some kind, standard magical fare, but she didn't know what the symbol as a whole represented. Even without understanding its significance, she recognized it for what it was, a type of sigil. This one felt older than those she'd grown familiar with during her internment on Sinclair.

In her last few hours on the island, the hospital's administrator had revealed to her that many of the sigils employed around the hospital were the modern and idiosyncratic work of the artist Austin Osman Spare. Spare had constructed his sigils, his "alphabet of desire," from bits of deconstructed language, taking phrases that expressed his wishes, stripping out recurring letters, and then compressing the remaining characters into a type of logogram, like an ampersand or a dollar sign, the administrator had explained, though with a more convoluted design and imbued with magic.

Spare believed that the act of creating a sigil served a dual purpose. First, it helped him focus his will, distilling each longing to its purest, most potent form. And by recasting his desire as a symbol incomprehensible to the rational mind, he ensured the sigil would take root in the viewer's subconscious—the subliminal sphere from which Spare believed the physical world emanated. Alice couldn't vouch for his rationale, but she'd experienced the results of his efforts firsthand. A combination of his sigils had prevented her from accessing her own magic during her time on Sinclair.

The design before her eyes, superimposed over her own blurry reflection, appeared a baroque and senseless design, but her heart told her she was in the presence of something sacred. It felt far weightier than the ones scattered throughout the hospital, like it carried the aspirations and faith of generations. Alice knew the symbol didn't belong to her, or even to her people. She touched the pane, tempted to wipe it away rather than to risk misusing it. And yet, she sensed her very existence might somehow depend on it. Alice sent up a silent plea for forbearance and committed herself to approaching the object, and those to whom it rightly belonged, with respect.

Behind the symbol, behind her own eyes, the seven stars flared up, burning with greater luminance than she'd ever witnessed before, the sky in their vicinity changing from black, to midnight blue, to rose. The stars expanded in size, each of them swelling to the relative size of her fist. Some force had changed them, and she knew it had changed her as well.

From below her window came a cry, then utter silence. No scratching, no cursing, no pleas for forgiveness or offers of clemency from her tormentor.

Alice watched in wonder as strips of night were torn from the sky, leaving a summer cerulean in its place. It took a moment, but as her dazzled eyes regained their focus, she realized that what she'd perceived as darkness had been woven from the hungry spirits hovering around her, waiting for her to join them, to become one of them. They hadn't left at all. Now they seemed to have given up on her, or to have been forced to do so. The shadows lifted—at first only one or two at a time, but then en masse—like ashes floating up on a warm current of air, growing smaller as they drifted farther away.

Alice pressed her face to the glass, needing to see, but unwilling to open the window for fear their peel-away exodus might be a trap, that the spirit that had masqueraded as Sabine might still be down there, ready to scale the wall with her sharp claws in a final desperate attempt to claim her. She went up on her toes to get a better view, a sense of déjà vu washing over her as she did. Smoke rose from a pile of ashes beneath the house. Alice intuited that the ashes were all that remained of the Sabine who'd shared her life.

Her deliverance from the spirit had arrived with such great swiftness and exactitude . . . She was taken aback, unable to untwine her fear of the impostor from her tenderness for her beloved. Perhaps that conflation was the source of the misplaced sympathy she now felt. Or maybe it sprang from the uncomfortable awareness that the twisted spirit who'd plagued her had started out as a person not so very different from herself.

She turned away from the window, catching sight of herself once she did so, as if a mirror had been suspended before her that showed her reflection—first from above, and then from behind. Vertigo sent the world around her reeling as she realized that she was seeing herself and seeing *through* herself in the same instant. She reached out to steady herself against a chair, breathing deeply and willing the sensation of spinning to pass. A moment of reorientation came as the scene seemed to fold in on itself, returning her normal sense of perspective.

A new terror drove her to her knees.

Before her stood the gaunt form of Babau Jean.

She looked up into blank, black eye sockets visible through his white, masklike face. There was no trace of Celestin in this creature standing over her. She sensed that this was the essence of the beast. The union with Celestin had been broken.

Logic told her that she should scream at the sight, that she should fight her way up and flee. Only her world had been diminished to this small square of space. She had nowhere left to run, and nothing left to drive her to do so. She waited on bended knees, not trying to rise, not trying to fight. If this was the end, then at least she would end this life as herself, not spend an eternity seeking out others to feed from and destroy.

Babau Jean approached her with a halting step until he stood within reach of her.

You're afraid?

Yes, I'm afraid. She responded to his silent question.

He reached up and pierced his own flesh with his razor-sharp nails, peeling away his glossy, bone-white features. She couldn't see—or perhaps just refused to see—what lay behind his flesh.

He knelt before her and smoothed his own skin over Alice's face. He reached out and took her in his arms.

One moment, she was lost in his embrace. The next, she was seeing through his eyes.

ELEVEN

Yeah, it did feel good. Damned good.

Evangeline stomped down Bourbon Street toward her club, the soles of her flat sandals beating out a warning, announcing the approach of a woman who—by God—was not going to take one more piece of crap from one more person. At least not today, and maybe not tomorrow either.

Variegated local day drinkers and tourists, some of whom were even wearing those god-awful Bonnes Nouvelles T-shirts bearing her caricature, milling about and gawking in windows, took notice of her and started showing better than normal sense. A few cautious glances in her direction, and the crowds parted like the Red Sea at low tide.

She'd locked herself away, ashamed and blaming herself for what was being done to her. That was over, too. The molting sisters and their bastard accomplice saw it as their right to manipulate her, to twist her mind and break her body. She might not yet know how to swipe back at them, but once she figured it out, she'd go after them like a scalded hellcat. Until then, she vowed to herself that she'd take every measure she could to resist this thief, this usurper. Right now it seemed existence was the best form of resistance.

She was going to start reclaiming her life, right here, right now. She was going to beat them. Sooner or later, she'd regain control. Even if it took years.

Years? a tremulous voice whispered in the part of her mind that had remained conscious through the breaking of every bone. Could she survive years of this?

She stopped in her tracks, clenching her fists, then forced herself to relax, breathing out the fear and lingering fatigue. She didn't have to survive years. She just had to survive one more damned day. One more hour. One more moment. She'd break it down, parse it into as many morsels as it took. This power wouldn't have the upper hand forever. And when the tables turned? Well, by God . . .

The thought pushed her forward.

She could see Bonnes Nouvelles a few odd yards ahead when a car blared its horn. Evangeline looked over and spotted a familiar, though unloved, face. Reverend Bill, the wretched old hypocrite who spent half his life camped out in front of the club, shouting scripture and condemning her, and the other half with his lips wrapped around a bottle, was stumbling toward her. It didn't help any that the old man reminded her of her dad, if not in appearance, for sure in behavior. Either someone up there felt she needed not one, but two wild-eyed fanatics to swill liquor in her presence and promise her she'd spend eternity burning, or she'd been born lucky.

Reverend Bill had started his "ministry" on Bourbon Street around five years ago, targeting her and her club for special attention right from the get-go. Even now, with a city council doing their damnedest to drive clubs like hers off Bourbon, there were still more than a half dozen of them planted in a zigzag up and down the street, including a new one "for the ladies" that featured male dancers. Still, Reverend Bill didn't pay the rest of the other clubs combined a tenth of the attention he gave Bonnes Nouvelles.

Now here he was again, bottle in hand, wobbling and weaving his way down the center of Bourbon, calling out her name, wild and desperate, like he was screaming murder or trying to alert a sleeper on an upper floor to a fire raging below. At least he was shouting her real name this time and not one of his tried-and-true pet names for her—Jezebel, Great Whore, or the one that had real teeth, Trailer Park Trash.

She shook her head and held her palm out facing him. "Today is not the day, old man," she said, picking up her pace and making a bee-line for the door. She didn't move fast enough. Reverend Bill sprinted, tripping as he stepped up onto the sidewalk but managing to right himself. Any normal day, she would've taken a reflexive step back. Today she dug in. "I am warning you . . . once."

He fell to his knees before her. Then he set his half-full plastic one-seven-five of crap bargain Russian vodka to the side and prostrated himself before her, stretching out his arms, planting his face on the ground.

"Get up," she said, fighting the urge to kick at him. "I said, get up."

He pushed himself up to his knees, caught hold of his bottle, and emptied its contents at her feet. This time she did jump back, but only to keep his swill off her shoes. "A sacrifice to my queen," he said, then dropped the bottle. It bounced once and rolled into the street. Reverend Bill stayed right where he was, looking up at her with glassy, adoring eyes. He seemed to be awaiting a benediction from her.

"There is something wrong with you," she said, stepping around him, like she used to when she needed to pack her lunch for school and her dad was passed out on the kitchen floor. She didn't look back.

The doors to the club were wide open. The low thump of bass greeted her. She tossed a glance at the stage. Tina was there, a red crimped-tinsel wig on her head and a bored look on her face. She wasn't even trying. Her mind wasn't in the game. Evangeline scanned the room. In all fairness, there wasn't much game there. Still, a good dancer always gave one hundred percent.

"Where's Hugo?" she called out to Matt, the bartender, as she passed by.

"He's in back," the bartender responded, the hint of a Cajun accent slipping out in those three syllables. Matt didn't have a lick of Cajun in him.

Evangeline stopped and looked back. A tall fellow with broad, square shoulders and dirty-blond hair—an untamed herd of cowlicks—busied himself with dropping white votive candles into a double row of clear glass holders. Evangeline had been riding a roller coaster already today, but now she felt like she'd been slapped and spun around. Even in the low neon light she could tell his eyes were aqua blue, nearly turquoise. He was about the prettiest damned man she'd ever seen, but right now she was in no mood for pretty. "Who the hell are you?"

Those aqua eyes flashed, and a smirk rose to his lips. He gave her a curt bow, then a wink. "Lincoln Boudreau," he said, "quite literally at your service."

"What happened to Matt?"

"Your boy Hugo fired that *couillon* going on a month ago."

"Fired him?"

"Yes, ma'am." He protracted both words, drawing them out into a dare. Her mind turned to hot August days and skinny-dipping. "That is my understanding."

Evangeline caught herself looking him up and down, then flushed when she realized he was doing the same to her. Her pulse quickened beneath his gaze. *Electricity.* That was what it felt like. Sparks and hot bright lights. She'd never felt this way around a man before. Not with Nicholas. Not even with Luc. She tried to focus, to hang on to the anger that had carried her here. She would not get all caught up in this strange fire.

Pursing her lips and forcing her eyes to focus on the candles lined up on the bar rather than on the man behind them, she did her best to convey the message that she had no interest in him. She waited a moment, then let her eyes graze him before landing on the bottles, one in particular, behind him. "Well, Lincoln—at my service—Boudreau, I'd like you to do me a favor."

"You're the boss." The way he said it conveyed both his willingness to help in this and a willingness to take other, more personal orders.

"Funny you should say that," she said, though she didn't even consider explaining the scene she'd faced on her way here. She nodded up at a large clear bottle with a silver cap and blue lettering. "Has that one been opened?"

He pulled it down from the shelf and held it up. "Don't think so. It looks full to me."

She nodded. "Okay, then. There's an old man outside. Bald on top, white fringe three quarters round. You take that out and give it to him."

Lincoln rested the bottle on his left palm, tightening his grip on the bottle's neck with his right. "Sure thing. Anything else?"

She paused and turned to gaze out the open door. She couldn't see Reverend Bill, but she could sense he was still lingering nearby. "Yeah. Tell him his queen isn't interested in any damn sacrifices."

He looked down at her with raised eyebrows and a small frown, but like the good soldier that he seemed to be, he carried the bottle to the door. He glanced left and right, then headed out in the direction of Bienville Street. Not two minutes later he came back through the door, dusting his hands as he circled back around the bar. "Package and message both delivered."

"Much obliged," she said, as a sense of familiarity crept upon her. Now that the surprise had faded, she was sure she'd seen this man before. "I know you, don't I?"

"Really?" He shook his head, his eyes narrowing. "You run a bar, and that's your best line?"

"It wasn't a line," she snapped, then regretted doing so.

He held up his hands, signaling surrender. "Just trying to make you laugh and failing miserably in the effort."

It was true. She felt certain they'd met somewhere before, but there was no denying she'd trotted out the oldest pickup line in the world. "I'm sorry. I'm a bit on edge right now. I know it was a joke, but . . ."

"It's okay," he said, waving her apology off. "You're right. We have met before." He leaned up against the bar and started whistling a tune she'd listened to maybe a million times when she was a kid. "Evangeline." She remembered. The day of Vincent's memorial. The fellows—brothers, she'd guessed—playing on the street corner over by Jackson Square. This Lincoln had flirted with her, and she had flirted right back. Seemed like a thousand years ago now.

He straightened, seeming to spot the spark of recognition in her eyes, and traced his finger in a slow snaking line along the bar. A gesture either innocent or seductive, all depending on whether she was open to being seduced. "You said I should come find you." He shrugged. "So I did." He turned away and began to arrange the bottles on the shelves behind him, turning them so their labels faced straight out and adjusting their spacing to cover for the absent bottle of vodka. "You weren't here," he said without looking back. She found herself straining to hear him over the music. "But the job was."

He snatched down two bottles of rum, one dark, the other light, and mixed a Hurricane, slipping it to a customer who'd just entered and approached the bar. The customer's face showed surprise, but he pulled out his wallet and left a ten on the bar. Lincoln's eyes followed the man as he took a seat near the stage, then fell back on Evangeline.

She caught a glimmer in them.

Sure enough. Another witch boy. She should've known it from the second she'd laid eyes on him. The first time.

She was almost as annoyed as she was intrigued. "Bourbon Street. Hurricane. Lucky guess."

He shrugged again, but held his tongue.

Today was not the best day, and now was sure not the time, but she decided the presence of an unfamiliar witch in her own establishment didn't leave her with much choice. She wasn't going to try to glean any specifics about him or his life that she didn't have the right to know, but she needed to be sure she could trust him.

She lowered her guard a touch and reached out to him with her mind.

"Oh," she said, an involuntary expression of surprise. Her magic and his embraced each other, the union creating something she sensed neither of them would be capable of on their own.

Sparks, literal ones this time, shot from every direction and the club went dark. The music stopped cold, replaced by moans of dismay from the few guys peppered around the stage, and shocked profanity from Tina. Lincoln already had one of those long-tipped butane lighters in hand, and he started lighting up the candles he'd put out on the bar.

"I can see a bit ahead." He pushed one of the candles to her. "Sometimes. Not always and not too far. Longest stretch, an hour or two. Most of the time ten, fifteen minutes." He illuminated another candle, placing it and a few others on a tray.

She didn't want it. She wasn't ready for it. Their timing was three-hundred-and-sixty degrees of wrong. Still, in the moment their magics had touched, she'd known she would fall in love with him. From the confident smile the flickering candlelight revealed, he damned well knew it, too.

He took the tray and made a circle of the club, putting down a candle on each of the occupied tables, and handing the final one to Tina. The silhouette of her body leaned in toward his. "Thank you, sugar." She held the candle up to his face, caressing his cheek with her free hand.

"My pleasure," he said, and Evangeline cringed at the words, anticipating Tina's inevitable response.

"It could be."

He lingered near the stage for a moment too long before returning to her. Another message successfully conveyed.

"We have rules about fraternization," she said, needing to break the silence and feeling the sudden urge to douse him with a bit of cold water. "Staff are not allowed to see each other."

"Well, that's a damned shame," he said, whipping off his apron and laying it on the bar between them. "'Cause you strike me as a woman who wants a man with a regular job."

Their eyes locked. Evangeline realized they were playing chicken.

"Tell me. How far ahead did you see? When we touched—"

"You mean when you touched me," he said, going back behind the bar and spreading the remaining candles out evenly.

A movement in her peripheral vision alerted her to Tina's approach.

"'Bout time you comin' back," she said and tapped the bar. "This place is going straight to hell." She looked up and smiled at Lincoln. "Usual, sugar?" Evangeline recognized the word "usual" as an expression of more than familiarity. She was marking territory. Lincoln filled a tumbler with diet soda and set it on the counter. Tina reached out and traced her finger down his wrist and hand. She lifted the glass like she was about to make a toast. "Don't worry, Vangie. I'm a good girl. I still follow the rules." She lowered the glass and started walking away. She stopped, looking back over her shoulder. "At least some of 'em."

"Do not call me Vangie."

Tina gave a crisp toss of her metallic wig. "Sure thing, sugar." She sauntered back toward the stage.

The lights flared to life, and the pounding music started back up, almost drowning out the cheers as a revitalized Tina started to put a little life into it, though Evangeline suspected the added sauce was for

Lincoln's benefit. Or maybe for hers, so she could witness his appreciation of Tina's efforts.

Evangeline cast a surreptitious glance in his direction, but he had his back turned toward the stage. She swiveled around to find a more compact, though—Evangeline sensed—no less potent, version of Lincoln heading her way. The brother, she decided, flashing back once again to the day she'd come across them near the square. "What's going on out—" he called to his brother, but stopped short as his eyes landed on her. "'Lo there, boss." He gave her a three-finger Boy Scout–style salute.

The door to the back part of the club swung open again. "Well, as I live and breathe," Hugo said, combing his mussed hair with his fingers, then fumbling with his misbuttoned shirt. "If it isn't the Lady Lazarus come back from the dead to grace us with her presence." He was putting on a show, trying to sound miffed at her, but she could see the gold flecks of joy pumping through his aura. "I see you've met the new members of the Bonnes Nouvelles crew."

"Not formally," the brother said, reaching out and pumping Evangeline's hand. "Wiley Boudreau. Damned pleased to meet you."

"Wiley?" she said, tugging her hand back.

"Like the cartoon coyote," Lincoln said. "His real name is Washington, but when he was six he ran clean through a sliding glass door."

"Didn't get a scratch, but you could see my outline where I broke through. And," he said, offering up a copy of his brother's shrug, "the name stuck." He slipped back to Hugo's side and wrapped his arm around his shoulders. Evangeline realized those gold sparks might have less to do with her than she'd thought.

"Are you back, then?" Hugo said.

"Not quite," she said. "That's something we need to talk about. Alone. I'll drop by again tomorrow. At least for a while. Later."

Hugo leered at her with a knowing smile on his lips. "I thought you might." His eyes shot over to Lincoln before pinging back to her. His head tilted a little to the side, his expression smug enough to make her want to smack him. Before she could give in to the temptation, he turned to Wiley. "I guess we should get back to . . . taking inventory." He smiled. Wiley smiled back.

Hugo took off, letting Wiley's arm slide off his shoulders. Wiley flashed her a smile that had no doubt broken many a heart. "That's right. Inventory. Gettin' back to it," he said, then nodded in her direction. "Good to meet you, boss."

"Technically," Evangeline said, watching the two cut through the club toward the door that led to the office and stockroom, "Hugo isn't an employee—"

"Far enough," Lincoln interrupted her.

She turned toward him and shook her head. "Sorry?"

"Your question. My answer. I said I saw far enough."

TWELVE

Alice felt herself merge with Babau Jean.

She wore him like an overcoat, or better yet, inhabited him like a diving bell capable of protecting her in depths she couldn't withstand on her own. Still, even as he enveloped her, he reached up through her core like an axis mundi, connecting her to every world along the Dreaming Road.

They'd long shared a rapport, Alice and this entity, one she had been unaware of until this moment. Perhaps it came as a side effect of the quasi-symbiotic relationship Celestin, her biological father, had shared with him. Or perhaps Babau Jean had worked behind Celestin's back to create a sympathetic vibration between them. A silent glow of pleasure confirmed the latter supposition. Celestin had forced himself upon Babau Jean, trapping him much as he had trapped Alice. Babau Jean, Alice understood without asking, had been trying to throw his rider for decades. Now, without warning or explanation, Celestin was gone.

The edges of the room grew dim, its center flaring as bright as a nova. The center melted and rolled back toward the edges until there was nothing left of her illusory apartment. Another image reached out to embrace her. Babau Jean's Mahogany Hall, his recreation of the long-gone Storyville brothel, flickered to life around her.

An epiphany struck her, and she laughed.

They laughed.

It was so clear to her now. The Dreaming Road was a single sphere haunted by innumerable overlapping, sometimes interacting, hallucinations . . . although "hallucination" didn't seem to be quite the right word. "Hallucination" drew a line between the objective and subjective. It felt too binary. Either a yes or a no. Here, each fabrication held its own kernel of realness. Babau Jean offered her a better vantage point: when all is possible, no world can be entirely real, and none completely unreal.

The Dreaming Road was inherently neither sanctuary nor prison. Both perceptions of it were perversions of its true nature. The Dreaming Road was a bridge. The bridge over which magic crept into the common world.

No. That wasn't quite right either. She felt the sharp certainty of the revelation dissolve and run through her clutching fingers like water.

Alice grasped at the vision's unraveling threads before they could slip away.

The worlds perceived as real and the worlds understood to be fantasy; there would always be an interaction between them. The Dreaming Road wasn't a place at all. It was the dance between the two. *No. Not a noun. A verb.* It was interacting, dancing, influencing, interjecting, molding, circling back around, and feeding on itself.

A crank phonograph came alive, scratching out an all but forgotten tune.

She sensed Babau Jean was trying to tell her something about himself, but he didn't just want to convey the information—he wanted her to understand as only one who'd shared his experience could.

She crossed to the turntable, lifting the needle and touching the record to stop its spin. The record's red and gold label read "Beautiful Dreamer." A feeling, *his* feeling—confused, aching, forlorn—crept up on her. He struggled to find a point of comparison in her own experience, but there was no need. She already understood how he felt. A homesickness that isn't the result of wanderlust, but is instead a reaction to abandonment, to seeing "home" ripped away.

A book sat beside the phonograph. She traced a finger over its faded slate-blue cover where the author's name was presented as "Mrs. Shelley." Her first thought, *Mrs. Shelley, indeed,* gave way to the realization that she had never read *Frankenstein* in the common world. She'd been too young before her time on Sinclair, and due to concerns the novel might "trigger" some patients, it wasn't one of the books included in Sinclair's otherwise extensive inventory of classics. She again felt Babau Jean's proud glow, alerting her that it was he who'd slipped the paperback copy of the book into the bubble where Celestin had imprisoned her. Babau Jean had been attempting to share his story with her all along, to alert her to his desire to free them both from Celestin's control. Of course, there had never been a literal book. The paperback was how Alice had interpreted the knowledge seeded into her consciousness by Babau Jean. *When is a book not a book?* An incipient riddle began to write itself.

A mirror appeared behind the table. A handsome youth with wavy black hair and a deep tan complexion stared back at her. She caught a glimpse of herself lurking in his bottomless black eyes. Those eyes blinked and, upon opening, showed a bachelor-button blue. Another face, a rosy pink beneath corn silk hair. Then another. A prominent forehead and a fighter's crooked nose. A moment later, a weak chin, hazel eyes, and freckles. The permutations continued until Alice understood he was relating the story of his origin. He'd been created after the Civil War by a mad doctor set on profiting from the grief of widows and broken-hearted mothers. Babau Jean would enter their opiate-laced dreams of loved ones, impersonating the departed. In so doing, he would draw life force from the dreamers and transmute it into magic for his master's use. Each withering dreamer slowly became a murder victim, a soft sacrifice.

He'd worn so many faces. Looked through so many different eyes.

The handsome youth reappeared, and Alice understood this face was the one he'd chosen for himself.

A pop. A cork escaping a champagne bottle. A woman's throaty laugh. Alice turned from the mirror toward the hall. The laugh belonged to the beauty she'd witnessed the first time she'd seen this mirage. The woman appeared even more radiant, despite being bereft of her fabulous emerald necklace. She raised a glass to Alice in salute.

A full band appeared on the dais in mid-tune, their Dixieland swelling up around them. Women circled around her. Their heady scents played a raucous but pleasing composition that pulsed right along with the Dixieland—with contending bass notes of rose and jasmine, beating-heart middle notes of geranium and lilac, and trilling citrus high notes of bergamot and sweet orange.

Soft hands caressed her. Soft lips pressed against hers, and she was enraptured by it all.

The thunder of artillery. Lulu White's bordello was suddenly gone. War was everywhere, and the other world had deserted them. They hadn't moved, but concrete reality was shriveling and pulling away, growing smaller, dimmer, gone.

Loss. Panic.

Alice looked out through Babau Jean's eyes as the two of them revolved at the center of a dark, icy abyss.

Cold. Hunger. Fear. Rage.

The cries of anguish issuing from Babau Jean's lips were not hers. They sprung from his own sense of desolation.

Alice realized he'd allowed himself to forget he carried her with him, that for Babau Jean this was more than a simple recounting. He was reliving his terror so that she could taste it, so that she could truly understand him.

Scintillations, like the phosphenes perceived when an eye is rubbed, floated all around her. They grew sharper, brighter, like the spark of a flint striking steel. Babau Jean snatched at them. He caught one, and it expanded in his grasp. He held it up to examine it, and Alice realized it was a kind of window opening into the common world. But it wasn't an actual window. Babau Jean grasped a *mirror*, one connected to a mirror on the other side, and they were peering through it. Each and every mirror served as a window into the ethereal plane. The innocuous looking glass was a natural collector of psychic energy, enchanted by the intent and repeated focus of those it reflected, and their keen feelings—vanity and self-loathing, fear and pride.

She understood now why the Dreaming Road had first revealed itself to her as Versailles's Galerie des Glaces—the mirrored hall she'd often imagined visiting, but in actuality never had. In her dream, she'd spied on the Dreaming Road in an inverse manner to how Babau Jean followed events in the common world. Even then, he had been trying to speak to her. He'd brought her dreaming self to his private domain, but for what purpose? What had he wished to show her in his Storyville recreation?

Babau Jean pounded on the glass, clawed at the silver backing. There was a face on the other side, a young woman pinning back her wavy, platinum hair. Alice caught sight of the pink and black tile wall over the woman's shoulder. For a moment the woman froze, then she began backing away, shaking her head as she did. Her mouth worked its way open as a scream began to build.

Babau Jean startled and dropped the pane. But the woman's terror had strengthened him. He caught another spark and peered through it. A boy in a blue short-sleeved shirt and jeans walked around on his knees, a silver and red tin rocket ship clutched in both hands. He rose, lifting the rocket over his head and zooming around the room. A woman with a helmet of bouffant brown hair came into view, her hands stuffed into oven mitts. She set an aluminum tray on a small yellow table, then tugged off her mitts. She tucked them under her arm as she crossed the room to a wooden cabinet that housed a sheet of glass resembling a circle with a cropped top and bottom. She switched a knob, and a light at the center of the glass sparked on, expanding from the center until it formed a full, albeit grayscale picture. The woman turned back, and the look of surprise on her face as her gaze fixed on the mirror exploded into wide-eyed terror. She dashed to her boy, swept him into her arms, and fled the room.

Fascinated, warmed, Babau Jean dropped the pane and clutched another.

A young man with thick, spiky black hair and the palest of skin rocked back and forth before the mirror.

Time in this nowhere seemed elastic. Between the first woman's hairstyle and the wooden console television, Alice estimated they'd jumped around three decades. Myriad silver spyholes shimmered all around them, each within easy grasp, but there were even more muted, shifting images that shot past like satellites, far beyond their reach. These, Alice sensed, belonged to an age that remained sealed to them, an age that she would perceive as "the future" if her feet stood solidly planted on the common world's timeline.

The guy they now beheld wore a plain white T-shirt. There was no way to know. Based on his appearance, their encounter might be happening in the common world's present or thirty years earlier.

Then Alice made out a rubber tourniquet around the man's left arm, and an emptied glass hypodermic with a silver plunger in his right hand. Alice had seen her share of hypodermics during her years on Sinclair. The outmoded glass needle implied that this day had long since passed.

The man clenched a cigarette between his teeth and stared forward into the glass, his shrunken, porcine eyes lost in the dark rings around them. He looked upon Babau Jean as he might his own reflection, without bewilderment but with a slight dissatisfaction. Without looking away from the mirror, he set the hypodermic down on its carrying case, then undid the tourniquet, letting it drop to the floor. He stood there, propping himself up against his sink and staring into the glass until his cigarette turned to ash, and the ash fell away. He spat the butt into the sink, looked over his shoulder and called something out, a muffled sound Alice couldn't decode, then turned back. Leaning in, he placed his hand against the glass.

Babau Jean caught hold of the hand, and only then did the man cry out and try to pull away. But it was too late—Babau Jean dug his fingers into the man's arm, blood spurting where his sharp nails pierced the man's flesh. He let the struggling man do the hard work of pulling them through the mirror. Like being reborn, they were suddenly in this new world. Babau Jean released the man, who clutched his wounded arm and backed away. His lips were moving, but he wasn't speaking. He made terrible, terrified guttural sounds as he retreated. Then he tripped over his own feet and fell backward, his head hitting the lip of a filthy clawfoot tub. Hidden deep within Babau Jean, Alice shuddered at the sound of the man's skull cracking.

The man slid down the side of the tub, then lay supine on the floor, his head propped up by the leg of the tub, his right leg jerking, his right hand slapping the floor.

They drew near him, and Babau Jean knelt over him, straddling the man with his knees. There was, Alice sensed, no more than a moment's light left in the man. Babau Jean traced a bloodied finger along the man's temple. Then he leaned forward and pressed his lips over the dying man's mouth, breathing in his last breath.

The breath raced through Babau Jean, warming him, strengthening him. He pushed up from the corpse and rose. The world of color. The world of light. They were again his.

Then he caught a glimpse of himself in the mirror. His handsome features bore a subtle change that combined the women's looks of terror with the dead man's pallor—as if he became that which he fed on. Babau Jean reached up and touched his reflection. As his fingers moved from the glass to an almost unnoticeable discoloration of the skin beneath his eyes, it struck Alice that these slight changes were the beginning of Babau Jean's frightening, masklike face. She also recognized it was too late to change the course he'd long since taken.

Alice realized how much she shared with the monster. How Babau Jean, twisted, broken, and consumed by darkness, had never been the true monster. Until he'd been driven to be.

"Until he chose to be," a woman's voice came from behind her. "Exactly as I, too, chose to be."

As Alice spun around, the sad, squalid bathroom evanesced, becoming the impeccable, luxurious Mahogany Hall. She stood as herself, the protective shell of Babau Jean gone. The band still played, though the volume had fallen, the tempo slowed. It was a hymn, one she'd heard played on the way to Précieux Sang Cemetery with Celestin's body.

The beauty drew near, now wrapped in a floor-length, floral peignoir in gold lamé. Her onyx eyes sparkled as she tossed back her dark curls. "As you yourself might have done if I hadn't intervened," she said, moving past Alice to recline on the divan Alice intuited was customarily reserved for the victims whose life force fueled this world. For years, Celestin had changed them out like batteries, snatching up a new dreamer as soon as the old one was spent. In silent response to an unspoken question, the beauty lifted her lithe arm, making a languid gesture over her shoulder.

A bier with a silver casket sat before the dais. "Our final dreamer, I'd imagine," she said, lifting her chin in brave defiance of her own implied demise. Her forehead smoothed, and her eyelids lowered as a small smile came to her lips. She seemed serene, resolved to her tragic fate. "You've forgiven your monster for his crimes. Or at least you've begun to. I wonder if it's possible that you might someday begin to forgive me. Perhaps if I could make you look through my eyes as Babau Jean has made you see through his?"

The beauty held her hand out, beckoning for her to come closer. Alice hesitated, and the beauty lowered her hand, the light fading from her eyes as she accepted that Alice would not suffer her touch. "I tried to warn you," she said, pique lining her every word.

"Warn me?"

The beauty's finger pointed upward, to the ceiling. Alice saw her own name flash overhead in a snaking crimson script. "It was the best I could do," she said with a toss of her curls. "And, oh"—her face stiffened as her eyes opened wide—"I paid for my little gesture. He made me pay." Alice cast an eye around the space, looking for Babau Jean, the author of this replicated world, surprised to find he had slipped away, leaving her alone, exposed. The beauty chuckled, a laugh as slow and as sad as the hymn the band was playing. "No, not that hopeless old bogey. I'm talking about the real monster. Celestin Marin."

"I don't understand what you want from me," Alice said as the beauty pushed up on the divan and leaned forward. "Who are you?"

The beauty rose, closing the distance between them in the blink of an eye. "Are you so deceived by outward appearances, my darling girl?" She traced her finger along Alice's jawline. "Can you not recognize your own mother?"

THIRTEEN

Magazine Street restaurant. Private dining room. Lisette's eyes ran down the table, its crisp cover dazzling white even in the restaurant's intimate lighting.

This dinner was Fleur Marin's attempt to bring the Marin and Perrault—note the order—families together. Lisette's father's words still rang in her ears. There was no denying that whenever the two families "came together" they tended to come back apart covered in blood. No, this event was probably not the best idea, at least not from the Perrault side of the equation. But Remy had wanted them to come, so come she had.

Was Fleur trying to rip a bandage off or stick one on? Either way, she was plenty smart enough to know a sea of wine couldn't wash away the past, all of it dark, and a lot of it pretty damned recent. The damage Fleur's parents had done to Lisette's family could never be forgotten or, for that matter, completely forgiven. Fleur understood that. She had to.

After Lisette's odd morning, she might've forgotten this bury-the-hatchet dinner altogether if Remy hadn't texted her three times this afternoon, first to remind her of time and place, then to coach her on the topics she wasn't to bring up, then to remind her again about the time. She might have been annoyed, but it was nice for a change that he was the one nagging her to get something done and done right.

Still, she was more than distracted, her mind darting about in a cycle of attesting to, then denying the connection she'd discovered— the connection she felt she'd been led to discover—between the city where she'd lived her entire life and the world of spirits. Either someone had rigged New Orleans from its very inception to serve as a doorway between the common world and the Great Beyond, or some force had bent the city from its founding to fulfill that same purpose. Chicken first or egg, something or somebody was looking to cross over. Lisette couldn't help but wonder which direction.

Lisette and Manon and Michael, Manon's gay boyfriend from the café near Vèvè, were the first to arrive. Remy, Lucy, Fleur, and her nephew Hugo were coming together, and Isadore should be well on his way. Lisette checked the clock on her new phone for the third time. In nine minutes.

Lisette had offered Fleur her father's regrets without even considering passing along the invitation, so Fleur had invited Manon to bring along a date "to even out the table." Lisette's girl had invited her favorite purveyor of overpriced coffee drinks. Isadore was driving in from Baton Rouge, where he'd been called last minute to make a bid on landscaping a big new housing development, so Lisette had asked Michael if he'd mind her riding along with them. Manon couldn't say Lisette had made him feel unwelcome if she'd asked him to be her escort.

Their waiter—one of the four, he'd explained, who would be serving them tonight—was making a show of decanting one of the wines he'd told them Fleur had selected for the evening, a Cabernet-Merlot blend whose vintage had Michael sitting on the edge of his seat like a six-year-old at the circus.

Fancy restaurant. Private dining room. Four waiters for eight diners. A chance, Lisette decided, to see how "the other half" lived. The waiter set the bottle on a silver coaster, then filled their glasses from the decanter.

She'd felt a bit disingenuous accepting the invitation. She'd begun to consider Fleur a friendly acquaintance, if not an outright friend. Still, the only reason she and Isadore had agreed to the dinner was they hoped the implied blessing of their son's romance with Fleur's daughter would dump a cooling bucket of water on it. Lisette reckoned things might have worked out differently for the Capulets and Montagues if they'd agreed to sit down for a meal together.

Well isn't she a shady one, Lisette thought as it dawned on her that Fleur had likely arrived at the same damned conclusion.

"Eight hundred dollars," Manon leaned over and whispered into Lisette's ear as the waiter carried away the not quite empty bottle. Lisette didn't question it. Manon worked in hospitality, so she'd know the price.

"No wonder our waiter friend is saving a taste for himself." Fleur was trying either to impress them or to buy their goodwill. Or maybe Senator Endicott's soon-to-be ex-wife was so removed from the real world she thought it normal to drop more than what most of the people Lisette knew made in a week on a single bottle of wine.

"No, Mama." Manon pulled her shoulders back and looked down her nose at her. Lisette knew that look. She'd embarrassed her daughter once again.

"Tannins," Michael said, an obvious attempt at explanation that meant nothing to her. "Sediment," he added when she didn't respond. "Older wines can collect sediment at the bottom of the bottle."

"Eight hundred dollars, and they can't even bring us a clean bottle of wine?" She said it with the sole aim of provoking Manon, but then Michael started laughing.

"Ugh. The two of you." Manon widened her scowl to include them both.

Lisette tasted her—she jumped through the calculations—one-hundred-forty-dollar glass of wine. Then she took another, deeper sip. Maybe it was the wine, or maybe it was Manon framing them as accomplices, but Lisette found herself liking this Michael even more. Still, it made her sad that her girl was wasting all her time on a dead-end man, when she could be out with someone who might grow into a life partner. Lisette knew better than to go there with Manon, though.

"I'm so sorry for being late." Fleur came sweeping in, Remy and Lucy in tow. "To my own dinner party, if you can imagine it." Fleur wore an expensive-looking crimson and black floral cocktail dress with cap sleeves and a flare skirt. She'd changed her hair since Lisette had last seen her. It was still shoulder length, but looked a shade lighter, now almost a chestnut brown. Neat, perfectly trimmed bangs. The rest meticulously tousled.

Fleur looked younger. Good for her.

Lisette knew she looked every bit as good in the black sleeveless below-the-knee dress she'd worn to every special event in the last three years, without putting in one-tenth the effort Fleur had. She'd be even more sure of that as soon as Isadore arrived to compliment her in it.

Michael rose to greet Fleur. At least he'd been raised right.

"I was waiting for Hugo, who can't make it. He sends his apologies. Some kind of last-minute crisis at Evangeline Caissy's establishment." She held up her hands and shook her head. "Don't ask me." She glanced around the table. "Isadore?"

"He's on his way," Lisette said to reassure them both.

"Thank you so much for coming." Fleur crossed to stand before Manon. "Manon, it's lovely to meet you again, this time under more pleasant circumstances." Fleur offered Michael her hand. "You must be Michael." Michael looked confused, like he wasn't sure if he should shake Fleur's hand or kiss it. Fleur seemed to pick up on his discomfort and saved him by taking a couple steps back and clasping her hands together. "I must say, Manon, I expected you to be beautiful, but look at you. You are positively radiant. Glowing."

A nervous smile rose to Manon's lips. "Uh . . . thank you." Manon's voice crept up at the end, making it sound more like a question than a response. Glowing? Lisette turned to face her daughter, searching for the bliss she had failed to notice. Manon cringed and pressed back into her chair.

Remy bounded to Lisette's side of the table and placed a kiss on her cheek. "Thanks for coming, Mama."

"Wouldn't have missed it, baby." She decided a little white lie wouldn't hurt. "You know I've been looking forward to this." He shot her a look that told her he'd caught her fibbing but was glad she was making an effort.

Lucy drew up beside her mother. The two resembled each other to an absurd degree, except for coloring. Lucy had inherited her grand-mother Laure's dark-blonde hair and fair blue eyes, though some color-ist had helped Lucy kick the blonde up a notch or two. Lisette prayed the hair and eyes were all Lucy had inherited from her grandma. "Good evening, Mrs. Perrault. It's good to see you."

"Good to see you, too, *ma chère*," Lisette said, surprised that she actually meant it. Ah, what the hell. Sins of the fathers, or in this case grandparents, shouldn't be placed at this young girl's feet. With the thought, Lisette's eye fell to Lucy's white, crystal-covered pumps, which must've cost, by Marin standards, three, maybe even four bottles of wine. Lisette patted Remy to signal he should return to his date.

Lisette's phone sounded with the "Your husband is attempting to reach you . . ." ringtone Remy had assigned to his dad. She leaned over and snatched the phone from her purse, tapping the screen before it could call out again. A text message. She scanned it. He wasn't coming. Someone had shattered all the windows in each of his six company trucks. Happened all at once. Rounding up the guys at the office to try to get to the bottom of it. "Oh," she said, disappointed and concerned. What in the hell was going on today?

"Bad news?" Fleur said.

Lisette tried to smile, but failed at it. "Nothing serious," she said to assure the kids, "but something's come up. Isadore won't be joining us." She sensed Manon tensing up beside her. "It's nothing, baby. Something with a couple of the trucks at work. That's all."

"Accident?" she said.

"Yeah." Lisette patted her hand. "Something like that, but nobody's hurt." She assumed nobody was hurt. Isadore would've told her otherwise, wouldn't he?

"What a shame," Fleur said. "He'll join us next time." Lisette nodded in agreement even though she felt pretty darned sure neither of them expected there to be a next time.

Fleur drew near Lisette, leaning down to kiss her on each cheek. A bit more intimacy than Lisette had been prepared for, but she could roll with it. "You look so beautiful," Fleur said, grasping Lisette's hand and holding it out as Fleur examined her. "That dress is absolutely perfect on you. Isadore doesn't know what he's missing." Actually, Lisette reflected, he did, but she breathed a bit easier having passed Marin muster.

Fleur noticed the wine Lisette had only just begun to drink. "Oh," she said, feigning, Lisette felt, surprise. "We're drinking red?" She flashed the waiter a confused look. He gave a slight nod of his head, communicating a bit of information Lisette failed to grasp.

"But you don't seem to be enjoying the wine," Fleur said. "Would you like something else?" Her tone implied that she was attempting to give a helpful hint. Before Lisette could even respond, Fleur continued. "I thought this might go well with the main course. Of course, it's so hard to know sometimes. I've visited the *domaine*, but I understand the year might not have produced their best *recolte*."

"No, no," Lisette said as Fleur snatched up the glass and swirled the wine beneath her nose. "It's delicious." She looked to Manon for confirmation.

"Yes, delicious," Manon said with a bright smile, though it looked to Lisette like she hadn't touched her glass.

Fleur smiled down at them as she returned the glass to the table. "I'm so glad. Shall we?" She returned to the other side of the table, and a new waiter slipped over to pull back her chair. "Thank you," Fleur said, looking back at him as he slid her chair forward. The waiter then repeated the process, this time for Lucy.

"Lucy," Fleur said, her voice gracious yet firm.

"Oh, sorry," she addressed the waiter. "Thank you."

"You're very welcome, miss."

Remy hesitated, like he was waiting for the waiter to help him. Lucy smiled and nodded at the chair, a signal for him to sit. He flashed a self-conscious grin before taking his seat.

Lisette still couldn't decide if Fleur's choice of restaurants came from a desire to offer them the best, or to keep them off-kilter. No, Lisette decided, looking at the sincere enjoyment on the woman's face. Fleur Marin almost-ex-Endicott thought everybody lived this way.

The first waiter returned, this time with a bottle of white. Fleur faced Lisette. "I've requested the charred oysters as a starter, so I hope you won't mind switching to the Chablis when they arrive. The tannins in the red. Well, you understand."

"I don't mind at all," Lisette said, with a wide smile. Oysters and Chablis. They were moving into familiar territory. She now understood the moment of silent inquiry that had passed between Fleur and their waiter. They'd made a faux pas by insisting on the Cabernet-Merlot rather than the proffered Chablis. Lisette gave Manon a cautious, though accusatory, side glance. It'd been Michael who pushed for the red, so at least the first fancy restaurant misstep hadn't been Lisette's.

The waiter filled Fleur's glass, even as Fleur held her hand over Lucy's. Fleur leaned in toward Lisette. "I promised Lucy she could have one glass with dinner, provided that you and Isadore agreed it would be okay for Remy, too." Remy looked at her with expectant eyes.

"One. I repeat. One."

Fleur nodded at the waiter, who poured for Lucy. Lisette glanced over at Manon to catch her expression. Lisette was surprised to see that Manon's own glass of red wine was now only half full; Michael's was full. She was about to comment on it, but Remy caught her attention. He was leaning forward on his seat, excited. "Did you all hear about the 'Doll House'?"

Silent glances and shaking heads all around. Even Lucy gave a slight shrug. "Man, where have you been?" His voice resounded with excitement. Lucy gave him a quick warning look, and he lowered his voice. "It's been all over the news this afternoon." He looked at them like they'd never heard of Christmas. "Some mortician has been using taxidermy to turn dead bodies into dolls, but the creepiest part is maybe not all of them came to him dead. He may have killed some of the people himself."

"What?" Lucy said, her face scrunching up with disgust, or maybe disgusted fascination. "Why?"

"News said he must be crazy." He yanked out his phone and started to search, Lisette reckoned, for the story.

Well, if the news is calling him crazy, he must be white, Lisette thought. Whenever a white man did something horrible, they always called him disturbed and started discussing his motivations. A black man does something horrible, and well, he did it because that's what black men do. "How terrible," Lisette said, repackaging her thoughts for mass consumption.

Fleur leaned forward and turned toward Remy. "What a dreadful story." She gestured toward his phone. "Not at the table. Off. We're here to enjoy each other." She looked at Lisette. "How about everyone under the age of, shall we say"—she paused, seeming to do a calculation of some sort—"thirty-five, has to turn their cells off until after dessert?"

Lucy turned on her mother with a toss of her hair. "Why not those over—you so wish—thirty-five?"

"We're mature enough to control our impulses." Fleur looked around the table. "Come on. Come on."

Lucy growled and rolled her eyes, but dug out her phone and powered it down. She turned to Remy. "Come on. You, too. This is your fault. You and your macabre small talk." He slid his phone over to her, letting her do the honors.

"Manon, Michael?" Fleur said. "Come on, you two, time to set a good example for your juniors."

Manon made a sour face, but obeyed. Fleur doggedly focused on Michael, a silent tilt of her head both a question and a demand. "Not me," he said with a chuckle. "Turned thirty-five in July." Lisette felt her jaw drop. She would've guessed ten years younger.

Fleur straightened, her eyebrows rising with surprise.

"I've got ID if you want me to prove it."

"No, no. I believe you. It's only . . . Well, nothing." She smiled with benevolence at Michael and Manon. "You two make such an adorable couple," Fleur said, addressing Manon and Michael. "How long have you been seeing each other?"

Lisette laughed. "They're just friends. They're not together that way."

"Oh, I'm so embarrassed," Fleur said, her face flushing. "I'd assumed . . ." She placed her hand over her heart. "Mea culpa." She took a sip of her wine. "Topic change to cover for my gaffe." She leaned in, laying her hand over Lisette's. "I hope you don't mind a little shop talk, Lisette."

"Shop talk?"

"Of a sort. I was chatting with Daniel today." She focused on Manon and Michael and waved away any questions. "He's an old family friend." Looked like she wasn't ready to address the origins of the family's manufactured domestic, at least not in public. "We were discussing a point about New Orleans, something I thought you might know a thing or two about."

"I know a little bit about a lot of things," Lisette said, her tone betraying the caution she felt, "and a lot about a few, so shoot."

Fleur leaned back and touched the stem of her wineglass. She lowered her eyes, looking sheepish. Something told Lisette her reticence was only for show. The woman was fishing for something. "Well, it's nonsense really," she said as her amused, sparkling eyes jumped up and pinned Lisette to her chair, "but Daniel was saying local legend has it there are seven gates, actual physical gates right here in New Orleans that link this world to . . . well, I don't know . . . an underworld of some type."

Lisette jolted. This was way too much of a coincidence. Bells and whistles and dire warnings from her father about getting involved with the Marin family sounded all at once. Lisette reached for her glass, only to find waiter number four clearing it from the table. She was lost in a sea of expectant silence. Even the kids were paying attention. Lisette examined the table like a chessboard, calculating her move.

"I believe your friend was speaking of the Gates of Guinee," Lisette said, trying to sound cool. She settled on a way to both tell the truth and offer a bit of misdirection. She forced a—she hoped—not too fake smile onto her face. "Sure, there are those who believe that they are actual portals, and even some who believe they're all right here in the area." That part was true. The stealthy waiter slipped in and placed a glass of Chablis before her. She grasped it and took a sip. She set the glass down, making a tiny *mmm* sound and flashing Fleur an appreciative smile. "Others hold that the gates are a metaphor for the seven days after death, the time it takes for the soul to understand itself as being separate from the body it vacated." That part was true, too. Her sole lie was one of omission. Lisette had never believed in literal gateways, but after Papa Legba brought her the map this morning, she wasn't so sure anymore. She'd begun to wonder if they might not somehow be both real and allegorical at the same time.

Two of the waiters returned with the promised trays of oysters.

"Oh," Manon said and pushed back from the table with such force Lisette's wine sloshed in its glass. Lisette reached out to right it before it could topple. "Excuse me," Manon said, her face turning gray. "I'm sorry. Ladies' room?" she asked the waiter as she rushed past him.

"By the kitchen," he replied, but Manon had already shot like a bullet in the direction he'd gestured.

"I don't know what's gotten into that girl," Lisette said, rising. "I'll go see if she's all right."

"No, Mama." Remy raised his hand and waved her down. "You sit back down. She's okay."

Lisette hovered over her seat. "How could you know that?"

"Almost two years," Michael said, apropos of nothing. Lisette realized he was talking to Fleur, even though his eyes were fixed on her. "We've been together almost two years."

Lisette fell back onto her seat.

"I'm sorry, Mrs. Perrault," Michael said. "We've been looking for the right time, and the right *way*, to tell you. I'm afraid this is neither, though at least now you know."

Lisette gaped at him, unsure of what to say.

"I love Manon," he said. "We love each other."

Lisette turned to Remy. "You knew about this?"

"Yes, ma'am." Two words confirming his betrayal but offering as little information as possible.

"How long have you known?"

He shifted in his seat, lowering his eyes. "Going on two . . ."

"Two what?" she prompted, her words coming out sharp and angry even to her own ears.

He looked up, his brow furrowed by guilt. "Going on two years."

They sat in silence for a bit. Lisette couldn't hazard how long. She was too busy replaying various moments in her head that should've—but hadn't—given her a clue.

Manon returned to the room and seemed to pick up on the situation in a flash.

"She knows," Michael said all the same.

"I can tell she knows. Look at the vinegar face she's making." She stood, hands on hips, facing Lisette down.

"Goodness," Fleur said, with a nervous titter. "I seem to have stuck my foot in it . . ."

"This," Lisette snapped, "is not about you." Fleur raised both hands in mock surrender.

"We'll talk about this later," Manon said, circling the table to her seat.

"I'd like to talk about it now," Lisette said, even though she didn't really want to. Her dander was up, and she was already imagining how Isadore would react to this news. "How could you not share this with me? Your own mama."

"I tried to," Manon said, as Michael rose to help her back into her chair. "About a hundred times. You didn't want to know. You'd already jumped to your own conclusions." She looked up to Michael. "She thinks you're gay. I let her, 'cause it was just easier that way."

The phone in Fleur's purse began to buzz, but she didn't touch it.

Michael looked around the table with a blank expression. "No, not gay. Just well-groomed."

Lucy gave a tinny laugh. "Then maybe you could give Hugo some pointers. He *is* gay and still a total slob." Lucy took the temperature of the table and then lowered her eyes. "Sorry. Trying to bring a little levity to the situation."

Fleur turned to Lucy. "Perhaps we should give the Perraults a moment?" Her phone started up again.

"We don't need a moment," Lisette said as one and one came together to make three. Manon had switched her full wineglass with Michael's half-empty one. They'd finally come clean about the relationship. Her girl was pregnant. And pregnant by a man fourteen years . . . fourteen years . . . her senior. She was jumping from college graduation straight into a baby shower. "It's gonna take a hell of a lot longer than that."

Fleur's phone stopped buzzing and started beeping.

"Someone seems to want you real bad," Lisette said, the words coming out in a growl. "You should probably see to it."

Fleur nodded as she reached for her purse. Lisette realized Fleur was happy to have something to do other than squirm in the face of the Perrault family drama. She looked at her phone, thumbing down the screen even as the alerts kept beeping. She rocked back in her seat.

Lucy looked at her mom. "What is it? Is there something wrong?" A pause. "Is it Dad?"

"No, dear, it isn't your father. It's Daniel. He says the police are at Nicholas's house. He needs us to come."

"The police? Why?"

Fleur glanced around the table, her eyes resting on Remy. "Your Doll House?"

"Yes, ma'am?"

"Where is it?"

"Right here in New Orleans," he said, sounding confused. "Freret or maybe Uptown. Somewhere around there. Not too far from Précieux Sang."

Fleur grasped the edge of the table. "I'm sorry," she said. "Come on, Lucy. We have to go."

"Not until you tell me what's happened."

Fleur's brow furrowed as she focused on her daughter. She seemed to be struggling to find the words. "It's only . . . They've found your aunt Astrid."

FOURTEEN

Most days Nathalie didn't drink alone, but hell.

The pub had a patio where people could bring their dogs, so she took a seat there, wanting to live . . . what was the word she'd picked up from the fellow she drove to the airport last week? Vicariously.

Nathalie wanted a dog. She wanted one bad. She used to think she wanted a dog and a cat, but the last couple of days had put her right off cats. At least for a while. But a dog, that was a go. Once she got her employment situation worked out, assuming she didn't end up in St. Gabriel on death row for murdering Frank Demagnan and defiling his corpse, she'd go get herself one. Go to the pound and pick up the goofiest, most muttsy dog she could find.

Maybe she'd leave her second-floor walk-up with its prime view of Odd Fellows Rest Cemetery and find a little house with a bit of a yard for the dog to run in. Even a bit across Highway 10, she'd seen you could rent a sweet single shotgun in Dixon, one with a small yard, for less than what she was paying now. She could maybe even get a better deal if she offered to help the owner fix it up and handle small repairs. She was good at that kind of thing.

A large-screen TV was playing a hockey game, and a trio of guys shouted at the screen. Nathalie had taken a seat behind them, next to a couple with a frisky yellow Lab puppy that was now doing its darnedest to reach her. He'd woven his leash around the legs of his peoples' chairs like macramé, but was straining on the last six inches of line he had left. His mom turned to see what he was fussing over, and smiled at her before bending over to undo the tangles in the pup's leash.

Nathalie began to see herself with a feisty pup—no, she knew herself, she'd find the grayest muzzle to take home with her. It was her daydream, though, so why the hell not take one of each?

Nathalie began to see herself in that cottage, sitting in a lawn chair in the yard with a beer in one hand, throwing her dogs' tennis ball with the other. The pup would chase it, then drop it in front of the old guy so he didn't feel left out.

Someone else suddenly entered her daydream. Golden sunlight backlit Alice Marin's chestnut hair like a halo as she came down the back steps to join her in the yard.

Gonna stop that one right there, Nathalie checked herself.

After she'd fled the mortuary, Nathalie had spent a long time looking at Alice's photo, at first wondering if perhaps she was wrong and the innocent face *could* belong to a murderer, but then posing simple questions about Alice and her life. What type of ice cream did she prefer? What did her voice sound like? How did her hair smell? It started out as an innocent-enough activity—a good way to distract herself from the image of Frank struggling into the room, already dead, but not quite dead enough. All too soon, though, Nathalie's imagination began crafting answers to those questions. She had created an Alice, but the Alice she'd envisaged wasn't the real one. She had to face up to that. On the bright side, at least she'd called it right on the question of murderer or not murderer.

Nathalie had done this before, building a fantasy about a woman based on nothing more than a few cursory impressions, disregarding the warning signals her intuition and common sense might wave before her eyes. Half the women she'd fallen for over the years had been unavailable on some level or another; with the other half, she'd fantasized her way into loving women who didn't even really exist. This Alice Marin was both. Unavailable and the perfect blank, if beautiful, screen for Nathalie to project her fancies onto.

Nathalie had had enough of loving someone who wasn't there. And while she'd enjoyed far more than her fair share of strange, she still didn't know what to make of this talk of "liminal"—that word would cost you a twenty—dimensions. This "gravity of rightful destiny"—she heard the words in that Daniel fellow's sincere, though a shade too desperate not to be creepy, voice. That gravity thing was nothing more than invitation to heartbreak . . . hers.

She had her own issues. Even now, New Orleans's finest were probably swarming all over Zombie Frank's study, picking up her prints, strands of her hair, even fibers from the damn borrowed suit pants she was still wearing. That brought her back full circle to the reason she'd come to this pub in the first place: to pull herself together before that visit to the police she'd been putting off, in the hope that if she relaxed a bit, inspiration for a plausible story—it helped, she realized, if she didn't think of it as a lie—would strike.

"Ma'am?" A voice pulled Nathalie back. A young guy. Her waiter, standing right in front of her. "You doin' all right today?" She realized he'd been trying to get her attention for a while. The few stray thoughts leaking out of him told her he wasn't just being polite. He thought there might be something wrong with her.

She smiled to reassure him, then noticed the couple with the puppy had gone. In fact, at the moment, she was the only customer left on the patio. "I'm . . . sorry," she said, pulling herself together, looking for a quick excuse to offer the guy so she wouldn't draw more attention to herself. "I've been having a bit of a day." She pointed at her temple and twirled her finger. "Left me feeling a little *dingue*." *Yes. I'm crazy, but normal crazy. Not the kind of nuts you're worried about.* She hoped he'd drop it, but no. She heard the buzz in his brain before the words formed.

"Which is it, money or love?" He leaned against the back of the chair across from her, his hand on the backrest. For a second she thought he might pull it out and join her, but he hung there, awaiting a response. Most days, she'd love nothing better than to chew each other's ears off, but just because she didn't think she was the kind of crazy he'd been worried about, didn't mean he wouldn't disagree on that point if she started yammering on about crawling corpses, disappearing cats, and the beautiful stranger trapped in a world of dreams.

"Bit of both, to tell you the truth. Beer?"

"Got a preference?" He flipped the drink menu over.

"Naw. I mean, no, thank you." She pushed the laminated card to the side and looked up at him. "Bring me what you'd have."

He nodded, backing away. "I'll bring you one of our local brews, that way you can tell all your friends we gave you 'The Boot.'" He smiled, waiting. She could tell he'd used this one before. "Hey, the Canadians here earlier laughed."

"Yeah, sorry," she said. "That one's only gonna work on the tourists."

He shrugged. "Wow, a tough room here tonight." He stood there for a moment looking at her. "Tell you what," he said. "First one's on the house. I think something grease fried and covered in hot sauce, too. A little heartburn to help you forget your heartache."

"You don't have . . ."

He held up a hand to stop her. He winked. "Family's got to look out for each other, right?"

Nathalie's eyes began to moisten at the kindness. Lucky for her he'd already headed to the bar to put in her order.

Family's got to look out for each other.
Hell.

Nathalie was sure Daniel meant well—although she wasn't so sure about his cat. He was right. Alice's daddy had sure handed her a raw deal. Nathalie would help if she could, but . . .

Well, all right, maybe she wouldn't. Daniel had fallen on his knees before her, and she'd still given him a flat-out no.

Nathalie thought of the young woman in the photo. The picture she'd stolen from Frank's place. The picture Daniel had insisted she keep, so she could remember the face of the "little girl"—his words, not hers—that she was condemning to "eternal darkness." Daniel was so dramatic when he spoke, she'd assumed he was exaggerating for effect. In retrospect, Nathalie wasn't so sure. All this other stuff, *chwals* and witches' balls, living vèvès, and who could forget Zombie Frank? None of it was an exaggeration. What if she truly was Alice's last hope?

"Somewhere between dreaming and death." That's where he wanted her to go, but to Nathalie, this "somewhere" seemed like a place where Babau Jean would feel at home. Well, if the whole gravity thing could pull Alice out of the mess she was in, how could Daniel be so sure it couldn't pull Nathalie in? Until now, the glass separating Nathalie from Babau Jean had always held, but if she did as Daniel asked, she might find herself standing on the same side as the monster.

Ah, hell. She was just making excuses. It wasn't Babau Jean that scared her.

Forget Daniel's guaranteed, A-1, five-star fairy-tale ending. Nathalie had never been the kind of woman to turn her back on someone in need. She never asked what was in it for her. Take out the hoodoo. Take out the magic. If she saw a young woman, Alice or not Alice, in a burning building, Nathalie would walk straight into the fire. If somebody were drowning, she would dive into deep and muddy waters to save them. So how had she managed to turn her back on Daniel's pleas? How was this different?

Maybe 'cause she was afraid that she'd feel this thing Daniel was so sure she should—and Alice wouldn't. That her supposed soul mate might want nothing to do with her. Then she'd know without a single doubt that she was going to be alone. Forever. That's why she didn't want to take the risk of helping Daniel help Alice.

Well, didn't that make her a total crap person?

Her waiter returned with her beer and, instead of the deep-fried wonder she now realized she'd been looking forward to, a remote control. "Here." He set the beer before her. "You want something to make you feel better about what you're going through?" he said, changing the channel from sports to local news. "Look no further." Remote still in hand, he crossed his arms over his chest and leaned back, focusing on the screen. A large-font "Breaking News Now"—phrasing that struck her as redundant—dissolved into a newscaster's face, a fellow who reminded Nathalie of her senior year's prom king.

"We're back again, bringing you a Five Alive update to the major story we broke earlier this afternoon," he said, then paused, seeming to take direction from a voice only he could hear. "We're going live now to Katie Cunningham at the scene." Nathalie took a sip of her beer as the camera panned back from Katie's fresh face to the big white house right next door to Demagnan Mortuary. Nathalie choked, and the beer came back out her nose. The waiter glanced down at her, but turned back to the screen, not noticing—or pretending not to notice—her wiping her face with the back of her hand. She set the beer down before she could do any more damage.

"That's right, Randy. We're here live in Uptown, where, in a bizarre incident today, the still unexplained, simultaneous shattering of a commercial truck's windows led to the discovery of the city's most gruesome murder scene since the infamous Axeman's spree." Nathalie felt all the blood drain from her face. "Behind me, you'll see the section of downed fence where the driver of a truck belonging to Perrault Landscaping crashed through, after losing control of his vehicle. The driver escaped the accident with minor injuries, but I'm told what officers discovered when they arrived on the scene shocked even the most stalwart of deputies." Her eyes sparkled as she clutched her microphone tighter and put on an *I'm about to say something very grave* face. As the camera pulled back, she gestured with her free hand to the fancy white Victorian behind her. "Law enforcement was attempting to contact the house's owner, when a cry coming from inside the house prompted officers to force entry. The source of the cry has not been discovered, but once inside they found evidence the media liaison has referred to as 'souvenirs' of apparent multiple murders."

"Wait," Nathalie said, as much to herself as anyone else, "she said 'multiple,' right?"

The waiter glanced back. "Mmmhmmm."

"Tell us, Katie," Prom King Newsman's voice rang out, though the camera stayed on the reporter, "have we learned the name of the property's owner?"

She put a finger to her ear, then nodded. "Yes, Randy, that's right. Through public records we've identified the owner as a Frank Demagnan. Mr. Demagnan is also the proprietor of the mortuary immediately behind the house in question. So far we've been unable to reach Mr. Demagnan for comment . . ."

"I should be going," Nathalie said, pushing up from the table.

Her waiter looked back at her with raised eyebrows. He turned. "Oh, darlin', I am so sorry. I should've realized this wasn't what you needed to be seeing right now. I just thought . . ."

"No, no," Nathalie said, heavy sweat staining her already stale shirt. "Nothing to do with"—her eyes drifted up to the screen, where they'd cut to a taped comment by the detective—"that." Nathalie heard Reporter Katie's perky voice saying, "multiple, unofficial estimates we've heard, perhaps as many as thirty."

Nathalie slid her chair beneath the table. "Thank you."

The waiter smiled at her, but she could see the genuine concern in his eyes.

Poor thing, he was thinking as she stumbled back to her SUV. Nathalie couldn't help but imagine the interview her waiter would give Reporter Katie once the police found out exactly how unavailable for comment Frank was, and came looking for his one and only employee.

She started the engine and shifted to drive without a clue as to where she was heading. The phone she'd left on the seat beside her began ringing, the vibration sending it sliding across the seat toward her. She put the car back into park and stared down at the screen. A New Orleans number. Not one she recognized. The phone fell silent, and the screen announced she had missed calls. Fifty-eight of them. Thirteen unheard messages. One was from her landlord. Maybe she was a coward, but she started there. She pressed play.

"Nathalie? Nathalie, you there?" Her landlord refused to use a cell and thought voice mail still worked like the old answering machines did. "Okay. I guess not." There was a dubiousness in his voice, like he suspected she might be standing beside the machine as he spoke. "Listen, girl. We're all real worried about you. The police called me. Asked me to open up your place for them." A pause. "Now, don't get mad. I know I'm s'posed to give you twenty-four hours' notice . . ." The old man sobbed. "They think something might have happened to you. And . . . oh, God, I hope not. You know I think the world of you. That new boss of yours. He's done some real bad things, girl. They got people keeping an eye out for your vehicle, but they said they're stretched pretty thin. You stop wasting those good people's time. You hear me? You call them. You tell them you're okay." Another pause. "Then you call me. Okay? I'll stay close to the phone." She heard him cough as he hung up.

All right, then. Time to face the music, she thought. "The Axman's Jazz" started playing again in her mind, and she flipped on the radio to kill the tune.

She'd go to the police department. It would be easier to convince them of her innocence if she met with them in person and could gauge their belief in what she was telling them.

First, though, there was an old guy she had to set at ease.

Nathalie had a blind spot, and that blind spot covered anything and everything that might be of any real use to her about what was headed her way. Sure, some stranger on the street, she could stop them and say, "Hey, I know this sounds kinda weird, but you might wanna tell your mama not to visit your aunt. At least not before next Tuesday." Most of the time she went on gut instinct, but in a lot of cases she could grasp the details. "Your aunt Toni," she'd added when delivering that particular message. "She lives in Mobile, right?" She'd seen the image of a casino, so that part had been a guess.

More than once she'd found herself smiling like a fool into a shocked or suspicious face. The woman she'd told about her mama hadn't even responded. She'd backed away, shaking her head and holding her hand out between them, index finger pointed at the sky.

Lots of people plain didn't want to know what was coming, but Nathalie tried to help where she could. She personally wouldn't mind a heads-up from time to time, but what she picked up about herself fell somewhere between a blank and a blur. She'd get an inkling or a rare flash of insight, but it would fade as soon as she tried examining it. Anything concrete? Oh, no, ma'am.

Had she possessed the ability to see into her own future, she would've known the police weren't looking for her because they thought she was guilty, but because Frank's last driver, some guy named Cutter, had been found in the Doll House, his severed head sewed back in place. He'd been wired for use as a lamp. She caught a visual of how that could be achieved, but couldn't bear to ask for confirmation of her concept.

The detective had decided to question her at his own desk, not in a formal interview room with cameras and recorders. That was a good sign. She made a point of looking directly into his red-rimmed brown eyes, trying not to shift her gaze to his shiny bald pate. It made it easier for her to read what he was thinking.

Nathalie wasn't dead, so she wasn't important. Her interview was a formality to be addressed, a mere box to tick.

A story formed in her mind. One that might sound just true enough.

Nathalie stumbled into it, treading with care through the officer's thoughts and feelings, building upon his expectations.

"Frank, Mr. Demagnan, that is—"

Still no sign of the freak. Images flooded Nathalie's mind. Photos the detective had seen of a beaming Frank posing with the corpses he'd mutilated. One image stood out in the detective's mind. *Like a damned family portrait. Even a goddamned Christmas tree.*

Selfies with the dead.

Nathalie could almost see the picture herself, her imagination filling in the blanks. So that's what he'd done to get himself cut up and sewn back together like Frankenstein's monster. Someone had discovered his playthings. Someone who'd decided to give Frank a taste of his own medicine.

"Sure, he creeped me out—" True enough, but the image she'd gleaned from the detective's recollections helped add an air of authenticity to her statement.

Desperate to work for him.

"—but hey, I needed the work. Can't be too choosy, right?"

She picked through the questions as they surfaced in the detective's mind.

Mr. Demagnan had called her up to his personal quarters out of the blue and told her he was closing up and taking off for vacation. Starting immediately. Two weeks. No. He hadn't said where, and she hadn't asked. Why not? She was angry. She might be part-time, but she still counted on the income. He wasn't paying her for her unwanted time off.

Permanent time off.

Where had she been? Why hadn't she answered her phone?

Day drinking. Followed by some night drinking. Sleepover with a friend. A friend whose name she'd not learned. A friend she'd probably not see again. Sly player's smile.

Yeah. She was a player. A regular Donna Juan.

A coyote dawn around noon. Coyote dawn? You know, you'd rather chew off your arm than wake what was sleeping on it—yeah, you can use it. Followed by a righteous hangover. She'd turned off her phone to keep her head from exploding. Wandered around looking for her SUV for like an hour. When she found it, she'd crawled in the back seat for a little six-hour siesta. Didn't have a clue any of this was going on until she caught the news at a bar she'd stopped by for some hair of the dog.

The balding brown-eyed detective sent her away with a pat on the back and a "You're a lucky little lady."

Nathalie wasn't little, and she'd never been too clear on what it meant to be "a lady," but she was a hell of a lot luckier than the detective could have guessed in a thousand tries. Someone had carried off Frank and his gun both. Must've done a good job of cleaning up the mess, too. Someone wanted the police to think the mortician was still alive. Or maybe—a chill ran down her spine—they'd collected all the pieces because they weren't through with Frank yet. Nathalie was glad those details fell into her blind spot. The less she knew about her accomplice in covering up Frank's suicide—and his murder before that—the better.

FIFTEEN

The warmth and humidity of the early fall air lessened as Evangeline rose above Vieux Carré rooftops, dim islands in a sea of neon light. She left behind the scent of Rampart Street piss, swooped down over Armstrong Park's lemony, peppery, ever-blooming rose garden, then struggled up on uncertain wings into the cold air currents. Winds wearing the muddy perfume of the Mississippi drove her forward as she angled northeast. She navigated using the speeding flares of headlights on Highway 10 as beacons, though her destination was unknown to her. The destination didn't matter. She'd been called to the sky, and she couldn't resist. At least not yet.

Despite the city glare, despite the madness below and in her mind, stars still shone above her. She tried to hold on to her sense of self by scanning for familiar patterns through a still unfamiliar wider avian field of vision, but the time of night and time of year had colluded to send the Big Dipper north to fill its cup, even as they drove Orion's belt below the horizon.

Cassiopeia ruled the sky.

Tonight, there had been no pain. In a single heartbeat, Evangeline had shimmered from one form to another. It was her reward, she knew, for the violence she'd given in to this afternoon.

She'd broken the windows of a single truck. Nobody had gotten hurt. And those idiots had sure as hell earned themselves a wakeup call. Evangeline knew these were rationalizations—she had knowingly committed an act of violence, and worse, she'd enjoyed it. Her painless transition tonight was like a treat given to a pet who'd performed as its master desired. She was being trained, escorted step-by-step on a gradual descent into darkness. The timing of the freebie wasn't lost on her either. They'd reached the end of the cycle. This was the last night this moon that the shift could be forced on her. She reasoned that it had to be. Otherwise her tormentors would've kept it up every night, wearing her down, trying to break her. Celestin and Margot weren't letting up on her out of goodwill. They had no choice but to give her a breather, but they wanted to give her something to think about. The message was clear: last night's change could be her last bone-cracking, painful shift. The choice was hers.

The twinkling lights of homes and shops below thinned, then disappeared. Grunch Road lay, or at least used to lay, not too far from here. She rose higher and drifted a bit south, trying to veer away from her suspected destination. She could sense her tormentors playing with her, letting her test boundaries for the pleasure of slapping her back on course if she strayed too far.

She felt the slack tighten as she approached the deserted remains of the amusement park.

The park had changed names a few years before Katrina, but she still thought of it as Jazzland, because that's what Luc had insisted on calling it. *Luc.* His face, his black-blue eyes, surfaced in her memory. For a moment, she was with him again. For a moment, the magic keeping her in a crow's form failed and she had full control of herself once more. The wind rushed up toward her as she began to plummet from the sky. In that moment, she knew ecstasy. She would crash. She would die. But she had no fear.

Death would bring freedom.

A rough, invisible hand jerked her skyward, like a yo-yo that had reached the end of its string. She'd discovered one of the limits set for her.

The force swung her like a pendulum, and she began to spiral downward, gaining speed with each pass, even as her field of vision narrowed. Her tormentors were toying with her, no doubt to underscore how powerless she was. The ground grew closer and closer. Evangeline braced herself, expecting to be dragged face-first along the rough pavement, but at the last possible moment they righted her and set her down lightly on her feet.

The magic had deposited her inside the deserted park, near the basin, beside the ruins of the old gazebo. Above the vines and brambles, she could make out the basin's far edge, where the Ferris wheel still stared like an unblinking, all-seeing eye. To her right, the white towers of the bungee ride framed a gateway to nowhere.

From above, the park's dominant feature, its dilapidated roller coaster, appeared to trail off into a double teardrop, but from ground level its wooden frame loomed high like the skeleton of Leviathan—fallen where it had been slain moments before it could take sanctuary in the muddy pond the park managers had once branded as a lake. Movement at the water's edge confirmed her suspicions. With the dragon dead, the basin and the lake were now alligator territory.

She could hear the roaring and rumbling of automobiles as they careened along the highway near the far edge of the park. Rather than connecting this space to the world beyond, the white noise seemed to cut off the abandoned park from the world around it. The wind picked up, teasing her naked skin into gooseflesh. She wrapped her arms around herself, her own touch bringing comfort if not additional warmth.

Flags, now no more than tattered rags, still fluttered, a frenzied flapping in the winds rushing from Pontchartrain to Chandeleur Sound. Old bones creaked in the abandoned rides, straining rusting joints. The chains of the swing ride rattled, its seats long since removed. As if in reaction to the clanking chains, Evangeline's memory conjured the ghost of a sunny day, overlaying the bleak and deserted scene before her with happy, dawdling crowds, rambunctious children, and melting ice creams. Bits and pieces of a day remembered. Bits and pieces of a day imagined. The comforting fiction heartened her, but soon the effort of maintaining the happy illusion started to drain her. She let the mirage slip away, and again she felt alone and exposed.

A door slammed behind her, causing her to startle. She forced herself to regain composure before turning, not wanting to give in to fear—or at least not show that she had. When she did swivel around, she found herself facing Festival Hall, a galleried two-story structure built to resemble those in the Quarter. No, at the end it hadn't been called Festival Hall. Like the greater park, the hall's name had been changed, too. In its final years, it had been known as the Orpheum. *Fitting,* reflected the tiny part of her mind that wasn't panicked. Like Orpheus, a dead lover had landed her in Hades. The door, one of the Orpheum's entrances, opened and slammed again—then, as if divining that it had her full attention, it eased wide open.

Evangeline realized that the park wasn't an improvised stop at all. It had been the destination all along. She'd anticipated a tour of Grunch Road, so she'd strayed south of it. Still, she'd ended up right where Celestin and Margot wanted her. They had turned her own expectations against her. All right, then. Lesson learned.

Come and see. A taunting voice whispered in her mind. It was the same invitation the angels made to John the Revelator at the breaking of each of the seven seals. Her drunk fanatic of a father had made sure she knew her Bible. Celestin and his feather-bound ally were certainly familiar enough with her history to understand this allusion would resonate with her.

Come and see. The words echoed again, this time in her father's impassioned voice as it had sounded coming from his pulpit.

The broken seals ushered in end-times.

Come and see. A strong tug pulled her toward the open door. She stumbled forward, unable to stop or even right herself until she stood inside. Although she hadn't thought of this place in years, once inside, she remembered it as it had been. The floor was even, not pitched like in most theaters, as the space had once been set up dinner theater–style with tables rather than rising rows of seats. The call dragged her along the floor, heedless of the broken beer bottles left by recent trespassers and the detritus washed in by the flood more than a dozen years ago. The pain of sharp edges meant nothing to her now. She tried to dig in, stand her ground, but still she lumbered along like a puppet on strings. Eager for even a false sense of control, she picked up her pace instead, rushing forward.

The hall was dark, even darker than the outside, which benefited from the city's ambient glow. For a few moments, she couldn't see much of anything, but soon her eyes adapted to the lesser light. On the stage, she made out the set from the theater's final performance, a rounded arch and cogs made to look like clockwork, framing a circle edged with Roman numerals. She heard a pop, and a flare-like ball of lightning exploded to life over the stage, dazzling her eyes. She blinked to clear her vision. A moment before, she had been certain the stage was empty except for the set. Now the brilliance illuminated a trio of bodies.

Evangeline gasped and staggered back.

Margot and Mathilde stood before her, each caught in mid-transformation. Woman-sized chimeras with the wings and talons of a bird, the head and torso of a human female. They stood side by side, the tips of their wings touching, their mouths stretched wide in a silent mimicry of derisive laughter. She didn't need to touch the women to know they were, after hundreds of years, dead. Their empty eyes were trained on a desiccated corpse kneeling face forward on the proscenium before them. The body held his hands out toward the audience as if in supplication, perhaps begging for mercy or maybe only soliciting applause. He wore an expensive-looking suit and a ridiculous white construction-paper mask. The mask had two rounded slits for eyes and pointed yellow tips along the top suggesting a crown.

Evangeline rushed forward, nearly stumbling as she mounted the four steps to the stage. She focused on the corpse's paper mask and leaned in to try to make out the word scribbled in green crayon along the band holding the mask in place.

It wasn't just a word. It was a name. *Alice.*

She steeled her nerves and snatched at the mask, breaking its band. The man's features had already begun to flake away, but there was no mistaking the face.

Before her knelt the corpse of Celestin Marin.

The great Celestin Marin, who'd slaughtered dozens of his fellow witches in his effort to claim their magic and escape death. The man who'd murdered his own grandson for power, and his own son just so he could hide behind his son's features.

Evangeline took a step back, freezing when she realized there was someone home behind Celestin's shrunken eyes. He had been wrenched from the safety of Babau Jean's form and trapped, aware, inside his own decaying corpse. Evangeline couldn't have envisioned a more fitting punishment for the man. It was almost as if the gravity of his rightful destiny had caught up with him and returned him to his natural body.

Who? The question broke the surface of her shock.

It hadn't been Celestin or Margot after all. The whispery voice, the irresistible will, they belonged to another. One who'd been strong enough to crush them.

Three of the greatest evils she'd ever faced stood vanquished before her. A poetic justice may have been served, but the thought could bring her no peace. That their judge could be the same as the source of her agony only kindled her fury. The light above her began pulsing, then strobing, reacting to her building rage. She screamed—sharp and shrill and bloodthirsty—a harpy's lamentation.

I am the balm for your suffering.

The words silenced her in a heartbeat. The force that had been tormenting her, twisting her body in the hope of twisting her soul, remained nearer than her own shadow.

Struggle begets pain.

She understood now. This scene hadn't been intended as a torment. It was an appeasement, an offering. The power driving her transformations was presenting itself not as her nemesis, but as Nemesis, the spirit of retributive justice. More importantly, it was working in her favor.

Unlike in Celestin, not a single spark of life remained in the sister witches. Still, their wings began beating in unison. Fed by a power other than their own, like the amusement park's dead animatronics, the pair parted and rose up, one on either side of Celestin, to gaze down on him like a travesty of a Nativity scene. They hung in midair as the strobing of the light slowed, gradually returning to a cold, steady beam.

Evangeline failed at first to notice, but a fine ash had begun to float up around the sister witches. Speck by speck, her childhood terrors were disintegrating, both flesh and bone falling away to dust. A gust of wind roared across the stage, finishing them and scattering their dust till there was no distinguishing between the sister witches' remains and the thick layer of grime that already coated the place.

A loud, shrill whistling suddenly filled the air all around her. She threw her hands up to protect her ears, and the light vanished. The force that brought her here pulled away, deserting her with Celestin. Or perhaps it had abandoned Celestin with her. Her light-deprived eyes fell on the witch's body, now a black silhouette on a background of shadow. As she studied his contour, the message grew clear. Celestin was hers, given to her to do with as she would, free of the power's interference or influence.

Swamp witch. That's what Celestin had called her. *Dalliance.* He'd used it as he laughed in disbelief in Luc's face. *Good enough for a dalliance, but certainly not to marry.* All these years later, the memory still caused her face to flush in shame. She felt her shame turn to anger, red sparks building and dancing along her fingertips. It suddenly dawned on her that she wasn't remembering the moment from her own perspective, but from Celestin's. He was willing her to relive all the raw moments from their shared past. Offering up intimacies she'd not been privy to before. The fake olive branch he'd given to Luc to bring him closer. That the idea of Luc rutting with her had made it a pleasure to kill the boy.

She yearned to watch the last spark of Celestin Marin shrivel up and fade. To end him once and for all. The sparks on her fingertips now sizzled like a sparkler, burning hot enough and bright enough to warm her body and shed light on Celestin's face.

You're weak. Weak. The words echoed in her mind, but the thought wasn't hers. It was Celestin's. She watched as the fear in his eyes turned to disdain, the same superior glint she'd caught there when Luc had first introduced them. Celestin was pushing her to wrath. He *wanted* her to strike out. She couldn't deny the temptation she felt, but she also couldn't bring herself to destroy him. A part of her had once believed his words. A part of her always might, but that part of her had led her down enough dark paths, and it no longer got to run her life. The energy at her fingertips fell away, leaving behind a faint scent of sulfur and a fluttering sensation in her stomach.

A beam of light landed on Celestin's face. "He's too big to use as a paperweight," a man's voice spoke from behind her. She was surprised to have company, but not frightened—she didn't have a single nerve left to jangle. She glanced back as he turned his flashlight on his own features. "It's me. Lincoln Boudreau."

"What are you doing here?" she said. She hadn't come here of her own accord, so let him be the one to explain himself, to justify his presence.

"Well," he said, shining the beam of his light on a duffel bag he was carrying, "I had the feeling you might be cold." He set the bag on the floor, and it slid to the end of the stage, then jumped up on its own to land by her feet. He turned his back toward her. "I told you I see things sometimes," he said as she knelt and unzipped the bag. A Bonnes Nouvelles T-shirt. Yoga pants. A pair of men's flip-flops. "Of course, I didn't anticipate the dead guy, but I did see . . ." His words trailed off. He was, she realized, doing his best to be a gentleman in a situation so singular and macabre that even the world's greatest optimist would struggle to promote it to "awkward." "I took the shirt from the club's inventory. You can deduct it from my pay." He paused. "'Course, I do hope you'll give it to me at cost." He made a tutting sound. "I mean really, Ms. Caissy. Thirty-two dollars?"

"They're collector's items," she said, amazed to realize that for an instant she'd almost forgotten about the rage-filled corpse kneeling beside her.

"Yeah, save it for the tourists," he said, committing, it seemed, to his grotesque choice of now as an appropriate time to flirt.

"I do." She glared down at Celestin. She could almost hear him chanting the word "whore" over and over. "They're the ones who buy the darned things." She pulled the extra-large shirt over her head.

"I know it's way big, but I was thinking you might wear it like a dress. Then I *borrowed* the pants. They belong to the new girl, Rose."

"Borrowed?"

"Well, without her permission or knowledge, but yeah. Borrowed. Don't snag them on anything on your way out of here."

"Remind me to fire you for theft later, okay?" She tugged on the yoga pants. Those fit fine. Better than most of her own clothes did these days.

"Yes, ma'am," Lincoln said and laughed. For the first time in a long while, Evangeline felt whole.

"You can turn around, Lancelot."

"Lincoln," he reminded her as he turned to face her.

"Oh, I know your name." She slipped on the flip-flops. They were twice the size of her feet. "Yours, I take it."

"Yes, ma'am," he repeated himself, though this time his tone carried a clear insinuation.

She felt her face redden again, but not from shame. He knew how to tug her strings. She didn't like it. She'd had enough of string pulling.

He turned his light on Celestin, and her eyes followed the beam. "*Pauvre couillon* there making a big *bahbin.*" Evangeline had to agree on two counts—Celestin's desiccated face had dried into a grotesque pout, and the old witch had certainly embodied every negative connotation *couillon* could carry. Still, she couldn't work up the sympathy to think of him as "poor." Not this man. Evangeline felt the weight of Lincoln's stare. "Looks to me like he'd like to be put out of his misery."

"I'm not sure he deserves that mercy."

Lincoln snorted. "Yeah, but what does magic have to do with mercy?"

"What does this have to do with magic?"

"Ah, come on. Old guy may not be able to use it himself, but that body there is pulsing with power. You've got to feel it." Lincoln held his free hand out, palm forward like he was warming himself before a fire. "You could draw that right out of him. Keep you in juice till long after that red hair of yours has gone snow white. With that kind of magic, you could own this town. Maybe even the whole Gulf region."

Evangeline *could* feel the power, a sizzling dark aura that coated his body like shellac. Unconsciously she'd been trying not to, but now that Lincoln had forced her to pay attention, she couldn't ignore it. What she sensed sickened her. She stepped back, revolted, drawing her arms in around herself. "No," she said, fighting back rising bile. Celestin's aura might look like an impenetrable shell, but she could sense the individual strands of magic he had woven together, see each murdered witch he'd stolen from. "Not that power. It's poison."

"You sure?" Lincoln said. "There're plenty witches who'd take the risk. Even those who wouldn't take it in bulk would pay a pretty penny for a piece of him. You could carve the old bastard up into some pretty powerful relics."

Evangeline knew he was right. Though Celestin's body had lain in a vegetative state for many years, he had remained a center of power. His coven had salivated at the thought of creating relics from his remains. Now, he carried the power of dozens. Some witches might wage war over his little toe, but they wouldn't be fighting her for any part of him. "I am sure. Darkness like that? Even a small dose is gonna take root and grow." And there, she realized, was the reason Celestin had been handed over to her. She had been fixating on the shame of powerlessness. Her tormentor had broken her down, then offered her a deep well of magic, a gift that, like the Trojan horse, carried her own undoing in the acceptance. "No, I want nothing to do with it."

"You're the boss." Evangeline imagined she could hear a tinge of relief in Lincoln's voice. "Okay, then, what're we gonna do with the old guy?" It felt good to hear him say "we." She'd file that bit away to process when she had the strength to think on it. Maybe in a decade or two.

"I don't know." She studied the deep lines on the flaking, leathery face. "We can't leave him here."

"Sure we can," Lincoln said. "We could walk out of here right now. Get in my truck and drive." She could almost see the fantasy building in his mind. "Get the hell out of Louisiana and keep going till we hit a coast. Los Angeles. New York. Seattle. Savannah. I don't care."

She turned toward his wistful voice, straining to make out his features in the shadows. "Who are you?"

"You know who I am." His voice came out in a whisper, like they were conspiring together. "You saw it, too. I'm the man who's going to ask you to marry him. And you're the woman who's gonna say yes."

Yes. She had seen. She had *felt*. But she'd understood it was only a likelihood, not something written in stone.

Whore. Whore. Whore. She sensed, almost heard, the word rising off Celestin like a toxic stench.

She glared down at the old man's body, shocked to see a smooth stone bounce off his forehead. Celestin, still frozen with his arms extended, teetered and fell to his side.

"There'll be no more of that, old man," Lincoln bounded up the steps to the stage. His flashlight shook in his hand, its beam jumping over the toppled corpse. "I got a pond not fifty yards from here full of *cocodries* who'd find you a tasty little treat." He squatted down before Celestin. "Whoever stuck you in there, old man, bound you up good and tight. I bet you'd be awake for every bite those gators take. Maybe even after. Maybe you'd still be connected to this bag of bones deep inside them. Or when you come clean out the other end. Tell me. How many bits do you think they'd have to chew you up into before you stop being you?" He nudged Celestin's shoulder. "One more comment from you, and we're gonna find out."

"It's gone too cool out there now," she said. "Alligators won't be feeding."

The beam of his flashlight darted to her feet. "Well, hell," he said, rising. "You know that, and I know that, but this here *bibitte* probably didn't."

Evangeline laughed despite herself.

"So, we're not gonna steal his magic," Lincoln said, the statement meandering back and forth between a confirmation and a question, "and we're not gonna strip him for spare parts."

"No, and we're also not feeding him to the *cocodries*." She stretched the word out. It felt at home on her tongue. She'd spent so long running from her background, it felt good to reclaim at least a shred of it.

"'Course not. Might make the gators sick." He looked down at Celestin, studying him like a school boy examining a bug. "Okay, then, what are we gonna do with him?"

Evangeline had already come to her decision. She couldn't trust Fleur with the choice. Fleur would gorge on her father's dark power, ruining herself to save her daughter. That was reason enough to protect the woman from herself, but it wasn't the only one. As much as Evangeline hated to admit it, soon it might be her turn to go to Fleur for help. There was only one thing to do. "The man spent years judging me. I'm gonna see to it that the favor is returned."

Lincoln turned the light on his face to illuminate his exaggerated confusion. He shook his head. "Would you mind elucidating?"

"He's guilty of probably a thousand different crimes." She knelt beside Celestin and tapped his nose with her finger. "You and I are going to see to it that he gets his day in court."

SIXTEEN

"You could see this place from space," Lucy said as Fleur pulled up to Nicholas's house.

Her daughter was given to youthful exaggeration, but she did have a point. Every light in the house had been turned on.

There were not one, but two police cars parked in front of Nicholas's house. Each had a uniformed officer behind the wheel. Two houses down sat a familiar-looking black SUV, but those things all looked alike to Fleur. Maybe it was an unmarked police vehicle.

"Nothing screams 'nothing to see here' like bathing yourself in six million watts."

"Daniel is nervous." Fleur was a bit nervous herself.

"And acting like he's got something to hide."

Fleur shifted into park and killed the engine. "He was the last to see Astrid. Maybe he does." She'd started the statement as a joke, but by the time it was halfway past her lips, she had begun to consider the possibility. There wasn't much that would astonish her anymore—other than the alacrity at which the unimaginable could become the everyday.

Still, it gave Fleur pause that Astrid's body had been right here in New Orleans the entire time she'd been missing.

Astrid had disappeared almost twenty years ago. Everyone assumed she'd taken to the Dreaming Road, but that assumption might have been false. Maybe Demagnan had discovered her physical body after she'd separated her consciousness from it, or maybe he'd killed her. Either could be the case, although the police wouldn't even entertain the first possibility.

Lucy laughed as she opened her door. "Yeah. Right. Daniel."

In unison, the uniformed officers turned in their respective seats and leaned down to get a better look at Fleur and Lucy as they started down the walk. Simple curiosity or suspicion? Did they suspect that Demagnan might have accomplices?

Lucy went ahead of her, but stopped at the already ajar door. Fleur joined her, wondering if they should knock first or slip in unannounced, but the door swung all the way open before Fleur could do either. Daniel met them in the foyer, a tray of finger sandwiches balanced on his hand.

"Ah, here," Daniel called at top voice over his shoulder. "Here's someone who can help you." Then, in a low whisper, he added, "What took you so long? The detectives want someone to *go with them* to identify the body." Daniel pulled an exaggerated wide-eyed face, Fleur was sure, to remind her that he couldn't even make it past the sidewalk without being snapped right back into the house.

"I'm surprised there is a body *to* identify," Lucy said. "It's been like a hundred years, right?" Her math might be insulting, but she had a point. Astrid had disappeared long ago. It seemed she should have crumbled to dust and bone by now.

Daniel's comical look turned to a grimace. "Well, Mrs. Marin always was a well-preserved woman." He turned on his heel and headed into Nicholas's formal sitting room. Fleur followed the anxious servitor, with Lucy on her heels.

A barrel-chested plainclothes detective sat on the edge of an antique settee, clutching a small, delicate china plate between his thick fingers. He looked like a prize fighter who'd been pressed into attending his young daughter's dolly tea party.

Another detective in a rumpled gray pantsuit returned the cup she'd been holding to its saucer and rose from the Bergère chair Nicholas had inherited from their grandparents—the Bergère chair that would, if Fleur got her way, soon make its way back to the Garden District house where it had started.

"Detectives Collins and Morel"—Daniel nodded first at the woman and then the sausage-fingered man—"this is . . ."

"Mrs. Warren Endicott," Fleur said extending her hand. The divorce would be final next week. This would be the last time she could throw around the weight of the senator's name, but she might as well take it out for one last spin. Fleur clocked the surprise on her daughter's face, but Lucy, blessedly for once, kept her own counsel.

Morel remained seated in his self-conscious pose, but Collins crossed to them and shook Fleur's hand. "Mrs. Endicott," she said, her tone suggesting both a question and a confirmation at once. Collins had done her homework. "I assume your"—she glanced over at Daniel— "assistant . . . has informed you about why we're here."

"It was a shock," Daniel broke in, "even to someone like me who's never met Mrs. Marin, but Detective Collins broke the news with the utmost sympathy and tact." Par for the course, Fleur thought. They'd left it to the woman to deliver the bad news. Easier for a family to hear about a death from a sympathetic female. Yeah, easier on the male officers who didn't have to do the dirty work. "No, I mean it," Daniel continued. "Is there a site where I can leave a review for you? Five stars, I promise."

Detective Collins's eyes darted to Fleur, her raised brows telegraphing the question "Is there something wrong with this guy?"

"Oh, Daniel," Fleur said, "I do appreciate your trying to lighten the mood, but now is not the time for levity."

Daniel's head tilted to the side like a confused pup's, then he caught on that he'd committed a faux pas. "Oh. No. Of course not, Mrs. Senator . . . I mean Mrs. Endicott. Pardon me."

Collins turned to face her partner, then back to Fleur. The detective's expression had gone blank. "I think it might be better to start afresh—make sure you have been properly alerted to the situation." She cast a cautious side-eye at Daniel. "We've come to notify you that we've discovered your sister-in-law's remains at a site in Uptown."

"The Doll House," Lucy interjected, her morose interest in the matter burgeoning with the awareness that she had a personal connection to it.

Collins gave Lucy a patronizing smile. "I'm aware social media has begun to popularize that tag."

"People are saying the guy built tableaux by posing dead bodies around the place, but dead bodies rot, right? It seems like the neighbors would've picked up on the smell."

"Taxidermy," Detective Morel spoke up for the first time.

"That"—Collins dragged the word out as she spun back on her partner—"has not been made public knowledge yet." She turned back and fixed Lucy with her gaze. "I'm going to have to ask you to keep that detail quiet for now." She turned to Fleur. "Perhaps it would be better . . ."

Fleur cut her off with a raised hand and a nod. "Daniel, perhaps you could take Lucy to the kitchen and whip something up for her? I'm afraid this tragedy"—she tried her best to make it sound like she meant it—"preempted our dinner."

"Hello. Plate of sandwiches. Besides, so not hungry," Lucy said, and crossed the room to plant herself on the settee next to the awkwardly perched detective. She turned to him. "Hello." She flashed him the bright smile that always landed her anything she wanted. Especially when she used it on Fleur.

"All right," Collins said, resignation in her voice. Or maybe she was just tired. Examining dioramas built using preserved corpses would have to take it out of a person. "Though I must caution all of you," she gave her partner a severe look, "that any information we share with you, we do so to facilitate our investigation, not so you can go all big orange loudmouth with the little blue bird." She paused and focused on Lucy. "Do we understand each other?"

"Well," Lucy said, her head tilted and a slight crease down her brow, "when it comes to social media, I'm more inclined to go with the little ghost guy, 'cause those messages . . ."

"Do we understand each other?" Collins barked at Lucy.

Lucy pushed back into the settee. "Yes, ma'am."

"Good."

The second Collins turned her back on Lucy, Lucy shrugged and looked at Morel with wide eyes and a slightly open mouth. A silent "What's up with her?" Morel shrugged back in response.

Collins seemed to have a preternatural ability to sniff out disrespect. Fleur could see her getting ready to check in on Lucy, so she spoke up fast. "I understand you need a family member to identify the body."

"Yes," Collins said, "but it's a bit more than that. We're trying to reach your brother Nicholas, but Daniel here tells me he's gone off grid. I'm hoping you can put us in touch with him. It would help us to be able to talk to Mrs. Marin's husband."

"I'll contact him right away."

"Perhaps you can give us his number so that we can call him now?"

"It isn't as simple as that."

"Mrs. Senator," Collins said. Her voice was too weary for her sarcasm to shine through, but Fleur stiffened all the same. "It would be easier if you could just call . . ."

If that's the way she wants it, Fleur thought, as any sense of sympathy for the officer drained away. Fleur was pretty damned tired, too. "Detective"—she slipped into the tried-and-true role of congenial politician's wife—"I'd be more than happy to give you his number. It's only, as I'm sure you, as an investigator, will soon conclude, Nicholas has turned his cell off."

"Why would he take off like this?"

"A few months ago he suffered a one-two punch to his ego, one romantic and one . . . professional. It seems to have triggered a midlife crisis, and now my big brother has gone off to find himself. He withdrew a fat stack of cash, packed up his car with camping gear, and vanished."

"Then how do you intend to contact him?"

Fleur smiled. "ESP."

"No, really . . ."

"Through friends. There are family friends spread out all over. I'll put out feelers." She brushed back the bangs she was still trying to get used to. "I'm sure he'll be in contact with one of them sooner or later."

"Sooner would be better."

"I'll do my best to make that happen." She held up two fingers. "Scout's honor. Is there any other way we can assist you?"

"You have a nephew and a niece? Astrid's children?"

"Yes."

"It would be a great help if they could come by the station and submit to a DNA test. It could help with identification."

"I'm afraid my niece is incapable of doing so—"

"Out finding herself?"

"No. In a coma."

"Oh. I'm sorry."

"I'm sure Hugo, my nephew, will not hesitate to assist."

"Wait," Lucy said. "One question, two parts. Part A: How do you know the body you've found belongs to Astrid? Part B: If you know the body you've found belongs to Astrid, why do you need Hugo's DNA to identify it?"

"That's actually two questions—" Daniel began.

"Whatever." Lucy cut him off.

Collins lowered her head and bit her lip. Fleur could tell that the detective was debating if she should answer Lucy's questions. Her lips pulled into a pucker, then she looked up at Lucy. "Demagnan kept very good records, annotated before and after pictures. He tattooed his victims' names on the back of their necks. A permanent reminder, I guess, in case any of his notes got misfiled."

"And the DNA?" Lucy pressed when the detective fell silent.

"He didn't keep the bodies intact. A taxidermist has to remove the organs, then refill the cavity with special wood shavings. I found out today they call the stuff 'excelsior.'" A slight shake of her head. "See, you really do learn something new every day."

"What did he do with their organs?" Lucy asked with wide eyes.

"Oh, he kept them. At least some of them. That's why we need the DNA. Seems that he may have sold the rest."

"Sold them?" Fleur said, the full picture dawning on her. The missing witches. The black-market relics.

"Seems there's a market for everything these days. It isn't only the internal organs. Most of the bodies are missing their original limbs. Demagnan replaced the missing bits with parts of old mannequins. We have no way of knowing if the missing parts have been marked to show . . ."

"Provenance." Fleur finished the detective's sentence for her. Collins couldn't know it, but this was the term used when dealing with preserved relics.

Collins nodded. "That's the word I've been searching for." She reached into her jacket pocket and pulled out her phone. She studied its screen for a moment before looking back at Fleur. "There are developments we need to attend to." She turned to her partner, who shifted to his feet but seemed at a loss as to what to do with his china.

"I'll take that," Lucy told him, flashing another patented smile. Fleur could read her without even trying. Her daughter might have no magic, but she knew how to make friends and influence people. Warm smiles, small kindnesses, positioning herself as a fellow sufferer of Collins's surly nature—Lucy was building a sense of comradeship with Morel that she might benefit from at a later date. Her daughter's barefaced methods wouldn't work if she were in the least bit disingenuous, but Lucy's every act was sincere. Fleur could never get over how her daughter had managed to become the perfect balance of compassionate and self-serving. Morel passed the plate to her and returned her smile. The man was hooked.

"If you could," Collins said, drawing Fleur's attention back to her, "start putting out those 'feelers' to reach your brother as soon as possible."

"Immediately," Fleur said, her senator's wife's smile in place.

"Please give this to your nephew." She fished a business card from her pocket. "It has my direct number. Ask him to call me as soon as . . ."

"As soon as he's sober." Lucy jumped in. She met Collins's surprise with a world-weary expression. "Just setting expectations. It may be a while before you hear from him."

"Lucy, dear," Fleur said, feigning shock while playing off her daughter. Lucy knew what she was doing. She was buying time, in case they needed it. Fleur sighed. "My daughter has no sense of decorum, but she's right. Our Hugo often finds himself needing to sleep off a bender."

"He doesn't come home to do this?"

Fleur chuckled, then copied Lucy's expression. "He doesn't need to. When you meet Hugo, you'll understand why he never faces a shortage of welcoming beds." She pressed her hands together. "Not to worry. I'll see to it he calls you as soon as he comes around." From behind her facade, the truth crept out. "This is going to hit him hard. I do hope you'll appreciate that beneath all his smugness there's a very sensitive soul . . ."

"And then another layer of smugness," Lucy said, taking Morel by the arm and escorting him to his partner's side.

This time Lucy had managed to take her by surprise. "Yes. That's true as well, but please don't be callous toward him, even if he seems uncaring. They were never close, and Astrid disappeared when he was a young boy, but she was still his mother." Fleur was speaking as much for Lucy's benefit as for the detectives'.

"We'll use the utmost tact," Collins said. "In the meantime, it would be extremely helpful to have a confirmation of identity from a family member."

"I'll be happy . . . ," Fleur began. "Well, perhaps 'happy' is the wrong word, but I'll do it. Now if you need . . ."

"Now doesn't work," Daniel said, sounding anxious, but trying to cover it with a wide smile. "Sorry. I worry Hugo might come home before you return . . . He'll know something's wrong. I'll make a mess of telling him, and you can't possibly want him to hear the news from Miss Incorrigibility here."

"Hey . . . ," Lucy protested.

"Truth," Daniel shot back.

Lucy glared at him, but then her expression softened. "Yeah," she said, "he's right. I'll do more damage than good if I try."

"First thing tomorrow?" Fleur addressed the detectives. "Once we know the lay of the land around here? I may have news about Nicholas. With any luck, Hugo will have stumbled home by then as well."

"Yes. Tomorrow's fine." Collins checked her phone's screen once more. "I'm not even sure the morgue is ready to show the body anyway." She looked at Morel. "We have to get back."

"I'll walk you out," Fleur offered.

Collins paused, seeming to study Fleur's face. Whatever she was looking for, Fleur hoped she wouldn't find it there.

"Not necessary." Collins flashed her a precise and, Fleur felt certain, calculated smile. "We're detectives, we can find our own way." A glint of sincerity rose to her eyes. "I am sorry for your loss. We'll get Demagnan. You have my word." For an instant Fleur felt a true human connection to the woman, and then it was gone. Frost covered Collins's features. "Tomorrow. First thing."

"Without fail," Fleur promised, even though what she meant was "if I don't have something more pressing to deal with."

"Thank you," Collins said. "Come on," she commanded Morel. He followed, though not before casting a look in Lucy's direction. Lucy went slack-jawed and wide-eyed, sarcasm and sympathy intertwined. That was her girl. Morel gave an almost imperceptible nod, then followed his partner out of the room.

Fleur held her finger up to her lips, listening to the receding footfalls, waiting for the click of the door. Daniel crossed the room and stood beside the window, watching. "They're pulling away." He turned to her. "You'll be using ESP to reach Nicholas, of course?"

"Of course." Fleur began rubbing at the knot that had formed in her shoulder.

"She's wound a bit too tight," Lucy said, "but I like him."

"I didn't see a ring," Hugo said, appearing right behind her.

Lucy jumped. "Shhhh . . . shimeny." She turned and slapped his shoulder. "How many times have I told you not to do that?"

"Evidently not enough." He circled around Lucy and walked to the tantalus bar set resting on the side table. He undid the latch and selected the center of the three decanters. Bourbon. He pulled out the stopper and tipped the bottle to his lips, his Adam's apple jumping as he drained the equivalent of a tumbler's three fingers in a single go.

"Oh, Hugo," Daniel said in dismay. "I raised you better than that."

"Yes," Fleur said, "if you're going to drink yourself into a stupor, at least use a tumbler."

Lucy clapped, then assumed an innocent look when Fleur turned on her. "What? It's nice to see I come by it naturally."

Fleur would've scolded her if she weren't correct. She approached her nephew instead, touching his hand first, and then grasping the neck of the bottle and setting it beside its stopper on the table. "I'm sorry," she said. "That came out . . ."

"Honest and without filter?" Hugo's face turned gray and impassive as he looked down at her. *Imagine it. Hugo. Looking down at me.* She could still see him in that ludicrous short pants suit Astrid had dressed him in to attend her wedding to Warren.

"It's okay," he continued. "You've left D.C. You don't have to practice dissimulation anymore." He'd been a little boy when she left New Orleans. She had spent some months of his young life with him, right after Katrina when Nicholas had sent him and Alice to stay with her and Warren. Other than that, she'd missed seeing him grow up, catching him at one- to two-inch increment increases in stature. Now he was full-grown and more of a needy little boy than he had been all those years ago. "And by 'dissimulation,' I mean lying to everyone, including yourself."

She ran her hand down his arm. "How much did you hear?"

"Hmmm . . . let's see. Daniel crapping crackers until you got here. Lucy coming on to Officer Mushroom. Oh, and Mom's corpse stuffed and mounted." His head tilted to the side. "Did I miss anything?"

Fleur retrieved the bottle and handed it back to him. "No," she said, crossing to sit on the Bergère chair that, when all was said and done, didn't matter to her one damned bit. It wasn't, she realized, even comfortable. Nothing more than a piece of scenery, and Fleur was sick and goddamned tired of worrying about appearances and putting on shows for others' benefits.

"I saw the cop cars outside," Hugo said. "No sirens. No lights. I decided to go into Casper mode till I knew what was up."

J.D. Horn

Fleur realized this explained why the door had been ajar when they arrived. "We thought you would still be tending to Ms. Caissy's club."

"Not to worry. I left both the woman and her bar in good hands." Color returned to his face, and a warm gleam to his eyes. "I can personally vouch for a couple of those hands." Hugo was back, Fleur thought, but then he flickered out again. His eyes lowered. He put the stopper back in the decanter and returned the bottle to the tantalus. He turned to Daniel. "Didn't you text them?"

Daniel's eyes widened. "No. I didn't have the chance. I'd only messaged you when the officers arrived."

"Message us about what?" Fleur tensed, not sure she could take another surprise tonight.

"Alice," Daniel said. "That's why I couldn't let you leave. We're going to bring her home. Tonight." He glanced down at his wristwatch. "In precisely two hours and twenty-seven, no, twenty-six minutes."

168

SEVENTEEN

Nathalie had been clear, sincere—and, to her shame, mildly profane—when asking both Daniel *and* his cat to kindly leave her the hell alone. Upon leaving the Marin residence, she'd wished them much luck in their efforts, but made it abundantly clear she wasn't ever coming back. They were on their own. Sorry and sayonara.

She might not get clear glimpses into her future, but either someone in Alice's house could, or Daniel had picked up on something in her character that she hadn't seen in herself, because it sure looked like someone expected her. Nathalie stood at Alice's door, watching it creak open before she could even make a fist to rap.

A pair of twins holding hands stood together in the center of the foyer. They were middle-aged and kind of plastic looking, like their appearance had taken a lot of artifice. They wore identical outfits, floral-print smocks, teal with oversize navy flowers, navy mid-thigh shorts, and brown pumps. Nathalie noticed the heels of their shoes were different lengths, lifting one of the two an inch higher to give the pair the illusion of being the same height. Their jet-black hair was cut in the same flapper style. Their lips had been painted into bright red hearts. Other than the difference in their height, the only way Nathalie could've told them apart was that one seemed to be wearing heavier foundation makeup than the other. They gazed at her with the same inscrutable expression.

Nathalie felt a thousand tiny pinpricks rushing over her. *New witch. New witch.* Their shared thought tickled her brain. It felt like she'd walked into a spiderweb that could pass straight through her.

"I'm not a witch," she said, bracing herself against the doorframe. The two cast a glance at each other before turning back to her, matching incredulous smirks lighting their faces. A force shot out from them and tugged her over the threshold. The door slammed behind her.

Nathalie held her hands up, ready to fend the pair off. Hot white sparks danced along her fingers. She turned her hands and gazed down at her palms in wonder. The veins of her wrists were glowing, as if the power in her hands was pulsing in her blood.

Nathalie looked up from her hands to see the twins watching her with unabashed amusement. The two rested their heads together. *Not a witch. Not a witch.* Their matching thoughts the punchline of a private joke.

No longer sensing a threat, she felt the force within her recede. A glance down at her hands revealed they'd returned to normal—or at least what used to be her normal. She felt another volley of the twins' magic hit her. Recollections of years long past rose up around her and raced by. The pair of matching witches moved around in them at will, touching and moving objects like props, examining the people who haunted her memories. Nathalie knew she should be angry, but she was too darned shocked.

"Nathalie?" a voice pulled her back. She looked up to find a young woman—pretty, blonde, and familiar—calling to her from the second-floor landing. Nathalie lowered her hands and nodded her response. The girl beamed down at her. "Be right with you." Nathalie watched as the young woman swept down the steps in the most ridiculous heels she had ever seen—more like stilts than shoes. Last July, Nathalie had driven this blonde girl and her mother to a memorial down by the river. They'd emptied the mother's brother's ashes into the Mississippi down at the end of St. Ann Street. She drew nearer, studying the twins as she passed them.

Nathalie scoured her memory for the young woman's name, retrieving it at the same moment the girl spoke again. "Hello, there. I'm Lucy."

Lucy and her mother were friends with Evangeline Caissy—and the Perrault family, too. Nathalie hadn't made the connection between the beautiful, delicate young woman in the photo and these people. Daniel had spoken of the gravity of rightful destiny, saying its force had been drawing Nathalie closer and closer to Alice, but in a flash, Nathalie comprehended that Alice figured as part of a larger puzzle.

She felt as if a noose were tightening around her. Adrenaline urged her to bolt.

Nathalie looked from Lucy to the twins.

Lucy followed her gaze to the pair. "Crazy, right?" she said. "You have to have amazing legs to pull off that look. I hate you both." The duo, pleased with her malice-lined compliment, smiled and curtsied in unison before turning and walking off toward the rear of the house.

Lucy turned back to Nathalie and gave her the once over. She pointed at Nathalie. "Wait. I know you. Oh, yeah . . ." Her smile fell flat as she remembered the circumstances in which they'd met, but by the next beat she was beaming again. "Wow. So, *you're* the one with the . . ." Her brow furrowed and she snapped her fingers a few times. "The gravitational destiny rights."

"I think you mean 'the gravity of rightful destiny,'" Nathalie corrected her, "but I don't think it's something I own. It feels more like something happening to me."

Lucy folded her arms over her chest. "Welcome to the family. The less you struggle against the undertow, the better your chances of survival."

"There you are," Daniel's exasperated voice caught her attention. He bounded down the stairs to the foyer. "Good heavens, girl," he said, addressing Lucy. "You know we're on a tight schedule."

"Hey." Lucy threw up her hands. "I came down to fetch her like you told me to. The Twins were the ones batting her back and forth between their paws."

"We'll overlook that," Daniel said, patting Nathalie's shoulder with a soothing touch. He pulled back as his brow furrowed. "They didn't have to come." He said it loudly enough for them to hear, his voice defensive, then leaned in and whispered into Nathalie's ear, "Their magic is worth the inconvenience." She sensed it was an intimation aimed at drawing her further into his well-meaning conspiracy.

Daniel grasped Nathalie's arm, a manic smile on his face. "Now, if you please," he began, tugging her toward the staircase, "it would be of great help if you could spend a little time talking to her, so she gets accustomed to your voice."

"Her?" She dug in her heels, bringing them to a lurching stop.

He looked at her with an annoyed grimace. "Alice, who else?" He tugged Nathalie up the first few steps. "She's in her room. At least her physical form is."

"What is she supposed to do?" Lucy said, coming up behind them. "Wake her with a kiss?"

"If only it were that simple." Daniel sighed.

"Actually," Nathalie said as she tried to pull her arm out of Daniel's vicelike grip, "the whole fairy-tale thing has always seemed kind of creepy to me. I mean, kissing a defenseless person who has no way of telling you if she wants to be kissed—"

"She does have a point." Lucy cut her off.

"We're all on the same page with that"—Daniel paused on the steps between them—"but no one is forcing their attentions on anyone." Catching sight of his own tight grip on Nathalie's arm, he released her. "Please, follow me."

He mounted the final steps, and Lucy came up beside Nathalie, flashing a smile that was no doubt meant to be reassuring. She placed her hand on Nathalie's upper arm, and a chill shot through her. *Dead.* Nathalie pulled back, though she did her best to return the smile. She didn't understand the stray thought, but she hoped, no, felt that it wasn't linked to Lucy's future. Death was a part of her past, but it still followed her as close as a shadow.

"I know you don't know Alice," Lucy said, misinterpreting Nathalie's discomfort. "Heck, even I don't know her well, and she's my cousin. But she's worth it. Whatever Daniel asks you to do, Alice is worth it."

Nathalie reminded herself for like the twentieth time today that if Daniel's plan worked, if they managed to bring Alice back to her body, the Alice who came through wouldn't be the woman Nathalie had imagined in her self-indulgent fantasies. Daniel stopped before one of the doors and eased it open. He waved Nathalie forward, then guided her into the room with a hand on the small of her back.

And there she was. Nathalie froze in wonder before Alice. The beauty from the picture, though her eyes were closed, not sparkling with humor and warmth. Her skin so pale, her delicate features gaunt. Nathalie's eyes traced the line of Alice's long, graceful neck.

A movement. Nathalie noticed the tiny ball of gray fur curled up on Alice's chest. The cat, the one that had been stalking her since she'd arrived at work yesterday—how could it have been only yesterday?— looked up at her with its oversized peridot eyes. The cat, too, seemed lessened. Weaker. An instant connection formed between them. Could a cat feel relief? Gratitude? It relaxed, its eyes going empty and closing.

Daniel dashed forward and snatched the cat into his arms. "No more," he said, raising the animal's tiny head to his lips. He placed a kiss there. Its eyes fluttered open, but it seemed woozy, pushing back in his arms to look at him before surrendering to his embrace. Daniel caressed the feline's fur with gentle, caring strokes.

"Wow," a surprised voice spoke from behind her. Nathalie turned to see a muscular but compact guy with curly blond hair and a devil's blue eyes. This was a guy who took breaking hearts as his birthright, but that was all surface. At his core, he was a guy who'd been broken himself. Nathalie had seen him once before, she realized, at the memorial by the river, but other than for the obvious affection she'd noticed between him and Evangeline Caissy, Nathalie hadn't paid him too much mind. That day her focus had been on the Perraults, Lisette in particular.

Nathalie noticed the pupils of those devil blues were dilated. It was cool in the room, but there were beads of sweat on his brow. He had a slight resemblance to Alice, visible in the curve of his mouth, the set of his eyes.

"I never thought I'd live to see the two of you making nice," the newcomer continued. "I thought you two hated each other."

"Perhaps we misjudged each other. We are both secure enough to admit to our mistakes. Isn't that right, my dear Sugar?" He lifted the cat higher, and she rubbed her head on his chin. "She's been giving of her own life force, the silly thing," Daniel said. "She's trying to lend Alice's body her own formidable strength, but I'm afraid"—he held the cat out before him—"from time to time she overestimates herself."

The blond guy entered the room and held out his hand to Nathalie. "Hugo Marin. Profligate, iconoclast, least likely to succeed, and still the last man standing."

"And drama queen," Lucy said. "Don't forget drama queen."

"Alice's brother," Daniel explained.

"Oh," Nathalie said and shook his hand.

"Oh," Hugo parroted her. He winked at her, released her hand, and made his way to a chair in the corner. "Okay, Big D.," he said, running his fingers through his thick curls as he sat, "I've finished with the sigils you wanted me to put on the floor. Hope you don't mind, but I decided to carve them into the wood rather than paint them." A smirk rose to his face. "No doubt Nicholas will have a conniption fit when he gets back."

"I," Daniel said, "do not give a"—he paused, gathering steam—"damn. There, I said it. I do not give a damn what Nicholas thinks. About anything."

Hugo laughed. "Easy there, big fellow. Sounds like there's revolution in the air."

"Nicholas has driven me to wrath. He's deserted her. He's deserted you." The anger in his eyes faded into sadness. "He's deserted us all."

"Nicholas?" Nathalie said, regretting her curiosity the second it got the best of her.

"My uncle." Lucy pointed one finger at Hugo and the other at Alice. "Their dad." She nodded toward Daniel. "And his Geppetto." She lowered her hands. "Nicholas has been gone—like second-act Peggy Schuyler gone—for months. Oh, wait." Her eyes drifted up like she was considering a problem, and her head bobbed from side to side. "Truth in advertising." She turned her focus back to Nathalie. "Nicholas isn't really Alice's dad. He's her half brother. Oh, and Daniel isn't made of wood." She studied Daniel. "At least I don't think so."

"No," Daniel said, turning the cat over to Lucy's care, "I most certainly am not made of wood, though sometimes I think your head might be." Nathalie could sense a sharp retort building, but Daniel derailed Lucy before she could hurl it at him. "I do hope your mother gets back soon." He paced around the foot of the bed and looked out the window. He turned to face them, but then spun back around to observe a passing car. Placing his palm against the pane, he surveyed the street.

"Where did she go?" Hugo asked, slumping in his chair and wiping his forehead with the back of his hand.

"I sent her out for a few . . . supplies."

"Eye of newt?" Lucy said.

Daniel turned and crossed to Alice's side. He lowered his eyes and bit his lip. "Relics."

Lucy's mouth fell open. "Relics?"

Daniel turned his face toward Lucy. His eyes gleamed with an angry fire. "Well, forgive me, but we'll need all the help we can get. We're going to need all the relics we can lay our tarnished hands on."

"Where," Hugo spoke, "did you send her to collect these relics?"

Daniel reached down and took Alice's hands. "Demagnan's."

"Demagnan's?" Nathalie exclaimed in unison with Lucy and Hugo.

"You should've let me go," Hugo said. "There are cops crawling all over that place and the house next door. I could've slipped in and out without anyone noticing." He tried to rise, but fell back into his chair, fascinated by a speck of dust floating before him.

"Then there's that," Daniel said. "I'm guessing psilocybin?"

"And peyote." He held up his hand, rubbing the tip of his index finger against his thumb. "With just a soupçon of the synthetic stuff."

"LSD."

"Wanted to make sure we had all the bases covered."

"You're high?" Nathalie asked. She turned to Lucy. "He's high?"

"Oh so very," Daniel answered for her. "But this time it's for a good cause."

"It's always," Hugo said, and laughed, "for a good cause."

"Hallucinogens," Daniel said, ignoring Hugo, "will help him walk closer to the world where our Alice has been trapped. As I told you earlier, I've spent these last months studying my true nature, my true purpose. I can walk between the worlds of the Dreaming Road. I can go to Alice and bring her essence back with me. Inside me. But once she's within me, I'll lose control. She'll be riding me, like a . . ."

"Like a *chwal*," Nathalie finished his sentence.

"Well, I was going to say 'horse,' but your simile falls closer to the truth. Alice will have to guide me, but she's had no experience walking between the worlds. Worse, she may be in no condition to guide me.

Celestin abandoned his body of his own volition, to become an expert at guiding Babau Jean. He had years to hone his control of his '*chwal*,' but Alice doesn't have the luxury of time. With my last moment of control, I'll fling myself in Hugo's direction. If Alice is incapacitated, our best hope is that Hugo will be able to reach us."

"What if he fails?" Any pretense had fallen away from Lucy. She was scared beyond teenage cynicism.

"No need to worry about that," Daniel said, his voice too bright. "He won't fail."

"What if he does?" Lucy pressed.

Daniel and Hugo gazed into each other's eyes.

"I'm not sure what will become of me. I suppose that I may be able to find my own way back—perhaps borrow a trick or two from Babau Jean—but Hugo and Alice will be lost."

"They'll die?" Lucy's eyes teared up.

"Yes," Hugo said, but his answer came too quickly. A look passed between him and Daniel. Nathalie shuddered. Whatever would happen to them, she realized, would be much worse than death. Nathalie regarded Alice's peaceful, no, blank face. Nathalie couldn't read from the guys' thoughts what they envisioned as the worst-case scenario, but she knew she'd do all it took to make sure that scenario never materialized.

"How is this going to work?" she said, wrapping an arm over Lucy's shoulders. To her surprise, Lucy leaned into her. The cat raised its head and gazed at Nathalie.

A smile quivered on Daniel's lips. "Magic."

Despite herself, Nathalie smiled. "How, specifically, is this going to work? Exactly and in detail, please."

Daniel sat next to Alice and ran his fingers through her hair. "As with all magic, it's best that the conscious mind is kept somewhat in the dark. Suffice it to say it'll be a bit like mailing a letter. I'm the envelope. The magic channeled by Fleur and the Twins, the postage. And you, dearie, are the address." He stood and strode to the door. "I'm going to inspect Hugo's handiwork." He sighed. "We'd stand a much better chance of success if we could work the spell closer to the gateway."

Nathalie turned to him in confusion. "Where is the gateway?"

"Well, there are a few spread out around the globe, but the closest one is east of here."

Pieces came together in her mind. The bizarre stories about pale, red-eyed cannibals, shadow men, and time anomalies. Her own attraction to the abandoned stretch of road. "Grunch," she said. "Grunch Road."

Daniel's eyes widened in surprise. "Yes. Precisely."

"That's like a, what, twenty-minute drive? Let's go." She advanced on Alice, ready to lift her from the bed and carry her to Grunch Road on foot if need be.

"Whoa," Hugo said. "Hold on there, cowgirl."

She stopped and turned to face them. "What?"

Daniel's shoulders slumped, and he gave her a pained smile. "I may be able to pass through the worlds of the Dreaming Road, but in the common world, I can't travel more than a few feet from this house."

"Edge of the yard, to be precise," Lucy said, the cat punctuating her precision with a meow.

Nathalie shook her head. "Okay. I'll bite. Why not?"

"It's how I was created. The magic binds me to this spot."

"Okay. How?"

"How what?"

"How does it tie you to the house?"

"It's just part of how I was created."

"Let's step back. How were you created?"

"It's far too complicated for us to get into right now. You'll learn more once we begin the ritual."

"Big picture it for me."

Daniel seemed annoyed that she was pressing him.

"Dear old Mom and Dad," Hugo said, "manufactured him like you would any servitor spirit." Nathalie nodded to show she was familiar with this type of entity. She'd even encountered a rudimentary one once during a visit with her father's family, though the Boudreaus referred to them simply as '*domestiques*.'" It made sense now why she wasn't able to read him, but still she'd never suspected. He just seemed so *solid*. Quirky maybe, but real.

"Well, not quite," Daniel said. "We've always believed so, but Astrid delved into the magic of *The Lesser*—"

"What steps did they take?" Nathalie pressed.

"Astrid was an artist," Hugo said. "She painted a portrait of Daniel. Kind of like reverse engineering. Make a focal point that suggests the characteristic you want the—"

"The painting. Where is it?"

"Up in the attic," Daniel answered.

"The painting that was used to make you is still in this house, and you can't leave this house. Have you ever tried taking the painting with you?"

Daniel and Hugo turned to each other with the same expression, mouths hanging open, eyebrows arched to heaven.

"Tell me," Lucy said, "do you ever get bored waiting for the rest of the room to catch up with you?"

EIGHTEEN

"Mother?" Alice said, swallowing the word. "Astrid?"

The beauty swung her legs off the divan and rose, drawing near Alice. She reached out a tentative hand to touch Alice's cheek. "Yes, Astrid, if that is what I must be to you." She lowered her hand and stepped back. Her shoulders stiffened. It seemed to Alice that Astrid was bracing herself. "I don't expect forgiveness. That's too much to hope for. I was corruptible, and I was corrupted."

"But how?"

"You'll have to be more specific, dear," Astrid said, lowering her hand. "How was I seduced by darkness, or how did I end up a set decoration in our friend Bogey John's restoration whorehouse?"

Before Alice could answer, the party roared back to life around them. The air rang with the blaring of horns, and shrill, unchaste laughter. The pop of a champagne cork was echoed by a gunshot. A woman in a white lace peignoir clung to a thick-waisted middle-aged man, her apathetic eyes scanning the room as she joined her partner in a swaying motion too languorous to be called dance. A pistol dropped to the floor, and the suicidal poker player slumped down beside it.

Astrid returned to the divan, watching the scene with an indifferent air. "It will work itself out soon. It always does, even if we can no longer afford the illusion of cause and effect. The scenes in our wretched passion play have fallen out of sequence, but we've been granted one small mercy—the libretto has undergone a heavy abridgment. For one thing, I've been spared the dreary crowning of Mahogany Hall's last king of Mardi Gras," she said, her focus turning to Babau Jean, who'd returned. The face of the Beautiful Dreamer bubbled up from behind his shiny, bone-white death mask, only to sink back down again. "Though I'll do it for Jean one last time before the end." She smiled at the creature. Alice sensed it pleased him that Astrid had dropped the pejorative Babau from his name. "He *was* such a lovely creature once. Besides, I do owe him."

"Owe him for what?"

"For bringing us together, my dear daughter."

My dear daughter. Alice stiffened at these words, angered by the long-ignored ache they brought to the surface. Then again, they were just words. As empty and unreal as the shadow Sabine's "I love you." And no doubt just as dangerous.

A sound like the crash of cymbals drew Alice's eyes to the bandstand. It stood empty, but the four familiar players remained at the poker table. One of the tuxedoed cardsharps appeared to be in mid-deal, but Alice realized the action was reversed. The cards were flying back up off the table and into the dealer's hands.

"I sent him for you as soon as I felt Celestin's grasp over us break," Astrid said, her words both a challenge to and a defense against what she must have read in Alice's reaction. She paused, seeming to await a response from Alice, perhaps an expression of gratitude or pardon. Alice was fresh out of both. Astrid's attempt at reconciliation, if that had been her intent, failed to bridge the gap between her crimes and Alice's propensity to forgive. "I wanted you to have the chance to . . . well, I'm not sure exactly. To find answers you've been wanting? Perhaps to mete out some satisfactory form of punishment? Anything to help fill the hole I've left in your life. In these final moments when we can be together, I wanted to give you whatever you needed. I know—too little, too late, but it's my small attempt at making amends."

Alice's reticent, cautious nature counseled silence. Anything she said now, any weakness she might show, could later be used against her.

Astrid gave a slight nod, a recognition, perhaps, of the gulf that would forever lie between them. Tiny lines formed at the sides of her eyes as she shook her head. "I knew something was in the air the first time I saw Daniel traipse through here with his familiar, and I was right." She fumbled with the tie of her peignoir. "He didn't recognize me either. He took me for another shadow. Perhaps he was right." Her expression brightened. An act of will, Alice surmised, rather than a reflection of feeling. "You have quite an ally in Daniel. I designed him to be willing to walk straight into hell to save you children, and it appears he's done just that," she said with what Alice took for affection. "Dear, sweet Daniel. He's my masterpiece. A perfect shepherd for my little lambs."

"A shepherd. Is that why you put the mark of Damuzi on him?"

Astrid stiffened, her shoulders pulling back, her borrowed eyes sparkling. "The original shepherd."

"The King of Bones and Ashes."

Astrid nodded. A thin smile came to her lips. "Yes. That too. Damuzi represents both the watchful shepherd and the lord of the underworld, but duality is part of all our natures. How did you make the connection?"

"Daniel found a copy of *The Lesser Key* hidden in your belongings."

"That explains it. He's changed, our Daniel. Daniel is a creature of *The Lesser Key*. It appears that he's been both reinvigorated and tainted by his contact with it."

"Why do you say that?"

She looked at Alice through widened eyes, like she was surprised that she needed to state the obvious. "How else could he have managed to take Celestin down? I'm sure the old reprobate didn't go gently into that good night. Daniel must have fought tooth and claw to defeat him. All that matters is that Celestin has been dealt with, and his control over us—you, me, *and* Jean—is over. That is well worth any price Daniel might have paid."

Raucous laughter pealed from the bandstand. A tradeswoman led her client past the empty chairs, on the way, Alice deduced, to one of the private rooms. The musicians snapped back into place, one of the trumpet players in the middle of an improvised solo. The party returned to full swing as the dance floor flooded with identical copies of the same languid bacchant, each apparition partnered with an indistinguishable, formally attired admirer.

"Why did you create him?" Alice spoke over the din. "It wasn't to act as a nanny. Not really."

"Why do you think?"

"I don't know. Luc told me it was Nicholas's idea."

"Did he?" Astrid lowered her chin and smiled at her. "He was right to some degree. Nicholas wanted someone to care for the house, to watch over the boys. Someone who could be trusted implicitly. That last bit meant the task couldn't be delegated to a human being. No one is completely trustworthy, so Nicholas asked for my assistance to build the perfect help—a genial, loyal, responsible servitor spirit. I simply saw to it that he got more than he'd asked for."

"How did you do that?"

The party burst like a bubble, leaving them alone.

"To the uninitiated," Astrid began, as indifferent to the silence as she was to the sound, "*The Lesser Key* appears to repeat itself from front to back, back to front, but a witch who opens herself up to its spirit soon realizes the volume is a spiral leading down, a torus twisting itself into a Solomon's seal knot with as much hidden from view as revealed. We call it 'the occult' for a reason." A smirk punctuated her sarcasm. "Hidden in the book are the instructions for building creatures such as Daniel—in essence a servitor spirit, but so much more than a basic servitor that remains linked to its creator. Lifelike enough to fool many who should be able to spot the difference between him . . . and a real boy. Able to survive being separated from its source, and to tap into any ambient occult energy—light or dark. It was a bit of a game, really, creating Daniel. To see if I were skilled enough, powerful enough. To see if I could still make the magic work." She grinned. "For many of the same reasons, I suppose Nicholas pushed me to have Hugo. A haughty man needs constant reassurance of his own potency." The grin faded. "I didn't intend to use Daniel for the purpose *The Lesser Key* ordains for him. At least that's the lie I told myself."

Her face turned away. "You'll be free soon now. I can sense them, Daniel and the others, gathering on the other side." She pointed at a full-length gilt-frame mirror on the wall. "You'll feel a tug anytime now, and then you'll be lost to me forever." The mirror shimmered. First it reflected a door, an arched wooden one with oversize ornate scrollwork hinges that reminded her of the sigil she'd drawn on the window of her imagined loft; then it shimmered once more and became the door it had reflected. Astrid focused on her with wistful mien. "My little Alice, slipping home through the looking glass."

"What are you going to do?"

"What can I do?" She wrapped her arms around herself. "I'm going to ride this storm out till the end. Celestin may no longer be holding me here, but my physical body died years ago. There's nowhere left for me to go. Besides, it's better for you, better for Hugo, too, that I can't go back."

"Why would you say that?"

"Because, my dear, here where I'm powerless and soon to fade, I'm not a danger to you, but back in the common world some mama bears eat their young. I came oh so close to bashing in your pretty skull once. It wouldn't take much to return me to that place." She smiled and shrugged an apology. "The truth isn't pretty, my girl, but I may be the only person in your life who's never lied to you. I have nothing to gain from starting now. So, in the limited time we have left . . . full disclosure. No question too big or too small." She held up her hand and a serving woman appeared behind her, a flute of champagne on a tray. Astrid accepted the glass, and the servant and her tray disappeared. "I'm getting pretty good at bending this reality now that Celestin's out of the picture, but there isn't much juice left to keep it going. Jean may be able to scare up enough to feed his own existence, but without supplemental magic, he'll soon be lost again in a dim and empty hall, as broken and pitiable as he was when Laure first found him. I've promised him he won't be left that way again." She held the glass up in salute to Babau Jean. "We won't fade away, will we, my friend? You won't be alone ever again. Together, we'll go out with a bang." She lowered her glass and sipped the champagne.

"With a bang," she repeated, emphasizing each word as she reclined against the back of the divan. She turned her gaze to Alice. "This will be your one chance for answers. You won't see me again. Do you want to know how your mother came close to a shabby dinner theater performance of *Medea*, or will ignorance be your bliss? After all, if you don't know how much I was once like you, you'll have the comfort of believing you could never follow in my footsteps."

"I'm not afraid of your past, or of my future." Alice had faced her worst fears already. Nothing Astrid could spring on her could be more horrifying than listening helplessly as a demon who'd masqueraded as her love clawed the side of her illusory house, than counting the days until she, too, would flicker out and become a part of the very contagion attacking her. Any kind of monster Alice might now become would have to be a step up from there.

"Good for you." Astrid seemed pleased, perhaps even proud, that Alice hadn't chosen to turn away. "Let's revisit your original question of how . . . how I came to find myself here," she gestured around the room with a wide wave. "And how," she said, lowering her hand to her heart, "I came to be here." She tapped her chest. "It's the same answer. Celestin Marin.

"Celestin trapped me here because I disappointed him. He asked me to do the impossible. I thought I could . . . right up until the moment he said it was time to take your life. We knew we would have to kill all of you eventually. His children and mine. You were ours, so he thought it was fitting that I start with you. But you were so small, so perfect. I couldn't . . ." Her voice broke. She took another sip of her champagne. "It was, it turned out, a dry run for the real thing. A test of my commitment to our scheme. I failed the test. I failed him, so he punished me.

"Celestin disappeared me from the common world. By now I should've disappeared from the Dreaming Road, too, burned away to nothing or perhaps transformed into one of your hungry shadows. But Celestin knew what he was doing." A trumpet blared and Astrid paused, glancing about, but the party failed to resurrect itself. "I believe," she continued, "it was always his plan to bring me back in some form to the common world. He wanted me to be around to appreciate his final victory, so he imprisoned me here, in this reality fueled by the life force of dreamers Celestin poached from the myriad drug-addled fools wandering around the astral, and whatever scraps of fear energy Bogey John might pick up from terrorizing teenage slumber parties."

She gestured around the hall. "It's a repeating loop," Astrid said. "It pleased Celestin to trap me in the tale you witnessed when you saw this place in a dream. The last days of Storyville. Over and over and over again." She lifted her eyes, and Alice followed her gaze to Babau Jean's white death mask. "Jean's paradise, and my hell.

"This image," Astrid gestured the length of her body with a wide sweep of her free hand, "is that of Jean's favorite whore." Astrid's eyes softened slightly as she stared at Babau Jean. "That's what Celestin called me, you know. When he brought me here." Her jaw tightened. "Whore. A catchall insult for any woman who won't do as she's told."

Her focus returned to Alice. "Funny, isn't it? He punished me for not following through with something he himself couldn't do." She spoke as if it were the first time this thought had struck her, though Alice sensed it had occurred to her many times during her confinement, perhaps as many times as the Mahogany Hall loop had repeated itself. "I mean, he could've made light work of the task and drowned you in flood waters. No one would have been the wiser. But no. He built you a paradise to allow you at least the illusion of a long, happy life. A deadly paradise, but a paradise all the same."

"A paradise that would have eventually drained me of all humanity and left me a rapacious demon."

"Well, there is that. A dark ending for you, but one he'd never have to witness. Or perhaps he thought you would end up there anyway. Like father, like daughter. Like the mother whose spirit he drove to perversion, though how he initiated my descent requires a more detailed recounting." A balloon-back chair with deep red upholstery slid up beside Alice. Astrid smiled and nodded at the seat. "Please. I know this is all illusion, and that we are no more than two tiny sparks in an abyss, but that"—she motioned to Alice's feet—"is a bit distracting." Alice glanced down, surprised to see that she appeared to be floating several inches above the floor. She slipped onto the chair.

"Thank you." Astrid saluted Alice with her glass, then handed it to Babau Jean, who had appeared at her side. "Would you mind, dear?" she addressed the creature. Shifting her gaze back to Alice, she said, "We have no secrets from each other, Jean and I, but a bit of privacy will, no doubt, make both the recounting and the hearing of the inelegant cautionary tale of my life that much easier." She smiled up at him, then he, and the glass he held, dissipated into mist. "Where to start . . ."

Alice cast a glance at the doorway. The portal to the common world remained sealed by the impressive and seemingly impenetrable door. It appeared they had time. "At the beginning."

"At the beginning, it is," Astrid said with a sigh, as if capitulating to Alice's demand, though Alice sensed Astrid had rehearsed this telling so many times, it would be impossible for her to start at any other point.

Astrid's gaze softened. "It began with Nicholas and me. You may already know a lot about how things went wrong between us. You were too young to remember on your own, but I'm sure Hugo has shared with you. Perhaps even Luc did, too . . . before . . ." She fell silent, as if she recognized that there was no need to finish her thought. "The fierce rows that would come and go," she continued. "The even more vicious silences that would come and linger. I believe at the end we were happier when shouting at each other than when the house was quiet. To paraphrase the Russian chap, our family was unhappy in its own curiously unhinged way. Hugo remembers, I'm sure, even though he was barely eight . . ." She stopped midsentence, seemingly beset by a new train of thought. "I don't blame Nicholas for not searching for me. I wouldn't have looked for him either."

"Everyone said that you were unstable. That you chose the Dreaming Road."

"That would fit the narrative they'd created for me from the beginning. *Odd girl. Not one of us. Not really.* Wouldn't be surprised if Celestin kicked that story off."

"I wouldn't know," Alice said, though no doubt many of the witches of New Orleans had, at some point, made similar statements about Alice herself. Celestin may have invented this theme of the odd and fragile outsider, but Nicholas had adapted it to his own ends. Sobering that if it weren't for Celestin's scheming, Alice might have wasted away her entire life in a psychiatric care facility.

"No, you couldn't. Still, Nicholas should've known better. He knew *me* better. In life, I was a survivor, not a quitter. But it must've been a relief for him once it was finally over. I'm sure he didn't give a damn what happened to me as long as he was free. He no longer held any affection for me, and I suppose it's obvious that I returned his cold indifference at the time." Alice wondered about the ambiguous way she said "at the time." Had the years of absence softened her toward him? "I'm sorry. It seems when it comes to Nicholas I can't help but begin at the end. We were such a glorious failure. The rest of our time together pales in comparison."

"Why did you marry and have children together if you didn't love each other?"

"Oh"—Astrid looked at her with surprise—"but we didn't begin in ice. We began in fire. Once we were very much in love, Nicholas and I. I can't speak for Nicholas, but I was stricken by Cupid. What was the term Celestin liked to use? *Un vrai coup de foudre.* Love at first sight." One eyebrow rose, as if she were gazing back through time at the woman she'd once been. "We met in the taxi queue at New Orleans International Airport. Romantic, no?" Alice couldn't tell if she was being sincere or sardonic. Her tone was out of sync with the tender look in her eyes. Maybe a touch of both. "We recognized each other as witches, so we began chatting in the cloaked way one does. He was coming back from a ski vacation somewhere or other. I don't remember the details, but I do remember he had too much baggage for us to share a cab." She shook her head. "I should've taken that as an omen, but I was new in town. I knew no one, and Nicholas was so charming, so handsome. So charming and handsome, in fact, he never needed to develop any other interpersonal skills." She wagged a finger at Alice. "You'd better believe that circled back to bite me. Hard." She paused. "Tell me, is he still beautiful?"

"I may not be the best judge of that, but yes. Until recently he was dating . . ." Alice stopped herself before mentioning Evangeline's name. "He was dating a much younger woman."

Astrid sighed. "Damn. I'd hoped time would allow me that tiny satisfaction. He's still due a bit of comeuppance, then, but karma never seems to distribute itself evenly."

"You blame Nicholas for your actions?"

"No, but I blame him for his own. At the root of it all"—she shook her head, the lovely, features hardening—"lay Nicholas's ambition and sense of entitlement."

Astrid seemed unaware of the change occurring to the doorway, but Alice noticed a rattling. She glanced over to see the door shaking in its frame.

"I needn't tell you about that," Astrid said, recapturing Alice's full attention. "You've witnessed it firsthand. Still, I would've been better off if I'd never gone to New Orleans. If Nicholas and I had never met. Perhaps we all would've. Even you children might've been better off had you never been born." She waited, perhaps to see if Alice might be of the same mind, but Alice held her tongue. "I didn't go to New Orleans to look for a husband, you know. I was, like I sense you are, very independent. I went to New Orleans to take a position. Hearth and family were the furthest things from my mind."

"You were a painter," Alice said, realizing that Astrid's artistic skills counted as the sole source of pride she'd ever been able to take in her mother.

"Yes. Among other things. I'd gone to New Orleans to work as a conservator and restorer of the community's magical texts. The most valuable had been locked away, some for centuries, in a room behind heavy locks and magical wards. All of that, and it lacked air-conditioning or basic humidity control. In New Orleans. The degree of the collection's decrepitude was discovered when its previous caretaker died.

"The books and scrolls weren't merely coming apart in the physical sense; their potency was dulling from lack of use. Grimoires must be used to maintain their power. An untouched book of spells loses its ability to reveal its true, hidden contents," she said, her tone waxing pedagogical. "It's never just about the material itself—true magic comes from the witch's interaction with it. Even a decade of neglect can leave a perfectly serviceable grimoire not much more than an outdated and poorly illustrated travel guide to a hypothetical land. The New Orleans magical community needed an expert who could stop the decline and reverse it wherever possible. Many complained I was too young and inexperienced to take on the job, but I'd apprenticed in the Atelier

Magnusson." She lifted her chin high and spoke the name with such pride, Alice felt compelled to react as if she were impressed—to pretend she'd heard of the workshop. "Besides, I was the only restorer of any caliber willing to move to and live in the city for as long as was required to care for the texts in the proper fashion, so I was engaged to do the work. I came to understand that 'too young and inexperienced' was code for 'lacking a penis'—the gods help us, even among witches. They were lucky to find me, whether they appreciated that fact or not. I did good work for the witches of New Orleans. Saving those texts took a strong witch and a skilled artist with a deep love of books."

Alice recognized this aspect of Astrid in herself—she not only lived for books, but she had, in truth, lived most of her life *through* them. A thrilling, though fleeting, sense of kinship warmed her.

"I dove right in, perhaps at the expense of observing certain niceties that might have positioned me better with the locals, but I was young and full of fire. I had years of work waiting for me behind those locks and wards, but I was up to the task. It wasn't all work, though. Against all odds, Nicholas and I began seeing each other." She traced a finger down her forearm, as if trying to remember the sensation of his touch. "A bit of a fairy tale, our romance. The drab little field mouse catches the eye of the crown prince and snatches him out from under the belles in their shimmering gowns." Her nose wrinkled up like she'd smelled soured milk. "Celestin and Laure disapproved of me. Foreign, and not the right kind of foreign. An orphan without title, without fortune—and worst of all—without pedigree, but there was another reason for their displeasure. I was some years older than Nicholas. Eight, if you must know."

She shook her head. "Laughable, really. If I'd been the man and he the woman, no one would've even blinked at the age difference. It didn't matter to me, and it certainly didn't matter to Nicholas. We grew inseparable. It was all so new and exciting. Before I knew it, I was pregnant with Luc—I do hope someone has warned you that no birth control will work if a witch wants to have a child."

Not a problem, Alice thought, but Astrid continued before she could speak the words aloud.

"And I did want his child. I loved Nicholas with every fiber of my being. I wanted to make a child with him, *et voilà.*

"Celestin fumed that I'd entrapped his son. Laure mourned the 'unfortunate, inappropriate match,' perhaps even more than he did. Mothers always have a special connection to their firstborn son. We place so many hopes in that first basket. But appearances, appearances! Laure insisted Nicholas 'do the right thing' by me." She laughed, tossing back her dark curls. "A creature of a different age, she was. Still, for once, and this was perhaps the only time, her wishes aligned with my own. Nicholas and I were married within six months of our first setting eyes on each other. For a while, a brief while, we were very happy. Nicholas burned bright, but not for long. He found a new passion."

"Another woman?" A faint scraping sound on the periphery drew Alice's attention to the doorway that stood between the common world and the Dreaming Road. It had begun to creak open.

"No. Not another woman. Power. Nicholas became obsessed with it. It started out as contempt for his father's practices and ended with him deposing Celestin as the head of the Chanticleers. I wanted nothing to do with his challenge to his father. Even as Nicholas's wife, I was still viewed as an outsider, and to be honest, I viewed myself as an outsider as well. Nicholas's desire to dethrone his father consumed him. So I focused on Luc. One of us had to. It seemed that Nicholas had only two uses for Luc—to prove his own virility and to preserve his legacy. I chose to stand outside the controversy and care for my son. And I threw myself into my work. I took pleasure in resurrecting things of magic and beauty." She paused and gave Alice a quizzical glance. "I assume the collection survived your disaster, that Nicholas would see to that."

"I believe so, but I can't say for sure."

Astrid nodded. "No matter. I once would have cared deeply, but no longer."

"If they held power Nicholas could use, I'm sure they were kept safe."

"And if they no longer mattered to him . . ." She clenched her fist. "I apologize," she said, relaxing her hand. "Perhaps I do still care. A little." Alice felt her mother turn inward, once again seeming to relive the moments she recounted. "I started my efforts, as one does, by composing an inventory, then performing a triage of the works. I had, I thought, a complete catalog of every text there. You can imagine my surprise when I later came across a copy of *The Lesser Key*. It shouldn't surprise you to learn Celestin had slipped it in. A bit of vengeance against his renegade son. I didn't learn that detail until later . . . until it was too late."

The door now stood open far enough for Alice to catch sight of a slice of night sky, spangled with an abundance of silver-blue stars.

"Celestin was right," Astrid continued. "He saw a darkness in me I'd always refused to see in myself, and *The Lesser Key* found fertile ground there. Oh, sure, I sensed the tome was dangerous. I hid it away in a safe place to protect others, but deep down I knew I was saving it for myself. I tried not to think of it. I resisted it for years. But it spoke to me every day. It played upon my disappointments, promising to give me back everything I'd ever lost. To right every wrong I'd suffered. It was my pain as much as my pride and greed that allowed it to take root in my heart. No," she said, holding up her hand as if she were cautioning Alice, "that isn't quite true. I already carried darkness in me. It's all about the progression: *The Lesser Key*, the subtle descent from where it found you to where you're ready to receive 'the greater key,' if you will, *The Book of the Unwinding*—"

Astrid's words were cut short.

For a moment Alice felt the familiar comfort of Daniel surround her. Whereas her immersion with Babau Jean had made her feel like she was inside a pressure suit, this was more like being swaddled in a soft blanket. Then Daniel was gone, and Alice found herself tumbling from the sky, below her a sea of twinkling red lights.

NINETEEN

Fleur picked her way along the overgrown lane that had once been Grunch Road. It had never been much of a proper road, more a convenient byway where teenage lovers could explore each other. The spot's notoriety had lent the lightless stretch an undeserved air of sexiness, and stories of red-eyed man-eaters and murderers with hooks for hands had gilded it with a seductive patina of danger that had only helped increase its notoriety. She'd never believed Grunch Road to be unique. Every city, every town had its own version of the bucolic lane. At least they used to. There was less sexual repression these days, and with the advent of the internet, teenagers had much easier and more private access to information. Maybe young people these days didn't need to recast their anxiety in the guise of monsters and murderers.

Fleur blessed the cooler days, but tonight, in this eerie place, she missed the hot weather song of cicadas. Other than the muffled, arrhythmic cadence of her companions' footfalls, there was silence.

Fleur could sense that in its desertion, the path had been reclaimed by spirits. Grunch Road no longer belonged to man. She felt the spiderweb sensation that often announced the presence of elementals or even interstitial beings—incomplete entities that sometimes existed in the common world and sometimes didn't. Their greatest yearning was to experience life as a human. They tended to be tricksters, though most were harmless. Fleur sensed she wasn't alone in her awareness of otherworldly presences. Even her voluble Lucy was uncharacteristically silent.

This wasn't Fleur's first visit to Grunch Road. She had come here a dozen times or so, long ago, with Eli Landry, the man whose arm she now held. The intervening years had streaked his chestnut hair with gray, but at the time he hadn't been much more than a boy, and Fleur herself had been a year younger than her daughter was now. Then they had come to the deserted road together alone. Now an entire entourage—Lucy, Daniel, Hugo, the Twins, and the latest wrinkle in her life, Nathalie—accompanied them, the latter carrying both of the shovels that Daniel had demanded they take along.

Alice, too, accompanied them in body if not in spirit, floating alongside them, buoyed by magic drawn from the relics Fleur had pilfered from the Demagnan Mortuary. She had employed a low-power variant of Hugo's stealth mode to gain entrance to both the Doll House and the adjacent mortuary, whispering a soothing chant as she approached the officers stationed outside the crime scene, acknowledging that while she might be unauthorized, she was harmless. Nothing more than a shadow, a trick of the light on their tired eyes. Noticing her would lead to more trouble than not, so they should simply turn away. And they had. The spell hadn't even taxed the modicum of magic she'd felt safe deflecting from Lucy.

The detectives had picked the Doll House clean, but in the funeral home itself, Fleur had discovered a hiding place they'd missed. In an alcove hidden behind a framed conté portrait labeled "Minnie Wallace," she'd found a coffer filled with dried hearts. Thirteen, in fact. Daniel had insisted on taking inventory. Eli walked beside Fleur, helping steady her with his right arm and clutching the handle of an overnight bag holding the coffer and its relics in his left hand. Fleur would commit the bag to flame before she'd ever use it again.

Daniel brought up the rear, clutching his copy of *The Lesser Key*—wrapped in his self-blessed kitchen towel and sealed in a plastic slider bag—to his chest, refusing to entrust it to any hand except his own. He'd pored over that dreadful book, wearing ridiculous pink rubber gloves he'd baptized in holy water of his own making, run straight from the tap and blended with wishful thinking. But Fleur felt sure it wasn't the sanctified latex or the towel that prevented the book's darkness from creeping into him. If anything, it was his own innate goodness that kept him untainted, though he seemed no longer to believe in that goodness. He'd learned he was a creature of *The Lesser Key*, created to allow the wicked to descend into death and return unscathed. If he had been born out of darkness, he questioned, how could he be innocent? The same question had been dogging Fleur for years, though it had grown more acute of late.

When Fleur and Eli had last come to Grunch Road, the lane had still been accessible from the highway, via the crossbow-shaped exit. Now the pavement petered out, leaving Grunch Road cut off from the main artery, a mostly forgotten vestige hidden by trees and tall, lush grass. They'd driven as close to the old road as possible, leaving them with only a hundred yards or so to travel by foot.

Fleur struggled to remember that last night she and Eli had found themselves here, but it was little more than a vague and blurry recollection. Their first pilgrimage to Grunch Road was a different matter. That memory had haunted Fleur on the lonely, loveless nights of her marriage.

They'd spent the afternoon at the old amusement park that lay only a stone's throw from here, then left behind the noise and flashing lights to come to this deserted lane. They'd come on a dare—one made to each other. Each thought the other would stop things before they went too far. Neither had. A frisson at the memory of those first touches brought hot blood to her cheeks. *First. First. First.* Eli had been her first. Her first love and her first lover. She wondered if Eli, too, remembered the heat. Fleur leaned into his hard shoulder, contemplating the life they might have had together if she'd mustered the courage to stand up to her father.

No, that wasn't true. She was tired of that same pathetic lie.

Coming home to New Orleans, learning about the extent of Celestin's insatiable hunger for power, had forced Fleur to face one uncomfortable fact—the proverbial apple hadn't fallen far from the perverse tree. She had made a conscious choice to marry Warren. She'd never loved him—love hadn't been part of the equation—but she *had* loved what he represented. Celestin had wanted his daughter to be First Lady, and Fleur . . . well, the idea had seduced her in ways sapless, bloodless Warren never could. Warren had been poised to realize his dream, too, but then the world had gone mad, and political savvy and experience were now seen as detriments. It seemed the electorate had lost their taste for adults . . .

She caught herself. Her mind was drifting, trying to relieve her conscience of an essential though unpalatable truth—that she had *chosen* to break Eli's heart. She'd chosen power and prestige over love. If that didn't make her Celestin's daughter, she didn't know what did.

Now, with the benefit of two decades of hindsight, Fleur realized she'd failed her daughter on two counts. First for selling her soul for position, and second for not setting her sights on a higher return. She should have held out for Madame President rather than First Lady, though the great Celestin Marin would've never entertained such an idea. He would've voted with great zeal to abolish the Nineteenth Amendment—and believed he was performing a service to all of womanhood in doing so.

Fleur glanced over at her daughter, navigating the rough terrain in a pair of thousand-dollar velvet platform sandals she'd worn on a single prior occasion and would never wear again. Lucy would complain that this trek had ruined them, and she'd probably be right. God forbid she change them before making the trip. Fleur was torn between annoyance at Lucy's sense of entitlement—a sense Fleur had to admit she'd sown in her—and pride that rough terrain or no, Lucy was making her own way, not relying on a man even as Fleur herself continued to do. Her daughter would always make her own way. Not just over this stretch of earth, but through the mess Fleur and Warren had made of her life, and whatever lay beyond that. More and more now, Fleur could spot the strong young woman Lucy was becoming, as it poked out from behind the visage of a spoiled teenager. Fleur admired that woman, wished she could be more like her.

No, I didn't make a mistake, Fleur reminded herself for the thousandth time. She'd done the right thing when she'd saved this child, regardless of the cost.

She returned her focus to Eli, studying his profile washed in blue by the night. She'd known he would come at her bidding. Without any explanation from her. If she were honest with him about her feelings, she knew he'd give them another shot, but Fleur couldn't put any energy toward a relationship. Not now. Not until she'd secured a strong enough source of magic to keep Lucy's heart beating. Eli looked down at her, and even in the darkness, she could make out the questions in his eyes. "Soon," the word escaped her lips, fleeing like a caged prisoner.

"I would hope so," Lucy said, looking back over her shoulder at Fleur. "This gross place is—"

"Ruining my shoes," Fleur finished the thought for her.

"Yeah, that too, Our Lady of Interruptus, but what I was going to say is . . . well, I'm not really sure. 'Wrong,' I guess. This place is just wrong."

No, the abandoned road was curious, weird even, but it was Lucy's sixth sense that was wrong. It should have died along with the rest of her magic when Lucy herself had died in Fleur's womb, not even leaving enough to serve as a relic. Fleur shuddered at the thought. In Lucy's presence, Fleur always disparaged her extrasensory perception as simple intuition or insight. Fleur couldn't afford to have Lucy asking too many questions, or looking into her lack of magic with any real scrutiny.

"Yes, indeed it is," Daniel said, his voice coming from behind them. "But it's perfect for the work we have before us."

Fleur felt the weight of a searching stare. She glanced back to find Nathalie focusing intently on her. The realization struck Fleur like a hard slap. *Nathalie knows. She knows.* There was no denying it. Somehow the newcomer had divined the truth.

Fleur would have to speak to her. Explain. She seemed a kindhearted and sensible woman, the type of person who would keep her own counsel. Still, it wouldn't do to have Lucy spending too much time around Nathalie. The witch didn't appear to have a spiteful bone in her body, but she seemed incapable of guile. Between Nathalie's open nature and Lucy's laser-precise insights, unfortunate truths might be discovered.

Fleur had set a glamour on Lucy to divert the attention of anyone who might pick up on anything odd about her daughter. Fleur's main concern wasn't that Nathalie would tell. Fleur was worried others might begin to take notice as well. She'd ask Nathalie what had alerted her.

Fleur couldn't dwell on the fact that if the glamour had weakened to the point where Nathalie could see through it, then the magic keeping Lucy alive was growing thin as well. She had to stay focused and have faith that Nicholas would find a source of magic that would allow Lucy to live a full, normal life.

Fleur hated that Lucy viewed her uncle in such a negative light. He might not have been a good father, hell, not even a passable father, but he had always looked out for his niece. Once it became clear that Nicholas had lost control of the coven, that he couldn't in secret continue to skim off a portion of the coven's combined magic to protect Lucy's well-being, he set out on his own to find another solution. There was no way Fleur could share the truth of Nicholas's wanderings, and without that knowledge, there was no way Lucy could see his desertion as anything other than selfish.

A suspicion crept up on her. A question she felt ashamed to pose, even to herself. Could it be that Nicholas only offered his assistance for selfish purposes? It allowed him to feel both magnanimous and avuncular. It kept Fleur dependent on him, forever in his debt. She pushed the thought away. His motivations, even in this cynical light, didn't matter. She would've made a deal with the devil himself to save Lucy. To be indebted to her brother was no great burden for what she received in return.

Fleur's eyes sought out Nathalie in the night. She was a bit behind them, beside Hugo. The Twins followed them, silent as always. She'd never heard their voices except when they sang with the Chanticleer Coven as it wove its spells. When the Marin family control of the coven was challenged, the taciturn siblings had shown themselves loyal. It was that loyalty that had saved the pair from Celestin's murder spree. Daniel had entrusted the Twins with carrying his portrait, though he followed the pair like a single shadow, refusing to be more than a few feet from it lest he be yanked away at this critical juncture.

The servitor spirit was preoccupied and—for Daniel—surly. He didn't want to waste any of the power they'd brought with and in them, but he had capitulated to using just enough magic to provide Alice a safe escort to the site of the working.

"Best to think ahead and be prepared," he'd said earlier as he slipped Lucy's Animalier backpack over his shoulders. His broad back strained the bag's straps. The contents he'd forced inside it stretched the bag almost to the point of zipper failure. Daniel had stuffed it with crystals and magic tools the likes of which Fleur suspected hadn't been used for generations. Fleur hadn't failed to notice the ruby-encrusted handle of the large athame Daniel had slipped into the sack, the knife's handle protruding from the red velvet in which its blade had been swathed. A blade like that spoke of sacrifice.

"We're here," Daniel announced without ceremony. With only a nod, he requested that the Twins prop his portrait against a nearby tree. He took *The Lesser Key* in his left hand and sloughed off the backpack, letting it drop at his feet. "We need to cut a pentagram into the earth."

"Pentagram. Old school. I like it," Lucy said, approaching Daniel and patting him on the back.

"Older school than you think." Daniel's cryptic response came with no explanation. "It has to be large enough to hold Alice at its center."

The Twins paced out a circle and, standing opposite each other, held their hands out, palms turned toward the earth. A harmony of voices rose, and sparks shot from their fingertips.

"Hold it," Daniel said. "Let's don't waste magic on the things we can do by hand. The pentagram is why we brought the shovels."

"On it," Nathalie said, handing one shovel to Hugo and setting about scratching a large star into the ground to serve as a guide. Hugo stared at his shovel as if he'd never seen one before, then fell to his seat, dropping the shovel by his side.

"Okay, I'll bite," Lucy said, turning a full circle. "What's so special about this particular spot?" That was her girl, always cutting to the chase.

Daniel knelt beside her and, setting *The Lesser Key* by his knee, unzipped the backpack. "The astral and the common world share a wall here." He pulled the athame from the bag and unwrapped the cloth that had served as its sheath. After spreading the cloth on the ground, he laid the athame on it. The knife was without a doubt worth a small fortune in financial terms, but it was clear Daniel valued it only for its intended use. If that use was sacrifice, what sacrifice, Fleur wondered, was he planning to make? "If the Dreaming Road were a house, I'd say that immediately beyond this point lies the foyer, and right here where you're standing is the front porch. Of course, there are many porches, and many foyers, too, but the separation is nothing more than illusion.

That's true both here in the common world," he wagged a finger at Lucy, "and in the astral realm, too. The many are, in actuality, one."

"E pluribus unum," Hugo called out, raising his fist to the sky and then looking up at his own hand like he'd witnessed a UFO.

"Yes, indeed. The founding fathers had knowledge of the astral and the Dreaming Road. Franklin in particular. But let's not go there. There are already enough conspiracy theories in the world for fascists to twist into propaganda. Let's not hand them another one gift-wrapped." He looked up at Eli, nodding at the bag he held. "If you could . . ." His words trailed off as Eli began to carry the bag to him. "Thank you."

"My pleasure," Eli responded, setting the bag on the ground.

Daniel, for a moment his old self, beamed up at Eli. "Why Miss Fleur, I do believe you have found yourself a keeper . . . again. This time, keep him."

The Twins began snapping their fingers in approval.

Fleur felt her cheeks flush as Eli returned to her. She hoped the night would hide the redness of her face from him. He stopped squarely before her. "What he said." He snapped his fingers and returned to her side.

"Please," Lucy addressed Eli in a petulant tone. Fleur knew her daughter well enough to know the annoyance was counterfeit. "Get her out of my hair." Fleur smiled, knowing that this was Lucy's way of giving them her blessing—the closest they'd ever come to receiving an official sanction. "Okay, we're on the porch," Lucy said, returning to the previous subject in an attempt, Fleur knew, to save her from further embarrassment. "What do we do, knock?"

"That would be the polite thing to do." Daniel grabbed Lucy's backpack and upturned it, tugging it even further out of shape and dumping its entire contents onto the ground. Fleur expected a protest from Lucy, but she didn't make a squeak. "However, sometimes politeness can get one killed." He began sorting through the items before him, setting packets of herbs to one side and crystals to the other. "Babau Jean has claimed the foyer as his own, and Celestin has claimed Babau Jean. You all got a glimpse of the foyer the night of the ball. Celestin bent it in so that it could share a temporary connection to the interior of the building where the ball was held."

He picked up a sandwich bag full of herbs and examined it. "I believe," he said, addressing Hugo, "this one belongs to you." He tossed the bag to Hugo, who managed to catch it despite his current condition. "To build upon my simile, it isn't too difficult to move back and forth between the foyer and the front porch. Especially at this precise geographical point," he pointed at the ground, "the door is always open, at least a crack. But beyond the foyer lie an ever-growing number of chambers, entire worlds, really, from which there is no exit. A new chamber is created every time someone drifts too far into the astral to find their way back." He picked his blessed rose rubber gloves out of the items he'd carried with them and slipped them on. "Again, there are innumerable chambers beyond, but they are all one. Any sense of separation is an illusion."

"Thank you, Mr. One Hand Clapping." Lucy's snark told Fleur that she was more anxious than she was letting on.

Daniel shrugged her sarcasm off. Not surprising, since he'd been created to have a strong sense of empathy. He must sense her unease, too. "You're welcome," he said without irony. "Sometimes," he continued, "it's an addict who floats a wee bit too high. Sometimes it's a witch who goes there on purpose." His face fell. "No witch would ever choose to take to the Dreaming Road if she knew what awaited her at the end of the dream. I used to suppose they eventually died in spirit, their physical bodies already long gone. But no. It's much worse. When a star goes supernova, it creates a black hole. When a witch burns through the last of her magic, a dark spirit is created. A kind of vampiric demon that wanders through the astral plane devouring any light it encounters."

"Charming."

He opened the plastic bag that held the cloth-enveloped grimoire. He unwound the dish towel and let it drop to the ground. "That's why there's no time to squander." He examined *The Lesser Key*, his face strangely emotionless as he did. "Last I saw Alice," he said, his voice dropping to a near whisper, "she was fading away, slipping into that darkness." He opened *The Key* to its center pages and placed it on the red cloth, next to the athame. "I tried to alert her to the precariousness of her situation. We can only hope she took my warning to heart." Before he bent back over the cloth, he paused and turned his face to the sky, searching the stars. Then he adjusted the cloth, aligning it, it seemed, with the constellations above. Once satisfied, he adjusted the placement of the book and the knife, then reached out and grabbed a small votive candle in a glass holder. Fleur's dark-adapted eyes judged that particular shade of gray to be yellow. He placed it on the cloth's right side, repeating the step by placing a red one on the bottom of the cloth, a blue votive on the left, and a green at the top. He'd aligned the cloth with the cardinal directions and placed each candle according to the element associated with its color. He was, Fleur realized, building an ersatz altar, relying on magical correspondences. Witches, real witches, had long ago dropped this practice, but it seemed Daniel was not taking any chances. "We must hope she listened." He rose, removing his rubber gloves and tossing them aside, not even watching to see where they might land. Fleur surmised that he didn't expect to need them again, but she wasn't ready to consider what that might mean.

Fleur cast a glance at Alice's body, still floating four feet or so above the ground. The Twins had stationed themselves by her in a protective stance, one at her head, facing back, the other at her feet facing forward. Perhaps they were right to anticipate an ambush. Celestin had wanted Alice removed from the common world. If he caught wind of what they were doing, he might well show up to prevent them.

"You mean she may already be lost?" Lucy said.

"I mean there's no time to spare. I hate myself for not understanding my own nature sooner. If only I'd—"

"The most common regret in the world," Fleur cut him short. Entertaining negative thoughts could only weaken him. She decided to give him a push forward. "How do we do this?"

"First we need the pentagram . . ." He paused, looking over at Nathalie, who stood leaning against her shovel. She motioned with a wave of her hand at a precise five-pointed star at the center of a perfect circle. The exposed earth held a faint shimmer. A collective gasp rose up from the group. Everyone, other than Nathalie, understood that she had charged it with the power of intent. Fleur had expected it would take the combined focus and powers of all present to complete that task.

"This okay?" Nathalie said, looking down at her work. "I could—"

"No," Daniel jumped in. He, too, stared at the earth, his eyes wide with surprise. "You did fine." He pulled a face at Fleur.

Fleur studied the unassuming woman. How could a light this bright have ridden in on such a dark horse? It seemed almost as if Nathalie had reserved whatever power she held for this very moment. Fleur had been unconvinced by Daniel's theory, but maybe there was something to this gravity of rightful destiny after all. "And next?" She addressed Daniel without taking her eyes off Nathalie.

"We position our girl in the pentagram. Head to upper point, limbs toward the other four." The Twins grasped Alice by the feet and shoulders and began to guide her toward the pentagram. "Easy, easy," Daniel called out, though the pair appeared to be taking the utmost care of Alice's empty form. "Wait," he said and motioned to Nathalie. "Better if you take her the rest of the way. No one else should cross into the circle."

Nathalie first seemed surprised, then nervous, but she approached Alice and touched her wrist. A glow, an actual luminescence, came to Nathalie's face.

New love, Fleur thought, *meet magic.*

Nathalie released Alice and pulled back, clearly shocked at the energy flowing through her, but Alice's dormant body followed her anyway, tugged along by the tangible strand of light linking them.

Daniel turned to Fleur, beaming with delight. "This is going to work," he said, as if before he'd given the working no more than an outside chance. "Go ahead," Daniel addressed Nathalie. "Step into the circle. She'll join you." Nathalie hesitated, her eyes full of uncertainty. "Yes, yes," Daniel said. "Go on." His enthusiasm carried Nathalie over the threshold and into the circle, and Alice floated to her side. As if on instinct, Nathalie knelt and Alice lowered to the ground before her. An aurora rose up around them—rose and gold—and then it turned into a white glow that descended and seeped into the star. The energy reached up and shifted Alice's arms and legs so that they were in alignment with the pentagram's points.

Daniel snatched up the crystals he'd brought along. At the edge of the boundary, above Alice's head, he placed a slab of agate. Fleur remembered the stone's correspondences: mental health, memory. He handed a stone to Nathalie. "Here, place this over her third eye." When Nathalie looked up at him in confusion, he added, "On the center of her forehead." The stone was an enormous diamond, no doubt intended to aid travel through the astral. Nathalie positioned the stone.

"That's the real Silverbell Coven diamond," Lucy said, pointing at the stone.

"Indeed, it is," Daniel said. "They traded it to Nicholas. I'm not sure for what, but it must've been something big. Doesn't matter now, though." He scooted around the edge of the circle and placed two blue stones, lapis, Fleur decided, outside the circle, one at the point of each hand. Fleur was growing concerned. Lapis could be used to assist with trance work, but this stone, like the agate, was usually used to treat brain disorders. Did Daniel expect Alice's return trip to the common world a risk to her sanity, or did he fear that she might already be too far gone?

He placed sharp pieces of obsidian at each of Alice's feet. The shiny irregular black stones would serve to ground her, and to draw out and capture any negative forces that might hitchhike along with her.

Daniel stepped back and stood akimbo, examining his work. "Good. Good," he repeated himself. His eyes fell to the ground, and he crossed to where the athame lay. He picked the knife up and tapped the tip of its blade against each of the drawings in the open book—the Queen of Heaven on one page, the King of Bones and Ashes on the facing. He tilted the blade, examining the unwholesome glow that now shone from its sharp point. Fleur's mind insisted that it was the blade itself glowing, but her intuition told her that the blade had instead become an insatiable devourer of light. The glow like the event horizon of a black hole. She fought the urge to take it away from him. To destroy it before he could put it to its intended use.

"What exactly do you plan to do with that?" Fleur finally asked. Daniel seemed surprised by her concern.

"What do you think I'd use it for?"

"I'm beyond guessing games."

"To protect Alice, Hugo, and myself." He traced the blade across his palm, creating a gash. A bright and beautiful white light shone from the wound. Fleur's ears picked up whispers in a language she was sure no one still living spoke, though somehow she understood every utterance. The blade, she realized, was rejoicing. "I've modified this old bit of scrap metal based on the formula presented in *The Lesser Key*. Now it can be used to destroy an entity conjured using the book. If the need arises, I can use it to remove Babau Jean." He closed his hand. When he opened it, the wound had disappeared.

"Or he can use it to 'remove' you," Lucy said.

"I shan't let him get his sharp claws on it," Daniel responded, then stuck his tongue out at Lucy and blew a raspberry. "Don't worry, love,

I'm tougher than any of you would guess." He shifted his focus back to Fleur and winked at her. "*Any* of you." Only then did Fleur realize how deep her concern for him ran.

"Hugo?" he called.

Hugo laboriously pushed up from the ground and made his teetering way to Daniel's side. He took Daniel's hand.

"Like we discussed?" Daniel asked. Hugo mumbled a response that Daniel seemed to take as an affirmative. "Be patient," he addressed Fleur once more. "This may take a while." He led Hugo to the pentagram, then knelt at the circle's edge, tugging Hugo's arm as a signal to join him. Hugo, addled, gazed down at him for a moment before sinking to his knees. Daniel nodded to the Twins, who'd drawn close to the pentagram. They began singing, a wordless melody that struck Fleur as the antithesis of the athame's chant.

"I'm coming for you, my little one," Daniel said, then drove the blade into the soil. An electric current shot out, running along the exposed earth like a track, then shooting up and connecting the stones Daniel had placed in and around the design.

A throbbing like a drum or a wild heart sounded around them. An excruciating, high-pitched whine caused Fleur to throw her hands over her ears. *The Lesser Key* burst into flame, the images of the Queen and King curling up and blackening in unison. A spark shot from the burning grimoire and struck Eli. He rocked back and forth, placing his hand over his forehead and weaving from side to side. For a moment it seemed he, too, would topple to the ground, but he righted himself. A deep rumble shook the earth, and Nathalie was flung from the circle.

A flash of blinding light swallowed the circle whole. Fleur, her eyes dazzled, turned away from it.

A scream, Alice's scream—wild and tortured—rose up out of the circle. Fleur turned back to the now dark pentagram. She tried to approach the design, but her feet felt as if they'd been turned to stone.

"He isn't breathing," Lucy cried. Fleur turned to see her daughter kneeling at Hugo's side. Lucy began compressions and then leaned over, pinching his nose and blowing into his mouth. She positioned her palm over his sternum, about to press down again, when Nathalie scrambled over to them.

"Move," Nathalie commanded. She shoved Lucy aside, raised her own fist, crackling bright with electricity, and brought it down against Hugo's heart. She raised her fist again to repeat the gesture, but Hugo rose up gasping.

A cry drew Fleur's attention to the Twins, who still stood at the edge of the pentagram. Eli knelt beside them, reaching in toward Alice. Alice was crawling, struggling to escape the pentagram as the earth behind her began to crumble and fall into a growing chasm. A dark figure rose up from the earth. A brief shimmer caused Fleur to perceive the form as a beautiful young woman, but the illusion was short-lived. The creature crawling up from the depths was no woman. It was a demon that shrieked as it clawed at Alice's ankles, attempting to pull her back down into the darkness.

"Take my hand," Eli called. Alice lurched forward, but her reach fell short. The demon caught her foot.

Fleur flung herself toward the circle, but she, too, fell short. A flash of movement passed before her. It was Nathalie.

Nathalie rushed into the pentagram, earth crumbling beneath her feet, and caught Alice by the shoulders, lifting her, but the demon would not be denied. It tightened its grip on Alice, even as Nathalie fought to pull her from the disintegrating circle.

With a loud cry, Nathalie pulled with all her might, landing herself outside of the circle. She'd managed to pull most of Alice past the boundary, but the demon still clutched her ankle in one claw, shrieking and tugging her.

"Oh, hell," Nathalie growled. "A little help here." Fleur scrambled to her side and caught hold of Alice's calf, even as the Twins aimed their combined powers at the demon's claw. Its grasp was weakening, weakening. As Alice's ankle crossed the edge of the circle, the demon's claw burst into flame.

If all the hatred and rage in the world could be condensed to a single sound, it was the cry that met Fleur's ears as the demon fell back into the void. The next moment, the yawning cavern disappeared, the pentagram and its bounding circle erased. The earth had returned to the state it had been in upon their arrival.

Lucy ran to her side and, falling down to her knees, threw her arms around Fleur's neck.

Fleur caressed Lucy's forearm, but her attention was fixed on Alice and Nathalie. Nathalie remained tense and ready for a fight, her arms still hooked beneath Alice's. Their eyes were locked.

Lucy released her and stood, making a full turn. "Guys," she said, "where's Daniel?" She cupped her hands around her mouth, calling out "Daniel," stretching the name out. "Daniel." This time the name came out short and sharp, edged with a growing panic.

Fleur pushed up to her feet and began scanning the area, her eyes locking on the tree against which they'd rested Daniel's portrait. She caught hold of Lucy's arm. Before the tree lay a pile of smoldering embers. The painting had been destroyed.

TWENTY

Lisette couldn't even bring herself to speak, so no way she'd be able to eat. It was the middle of the damned night, but Isadore needed his dinner, and she needed something to keep her from killing five-dollar-coffee boy.

Lisette glared at Michael and made a point of not looking at Manon, both sitting across from Isadore at the kitchen table. The three of them sat in utter silence, casting questioning glances at each other every odd minute or so.

Lisette had plenty to say, but she couldn't find the words. That didn't stop her from letting them know how she felt. Her sharpest, most impressive knife in hand, she'd already sacrificed an onion to her anger, and was in the process of disemboweling a pair of bell peppers when the boy piped up.

"Can I help you with any of that?" Michael asked. Lisette lifted the knife and slammed its sharp edge down on the cutting board in response.

"Mama," Manon said, using her name in an attempt to chastise her.

Her daughter's disapproving tone loosened Lisette's tongue. "Don't you 'Mama' me." She wagged the knife at Manon.

"He was only offering to help."

"Oh, I think he's helped enough already." The rice had come to boil, and so had Lisette. Snapping and popping came from behind her as water bubbled up over the edge of the pot. Lisette turned back to the stove and lowered the heat. She assaulted the pot with its own lid. Her eyes landed on the colander of shrimp in the sink, so she grabbed it and the deveining knife and crossed to the table. She slammed the colander down before Michael hard enough that a couple of shrimp jumped out and landed beside the strainer. Tilting her head, she squinted down at him in challenge. His eyes fell to the table, and he reached out to capture the wayward shrimp and return them to the sieve.

Before she could make it back to the stove, Michael started up again. "So, what's up with this Doll House thing?" Not one for silence, this fellow. A smarter man would know to keep his mouth shut until spoken to.

Isadore shook his head and rubbed his hand over his tired face. He shrugged. "Took me an hour to convince the cops I didn't know a thing about that Demagnan guy. And it took me another two hours to convince the reporters. Seems some folk don't really believe in coincidence."

"You do have to admit it's odd," Michael dared. Lisette knew what he was doing, all right. Keep them focused on the damage done to their business, and maybe they'd get used to the idea of him and Manon, skip right over the damage he'd done to their family. "It's crazy, isn't it? That all your trucks would be like ninja stealth vandalized at once, and one of them would crash through the gates of a psycho funeral director." Did he really think anything, even spontaneously shattering glass or murderous morticians, was going to make things go easier for him?

Manon placed a cautioning hand on Michael's forearm. He ignored it and charged on. "I mean, what happened with your trucks anyway?"

"Damned if I know," Isadore said, seeming to take the boy's bait. "The windows in every single one of them shattered at the same time." Isadore looked back at her. "Two of my guys blamed what happened to their truck on some crazy redheaded woman who picked a fight with them in the middle of the street, but nobody else had anything weird happen today, until . . ." He held up his hands. "Boom. Crack. Crash. Todd jerked the wheel and went through that freak's fence. And he wasn't even the worst wreck we had. Santos and Antoine were coming down Alvar Street and went off the road. They rolled over twice."

Lisette's heart skipped. This bit was news even to her.

"Are they okay?" Manon said. Santos was her favorite. He used to sneak her and Remy sweets when they were little.

"Santos is fine. That one has an angel looking out for him."

"And Antoine?" Lisette pressed him.

"Antoine got banged up pretty good. They're keeping him overnight at Tulane, but they say he's gonna be okay. They wouldn't let me in to see him. Too late and not blood. But I had to try. I had to check on him."

"Of course you did," Lisette said. "Antoine's as good as family."

"What do the police think?" Michael steered them in the direction he preferred, which—surprise, surprise—was away from family.

"Hell, nobody knows what to think. They asked if I had any enemies, and if I had any idea how these theoretical villains managed to pull it off. They're checking into the redhead story, but they seem to think one of my guys is a mad scientist with a grudge. Or maybe a magician." Isadore studied her with tired eyes. There was something rolling around in his head that he wasn't sure should make it to his tongue. "Demagnan," he said, diving in. "Wasn't that the name of the funeral home that buried Fleur Marin's father?"

"I wouldn't know," she said, her words coming out sharp and fast. "It was you and Daddy who attended the service." Truth was, she didn't know, but she understood the connection he was making. Lisette's daddy was probably sleeping it off somewhere right now, or he'd have already come knocking. She felt bad for snapping at Isadore. His question was his way of warning her of what would happen when her father caught wind of this.

It was a sure thing her daddy would consider the strange event proof positive that associating with the Marins was as dangerous as ever. Lisette hated to think her father might be right, but, well, even Isadore was creeping up on the same assumption her father was gonna jump to. Some folk really didn't believe in coincidence.

"Then there *is* a connection between you and Demagnan—a tenuous one, maybe, but still," Michael said, sounding like he'd just won fifty dollars from a buck scratch ticket.

Lisette was done with his shepherding them around the elephant in the room. She pinned her husband with her gaze. "What are we going to do about"—she waved her hand in the kids' direction without looking at them—"this."

Isadore was far too calm about this mess. He looked up at her and raised both hands palms up, shaking his head. "I don't think there is anything for us to do about *this*," he said, choosing the wrong damned time to sound reasonable, "other than maybe welcome Michael to the family."

Lisette stood there in a white-hot silence, staring him down. Of course they'd welcome the boy to the family. After she got good and ready to. Right now, she wasn't even in ready's neighborhood. Those two had made a fool out of her for years. Well, okay, maybe she'd made a fool out of herself, but they'd knowingly let her do it.

"Thank you, Daddy," Manon said, in the same Daddy's-little-girl tone she used whenever Isadore gave in to her without a fight, whether it was for a new phone, concert tickets, or even financing spring break in Miami her junior year in college.

"Thank you, Daddy," Lisette parroted her and went back to the cutting board. She pasted a half smile on her face as she focused on

Michael, enjoying watching him squirm beneath her gaze. As he fumbled with the shrimp, she dropped an entire bunch of celery onto the board, then grabbed a cleaver and chopped off the root end in one fearsome stroke.

"Isadore," she said, repeating her cleaver attack on the celery sticks, "maybe you should ask your daughter and her lover when they planned to tell us about all of this." A headache was forming, like a hot pin was being poked into her brain, but she kept hacking away, awaiting Isadore's response.

"It is a fair question," Isadore said, addressing Manon.

"Tonight, Mr. Perrault," Michael answered for her. Manon's eyes met Michael's. He laid the deveining knife, which he had yet to use, on the table and took her hand. "Right after dinner with the Marins."

"Because," Lisette said, dropping the knife to the board and advancing on him, "the only way to make the evening more delightful would be for us to learn you two had been carrying on in secret behind our backs. For two years." The headache was building quickly, so fast it made her nauseated. But she didn't have time for that now. "Give me that," she said, reaching out for the colander.

Michael caught her hand before she could touch the basket. "I know it was wrong to keep our relationship from you. I'm sorry." Lisette's neck was growing stiff. "We were afraid . . ." He paused and cast a quick glance at Manon before shifting his gaze back to Lisette. *Damn it. Damn it. Damn it.* Lisette could see the truth in them. "*I* was afraid you'd object. That you'd think I was too old for your daughter. Not good enough for her."

"Well, you are and you aren't," Lisette said, though without rancor. She drew a deep breath, and her hand relaxed in his.

"I know I'm not good enough for your daughter, but I do love her." The overhead light beamed down as bright as the sun.

Lisette patted his hand with her free hand, as much a reassurance as a signal to release her. "I know you do," she said. Tears brimmed in her eyes. She pointed at the colander. "You're making a mess on the table. Bring that over to the sink." She pointed to a cabinet. "Then reach me down the cornstarch from that cupboard."

Michael jumped up to obey.

A look passed between Isadore and Manon. Storm was over. All clear. Like hell. She pointed at Manon. "Just because I'm ready to think about forgiving him, doesn't mean it's going to be so easy for you. You, *ma fillette*, are gonna have to work a little bit harder."

"I know, Mama. I'm really sorry." Manon looked exhausted. She was bound to be. Lisette hadn't confirmed the timing yet, but now that her eyes had been opened to all she'd been disregarding, she estimated the pregnancy at around four months.

Lisette sighed, then circled around the table. She planted a kiss on top of her daughter's head, breathing her own little girl in, remembering the first time she'd held her. Now the girl had gone off and made her a grandmother. She squeezed Manon's shoulders and finished the circle, heading back toward the stove. She felt herself weaving.

"You okay, Mama?" Manon called out to her.

"Fine," she said with more irritation than she felt. Her headache pounded at her, like it wanted to break her skull clean open. She glanced back at Manon, and even that slight movement made her dizzy. "I'm fine." She gave Manon a reassuring smile. "Your mama's just tired." She closed her eyes before turning her head again, willing the headache to go away. When she reopened them, she focused on walking to the counter in a straight line. She could feel all eyes on her as she took each laborious step. Finally, the counter dug into her hip, signaling that she could stop.

"Maybe I should close Vèvè tomorrow? Go to your office and help with the insurance paperwork?" Lisette said. Her left hand had fallen asleep on her. It tingled for a few seconds, then started to go numb.

Isadore didn't answer her questions. Instead, he looked her up and down. "You don't look fine," he said.

Lisette raised her hand to stop him. "Nothing a good night's sleep and watching these two walk down the aisle before my grandbaby is born won't cure. Gonna need a place to live," she said, trying her best to think things through. "'Course, it won't work long-term, you two will want a place of your own, but you can live here till you find it. There's a little house over on Tonti that someone's fixed up real cute to sell. Right by the school. You should run by and check it out."

Silence. Another furtive glance passed between Michael and Manon. "What?" Lisette said.

"Well, Mama, it's only we've made other plans."

"Other plans." Isadore repeated the words before Lisette could.

Michael set the cornstarch on the counter and hurried back to Manon's side. *Well, this wasn't going to be good.*

"I know you've never thought much of me working at the coffee shop."

"I," Lisette said, her own voice like an icepick in her brain. She lowered her voice to a near whisper. "I have never looked down on you for working an honest job."

"No, I'm sure you haven't," he said, placing a hand on Manon's shoulder. "But I'm also sure you want more for your daughter. You want her to have a husband who'll show some ambition."

It was true, but it felt like a trap. Lisette held her tongue.

"I've been offered a much better-paying position: director of food and beverage at a luxury hotel. More responsibility. Plenty of room for advancement."

"Good for you, son," Isadore said, leaning his chair back on its two hind legs. He was more than happy to hear this. Poor guy had no doubt been calculating how he was going to put food in yet another mouth— or two. But here Manon's guy was stepping up. Lisette could almost see the relief wafting off Isadore, blurring his edges. "In the Quarter?"

Michael looked down at Manon. She nodded at him.

"No," Lisette said, giving the answer she felt certain she was about to hear. She reached behind her neck, trying to rub the stiffness away. "It isn't in the Quarter."

Manon reached up to take Michael's hand. "You remember Michael took that trip to Oregon a couple of weeks ago?"

No. Lisette didn't remember. She hadn't cared enough about the boy to put much energy into noticing his comings and goings. "Yeah," she lied.

"That's . . . that's where the job is."

"Portland, to be precise," Michael added.

"Well, yes," Lisette said, "let's do be precise." She tried to focus on her daughter, but the headache made that impossible. The pain had shifted to right above her left eye, stabbing into her. *A migraine maybe? I've never had one before, but . . . pay attention, dammit.* She rubbed her finger over the spot. "I'm sure Mr. Hipster Caucasian will feel right at home there," she addressed Manon, "but you do realize that Portland is *precisely* the whitest damned city in the country, and it's a pale white, too, 'cause it rains *precisely* fourteen months out of the year there." The pain in her head met the pain in her heart. That wasn't physical, though. It was only everyday, ordinary heartbreak.

"That's a bit of . . . ," Michael said with a nervous laugh, "well, actually that's quite an exaggeration . . . on both counts."

He was standing up to Lisette, he was. Well, good. About time he showed a bit of spine.

She put her hands to her temples and closed her eyes. Anything to block out the suddenly blinding light. Had Isadore changed the bulb for a higher wattage?

The pieces she'd put together began spiraling back out.

Focus. Focus. Focus. Her girl was leaving. She'd miss her. And it rubbed her raw that she'd get to see her first grandchild once, maybe twice a year, though that wasn't even the worst of it.

Vèvè. Lisette knew running the shop wasn't Manon's ambition—hell, it hadn't been hers either—but it had been the right path to take. She'd always hoped her daughter would come around eventually. That she would keep the memory of Soulange Simeon alive in this city. Instead, Manon seemed anxious to flee as far as possible from her roots, from her tradition. From her mother.

She opened her eyes to see two of everything, one eye reporting independently from the other. The room swirled around her and she fell forward. She heard Isadore's chair scrape the floor as he jumped up to reach her. Her vision normalized as he bent over her. One face. One beautiful face. He was terrified. Oh, how she loved him. He was shouting, but she couldn't make out his words.

Words. She regretted the way she'd behaved tonight. She'd been short with Remy. Told him he might as well go off with his little Lucy, because she was in no mood to deal with him. She struggled to remember if her last words to Manon had been kind, or if she'd still been chewing her out. Only moments before and she couldn't remember.

Isadore's face once more. If she could've smiled, she would have. She was happy that he'd be the last person she'd see. The thought was followed by the cold realization that she *was* dying, then a hot protest against that fact. She wasn't ready to die. Not by a long shot. She had a husband and a family. She was not going to leave them. She opened her mouth, trying to tell Isadore to hold on to her. Not to let go. But he faded from sight.

She was floating faceup in a dark sea. There were no stars above, nothing but red lights, burning rubies, bobbing up and down in pairs all around her. She tried to move her limbs, but, although she had sensation in them, they refused her commands. Only her eyes remained under her control. She scanned from side to side, trying to place herself. To discover the source of the lights. Those nearest her had slipped beneath the surface. She felt a jostling, and as she was lifted above the water, her body rose up to touch the cool night air. She was carried along by a quick, smooth motion, moving faster than the current. Then the water was gone. She was on land. Still moving. The ride grew bumpier, and she rocked from side to side. The jouncing movements widened her field of vision, allowing her to catch glimpses of the grouping of dark shapes that had come together to convey her along.

Overhead she could make out the dark lines of cypress branches. A weak light began to glow around her, illuminating the creatures carrying her on their backs. In the gloaming, she recognized the leathery flesh and bony scales of her convoy—alligators. Panic commanded her to rise, but her body remained stiff. She wanted to scream, but her mouth remained closed. Still, inside her mind, her inner voice cried out. An old myth bubbled up through her panic. The ancient Egyptians believed that the heart was weighed after death, and those found wanting were sent to the dim hall of Maat. There, the reptile god Ammut would consume their wicked, heavy hearts. Maybe the story the ancient Egyptians had believed was as valid as any of the others—maybe that was the fate that awaited her.

A heart. Pounding. Pounding.

Pounding, though her own was still.

The frenzied throbbing drowned out her thoughts, drowned out her internal scream. The light around her brightened, but she sensed this place never knew dawn. Whatever its source, the glow was nothing wholesome. Above the pounding, a shrill, cold whine soared and descended, a chilling tingle spreading across her breasts as this . . . force examined her, tasted her, and then rose again. The light flickered. Acrid smoke—the smell of burning tires intertwined with the stench of charring flesh—filled her senses.

Her litter came to a stop. A new rhythm, the snapping of teeth, sounded around her as the cohesive force that had brought her here broke into its constituent reptiles. Jostled from side to side, Lisette caught sight of the source of this foul place's dim light. The radiance came from the erratic dance of flames.

The beasts crawled out from under her, lowering her to the ground as they slipped away.

A face appeared above her. Human. Not Isadore.

An unfamiliar young white woman, one Lisette might have thought beautiful if not for the madness in her eyes, bent over her. In the firelight, the woman's hair glowed, not quite red, not quite blonde. Strawberry. *Blond vénitien*. That's what her mother would have called it. Her mother. What would Soulange do in her place? Lisette's spirit called out, but no answer came. She hadn't expected a response. Not really. Lisette knew this place where she'd landed was nowhere near where her mother had gone.

The woman pressed her cold lips to Lisette's. Then she pulled away, hunching her shoulders and reaching out her hands, her fingers hooked like claws. She shot backward and upward into the air. Her skin milky, nearly opalescent, she hung overhead like a baleful moon. Manic laughter sharpened into a cackle and rained down on Lisette.

This creature, Lisette realized, was no god. This was a witch. Not the polished, polite, contemporary type who used magic to gain privilege, but the old-school cut-your-heart-out-and-roast-your-children variety her mother had warned her about.

A tall flame jumped up beside Lisette. It was, she sensed, a child of the inky blaze lending this place its weird twilight. The strange fire gave off cold and, like its source, burned darker than the surrounding gloom. It struck her that rather than being a source of light, the shadowy inferno was the devourer of it. Any luminescence in this world came from the death throes of the true light these wicked tongues consumed. The flame spread out in a zigzag fashion, tracing a shape around her. Lisette's eyes couldn't follow its full path, but from its jerky motion, she decided she was being surrounded by an inverted pentagram of fire.

From above, the witch shrieked, "A loss of fertility to seal the lock."

Voices, a blend of masculine and feminine, none familiar, came at her from each point of the star. They'd approached without her noticing, or perhaps they'd been there all along. She strained to turn her head, to get a glimpse of these witches, but her body remained rigid.

"A new conception," they chanted in unison, "to break it."

The witch above bobbed up and down on invisible currents. "A loss of reason to seal the lock."

"A return to lucidity," the voices on her periphery called out together, "to break the seal."

They seemed to be following a type of a versicle and response. Lisette's mind resurrected a fragment of a catechism from her schooling at Queen of Heaven Elementary. *He is the beginning, the firstborn from the dead . . .*

A flute-like trill joined the incessant, high-pitched whine. The throbbing beat grew louder.

"A loss of love to seal the lock," the witch above screamed, the pitch of each word in discord with the whine, albeit in what seemed to be a measured, intentional dissonance.

These words sizzled in Lisette's ears. She'd suffered a loss of love herself. Her love with Vincent Marin had been sacrificed to seal the spell that would maroon *The Book of the Unwinding* between the common world and the Dreaming Road—existing in both at once, though fully in neither. Laure Marin had supposedly led Lisette's mother to believe the book needed to be hidden from her daughter-in-law Astrid, but Lisette didn't trust Laure's version of the story one bit.

"New love found," the voices said together, "to break the seal."

These people, or witches, or demons, or whatever they were . . . they were trying to undo the spell.

"No," her mind cried out from indignation as much as fear. She should not have had her young heart ripped out, even if that pain had led her to Isadore, and sure as hell her mother should not have died to protect the Book for less than three measly decades.

"A loss of life," the words from above drowned out Lisette's inner voice, "to seal the lock."

In a blink, the witches from the periphery were on her, leaning over her. She could see flesh, though the night helped to disguise its tones. Faces were hidden from her, their features blurring, shifting.

Five hands reached down, each taking its turn slapping her on her breast over her heart.

"A return to life," was all she heard, followed by a beep—steady, even in pitch. She felt cool. Dry. Her eyes fluttered open, though she didn't remember closing them. Bright light. That same beeping again. White sheets. Metal railings. She lay in a narrow bed, wires attached to various points on her body.

A hand grasped hers. Her eyes focused on the face looking down at her. Isadore.

She heard Manon calling out for a nurse.

Tears streamed down Isadore's face. "There you are. There you are," he repeated himself. "You didn't think I heard you, but I did. I was holding on as tight as I could. No way I was letting my girl go."

TWENTY-ONE

The headlights of Lincoln's pickup illuminated the stretch before them, but the road came at them almost too fast for Evangeline's eyes to follow. The dotted white line on the road maddened her. It indicated that she could change lanes at any time, but that was clearly a lie. Evangeline never used to believe in destiny, but of late it was pretty damned clear a guiding hand was playing with her, tugging her in a crooked line to a predetermined fate. Maybe she should surrender, but the thought of losing her free will pissed her off to no end. Be that controlling force a god or a man, Evangeline was going to resist the bastard at every turn.

Evangeline looked back over her shoulder at the dim outline in the darkness of Celestin Marin's haunted corpse wrapped in a tarpaulin. "Thank you for the clothes. And the ride."

"'Course," Lincoln said. Evangeline turned to study his profile. He took his eyes off the road and faced her, but the shadow prevented her from reading his expression. She didn't need to use her eyes to understand his thoughts. His feelings for her radiated from him; his aura, rose with flecks of gold, reached out toward her, not touching but hoping to be touched.

She looked away. Beyond the passenger window, a shifting black line of trees marked their progress. "It would've been a lot faster to take Lake Forest."

"This is the first time I've come out here. I figured it might be better to return the way I got to the park." His voice dropped to a low, grumbling mutter. "You could've given me directions."

"You could've asked."

A warm laugh turned her head. The headlights of a passing semi illuminated his face. For a moment she could make out the crinkles at the corners of his eyes. "I can tell I'm not gonna have an easy road with you, Ms. Caissy. Good thing I like a challenge." He turned back to the road.

A pang hit Evangeline's heart. Whatever he'd seen earlier had convinced him that their future was guaranteed. He saw a straight line, but Evangeline knew *nothing* was guaranteed. The happiness he'd seen them share was nothing more than a potentiality. A strong one, no denying that, but life had thrown her too many curves for her to jump into something without caution. Once she'd been certain her future belonged to Luc Marin. With Nicholas, she'd never suffered from the delusion of certainty. Every moment with him had been a question mark. Still she'd clung to him desperately and, to a large degree, blindly.

Lincoln seemed to feel certain her heart would soon belong to him. Right or wrong, he'd have to face up to the reality that her heart came used, as-is, and without warranties.

"I didn't count on having to drive all the way to Eden to find a turnaround. Not many exits out this way."

"Not much out this way to exit to." She scanned the empty darkness that ran one hundred eighty degrees ahead of them. "At least not anymore. You should've gone straight across coming off Michoud instead of getting back on the highway. You'll have another shot soon. I think the next loop around may never have reopened, but there's another one after that before we hit Pontchartrain."

"See, that wasn't so hard, was it?"

"You know the night I've had." Her words came out in a harsher tone than she'd intended, but hell. "You might want to keep the sarcasm to a minimum if you want a second date." He lifted his chin and pushed back into his seat. She could feel the smug satisfaction wafting off him. "What?"

"Nothing. Just pleased to know this counts as our first."

A shrill whine worked its way into her consciousness. Now that she'd become aware of it, she realized it had been there the entire ride. She looked at the ancient AM radio in the dashboard. "You know what I mean."

He tilted his head to the side and glanced over at her. "*Ben ouais, sha.* Maybe even better than you do."

"You are lucky I feel I owe you for helping me out."

"Nope. I'm lucky just to be sitting here next to you. You don't *owe* me anything. 'Course our second date might be more romantic if we don't bring a corpse as chaperone." She was too distracted by the annoying sound to follow his words. She grabbed the radio's power knob and gave it a hard left twist. The radio was already off.

"That thing works. Mostly sports and one-sided propaganda passing for news, but there are a couple of music stations. Go on. Turn it on, if you want."

Evangeline shook her head, then realized his eyes were focused on the road. "No. Don't you hear it?"

"What?"

She raised her hand to her ear, surprised that the whine got louder and higher as she did. "That sound. That squeal." Like an unwanted souvenir carried from a dream into the waking world, she seemed to remember that drone, though its significance skulked at the edge of her consciousness.

Lincoln went silent, tilting his head first to the left, then the right. "Nope. Nothing. Probably the wheels arguing with the asphalt. Not to worry," he said and patted the dashboard. "Old Bud here might complain a bit, but he'll get you home." He patted the dash a second time, this one, she reckoned, for good luck. "Besides, we have bigger concerns than Old Bud."

He was trying to comfort her, to distract her. She wanted to be distracted, so she bit. "Such as?"

"That Hugo boy of yours. He's getting close to Wiley. I need to know if his intentions toward my little brother are honorable."

"Unlikely." She found herself looking down at her hand and, unable to help herself, she brought it up to cup her ear again, pretending to brush back her hair. "I don't think Hugo's had an honorable intention since junior high. He's self-centered and reckless." The whine grew louder again. She dropped her hand to her lap. "He'll never think of your brother's feelings first. Oh, he'll be sincerely sorry when he messes up, but that won't stop him from messing up again."

"Wow. You don't pull any punches, do you?"

"No, I don't. You'd be well advised to remember that."

"Duly noted." He paused long enough that she'd begun to consider the topic closed. "If Hugo," he continued, with the caution of a soldier crossing a minefield, "is such a mess, why do you give a damn about him in the first place?"

"Because every so often you get a glimpse beneath his shell, and what's there is beautiful. Maybe Wiley can pry off Hugo's armor, but I'm not going to lie to you. He's proceeding at his own risk."

"We Boudreau boys always do. Proceed, that is. And Wiley is as patient as I am, twice as stubborn, and maybe even three times as stupid. When he was ten, I caught the boy wrestling a gator that had snatched up his Braves cap off the bank." A thumping sound that Evangeline guessed was the engine's death rattle began. Lincoln took no notice of it. "Gator didn't stand a chance." The thumping grew louder, a wild heartbeat, a furious knock at a door. No, not the engine—something out there was demanding to be let in. The owner demanding access to his property.

Her own heart began to thud. She felt the bones in her hand begin to crack.

"No. Come to think of it"—Lincoln carried on, not noticing—"it sounds to me like those two have met their match."

This couldn't be. She'd made the change for the third time this month. The moon would next appear as a waxing crescent. The fingers of her left hand began to contort. *No! The force can't control me . . .* The thought froze in her mind as she realized the power had duped her, reinforcing a pattern over the last three months, so she wouldn't expect . . .

"Pull over," she commanded Lincoln, who turned toward her. She could sense his confusion. He continued driving as he processed the situation. "Pull over," she screamed as a wave of nausea hit her. She grasped the door handle and flung the door open even as Lincoln brought the truck to a screeching halt. Celestin's body was thrown up into the air. It tumbled over the top of the cab to bounce off the hood and onto the side of the road.

She didn't care. The agony was once again upon her. She sensed that an even greater force than her tormentor had triggered the change, but it was her tormentor who'd allowed the pain to return. The pain was a punishment. The realization burned in her mind with as much pain as the change brought to her body. She rolled out of the cab, the sensation of being stabbed by a thousand hot needles shooting through her as she landed on the asphalt. She lifted her head to the sky, screaming, falling silent as she realized the stars had all been replaced by bobbing red lights. *Familiar* bobbing red lights.

The space where she'd met the sister witches, where she'd watched Marceline destroy herself. She wasn't physically in that place, which meant that place was in her.

Lincoln's face appeared before her. *A foolish face.* He grasped her shoulders. His fingers felt like ten paper cuts. She hissed and pulled back. Her field of vision was widening. Her spine broke. She couldn't bear it. She couldn't bear it.

You can end it. You can end the pain forever.

"How? How?" she cried, but her voice had become the caw of the crow. Her arms snapped, then jerked out of their sockets. They reached up, unfurling as wings, flapping, lifting her to her feet even as her toes lengthened and bent into talons.

(Kill him.)

Kill him—her own thought echoed the other's voice.

She looked down at Lincoln, still squatting on his haunches before her. The whine fell silent. The drumming heart stopped cold. All that was left was the sound of the blood pulsing in Lincoln's veins. It was that pulsing that caused her pain. End the pulsing, end the pain.

(Murder.)

(Murder.)

(Murder.)

Lincoln rose to his feet. He took a step toward her.

No. God. Please. She tried to scream at Lincoln. To warn him. To tell him to run. To get back into his truck and speed away. To leave while she still had some control. But her cry came out as a demand for his blood, and intuition told her that if he ran, she would rise up on wing and hunt him. And she would relish the hunt. Catching him, snatching him up, tearing him apart in midair to watch his blood fall to the earth like rain.

He was speaking to her, but his words bore no meaning. A fool's chatter.

(Murder.)

Yes. Murder.

Lincoln slipped off his shirt, exposing his chest. She could see the pulse in his neck. Yes. That was where she'd tear into him first. She'd plunge her beak into him over and over until his head held on by a strip of flesh alone. She'd sink her claws into his tight stomach, catch

229

his intestines, and fly upward—see how far she made it before they snapped.

Lincoln kicked off his shoes, balancing on one foot and then the other as he removed his socks. He tugged down his jeans, removing his briefs at the same time. He threw them behind him as he turned to face her, arms held out to his sides, all of his tender flesh exposed. Vulnerable.

He had presented himself as a willing sacrifice. She heard a pop and felt a flash of lightning. He took a step closer. Then another.

"I believe in you," he said, his words warped and reverberating. No. This time he wasn't speaking at all. He was projecting his aura into her mind. The message hadn't been phrased in words but in a wave of pure feeling. He was reaching beyond the monster to touch her true self. This was no Prince Charming coming to save her with a magical kiss. This was a flesh and blood man, willing to risk everything to help her save herself.

Every bone in her snapped at once, then bound back together, the healing as horrible as the breaking.

(Murder.)

A shove from behind pushed her closer to Lincoln. He stopped approaching her, but he didn't turn. He didn't run.

His trust reached out to her like a calming balm. He took another step.

(Murder.)

No.

Her refusal rang out, echoing between worlds. Her tormentor could kill her. He could drive her out of her mind, but as long as she held on to a shred of herself, she wouldn't do his bidding. She would resist.

Another step. Lincoln stood in easy striking distance.

She threw back her head and stretched out her wings. She sucked in the foul night air from that other place and then screamed it out at the top of her lungs, rebelling against earth, air, fire, and water. Against the fixed and the mutable. Against what was above and what lay below. Flames rose up around her. She smelled the stench of burning plumage, but she didn't stop. A white light shot out of the crown of her head before turning back on her. Thunder met her ears.

Then it was over.

Lincoln stood before her, sweating, relieved, smiling.

"I believe in you, too," she said, then reached out to him with her very human hand.

TWENTY-TWO

White box, black bag, black-and-white cashmere scarf from last year's winter season. Fleur had called it a lovely, thoughtful gift when she'd received it from . . . Hell, she had no idea who the giver had been. Only, you weren't supposed to bring flowers to the hospital anymore—pollen—or even green plants—mold—and between the breakfast visit to the morgue to identify her taxidermized sister-in-law and the fruitless efforts to reach Eli, who, it seemed, might have finally had enough of her, there hadn't been time to shop for something else. Besides, it was an exquisite scarf, and if not brand-new, it was at least unworn, and she knew hospital rooms could be chilly, especially when you were confined to bed, and dear God, dear God, dear God, please don't let last night's activities have any connection to Lisette Perrault's stroke . . .

Lisette had been worked up about her daughter's secret relationship. If there was a contributing factor to Lisette's attack beyond heredity and diet, surely that was it. Fleur had no concrete reason to connect the happenings on Grunch Road to Lisette's bad turn, but still she had a queasy feeling that a direct line ran between the two events.

"You okay, Mom?" Lucy stood on the other side of the open elevator doors, using her arm to prevent them from closing.

"Yes, fine," she said, an automatic response that had no relation to reality. The impatient buzz of the closing doors alert goaded her into movement. She hurried out of the elevator.

The hall was bright and sterile, and so elongated that Fleur's weary mind initially perceived it as a perspective drawing. She blinked, and the space snapped from two to three dimensions. Left wall taupe, right a well-intentioned though off-putting shade of moss. Floor, an angled checkerboard of white and light gray tiles set so that a nauseating diamond pattern led one's eye to the nurses' station at the hall's midpoint. "Has Remy gotten back to you?" Fleur said, prompting Lucy to check her phone's screen.

"No. Not since he said they were moving Mrs. Perrault to the eighth floor."

"Not to worry," she said to reassure herself as much as her daughter, "it's a good sign—a very good sign—that they've moved her out of intensive care. Lisette may have a long road to recovery ahead of her, but she's already underway."

Lucy sidled up to her and bumped her shoulder against hers. "Come on," she said in a tone Fleur knew well—the softening Mom up, we're-in-this-together, here-comes-the-big-ask tone she'd been perfecting since the age of twelve. "Isn't there something we can do—and by 'we,' I mean you—to help speed up the process? Just a little." She held her hand up before Fleur's face, her thumb and index finger in a loose pinch.

Fleur stopped and placed her hand on Lucy's shoulder. "No, *ma petite mendiante*, there is nothing *we* can do." She leaned in to whisper in Lucy's ear. "My magic is all but gone." She released Lucy and stepped back. "A spark or two, but the battery is nearly dead. You know that, *ma chère*."

"Don't think you can French your way out of this. I know what I saw last night . . ."

"You saw the cost of it, too. No more shortcuts. Not for us. Not anymore." She held the bag with her hand-me-down gift out to Lucy. "Here, take this. It will mean more to Lisette coming from you."

Lucy accepted the bag, but continued to search Fleur's face as if she didn't accept her rebuff, or at least the reasoning behind it. "Okay. Maybe not you, but what about the walking defibrillator? Nathalie's kind of like family now, right? Mrs. Perrault's kind of family, too. We could talk to Nathalie . . ."

"And by 'we' . . ."

"I mean we."

There it was again, the generous goodwill wrapped up in entitlement and ornamented with a bow of impatience. Lucy meant well. There wasn't a shred of self-serving in her wish for Lisette to make a speedy recovery, but she had to learn that life didn't work that way. At least not anymore. Besides, Fleur had her own thoughts about how Nathalie's magic might best be channeled.

"I wouldn't jump to conclusions about Nathalie or her abilities," she said, giving Lucy a nudge toward the nurses' station. "Sure, she seemed impressive last night, but it might have been the equivalent of a panicked mother lifting a car off her child. A show of adrenaline, nothing more." She started down the hallway, unable to resist glancing into the open doorways of the rooms they passed, though she only caught sight of the feet of narrow beds, or the occasional family member staring back at her through anxious, exhausted eyes.

"Yeah, but we could still ask, right? What could asking hurt?"

"Let it go, Lucy."

"And nevertheless, she persisted," Lucy said. Catching Fleur's hand, she turned her back and regarded her with a mixture of defiance and humor. Fleur was yet again faced with the knowledge that, for the good and the bad of it, Lucy was exactly the young woman she had raised her to be.

In this matter, though, Fleur could not capitulate. She riffled through available excuses to deny Lucy what seemed like a reasonable request. She put her finger on the best truth-adjacent one. "I'm sure Nathalie would want to help. If you ask her, she will most certainly try. But Nathalie is at best an amateur. She's had absolutely no training, and I'm assuming no practice either. What you saw last night was the use of a raw, imprecise force. Helping Lisette heal would require perfect precision, or the results could prove disastrous—possibly deadly, almost certainly debilitating. The risk is far greater than any possible gain." Fleur felt relief—and the stab of a guilty conscience—when Lucy's face fell. She was buying it. "Listen. The human body is a wonderful thing. It wants to be whole and healthy, and Lisette is a strong and determined woman. She already has those two things going for her. What we can do is see to it she also receives world-class medical care and any necessary rehabilitation. If the Perraults can't afford the best, we can. Your mother may soon no longer be a senator's wife"—she looked around them and drew closer to Lucy, lowering her voice—"or an eminent witch, but she's still one of the wealthiest and most influential bitches ever to walk this obdurate crescent of earth. Lisette can count me in her asset column as well. Okay?"

"Okay," Lucy said, and her tender caress of Fleur's hand said that she was both grateful to and proud of her mother. Then she dropped Fleur's hand and turned away, and the moment was over. "Kudos, by the way, on squeezing two of my SAT study guide words into a single sentence."

Lucy took off in the direction of the nurses' station, but stopped cold at the sound of her name coming from the room she'd just passed. Remy emerged from the room as Lucy approached it. Lucy threw her arms around his neck, the bag slapping against his back. To Fleur's surprise, Remy removed her arms from his shoulders and stepped back. "You shouldn't be here."

"We wanted to come," Lucy said, stepping toward him, trying to close the distance between them. He put a hand against her shoulder, keeping her from drawing nearer. Lucy's face flushed with frustration, and she dropped the bag to the floor. She studied Remy like she was trying to work out a difficult problem, then her body shifted into her preferred posture for confrontation—a widened stance, hands on hips, head tilting to one side. "I wanted to come," she said, though the tenderness had changed to annoyance. "I wanted to see how your mom is doing. But mostly I wanted to be here for you."

"I appreciate that," Remy said. His words were civil but cool. "But it's family-only visiting now." Lucy seemed to read even more into Remy's detachment than Fleur had. Her shoulders fell as the starch went out of her. Tears brimmed her eyes. Fleur knew she shouldn't interfere, that whatever had come between the two young lovers was an issue they'd have to work through—or not—but she couldn't stop herself. She stepped up beside Lucy and placed a protective arm around her shoulders. As she did, Manon appeared in the doorway.

"Yes, dear," she addressed Remy, trying her best to grant him the benefit of the doubt, blaming his coldness on the stress he must be under. She invoked the polished demeanor of a politician's wife. "We understand. We'll be going. We only wanted to give your mother our wishes for a speedy recovery, and to drop off a gift." Even as Fleur spoke, she felt the skin on her arms prickle up into gooseflesh that had nothing to do with air-conditioning. Fleur could read the blame in Remy's eyes. Did he see guilt in hers? Lucy grasped the bag and thrust it at him like a weapon. He stared at it for a few moments, seemingly uncertain of how to proceed.

Fleur looked past Remy to Manon, who stood with her arms wrapped around herself, scanning the three of them with red, sleep-deprived eyes. "It isn't much. A scarf to help Lisette keep off the chill in here." Manon started to speak, but stopped to wipe away a renegade tear. A smile—genuine but far from effusive—quivered on her lips. She nodded her response.

Remy accepted the gift with the same enthusiasm with which one receives a jury summons. "We'll talk later," he addressed Lucy. With that, he turned away, pushing past Manon into his mother's hospital room.

"Remy," Lucy called after him. When he didn't return or even answer, she swiveled to look at Fleur. Fleur couldn't be certain what lay behind Remy's behavior. She hoped that she'd misread the situation, that he was only worn out and worried about his mother. That he didn't truly blame her or, worse, Lucy for his mother's condition. Still, the tiny bit of Fleur that still thought like Celestin pointed out that regardless of the cause, this was an opportunity to end this inconvenient teenage romance without having to appear a villain to Lucy.

Then she looked into Lucy's eyes and told that tiny part of herself to go to hell. Her girl was confused, hurt, and angry. Fleur would not be like Celestin, using sticks and promises of carrots to maneuver his children into the positions that best served him. Regardless of the problems waiting for them down the road, Fleur wasn't going to meddle in her daughter's love life, but she would do her best to prevent Lucy from sabotaging it on her own. That meant getting Lucy out of here before she said or did something she might regret later. She squeezed her daughter's shoulders. "Come, sweetie." Lucy's features hardened, and for a moment Fleur feared she might dig her heels in and cause a scene, but whatever rebellion she'd begun to foment fell away. Lucy slipped out from under her arm and strode toward the elevators.

"Manon," Fleur addressed the cautious, uncertain young woman in the doorway. "Please tell your mother she's in our thoughts." A look of forced politeness crossed Manon's face, and Fleur decided to save her from what would undoubtedly be a white lie. "If you believe that it would be good for her to know." Manon's shoulders rose and fell as she released the breath that, in all likelihood, neither of them had realized she was holding.

Fleur turned away and followed Lucy to the elevator bank. She'd drawn up to her daughter's side when the doors yawned open. Alcide Simeon stepped out, his head rearing back in shock at the sight of them. Fleur grasped Lucy's arm and tried to navigate her past Alcide and into the elevator, but the older man blocked their way. "What in the hell are you doing here?"

"We're just leaving, please excuse us." Fleur modulated her voice, trying to find the right balance of confidence and humility, hoping to ease tensions and avoid a public confrontation. The elevator doors closed behind him.

"Oh, I'll excuse you two fine ladies all right, but not before I've had my say. For starters, what makes you think you even have the right to come here?"

"We wanted to help," Lucy said. Fleur pulled her back.

"Isn't that so very kind of you?" Alcide said, his eyes narrowing and the vein on his temple bulging out. "If you want to help my daughter . . . if you want to help my entire family, you Marins will stay away from us." He jabbed a finger at Lucy. "Leave my grandson alone. Don't drag him into your mess, too." He turned on Fleur. "For two generations now, your family has done its best to destroy mine. I know deep in my heart that my daughter is lying in that room because of you people."

Fleur's peripheral vision picked up movement, and she turned to see Manon hurrying to their side. "Please, *Granpè*. Let them go. There's no need to offend Ms. Marin."

Alcide's eyes flashed wide in indignation as his lips pulled into a snarl. He stretched to his full height and looked down on Fleur in disgust. "Oh, I certainly wouldn't want to offend the fine Ms. Marin now, would I?" He made a show of doing a bow and scrape. "I do apologize if you feel in the least bit slighted by my fight to save my child's life."

Manon flashed them a warning look. *Hold your tongues, and go.* It seemed good advice to Fleur, and she tugged Lucy over to the facing elevator.

"Oh, no, you don't." Alcide moved with surprising agility for a man his age, positioning himself between Fleur and the elevator button.

One of the nursing staff noticed their confrontation and started down the hall in their direction. "Is everything all right here?" she called. Her white, molded foam nurse's slippers muffled the sound of her determined steps, but she arrived at their side in a flash. She stationed herself within arm's reach of both Alcide and Fleur. "I asked if everything is all right here."

A glimpse into the nurse's eyes told Fleur this woman was both a person capable of near infinite empathy and someone with whom it would be best not to trifle. "Yes," Fleur said, "Everything's fine. I apologize for the disturbance." She cast a glance at Manon. "My daughter and I were just leaving."

The nurse scanned their faces. "Okay, then. You ladies can catch the next car." She focused on Alcide. "Excuse me." She reached behind him and pressed the down button. Turning to Manon, she asked, "Would you like to help me escort your grandfather to your mother's room?"

"Yes," Manon said, nodding. She touched Alcide's arm. "*Granpè?*"

Alcide would not be moved. He stood stock-still, glaring at Fleur. "You Marins are a cancer on my family. Always have been. Always will be."

"You know Mama wants to put history behind us."

"History?" He pounded his fist into his chest. "History? Her mother murdered your mama's mother."

"Mr. Perrault," the nurse said, her tone a warning.

"Mr. Simeon," he replied without taking his eyes off Fleur.

"Yes, I apologize. Mr. Simeon," the nurse said. "I'm sorry, but I do have to ask you to come with me, or I'll need to call security."

Alcide burst out in a bitter laugh. "You're going to call security on me"—he pointed at Fleur—"to protect her?"

Fleur heard a bing behind her and turned to see the doors had opened. She guided Lucy into the elevator first, then stepped in after her.

Alcide stepped toward the elevator, catching the door so that it couldn't close. He fixed Fleur with his gaze. "Maybe," his voice came out in a low hiss, "you are the *good* kind of witch. The kind who wouldn't intentionally harm my family." Manon appeared behind him, trying to tug him away, but he shrugged her off. "Maybe you aren't your parents, but the life you're living was built on your parents' actions. I'm warning you. Stay the hell away from my family."

The nurse came and took his arm. An orderly had joined her. "Mr. Simeon, I must insist."

He turned back to face her. "All right," he said, walking away. "All right. I've said what I had to say. I'm done."

The elevator doors started to close. Fleur broke. Hot tears flooded her eyes.

Manon dove between the closing doors and joined them as the elevator began to buzz. "I'm so sorry," she said. "I'm sorry he hurt your feelings."

Fleur wiped the tears from her eyes. "Oh, *ma chère*, I'm not crying because your grandfather hurt my feelings. I'm crying because everything he said was true."

Manon's face lit up in surprise. She stood there, seemingly struck dumb, until the elevator reached the lobby.

The doors opened. "Excuse us, dear." Fleur grasped Lucy's hand and led her around Manon and out of the elevator.

"Ms. Marin," Manon called out, causing Fleur to turn back. "Thank you for the scarf," she said. "It's a lovely, thoughtful gift."

Fleur heard a bing, and the doors closed between them.

TWENTY-THREE

The tombs of Précieux Sang Cemetery took on a golden sheen as the day drew to its close, with the sun making a last, brilliant stand in the western sky. Evangeline stretched out on the oblong patch of lawn that lay a yard or so behind the now locked gate. She propped herself up on her elbows, indulging in the animal pleasure of the cool grass beneath her calves and the warmth of the fugitive light on her face.

Life gave no guarantee that she'd see the sun rise again. What better place to remember that than here? Of course, she hadn't needed any reminders of her mortality of late. Seemed that every damned day delivered another flashing neon arrow pointing to the end. Take this trial, for example. Evangeline had called for a witch's judgment without really understanding what she'd set in motion.

She'd learned a few moments earlier that, as the witch who'd called for judgment against Celestin, it would fall to her to offer the first testimony. After her testimony, those present would seek a consensus to decide if her claim had merit or had been brought frivolously or out of malice against the accused. It turned out that since Evangeline had accused Celestin of multiple capital offenses, Evangeline could herself be put to death if she couldn't back up her claims.

The taking of a consensus was a prerequisite, but Fleur had assured her she need not sweat the outcome. There had been no shortage of witnesses to the massacre Celestin had carried out at the ball intended to memorialize him. In a warped way, it had worked as originally intended. Nobody was ever going to forget Celestin or his ball. Still, she needed to make a habit of asking more questions, especially in situations related to witchcraft, before diving in.

Evangeline wished she hadn't refused Lincoln's offer to accompany her, but the truth was, Bonnes Nouvelles was barely holding on. She needed someone she could count on to cover for her, so she'd left the club in Lincoln and Wiley's care.

She'd only taken a cursory look at the books, but that was enough to show her Hugo had been keeping the place afloat with cash from his own pocket. It would take her a while to pay him back. By all rights, she should offer to make him a partner, but she couldn't. God knows she loved the boy from the bottom of her heart, but she didn't want to be in business with him. Halloween was only three weeks out, and Bourbon would soon be bursting at the seams with revelers. A good share of the purse Halloween night wouldn't put Bonnes Nouvelles into the black, but it might at least pull it back from candy apple red into burgundy. Once the club was back in kilter, she'd find some way to start paying Hugo back, match the same interest she had been paying—no, that Hugo had been paying—the bank.

If she needed Lincoln, though, he'd know and he'd come. He'd promised, and that was good enough. That he wasn't already at her side reassured her she'd see the other side of this. Besides, the eagerness of the fifty to sixty witches milling about, waiting to give testimony about Celestin, was palpable.

Last night, it had seemed too dangerous to dangle a bounty of poisoned magic under Fleur's nose. It had seemed a much better idea to bring Celestin to face a fair judgment as delivered by his peers. She'd assumed they would sense what she had—the toxicity of the magic held by Celestin's corpse—and they would choose to dispel it, as the Chanticleer Coven had been tricked into believing it had done the day of Celestin's funeral. Dispel the magic, send Celestin off to whatever hereafter a man like that earned himself, and dump the body into the Marin family vault. Seal it up and call it a day.

But Evangeline should've known better. She had learned that according to the customs of the witches of New Orleans, if those gathered voted to hold Celestin responsible for his crimes, they would be able to carve the corpse up into pieces to pass out like party favors that could be used to augment the failing magic of those he'd harmed.

Until the witches had convened, Evangeline had believed that, regardless of what happened, Celestin would be freed from the torment of being imprisoned in his desiccating corpse. Now she understood that keeping Celestin's spirit bound to his body would help the relics maintain their charge. Perhaps even for generations. Celestin could be freed from his flesh prison until the first cut was made. After that first cut, it would be too late. No, now that she understood the lay of the land, Evangeline had no doubt as to what the verdict would be. What was left of Celestin would leave this cemetery wrapped in brown butcher paper, a portion of his psyche still attached to each relic. She'd been dealing with witches long enough to know that the single commodity rarer than justice in their community was mercy.

Last night, with Celestin doing all he could to rile her, she would've been fine with this fate. Today, Evangeline surprised herself by wanting to grant the old bastard leniency.

Evangeline could tell just by looking at them that most of the witches gathered had been raised in the golden fields of privilege. Regardless of how polite this type was to your face, they'd cut out your heart with a butter knife to preserve their crumbling position. If enough of them thought there'd be more to gain from coming after her than after Celestin, she was sure this preliminary consensus, this thing she didn't need to sweat, could and would swing like a heavy door against her.

Many of the witches she'd encountered over the years believed themselves to be above such petty ideas as good and evil. This bunch might not be quite so haughty, but they did seem to believe themselves immune to the darkness carried by the relics they coveted. Evangeline couldn't help but wonder if the force that delivered Celestin to her had known the seeds of evil could be spread with the ease of puffing on the head of a dandelion.

Many of those present couldn't even be bothered to hide their enthusiasm. Evangeline had witnessed one unfamiliar, chinless old man, whom Fleur had addressed as Mitch, standing over Celestin and salivating, literally drooling. He'd removed his glasses, accentuating his resemblance to a beige turtle, and walked his watery blue eyes over the corpse as if inventorying the prime cuts and ranking them in order of his preference. That sight was what had sent Evangeline rushing over to this welcoming patch of grass. She couldn't handle these freaks.

Evangeline closed her eyes, shutting out the radiance, and focused on the fading indigo negative the light had left behind.

"They don't believe you." Evangeline jolted as Fleur circled around her. "They're not buying your talk of a mysterious presence handing Celestin over to you gift-wrapped, but then you probably already sensed that."

Evangeline nodded an acknowledgment, but otherwise didn't budge.

"The night of the massacre," Fleur began, her tone cautious, "there were witnesses, I'm afraid, to your . . . transition."

Transition. Fleur was trying to be sensitive, but the word came out sounding like euphemism for a shameful, dirty act.

"And?" Evangeline's own shame bubbled up as anger.

"And some . . ." Fleur paused, seeming to wonder if it were wise to continue. She shrugged. "Some are conjecturing that there was a falling out between Celestin and your mother's sister witches. That, in fact, you've been in league with them all along."

"They're dead," Evangeline said, realizing that a part of her did, in fact, mourn the loss. These women had been her last connection to the mother she'd never really known. In an odd way, it felt like being orphaned all over again.

"The same coterie finds that fact a bit too convenient to accept at face value."

"Everything I've said is true."

"Yes, *ma chère*," Fleur sounded tired—no, defeated. "I know that, but even this dull bunch can tell you haven't shared all. Suffice it to say, you should watch your step for the next little while. Others certainly will be." Her lips twisted into a sad smile. "If only our deliverer had been Daniel, as Astrid seemed to believe. It was only after finding nothing but ashes where his portrait had been that I realized how fond I'd grown of him."

"I'm sorry about Daniel," Evangeline said, feeling a twinge of grief herself. "I'm sorry about all of this." Even though Fleur treated her with every kindness, walking her through the maze of traditions and arcane rules, Evangeline suspected that Fleur couldn't help but resent her for snatching away the abundance of magic Celestin offered. Had Evangeline chosen differently, Lucy could've lived to a ripe old age without Fleur having to constantly scramble to collect another source of power before the last gave out. But magic that dark . . . Fleur had to know on some level that the seething reservoir would draw her in and drown anything decent in her.

Fleur had positioned herself between Evangeline and the setting sun, eclipsing the light.

"Sorry about all what?" Evangeline heard Hugo ask. He drew up alongside her, giving her shoulder a squeeze, and she placed her hand over his. Always on her side, he was, even though he had to see her choice—to make what could have remained his family's private business a public spectacle—foolish, perhaps even selfish.

Evangeline lifted her gaze to meet Fleur's eyes, which telegraphed caution. Seemed she wasn't ready to share her secret with her nephew. Maybe she was worried that the more who knew the truth, the easier it would be for Lucy to learn, or perhaps there was another reason for her reticence. Either way, soon she wouldn't have a choice. But for now, it *was* her choice.

"For this parody of a trial," Evangeline said. "For rubbing your family's noses in Celestin's dirt."

"I think," Fleur said, "you mean what's left of our family. Celestin killed my brother and my nephew without remorse because it was expedient for him to do so. Because he needed them to die so that he could capture the magic in *The Book of the Unwinding*. I was next on his list. I wouldn't be standing before you now if I hadn't unintentionally stoked his inflated ego. I'm sure he only granted me . . . and Lucy, too . . . a temporary reprieve because he thought my rebellion against Gabriel Prosper reflected well on him. Then there's Nicholas. He would've killed him the night of the ball, too. Or eventually. That's a given. But few could know better than you how Celestin destroyed Nicholas without ever laying a finger on him."

Hugo squatted beside her, examining the grass, calculating, Evangeline surmised, the damage it could do to his light gray pants. He plopped down on his seat. "Celestin wanted me dead, too, but I didn't even merit the personal touch." He reached into his jacket pocket and pulled out a flask. "He delegated my murder to those crazy crones. If you hadn't flown my sweet pink cheeks out of that hall, I'd be dead for sure." This was as close as she'd ever heard Hugo come to expressing gratitude for anything . . . to anyone. He opened the flask and held it out to her. She sat up and accepted it, her fingers brushing his. That simple touch finally toppled the levee that had held back her unspoken shame. Guilt swirled in all around her, almost causing her to drop the drink.

She owed him the truth she'd been hiding from him, the truth that had been gnawing at her gut for months. She spat it out. "They wanted me to kill you." She risked a quick glance to see how he took the news. He looked sad. Tired. But not in the least bit shocked.

"Yeah. I don't speak bird, but I kind of picked up on that." He wagged his finger at the flask. "Go on. Doctor's orders."

She raised the flask, then lowered it. There was a bit more truth she had to share. "For a moment, I . . ."

"Got that bit, too. But you didn't. You wouldn't. Now drink."

She took a swig, nearly choking it back up. Nothing like straight vodka served body temperature.

"You did the right thing," Fleur said. There was a slight tugging on Evangeline's empathic power. Fleur was vying for her attention, inviting her to divine the meaning behind her words. She wanted Evangeline to know that she understood and approved of her choice.

"I'm not sure what I would have done in your shoes."

Another coded message. A thank-you. An acknowledgment that Fleur knew exactly what she would have done. She would have risked it. Laid claim to the full pool of blood magic, consequences be damned. She was grateful that Evangeline spared her this trespass.

"Celestin committed many crimes," Fleur said, closing the sympathetic channel she'd opened between them. "Now he'll face a trial by a jury of his peers."

"More like a jury of vultures," Evangeline said. "Do you even recognize half of these people?"

"Half, yes. They either attended Celestin's ball or had loved ones who died there. These are the witches who've recovered enough to be angry, but they're only the tip of the iceberg. If everyone left bereaved by that night showed up, the walls of this cemetery would strain and burst. Those who've come with hope of profiting off the pain of others will be sorted out in short order. Not to worry."

Hugo signaled with a wave that Evangeline should return the flask. She handed it over, and he offered it to Fleur, who refused it with a shake of the head. "Your loss, *chère Tatie*," he said, then took a long draught, shaking his head and wiping his lips with the back of his hand. He offered the drink to Evangeline again. "Awful at any speed, but no way I'm facing this unfortified."

Evangeline sat up and accepted the flask. She took a drink. It wasn't so bad now that she knew what to expect. She hoped that precept would apply to the rest of this ordeal. "I'm sorry," Evangeline said, "but given that throwing this fete might have killed me, I would like to understand the details."

Fleur smiled. "You're learning. Good." Her gaze rose, fixing on a point behind Evangeline. Evangeline glanced back to see Fleur was studying the witches awaiting them. "My guess is that a good twenty of those fine people have no standing in this case."

"Standing?"

"They," Hugo said, "weren't directly affected by Celestin's actions. If they weren't affected, they don't have the right to be here. They're tourists. Hangers-on hoping to walk away with a relic."

"That's why you'll demand that all who claim to have standing undergo the ordeal of *les Dents de la Vérité*."

"Really," Evangeline said, fighting back a laugh. "The Teeth of Truth?"

"Yes," Fleur said, her cautious tone telling Evangeline that she'd decided to sidestep, if not disregard, Evangeline's derision. "Think of it as New Orleans's take on Rome's *Bocca della Verità*." Fleur seemed to consider this an adequate explanation. She stood there, staring down at Evangeline, waiting for a lightning bolt of understanding to strike. Evangeline's blank expression must have finally signaled that no such flash would arrive.

"Well, there's no practical reason you would have heard of it," Fleur said, taking obvious pains not to make Evangeline feel stupid. Her attempt at tact made Evangeline's embarrassment burn even hotter. In a flash, Evangeline realized that there was a whole wide world out there, but every breath she'd ever taken had been Louisiana air.

"The *Bocca* is an old stone disk engraved with a vicious-looking face." Fleur paused, perhaps to give Evangeline the chance to envision the item. "A preposterous, ugly bit of classical masonry, really." Another pause. This one, Evangeline intuited, to help her internalize the appropriate degree of reverence with which she should speak of this carving—a lesser work whose craftsman's name had not survived the ages, but still, an object of which any member of the Marins' caste should have at least a passing awareness. "Experts posit that it started out with an entirely mundane purpose. Perhaps a drain cover." A bit of trivia Evangeline could later employ like a watchword or secret handshake to mark herself as a member of polite society. Fleur, Evangeline realized, was offering her expertly curated access to what Fleur considered a basic cultural signifier. "As the stone's original purpose was forgotten, a superstition grew up around it. People came to believe that it would bite off a liar's hand."

It seemed that Fleur had decided to take Evangeline under her wing. Was she attempting to make amends or taking pity on a girl who might have been so much more if she'd had a better start in life? Both thoughts pissed Evangeline off. Both thoughts made her like Fleur even more. In equal measure. Hell. It was always complicated with these people. She'd chew on that later. For now, she needed Fleur's guidance, if not about which fork to use, then for certain how to make it through an evening of witch politics. "It's only a superstition, though, right? The biting part, that is."

"Yes. At least it appears to have been now, but here in Précieux Sang, it's much more than that. There's a spirit of place here, a guardian.

You may have already sensed it. Maybe even noticed a shadow flitting past in your peripheral vision."

Evangeline felt a shiver up her spine, and her skin prickled up into gooseflesh. "Not so much," she said. "I would've scaled the gate if I had."

"Then he must like you." She pointed east. "There's a tomb, a few rows over that way, but it isn't really a tomb at all. No remains have ever been placed in it. It's the spirit's abode."

"The marble seal on the front is broken," Hugo said, rising. "There's a hole." He formed parentheses with his hands. "About this big."

"Those who wish to validate their standing in the case against Celestin will have to reach their hands into the grave."

"But nothing is gonna happen, right? It's just a harmless dare."

"Nope," Hugo snapped his teeth, then offered her his hand. She took it more to please him than out of any need for reassurance.

"It's a rare practice," Fleur said, her tone far too even, too reasonable to be speaking of a flesh-eating demon, "but so are these trials. When enough time passes between uses of the tomb, the truth is sometimes forgotten—or viewed as nothing more than an old witches' tale intended to scare children. Over the years, a few foolish hangers-on have lost a finger or two to the perspicacious elemental. Actual witches, overconfident in their ability to obfuscate or in their certainty that the indwelling spirit is a bluff, have lost hands. Some have even lost arms."

"Argh," Hugo cried out, stumbling forward and mimicking the scene Fleur had just described.

"Cute," Evangeline said.

Fleur watched on, nonplussed. "You do realize he only behaves like a twelve-year-old when you're around."

"I've always suspected as much." Evangeline's eyes wandered east, in the direction of the guardian's tomb, and she tried to guess which vault played host to the entity. As her curiosity reached out, the demon caught hold of it, infiltrating her mind and twisting her empathy to its own purposes. Evangeline gasped out a breath of icy air.

Loneliness. Hopelessness. Hunger. So very hungry.

She stumbled backward, but Fleur's hand shot out and grabbed her by the wrist, preventing a fall. For several moments, Evangeline struggled to catch her breath, her lungs feeling like they'd been filled with sharp ice crystals. "It's one of those things you said Daniel described," she said, gasping out the last of the frozen, sepulchral air. "One of the hungry shadows."

Fleur handed her over to Hugo and then circled around them, taking a few strides in the direction of the tomb. She lowered her head and held her hands out, palms forward. Her hands began to tremble, the shudder working its way through the whole of her body. She spun back toward them, wrapping her arms around herself. "Let's do keep this to ourselves. For now, at least." Fleur pinned her with her gaze until Evangeline answered with a nod. "Hugo?" Fleur said in a commanding voice.

"Sure," he said, though he sounded anything but certain. "Whatever you say, *Tatie* dearest."

"Good," Fleur said, turning on her heel. "We should get back to the others now." She began walking away, then stopped to look back at Hugo. "Be a gentleman for once and escort Evangeline, won't you?"

Fleur carried on before them as Hugo made an exaggerated show of bowing, then offering her his arm. "Madame."

Evangeline wrapped her arm through his, but held him back. "How could you know for sure? That I wouldn't hurt you? I wasn't in control. Not by a far cry."

"Simple. I knew I was safe, because I know you." He patted her arm. "Come on, crow girl. Don't want to keep the buzzards waiting."

TWENTY-FOUR

Fleur had come home from her confrontation with Alcide to find the Twins waiting for her, holding a garishly ornate yet official summons. A summons to the trial of the father she'd returned to New Orleans to bury.

Now she was back in the same cemetery where she'd participated in Celestin's entombment, doing her best to maintain the appearance of sangfroid, even though she was shaking apart on the inside. Fleur kept reaching out for an arm that wasn't there. Eli lacked either the stomach to face this farce or the heart to face her. She hoped it was the former, feared it was the latter, but would survive either way.

It was long past time to learn to stand on her own anyway.

It tormented her to know she'd come so close to a permanent, or at least near-permanent solution, only to see it snatched away. If she could've gotten her hands on Celestin, she would have stuffed the bastard's conscious corpse into the same priest hole where he'd hidden Vincent's body. Just desserts if ever just desserts had been served. She could've kept him whole, with his despicable psyche sealed up tight in his body. She could've plugged the spell that protected Lucy directly into that current, and Lucy might have been able to live out a full life, without ever knowing what her mother had done for her.

Still, Fleur couldn't find even an ounce of anger against the woman who'd stolen this chance. Evangeline Caissy was a good, kind person—good enough and kind enough to want to save Fleur from herself. But Evangeline was a babe in the woods when it came to magic. If Evangeline understood anything about resurrection spells, she would know that it was already far too late to save Fleur.

But what was done was done. One part of Fleur's mind now busied itself with calculating her next best move. Another part, perhaps even the part Evangeline had hoped to save, hid its eyes as Fleur prepared to take part in the desecration of her father's body. A third justified her actions. If Fleur could walk out of here with a powerful enough relic, she could buy herself and Lucy time. A lot of time. The right relic, maybe decades. Fleur was prepared to fight for the center of Celestin's consciousness. She'd walk away with his head or die trying.

Today had already started off badly, and after one hell of a night. Now she had to parse Evangeline's latest discovery. As she passed the row of the guardian's tomb, she stopped for a moment to study it from what she hoped was a safe distance. The entity Evangeline had sensed was not the familiar genius loci of Précieux Sang Cemetery. No, this new spirit must have devoured the cemetery's guardian. That there existed an unknown, formidable, and undoubtedly malevolent personage capable of delivering Celestin into Evangeline's hands was a disquieting enough proposition, but now, an even more unsettling concern began to take root in her thoughts. If Evangeline was correct that this being was one of the shadows poor Daniel had spoken of, how had a creature of the Dreaming Road found its way into the common world? Had it piggy-backed a ride with Alice? That would be better than what Fleur feared.

Unable to rely on either Lisette or Daniel for guidance on the seven gates, Fleur had made a desperate move—she'd turned the research over to Lucy, whom she'd left safe at home. She'd hoped it would help keep

Lucy occupied with something other than her ongoing, single-sided argument with an absent Remy. No such luck. Lucy returned with a quick, if cursory, report conveyed, in typical teenager fashion, over a series of texts: *Gates of Guinee. Portals to the underworld—or whatever. Seven. Scattered around NOLA. Probably in cemeteries, because dead. Right?*

The empty tomb with the gaping hole. Fleur remembered her parents pointing it out to her thirty years ago. From her current vantage point, it appeared unchanged, though those around it had weathered despite preservation efforts. Could one of the gates be here in Précieux Sang? Could the guardian of the cemetery have been here to protect it? If the guardian had been bested, what did that mean for the gate?

That would be a concern for later. One disaster at a time. She'd get through this, get what she needed, and then it would be time to dig deeper.

Hugo and Evangeline drew up beside her. Ahead of them lay a sea of avaricious eyes that Fleur could almost imagine glinting red in the dying light. "We'll forgo the ordeal." She nodded toward the tomb. "My instincts tell me that whatever has set up housekeeping in there will bite off anything put through the opening."

"Fine by me," Evangeline said, glancing at the tomb. She then dashed past the row, dragging a straggling Hugo forward. Fleur followed a few feet behind them.

As Fleur drew closer to the congregants, she began to pick up on grumblings and random bits of mumbled conversation.

"Still swanning about, like their time is more valuable than ours."

"Like they're some kind of royalty."

That, Fleur felt, was unfair. No family had ever faced such a shame in the history of New Orleans magic. She and Hugo had come forward, agreeing to speak out against Celestin's crimes, to air every last bit of Marin dirty laundry if necessary. The least these people could do in return was let them take their time.

"Ask me, all the Marins should have to stand. They're all guilty. One way or another." Fleur feared there was more than a grain of truth to this.

The gathering fell silent as they drew near.

Nicholas should be here. He could put a stop to this. Interesting. This thought had reached her not through her ears, but as a direct touch to her mind. She traced the thought to its origin, though she should have guessed. The Twins, dressed in identical gray jumpsuits, stood at the center of the gathering, one at the head of the bier that held Celestin, the other at its foot. Celestin had always referred to the pair as *les Fidèles*, and he'd been right to do so. They'd be Marin loyalists to the end, even if alliances within the family shifted daily. They'd come into the Chanticleer Coven under Nicholas, the usurper. Still, they honored the dethroned Celestin. Such devotion must be exhausting. Fleur realized she hadn't picked up on their thought at random. They'd projected it to her.

They were right on both counts. Nicholas should be here, and he could probably stop this trial from happening. Even as the deposed head of the vestigial Chanticleer Coven, Nicholas still held influence in this community. That was the exact reason Fleur hadn't alerted him, claiming she was having more trouble connecting with him than she'd thought she would—the same lie she'd told the police when she'd gone to ID Astrid's body.

In truth, Fleur couldn't take the chance that he might choose to stop the trial. Nicholas might find a different solution to her problem, and then again, he might not. Maybe Nathalie would be able to put a bandage on the issue, or maybe she'd refuse once she understood what Fleur had done to bring Lucy back. With some things, Fleur was willing to take calculated risks, but not with Lucy's life. Besides, what she wanted to take from Celestin, a loving grandfather would have offered of his own free will. Celestin had never given anyone anything for free.

She scanned the faces of those staring at her. Each stepped back as they felt the weight of her gaze land on them. Just as she'd suggested to Evangeline, a third of the people awaiting the proceedings had no business being here. The young fellow outside the gate, reed thin and half spooked, was no kind of sergeant-at-arms. If the Great Wall of Jeanette, as Hugo had called their former sergeant-at-arms, were still alive, these pretenders would've never made it past the gate, but Jeanette was one of the fallen . . . no, one of those who'd been slaughtered by Celestin's hand.

With an impotent boy in the role of enforcer, it looked like it was up to Fleur to handle things. A task that had become more difficult now that they could not use the usual test. The first step would be to eliminate competition. She'd long ago mastered the use of soft influence to get people to perform as she desired, but soft influence took time. Good thing she'd also perfected her strong-arm twist.

Stalk the herd. Take out the weakest first. Spook the rest, and let them peel off on their own.

Her eyes fell on two young women who looked to be no more than a year or two older than Lucy, their hair dyed in an amateur violet and magenta ombre. Black lipstick. Too much eyeliner, and black peacoats over black T-shirts and ripped jeans. A pound each of silver jewelry on them, and not an ounce of real witch between them. How had they even learned of this gathering?

Fleur decided to start with these two, the easiest marks, then pick her way through the others who lacked standing. As she approached them, she caught wind of lavender, heavy-handed patchouli, and, bless them, mugwort—the ingredients of the basic protection oil with which they'd anointed themselves. Fleur couldn't help but smile at their naiveté, thinking that their homemade perfume could protect them even from the degraded, some close to toothless, real witches gathered there. She pushed through to them. "The gentleman at the gate will let you out."

"Nicholas Marin sent us," the shorter of the two said with bravado, then puffed up with satisfaction like she'd uttered her first successful banishing incantation.

"Don't be absurd," Fleur said, unable to repress a laugh. The girls' attempt at chicanery was the first amusement Fleur had enjoyed in weeks. The very thought that Nicholas would even notice these two, let alone deputize them. "Leave."

They regarded each other, and Fleur knew they were contemplating standing up to her. On any given day, Fleur loved encountering strong, determined young women, even a brash duo like these two. This, however, was far from one of those given days. "Go," she commanded. "I won't repeat myself." She lifted her hand and let the tiniest of sparks—channeled static electricity—shoot at them. No chance it could harm them, but it had the desired effect nonetheless. The taller girl, the shakier of the two, grabbed the other's arm and dragged her toward the gate.

"Open it for them," Fleur called out to the gutless sergeant-at-arms, but he didn't make a move. He was craning his neck, gaping down the road at something the stone wall prevented Fleur from seeing. He gave a comedic yelp and stumbled backward. Fleur sensed he was about to abandon his post, and sure enough, he darted away in the opposite direction of whatever had given him a fright.

"Hugo," Fleur called and motioned for him to join her at the gate. Evangeline grasped his arm, trying to hold him back, but he patted her hand, signaling for her to release him. Instead, she went ahead of him, grasping his hand in hers.

A grating, clanging sound rang out from every corner of the park.

Fleur turned her face toward the guardian's tomb, then realized it stood silent. The assault came from outside. The bars of the cemetery's eastern gate were bending, the lock snapping as the gate's sides curled back.

The witches crowded together in the cemetery's center, unintentionally forming a protective barrier around the very man they'd come to prosecute. Irony one. Irony two—the young women Fleur had tried to intimidate into leaving now clung to her for protection, preventing her from reaching the gate. Poor fools mistook her for the most powerful witch there. Not even in the top twelve, not with nearly every volt of power she had dedicated to Lucy. If Fleur could've passed the pair on to Evangeline, she would have, but Evangeline and Hugo stood frozen by the growing hole in the eastern wall. Fleur wrapped an arm around each quivering girl.

The witches, the real witches, might or might not be able to fend for themselves, but her Goth duo didn't stand a chance. She turned the girls toward the western gate, hoping to escort them to safety, but on the far side of the long allée that bisected the cemetery, the western gate, too, was shaking, snapping, and curling backward. The sound of straining and breaking bars echoing off the tombs testified that the northern and southern gates were also falling.

Fleur realized she'd have to choose. She could transport the girls away from here. Not far enough to guarantee their safety, perhaps, but far enough to give them a fighting chance. Still, doing so might mean she'd lose her chance to save her own girl. A hand on her back. She looked over her shoulder to find that the Twins had deserted Celestin and come to her defense. Nice to know she rated higher in their eyes than her murderous father. "Here," she said, shoving the sniveling duo at them. "One for each of you." She was on the verge of ordering the Twins to keep the girls safe, but perhaps that wouldn't be possible. She couldn't get a clear read on the assaulting force, though the strands of its power seemed to intertwine with those of Précieux Sang's new resident. The two were perhaps related in source, though intuition told Fleur they weren't the same. She couldn't be certain. The only thing clear to her was that whatever was coming was big and full of power, more power than she'd ever encountered before. "Do what you can," she called to the

Twins, and sent them back toward the cringing circle that surrounded Celestin. Fleur ran to Hugo's side, amazed to see there was no fear in his eyes. He was beaming with pride, and Evangeline stood beside him, stunned with wonder.

Alice appeared before the open gates, her unshod feet hovering above the ground. A crackling cloud of silver lightning encircled her.

Horrifying. Glorious. The two words chimed in unison in Fleur's mind. Fleur blinked, unable to believe her eyes as the woman she'd long believed to be her niece stepped down to the earth as if she were descending an ordinary set of stairs.

"Now that's how to make an entrance, little sis," Hugo said, but Alice allowed him only a casual glance as she passed.

Fleur struggled to find her voice. "Alice, dear," she finally choked out. "I thought we'd agreed that you shouldn't be party to this. Not after all you've been through. Let us handle this."

"I changed my mind," Alice said, the words coming out in a discordant singsong.

"Please," Fleur said, nodding at Hugo. "Let your brother take you home." Alice continued, passing through Fleur's words as if she hadn't even heard them. Or perhaps they were simply of no consequence to her. "Lucy will be out of her mind with worry when she discovers you're missing."

"Lucy will be fine," Alice said without looking at her, answering a worry Fleur hadn't yet allowed herself to acknowledge. "*Everyone* here will be fine," she said, her voice cold, distant. "As long as they stay out of my way."

Alice stopped by the Twins and focused on the wards Fleur had given them. "You don't want this," Alice said, addressing the young women. "You don't want any of this." Alice glanced back at the wreckage she'd made of the gate. "Two blocks south. You'll encounter a woman waiting in a black SUV. Tell her I said to take you home. Tell her I don't need saving. Not anymore. No matter what she thinks she knows about me." In a flash, the young women were suddenly standing outside the cemetery on the far side of the gate's twisted remains, staring in at them with wide, shocked eyes. "Tell them to leave, Hugo."

Hugo lunged at the opening. "Boo." The pair grasped each other's hands like schoolgirls and took off running. The cemetery went so silent Fleur's ears could follow the sound of the girls' receding footfalls to the end of the block.

With a wave of her hand, Alice parted the crowd, leaving her a clear path to where Celestin lay. "Bring me the blade," she commanded.

No one moved. No one spoke. Still, a psychic clamor rose up from the crowd—even from those who'd come determined to find Celestin worthy of punishment.

"The Caissy woman hasn't even taken first oath," Mitch, the great lemming-in-chief, challenged Alice. Mitch considered himself a leader, which was only true if you considered leadership to be following the sentiment of the majority.

"That won't be necessary," she said without even looking at him. "Celestin is guilty."

"It is necessary," Mitch responded, coming forward, all the while taking a silent survey to make sure he'd have backup. "It's procedure. This community needs healing. We deserve our chance to air our grievances against this man."

Alice turned to him and laughed. "To hell with your grievances and procedure. Your procedure is nothing more than a way for you to absolve your conscience. To claim that justice has been done, even though you have no intention of leaving here without a scrap of Celestin's flesh. I have no need of that."

"We all have suffered at your grandfather's hands—"

"Father," Alice said, the fire in her voice having been exchanged for cold steel. "Celestin was my father."

A wave of shocked whispers rippled through the ensemble.

Alice looked the crowd over. "It's true. Some of you have suffered great loss because of Celestin. But you," she said, focusing on Mitch as her lip curled up in disgust. "Your great wound is nothing more than a paper cut. For you, this is no more than a bit of theater and a chance to walk away with a prize." She raised her right hand, and a sound like a gong rang out from every direction. The hilt of the athame their community had consecrated for the collection of relics shot into her hand. "Stop playing the victim, Mitch. And stop playing the hero, too." She held the knife up before her eyes and blew on it, her breath creating a discordant whistle as blade split air. She lifted the athame with both hands over her head, the point of the blade aimed at Celestin's chest. "What'll it be? Light or dark?"

"Let me do it." Evangeline rushed forward and laid a hand on Alice's shoulder. Alice hesitated, lowering the blade and resting it on the bier beside Celestin. "I don't mind," Evangeline said as Alice turned to face her. "What does it matter, really? Let's give them their damned pomp and circumstance, but don't take this all on yourself. You've been through so much." Evangeline dared to lay her hand on Alice's cheek. "We'll break the bond on him first, though, okay?" she said, nodding in encouragement. "I know he's a miserable bastard, sweetie, and he deserves the worst kind of punishment, but let's send him on. Let a greater power than us be his judge."

Alice's gaze softened, causing Fleur to feel a twinge of panic. Evangeline was right—Alice should not be the one to wield the athame—but what if she convinced Alice to release Celestin? If the bond connecting him to his body were broken, Fleur would leave here not much better than empty-handed.

"It's only," Evangeline continued, "I've done things in the heat of anger, things I'm not proud of, and I'm afraid you may not be thinking clearly right now. That when you get back to yourself, you may regret having done this."

For a moment Fleur thought Alice might fall into Evangeline's arms, but Alice stiffened, and her eyes lost the fleeting spark of warmth Evangeline's touch had brought to them. "There is no *me* for me to go back to. Celestin saw to that." Alice's eyes flitted around the crowd as if she were searching out a particular face. Nicholas, no doubt—her ever-absent, putative father. "Nicholas, too, in his own way."

Fleur knew the shortest line between herself and what she needed was Alice's rage. She should keep still, let Alice do what she seemed determined to do, but guilt, stone by stone, pressed on Fleur's heart, crushing her. She struggled to catch her breath. "And I did too, in my own way," she said, coming forward. Alice's eyes darted to her. "Through willful ignorance." Fleur drew closer. She could feel the air around Alice vibrating from a good six feet away. "Through inaction. Through being so caught up in my own life that I never gave my little sister more than a passing thought. Celestin's actions were monstrous. You may rightly find Nicholas's abandonment unforgivable. But I'm just as guilty of abandoning you. While I told myself Nicholas was seeing to it that you got the care you needed, I never once came to make sure of that. If I had, I might've realized you didn't belong in that institution. Saying I'm sorry could never even begin to make up for the ways I've let you down."

"Maybe not," Alice said, her expression impassive. "Though pulling me out of hell was a very good place to start." Alice turned away from her and grasped the athame. "You were saying, Mitch, that you've suffered at my father's hands?"

He coughed, already having slipped back into the ensemble. "Yes," he said. Then, with more surety, "Yes. We all have to some degree, even if you choose to belittle the pain of some."

Alice made two quick slices with the blade, severing Celestin's hands from his body. Fleur choked back bile, realizing that there was no going back now. Even though she, too, wanted this, her father's psyche would now be trapped in his dismembered body for years, for decades, perhaps even until the end of magic. What was done to any part of him would be felt throughout the whole of him.

"Here." Alice snapped up Celestin's right hand in her left and flung it at Mitch, who fell back, afraid, then darted forward to claim his bounty before the others could reach it. Alice took hold of his left hand and tossed it up into the air, where it burst into flame. The fire burned until his flesh and bone had both disintegrated into an ash that a conjured wind caught and scattered, coating all present with the residue. "No more hands," Alice said, her voice sounding so much like it had when she was a tiny girl, "no more suffering." She held the hilt of the blade out to Fleur. "Take what you need," she said, speaking up over the growing rumblings about Alice's waste of a fine relic. Alice's eyes locked with her own. *For Lucy.* These words had been sent silently, and Fleur sensed Alice had even encrypted the message so that no one else could hear.

Fleur accepted the knife, but turned to watch as this stranger, her sister, passed—this time without the aid of magic—through the gates to which she'd laid waste.

TWENTY-FIVE

Astrid's physical form had died years ago by the standards of the common world, but eons ago by her own. Now she wore Babau Jean like a comfortable sweater, passing with ease between the Dreaming Road and the common world. She'd worried the transition would prove awkward, that her return to the common world would be greeted by a steep learning curve, but she found Jean well broken in, even happy to have a new inhabitant, a new master. The creature had spent years trying to buck his former rider, but unlike Celestin, Astrid had asked permission, not forced Jean to accept her.

The creature possessed far greater physical strength than Astrid's mortal body ever had, and his senses were far superior to those she'd known in normal life. Looking through the eyes of Babau Jean, she observed the world in an expanded spectrum of color, and from a greater vantage point that had nothing to do with his towering height. The shadows that had once flitted on the periphery now revealed themselves to her in full relief. The whispers that had once been incomprehensible now chimed clearly in her mind.

It pleased her to know that Jean was the sole creature of his type left in the common world. Once the starting gun had gone off, the race to capture *The Book of the Unwinding* had begun. Now that it had returned to the world, now that the world was ripe for it, *The Lesser Key* had been supplanted. When *The Book of the Unwinding* came into the world, every copy of *The Lesser Key* and every creature conjured with its magic had been made redundant, reduced to ash. Every creature, that was, other than Jean. Jean was now attuned to her magic, and as master of the Book, Astrid's magic endured. He now counted as the last of his kind.

Astrid watched in amusement as Rose danced around the living room of their commandeered house, unable to control her joy at Astrid's homecoming. The old hag, once the most ancient crone in the Chanticleer Coven, had benefited from Celestin's blunder, his inability to control Soulange Simeon and her pathetic daughter. The blood of the sacrificed witches had failed to raise a new body for Astrid, but Rose's own bent, ancient body had been washed in the blood, baptized in it and renewed.

Astrid hadn't evicted Celestin from Jean out of revenge as much as out of necessity. Celestin had failed to provide her with a body to walk in this world, while he had a perfectly serviceable one at his command. And, of course, there was the matter of maintaining discipline. He'd failed her. She couldn't let that go unpunished. What did it matter if Rose benefited from Celestin's failure? Unlike that fool Demagnan, who, believing Astrid's cause lost, had abandoned faith and turned her physical form into a grotesque plaything, Rose remained a good and faithful servant.

Besides, the return of Rose's youth and beauty made her a perfect plant to keep an eye on that swamp witch Evangeline's comings and goings. To think Astrid's scheme hinged on a backwoods strip club owner who didn't have the sense to put her own self-interest first. Astrid hadn't found much to work with in the girl, but she'd begun to break her down. First a taste of agony, next a taste of power. The girl would come around.

Besides, Rose took great pleasure in her new part-time employment, dancing in the witch's strip joint. It was a source of amusement, really, to witness Rose reveling in the attention given to her by the strapping young men who stumbled into the bar. Poor dear had been denied a man's touch for decades. Now Rose was making up for lost time, selecting a different escort, sometimes two, to see her home. She acted almost like the teenager she appeared to be. Astrid would have to keep a close rein on her. At least for as long as she needed Rose. After that, it wouldn't matter what the old, new girl got up to.

Astrid looked away from the whirling Rose, glancing out the window at Celestin's former house. She had taken the house across the street for no other reason than it pleased her to. It amused her to see Fleur and her daughter passing by, unaware of her presence across the way and one floor up. Astrid could see Fleur's light dimming as her magic waned, and the girl was as good as a walking corpse. The second Fleur's magic failed, so would the girl's heart. Imagine. Fleur, of all people, performing one of the great forbidden spells—and getting away with it. But not for much longer. Her crime would be evident to all as soon as the girl fell.

The doorbell rang, and Astrid delighted at the mundane sound.

"I'll get it," Rose said, as if it weren't understood that she would—that this was her role. For now, perhaps it was best to let the fool consider herself above her station.

Astrid held up her hand. "Wait."

Rose paused, her cautious expression betraying her uncertainty. The truth was, Astrid simply wanted to hear the electronic bell chime once more. The common world teemed with simple pleasures she hadn't realized she'd missed—even something as banal as the chime of a lowly doorbell. There was a delay of ten to fifteen seconds before it sounded again. "Now."

Rose gave her a good hard look, as if Astrid was playing a trick on her.

The bell chimed again, though this time the chime struck her as impatient, demanding. The sound, once pleasant, now grated on her. She'd rip the bell out with Babau Jean's bare hands later. Rose seemed to pick up on the change in her mood and scurried downstairs to answer the door before she could grow any more agitated.

Astrid's human ears could never have picked up the words whispered on the threshold by the trio of conspirators, Rose and the two hapless men.

"The mistress isn't happy."

"You promised you'd let me tell her about the Book."

"Do you really think she'll go easier on you if she hears it from your own lips?"

"More likely she'll rip those lips off your face. *Tant pis.* They are such pretty lips."

Nor could her human ears have picked up on the trio's varied footfalls as they passed over parquet to rug and back to parquet. Rose's nimble steps leading the way, the younger man's confident—overconfident—stride. The older man's halting shuffle, the hesitant tread of a man being led to the gallows. Astrid smiled. He believed he'd failed her. He couldn't be more wrong.

The creak of the stairs announced their progress, though the feverish buzzing of their brains served as a far better sentry. They were suspicious of each other, each vying to be her favorite. Such fools. Their eagerness to turn on one another was her greatest tool to control them. She need never worry one of them would betray her, as they were all too busy policing one another, hoping to trip the others up.

Astrid turned her gaze back to the window, taking in the khaki-colored double gallery of the rose Italianate mansion that had once been

Celestin's. A bit to the right of the gallery, hidden by the foliage of a tree, was a room she could still envision in minute detail even though she hadn't been there since she'd last lain with Celestin. The pale green walls, the chandelier that had never been wired for electricity, from which two dozen candles would spill their dancing light, the ridiculous four-poster bed where Celestin had liked to be restrained. Degraded. Strange that the most powerful in this world often crave private humiliation, even though they would spill blood to prevent a public shaming. Celestin had spilled oceans of blood, and still he lay powerless, a prisoner in his own corpse, as his inferiors delighted in choosing his fate. Perhaps she should feel a twinge of sympathy for him, but it was all too delicious. So rare that one got to witness justice in its most poetic form. To the others, she'd attributed his punishment to his failure to provide her with a human form, but in truth his pride had been his undoing. A shred of humility would have saved him this end. The fool should have known a soft, spoiled man such as himself could never rise to become the King of Bones and Ashes, any more than Astrid could become the Queen of Heaven. Vain, pampered Celestin could never have understood a mother's willingness to perpetrate crimes for her child that she'd never commit in her own self-interest.

She would have relished watching his dismemberment firsthand, but passing by Précieux Sang would have been too much of a risk. Magic was failing the witches gathered in the cemetery, but there was no doubt they'd sense the power she'd carried back to the common world. With so many of them gathered in one place, it was quite possible she'd be discovered. Still, she might manage to watch the proceedings through her little birdie's eyes, if Evangeline didn't flit away. Astrid suspected the swamp witch lacked the stomach to watch the butchering for her own edification.

Astrid's three servants entered the room, one on the heels of the other. She was cognizant of the trio's nervous, perspiring presence, but they could wait. Now that she stood at the threshold of reaching a life goal, she wanted to savor this moment. *The Book of the Unwinding* was finally here, and it was hers, despite Celestin's bumbling and Laure and Soulange's cruel interference.

After some minutes had passed, Rose dared to break into her reverie. "Mistress," Rose spoke in a soft voice. "Eli and Michael are here to see you."

"As you commanded." Eli rushed to speak over Rose's words.

Astrid turned to face the three. Rose held back, not wanting to get caught in the crossfire. The witch was much wiser than her newfound giddiness let on. Perhaps the old girl couldn't be faulted. She'd suffered the decrepitude of the flesh, only to find herself returned to her prime. An octogenarian's wisdom and a youth's lust for life poured together into a teenager's body.

Michael stood in the front, his stance wide and comfortable, his arms crossed loosely over his chest. This one believed himself to be irreplaceable. Perhaps, for the moment, he was.

"I . . . ," Eli began, but Astrid held up her hand to silence him.

She turned her focus to Michael. "The Perrault woman?" He wasn't a strong witch, not even by today's degraded standard. But he did have one essential gift. He could get almost anyone, even someone as astute as Fleur, to perceive him as harmless. Fleur could sit across the table from him and see him as an ordinary man. And Lisette, overprotective mother that she seemed to be, had, much to Michael's chagrin and Astrid's amusement, perceived him as a safe and sanitized gay man. Certainly no one who'd have designs on her daughter.

"Her left arm is paralyzed. She's having difficulty forming words. The doctors say she'll recover"—he grinned and rubbed his chin—"though we know better."

We. Was it possible that this foolish child thought he might replace Celestin? Or worse? Did he, like Celestin, fancy himself worthy of becoming the King of Bones and Ashes? Fine. Let him believe either or both. Michael was a useful fool. Lisette Perrault might be the only person left capable of preventing her from prying open the seven gates. "You did well. Your attack was precise, damaging her without killing her." She lifted Babau Jean's long arm and pointed at Michael with the razor-sharp claw of Jean's finger. "Keep her debilitated, but alive. We don't want her power to be passed on to Manon. It would be dreadful if that happened, and then Manon learned the truth about who'd harmed the mother, wouldn't it?"

"I deceived Lisette with ease. How could Manon see what her mother missed?"

Astrid folded her pale hands, the nails of the fingers clicking against each other. She let the tiniest of smiles creep to her lips, exposing the sawtooth edges of her teeth. Michael blanched. There, message received. "For now, you are the devoted soon-to-be husband and son-in-law." She grated her teeth, enjoying the chilling whisking sound they made. "And father, too, I understand. Congratulations.

"Congratulations to you, too, Rose," she said, adding as much warmth as possible to the rasp her voice made as it passed through the otherwise mute Jean's lips. Rose took a tentative step forward, craving the praise, fearing the cut that might follow. "You've become part of the swamp witch's world. You are in the catbird seat to keep an eye on her and those Boudreau miscreants." The arrival of the Boudreau brothers in New Orleans had been an unexpected kink. Astrid had no doubt they'd been sent to kill Evangeline if she exhibited any signs of her mother's ambitious nature. Of course, she wouldn't—and that, it turned out, wasn't a problem. Evangeline's unshakable sense of decency had been nothing but a liability for so long, Astrid wondered at how, in the end, it had proved such an asset. Even more ironic, and convenient, that it had led the region's head assassin not only to spare the girl but to become enamored of her. Farcical, really, but then again, greater men than that Boudreau trash had fallen for the Cajun bar wench.

"Yes, mistress," Rose said. "It's lucrative, too."

"Never too late to lay away a nest egg, dear." She turned her gaze to Eli, his light blue button-down sticking to him, deep circles of sweat under his armpits. "Now, Eli. You were saying?"

"I, I," he stammered. "The Book." He rushed forward and fell on his knees before her. He raised his head, looking up at her through tearing eyes. He was a beautiful man, really. His terror made him all the more attractive.

Astrid reached out with the utmost gentleness, bringing Babau Jean's claws up to his chin, resting them with care beneath it. "Yes," she prompted him. "The Book?"

"I don't have it. I've failed you. The thirteen hearts you left for Fleur to find. They were there. I'm certain. I carried them to Grunch Road myself."

She reached up with her other hand and caressed his hair. "Oh, my dear boy. I believe you. I do."

A glimmer of hope reached his eyes. "The Book never materialized. I looked everywhere while the others were caught up with your . . . the girl." He bit his lower lip, waiting to see, no doubt, if he'd offended her. Astrid knew it bordered on classless, toying with these people who understood so little, but it had been so long since she'd had any fun. She gazed at him through Jean's bottomless black eyes, not responding in any way. "I went back last night, and again this morning. I've turned over every stone."

"Every stone?" she said. Her question was posed in jest, but still it flummoxed him.

"I'll go back. Right now. See if I could've missed anything."

"Not to worry. You missed nothing."

"But there was no book . . ."

Astrid raised a hand to quiet him. She could understand Eli's consternation. He'd been expecting a physical book, a volume of enormous girth and boasting an impressive width of leaf, bound in leather of uncertain, though undoubtedly sinister, origin. Something along the lines of the tome carried to New Orleans centuries ago by the sister witches and their indentured servant Delphine Brodeur. A decoy grimoire of no value that still sat moldering in the attic of the old convent, hidden behind shutters held closed by nails blessed by Pope Benedict himself. Utterly ludicrous, really, but a convincing enough ruse to fool generations of would-be dark messiahs. Oh, the sisters did convey *The Book of the Unwinding* to this eternally decadent city, but only one of them ever came to understand how.

It was Astrid's own fault that she'd allowed herself to trust Laure Marin with her discovery about the Book. But Astrid had been weak and in need of a mother figure's approbation. Foolish girl that she'd been. Astrid should have learned from her own upbringing that some mothers eat their young. Laure's betrayal shouldn't have come as a surprise.

"Tell me, Rose," she said. Rose startled, shocked and worried to have attention fall on her when she was savoring the downfall of another. "When is a book not a book?"

"I'm not sure I—"

"It's just a riddle, Rose. A simple riddle."

"I'm sorry, mistress," she said, shaking her head and clasping her hands together. "I was never clever when it came to the riddles."

She reached out and gave the top of Eli's head a slight tap. "How about you? Would you like to hazard a guess?" Eli stared up at her, his mouth working silently.

"A book," Astrid said, "isn't a book until it's freed from the mind that carries it. *The Book of the Unwinding* is here. Right here with us. We need only free it. Shall we do that, Eli?"

He nodded awkwardly beneath the weight of her claw.

"Good." She caused his limbs to stiffen, fixing him in place, then drove her nail into his scalp, making a quick, thin, spiral slice.

He screamed as blood poured from the gash. The blood rose up into the air, forming lines, then symbols, then spelling out words that none had read since they'd been scratched into the eternal ether by Theodosius's stylus.

"Rose, grab a blade and take over, won't you?" she said, never taking her eyes off the already dissipating warning—the Book could only be read once.

Rose scrambled to the altar and grasped a wicked athame.

"Oh, Eli. Dear, faithful Eli," Astrid called to him over his agonized cries. "You are so honored, so honored. Imagine if Fleur hadn't favored status over your devotion? Your life would have been of no importance. Now you're the bridge that will carry us through the final days of magic."

Rose approached them, but Astrid couldn't bear to look away from the splendor before her eyes. "I have the knife."

"Take your time, dear, and proceed in a spiral to his groin. The thinnest strip of skin you can carve, my dear. Then do the same with his arms and legs. Take each of the strips in a single strand. Don't let them break." She leaned in and placed a kiss on Eli's bloodied forehead, delighting at his salty taste. "He must be unwound." She waved a hand at Michael. "Go on, don't just stand there. Undress the man."

TWENTY-SIX

Lisette had always hated the smell of pumpkin pie, but that was before her stroke. Sitting here at her kitchen table, watching Michael and Manon pull together the makings of their Thanksgiving dinner, it smelled like a bit of heaven. Hell. Maybe she was just glad to be alive to smell it.

Glad to have a pleasant smell to mask the stench of charring flesh her memory had carried back from the dark place. Lisette worried she might not live long enough to forget it.

Manon put the mirlitons on to boil, then gave Michael a quick peck as he prepared to chop up the ham and shrimp that would serve as the squash's stuffing. Her girl looked over at her. "You doing okay there, Mama?" Manon was getting big. Fast. But still no wedding. They were holding off, Manon had told her and Isadore when they'd pressed, holding off until Lisette was better. Until things got back to normal.

Better. Normal.

Lisette seemed to take one step ahead then fall two steps back. She'd only made it home yesterday, after weeks in the nursing facility over in Algiers. Even with the expert care, she hadn't made much progress toward the recovery everyone—except maybe her doctors—kept assuring her she'd make. Now might be as normal as normal would ever get again.

"Ffff . . . Ffff . . ." Lisette tried to answer that she was fine, but this was as far as her mouth could make it. Sometimes she could form the words, sometimes she couldn't. She raised her right hand and waved the two off. She tapped her nose and nodded in approval.

"Smells good, Mrs. Perrault?" Michael asked, beaming at her.

Lisette nodded again, hoping her lips formed the smile she was trying to make.

Michael checked his wristwatch. Not a real wristwatch like folk used to wear, but one of those fancy combination watch, exercise tracker, heart monitor, telephone, and, for all Lisette knew, maybe it even had a built-in microwave oven, too. "Wasn't your dad supposed to be back with your grandfather by now?" His tone contained a measure of concern with a soupçon of contempt. "Don't suppose your granddad . . ."

"No," Lisette surprised even herself with a vehement objection. No. Her father hadn't started drinking again. Her attack had scared him back into sobriety. It was damned near worth it to have him back to the man she'd always known and respected. Wasn't anyone going to tear him down again. Certainly not in her house.

Manon shot Michael a warning glance. "I'm sorry," he said. "I didn't mean to imply . . ." He flushed red. "It's only that . . . Well, Mr. Simeon was hitting it pretty hard there for a while."

"He isn't anymore," Manon said. Her tone announced that any such talk was done, but then she looked over at Lisette. "He isn't, Mama. You can believe that."

I do, Lisette wanted to say, but had to settle for nodding.

Her father had been managing Vèvè for the last few weeks, doing his damnedest to keep the shop's doors open. Remy was taking shifts, too, when he wasn't in class. Manon would have, but she spent most of her time here, helping around the house, and now, it seemed, keeping an eye on Lisette.

Lisette was grateful for her daughter's assistance. Still, she couldn't help but feel a bit guilty. She'd never wanted to be a burden to her children, but hell, here she was. Michael had ended up passing on the Portland job. "We aren't going anywhere till you're back on your feet," he'd told Lisette with a plastic smile. "Not to worry. Another job—a better job—will come along. Maybe closer to home." He acted as if he weren't disappointed, at least when Manon was around, but Lisette could still sense a cloud of resentment emanating from him, like he suspected she might have brought on the stroke herself to keep them in New Orleans.

"Hey, Mama," Manon said in a playful voice. "You remember the Thanksgiving when Remy asked if he could take some food to that homeless guy he'd met in the park? You and Daddy said yes, thinking he'd just take him a plate, but he got his wagon out and took the guy our whole turkey?" She laughed and turned to Michael. "It's true. Twenty minutes before our guests showed up. Mama"—she laughed again, her face so bright, so beautiful—"walked into the kitchen to find the oven door wide open and the turkey gone. A coconut crème pie, too." She pulled a look of mock disapproval. "Though seeing as how it was little Prince Remy, he didn't get into trouble." Manon said that for Michael's benefit. Truth was, Remy hadn't been punished because Lisette and Isadore had realized they should've had their boy invite the man to eat with them. "Mama hurried up and fried a chicken for the guests. We had hot dogs and sweet potatoes." Her expression softened, and she got a wistful, faraway look in her eyes. "You know, Mama, I think that may have been the best Thanksgiving we ever had." Fat tears rolled down her cheeks.

"Ah, sweetie." Michael dropped his knife to the chopping board and approached Manon.

She wiped away her tears, forcing a smile. "Nothing. It's nothing. Just these danged hormones." Lisette knew that was only half true. Manon had been thinking on how close she'd come to not being able to share the holiday this year with her mother. Manon gave Michael a gentle push. "No one said you could stop working."

Michael sighed as he returned to his station. "The life of a sous-chef."

Lisette rubbed her left arm. She still couldn't move the damned thing, even though she often felt prickles of pain in it. She hated not to feel one hundred percent grateful, but she wished she could chase the boy out of her kitchen and spend the day cooking the meal with her daughter. Lisette would have made sure to share the secrets to her recipes, spices, and methods of preparation—the things she never wrote down when she shared the recipes with others. Make sure her dishes could live on even after . . .

Stop it. Lisette felt a fire rise up her spine. This wasn't like her, to be sitting here planning for her own demise. It felt almost as if this lack of hope, this outright morbidity was coming at her from outside herself. She froze. Was a sense of disassociation a sign of a worsening condition? Michael leaned over the counter, grinning at her. She tried to return the smile, but only ended up trembling.

"Speaking of Remy," Michael said, even though they hadn't been, at least not for a beat or two, "where is he? Not over at the Marin girl's, I hope."

Manon gave him a withering look.

"I'm just saying, your grandfather will have a fit if he even suspects it."

"There's no reason he should. Remy isn't there. He went out for a run, that's all."

"Three hours ago," Michael said. His tone fell a hair's width on this side of dubiousness.

"A long run," Manon said, chewing out each word. They stared into each other's eyes. A silent challenge. He shrugged. Lisette didn't get why

Michael would even care. She came close to suspecting him of trying to sow discord, but then again, Lisette had read the boy wrong from the beginning. Manon loved him. She had to place her trust in that.

Lisette knew Manon was covering for her brother, even though Manon herself would be the first to complain that the boy always got away with stuff he shouldn't be doing.

Lisette couldn't pinpoint the moment when she'd had a change of heart, and she certainly couldn't supply a precise reason why, but she found herself hoping that her boy *was* out with Lucy. If her Remy loved Fleur Marin's girl, Lisette was not going to commit the same mistake her own mother had made. The pair might be ecstatic together, or they might end up miserable. Lisette couldn't say, but she knew for damned sure that she wouldn't stand between them.

"We could use his help is all I'm saying. Or someone's help. Shouldn't her aide be here by now?"

Her. Michael had called Lisette "her." Like she wasn't sitting right here, ten feet from him.

"I don't know." Manon didn't seem to pick up on the slight. She grabbed his wrist and checked his fancy watch, even though there was a perfectly good clock on the wall. The same damned clock Manon had been using to tell time since she'd learned how. Manon sighed. "Yes, she's late." She came to the table and picked up her cell. "No message even." She started to dial.

"Holiday," Michael said, and Manon dropped the phone back on the table. "I bet she's blowing us off, so she can be with her family." Manon looked down at her phone, confused as it clattered against the wood. Lisette grasped that Manon hadn't meant to put the phone down, let alone drop it. It almost seemed like she'd been willed to do so.

"She wouldn't leave us in the lurch . . ."

"Why don't you help get your mother ready?"

Lisette tensed. She hated having to let her girl take care of her physical needs. It was a blessing that their insurance had covered a visiting aide. "I'll keep an eye on everything here." His lip curled up. "Maybe a nice sponge bath to help freshen her up." He focused on Lisette. "You'd enjoy that, wouldn't you, Mrs. Perrault?" He spoke to her as if she were a child. Or worse, an addled geriatric. He was piling indignity on top of humiliation.

Outside a dog began barking, howling really, though neither Michael nor Manon seemed to notice. The dog's bark grew a lot louder, like it had jumped their fence and landed beneath the window.

"You don't mind?" Manon said to Michael.

Lisette turned her face to the window. A man stood outside. A bent old man in a worn straw hat. He tapped the window with his cane, and Lisette felt sure her daughter would react, but she went and placed a kiss on the equally oblivious Michael's lips.

"Papa," Lisette spoke the word without difficulty.

Manon tilted her head, listening for signs of her father. "No, Mama, I don't think Daddy is back yet." Michael looked at Manon, raising an eyebrow but keeping silent.

Legba tapped the head of his cane against the glass once more. Lisette turned back toward the sound, though the others didn't. The little old man raised his hand and pointed at Michael.

"I don't mind at all," Michael said, picking up their conversation where they'd left off. "Go on. I got this."

Legba pressed his palm to the glass, then faded away.

TWENTY-SEVEN

Nathalie Boudreau knew better than to open that damned door.

She leaned a bit to the right, so she could peek through the café's window. Alice sat there, her back to the window, a ray of golden light caressing the nape of her slender neck. Nathalie almost cried at the sight.

If she turned around now, she could hold this moment, pure and unspoiled, in her memory. Never let reality reach in and ruin it. Already Nathalie could sense the storm brewing. No way she'd get out of this without losing something.

She'd had a long stretch of losing. From the moment her boss called her into his office to tell her that he and his wife had been praying real hard on things and decided they couldn't employ "her kind" anymore. Even though she'd never missed a shift and had always filled in without warning—and without complaint—whenever someone else called in sick at the last moment. Even though she'd stopped two robberies. Even though she'd taken care of the boss's dog when the same wife who'd prayed her into unemployment had been hospitalized for appendicitis, and again when she'd wanted to vacation two weeks in Hawaii. No pay. Just a box of chocolate-covered macadamias to thank her. A small one that still had the price tag from a dollar store in Kenmore stuck on its back.

"They not open?" a man spoke from behind her.

Nathalie realized she was standing there gaping through the window and blocking the door. "Oh, yeah. Sorry." She stepped aside and let the guy pass. He stopped and held the door open for her. "Thanks." She didn't mean it.

She touched the door like it was going to bite her and closed it behind her with great care. Still, the slight click managed to alert Alice to her arrival. The second Alice looked over at her, the ray of sunlight illuminating her neck disappeared, like someone had flicked a switch. Nathalie felt like someone had flicked a switch in her, too. She felt a smile quiver on her lips, just as sweat broke out on her forehead. Her eyes went wide in a "so happy to see you" set. She caught a glimpse of herself in a mirror on the wall.

She looked like an utter maniac.

She almost gave herself facial whiplash trying to adjust her expression to something near normal, ultimately settling for wiping her brow as she read the placard affixed to the bottom of the mirror's frame: "Our Favorite Customer." She let her eyes drift up to meet their reflection, growing even more embarrassed due to the redness of her face.

"Nathalie." Alice waved her over. "Did you just get here?"

Damn. Nathalie's abilities made it clear to her that Alice was trying to pretend she hadn't witnessed her lumbering clown show. "I . . . I'm sorry," she said. "To keep you waiting," she added, though she was even sorrier for her foolishness.

"Not at all," Alice said, then lowered her eyes.

For a split second Nathalie panicked, thinking she'd strolled in with her blouse unbuttoned or her trousers wide open. A quick pat down assured her all was well. At least on that front.

"I won't keep you long," Alice said, drawing Nathalie's eyes to her own.

"Oh, I got all morning," Nathalie said. "Evangeline's doing a lunch over at Bonnes Nouvelles for her employees and their families at noon." Nathalie turned a chair around and sat, draping her arms over the chairback. "I'm kind of both, you know? Two of my cousins have moved here, and they're working at the club. I didn't even know they were here, but Lincoln—that's my cousin—said he and his little brother Wiley came to town back in early June."

"I've met Wiley—"

"He's great, isn't he?" Nathalie knew it was rude to interrupt Alice, but she couldn't help herself. She could feel the rumbling on the tracks. The train was speeding her way—no room in the tunnel to get off the tracks, so her only hope was to keep running ahead. "Yeah, he and Hugo, your brother . . . well, you know he's your brother, they've really hit it off. Lincoln says he's never seen Wiley this serious about anyone before, and Hugo . . ."

"Hugo's in love." Alice reached over and laid her hand on Nathalie's forearm. "And he wants everyone else to be in love, too."

"Looks like he's gonna get his wish," Nathalie plowed on, even though on the inside she was screaming *Shut up, shut up, shut up!* at herself. "Lincoln and Evangeline. They're shooting sparks all around, too, if you know what I mean." She laughed. Her laugh sounded so, so stupid. "But that. The lunch. It'll be over by two, and the club doesn't open till nine tonight. Oh, that's what I mean about being both. Evangeline has hired me to work the door. Pretty cool, right? Then dinner with your family is at six . . . Fleur invited me, you know that, right? Really nice of her to include me."

"Nathalie," Alice said.

"Don't worry, though. I'm going to go home and put on something nice before—"

"Nathalie." Alice spoke her name, each syllable an emphatic request for silence.

Nathalie fell dumb. Damn. Here comes the engine. Should've known she'd never outrun it.

"It's about Fleur's dinner." Alice looked down at the table. She was searching for a way to let Nathalie down easy. No doubt, she'd prepared a nice speech, but Nathalie's blabbering had derailed her.

"Truth is, I'll end up having to shave it close," Nathalie improvised. "Having to run back home and change again before heading to the club. I'm glad we got to talk this morning, see. I feel terrible canceling at the last minute, but I didn't have a gig when Fleur invited me. I'd hate to do it over the phone. Would you mind taking her my regrets?"

"Regrets," Alice said, then looked up through the tears flooding her eyes. They ran down her cheeks, but she didn't pay them any mind. Nathalie reached out and took Alice's napkin, dabbing at the tears. Alice's hand brushed hers, and Nathalie felt her heart skip. This Alice had little to do with the idealized fantasy Nathalie had conjured. Sure, Nathalie had made a lucky guess about Alice's favorite flavor of ice cream, and Alice did in fact love dogs, but that was about it. It didn't matter though—this Alice was real, and that made her better than any fantasy. Alice was blooming before her eyes, revealing more of her true self to Nathalie with every encounter. And each revelation came as a gift.

Alice took the napkin from Nathalie's grasp. "People have controlled me my whole life." She wiped her eyes and crumpled the napkin, dropping it on the table like she was announcing crying time was done.

She lifted her hand and motioned around the room. "I used to own this place. Though then we called it 'Muddied Waters.' I can't even think what it's called here."

"Hank's," Nathalie volunteered, pointing at the window where the name showed in reverse, then instantly regretted having done so.

"Hank's," Alice said, lost between sadness and amusement. "I owned this place." She fixed Nathalie with her gaze. "For seven years." Nathalie understood the math of Alice's time on the Dreaming Road. In the common world Alice was going on twenty-two, but in terms of Alice's own experience, she was pushing thirty. Nathalie could hear the anger growing in Alice's voice, but then it seemed to fall away as quickly as it had arisen.

Alice glanced around the café. "I'd never been inside this place in the real world, so the interior was different. In fact, the layout was almost reversed." She pointed toward a corner behind Nathalie. "There were stairs over there that led to my apartment." She paused. "Our apartment." Her eyes drifted up little by little, like she was letting them mount the now invisible steps. "I ran the café with my partner, Sabine." She grasped the balled-up napkin, but didn't pick it up. "I let myself pretend that I was free there. Safe. Loved." She shook her head. "But it wasn't real. Any of it. Not the place. Not the time. And certainly not the love. My 'love' was a demon, a dark spirit sucking the light and life out of me."

"You're not the first woman to feel that way about her ex," Nathalie said before she could stop her fool mouth.

Alice looked up at her with wide, surprised eyes, then burst out laughing. She offered Nathalie her hand, and Nathalie damn near flipped her chair reaching out to take it. She grasped Alice's slight hand in her own, wishing to God she'd never have to let go, but knowing all along she was walking out of here alone. This was the moment to enjoy. This was the only guarantee.

"I thank you for helping me," Alice said. "I thank you for putting yourself at risk to save a stranger. My dear Daniel trusted you. He believed in your goodness. That tells me everything I need to know about the person you are." She lowered her light brown eyes. When she looked back up at Nathalie, a sparkle glimmered in her gaze. That sparkle destroyed Nathalie. So did Alice's soft smile. "Maybe there is something to this rightful destiny thing." She pulled her hand back, and Nathalie felt a chasm open between them. "But my free will has been negated just about every day of my life. I'm not going to be compelled into a relationship by any force."

"Not even love?" Nathalie put her hand on the table, palm up. Hoping, just hoping, Alice would once again rest her hand there.

Alice's smile held, but it hardened. "Especially not love. Not today. Maybe tomorrow, but not today." She clasped her hands together and stared down at them. "I can't think about destiny when my life has been hijacked." A dry chuckle. "At least twice. Maybe we will be each other's happy ending. I don't know. Right now, I don't even know who I am. I need time to figure out the woman I want to be and to start working on her."

Nathalie moved her hand, placing it alongside, but not touching, Alice's. "You've got it."

Alice rewarded her with a look of gratitude. Maybe this was it, a single genuine moment with all their cards laid out between them. Maybe this look was all of Alice Nathalie would ever have. If so, it would be enough. "You'll give Fleur my apologies?"

Alice nodded. "Of course."

Nathalie rose and rapped her knuckles against the tabletop. "You have a happy Thanksgiving, okay?" She turned and made her way to the door.

"Nathalie." Alice's voice stopped her cold.

She looked back. The ray of sunlight had returned, bathing Alice in a golden glow. That moment erased any doubt. Nathalie would wait till the end of time for this woman. "Yes," Nathalie said, struggling not to sound flustered.

Alice rose and drew near. "When you see Evangeline, will you tell her she should come pick up her cat? I know she feels bad about taking Sugar from me, but I'm not her home. Evangeline is."

"Sure," Nathalie said with a quick nod. She grasped the door handle before stopping again. She pulled her phone from her pocket and tapped the screen, opening the driver's app. "Hey, if you ever need a ride . . ." She closed the app. "No need to use this, actually." She slipped it back into her pocket. "I'll just know."

Alice shook her head. But by God, she was smiling. And that was a win.

EPILOGUE

No Hugo. No Alice. The scent of that man, the one who discomforts, everywhere Sugar went in this house. *Nicholas.* A low growl as his image shimmered. Flashes. This house. Almost memories of the time before.

She could not remember the man in the time before, but she remembered disliking him.

Tap. Tap. Tapping.

Every window scouted. No birds. No filthy squirrels.

She padded up the stairs. Stiff. Not easy. But necessary.

A voice tingled in her ears. She shook her head to shake it out. She felt pain. Not hers. Another's.

Man not man, smells of thunder, old crimes forgiven but cataloged. Not gone. Not yet. Trapped between. *Between* meaning not clear.

She waited on the step. Not to rest. To listen.

Tap. Tap. Tap. More need. Less loud. Weaker.

Gain the landing. Find the sound.

Door ajar. Scent of Alice. Silence. Door open. Hugo. No *tap.*

Door closed. She paused, sniffing along the crack at the bottom. Familiar. Faded. Nothing.

Light at the end. An open door.

More steps.

She hissed at the hateful stairs, but began to climb. The tap was now a scratching, almost too quiet for even her superior hearing to pinpoint. Still, she persisted.

Upward. The final step. A room above. Beautiful, musty-scented treasures.

Scratch. Scratch. Scratch. She followed the sound to a silver window shining inward. Not a good window. The kind that fascinated humans. She bumped her nose against a crack in the glass. Through the crack, Man not man.

No link. No anchor.

He made no sense.

She patted the glass, but unlike before, it did not open to let her pass. A beam of light, not gold, not warm, shot through the crack. She turned to discover its path.

A box on top of boxes. On top of many boxes.

Inside the box.

She understood. She scanned for a path to reach it. In the time before, she could have pounced without effort. Now she would have to climb. A trunk first. She jumped and paused. A second leap. Her goal just above. She went up on her hind legs and placed her front paws against it, readying herself. The box shifted, falling forward, breaking open.

Sugar spun. Tried to catch herself. Slipped.

Thump.

She rose and stretched, left front paw forward, right leg back. *Hateful boxes. Hateful stairs. Hateful time.*

Another scratch. The beam of light shifted to land on a sheet of paper. Sugar padded over to examine it. Below human marks, the nonsense lines they cut.

Above the nonsense, three figures, though not true. Recognizable not from appearance, but from intent. Alice. Simple. Small as she was.

In the time before. Sugar herself. A poor representation of her true beauty. And Man not man. Sugar purred in amusement at his awkward, oafish image.

A rap on the glass. Loud. Annoyed. Impatient.

Sugar clawed at the paper's edge until it curled up. She bit into the page and lifted it. She raised her head high, so the sheet wouldn't trip her, and slunk toward the silver window. The crack in the window widened. Cold white light spilled through, blinding her. She squinted and, clamping her jaw down tight on the page, bounded over the edge.

ACKNOWLEDGMENTS

The mad dream of The Witches of New Orleans continues. I'd like to thank Jason Kirk at 47North for giving me the freedom to march boldly into places where many editors would fear to tread. I'd also like to thank Angela Polidoro for, as usual, making me look much better than I am, and my beta readers, Pat Allen Werths and Evelyn Phillips.

A heartfelt thank-you to all those who resist and persist for helping resuscitate my faith in humanity.

Finally, I'd like to thank my loves, Rich Weissman, who continues to be the world's most understanding spouse, our daughters, Becky and Maddy, both of whom will have graduated law school by the time this comes out, and Kirby Seamus, the rescue Chihuahua who, in a very dark moment, brought a ray of light into my life.

ABOUT THE AUTHOR

Photo © 2017 Mark Davidson

J.D. Horn is the *Wall Street Journal* bestselling author of the Witching Savannah series, as well as the first book in the Witches of New Orleans trilogy, *The King of Bones and Ashes*. A world traveler and student of French and Russian literature, Horn also has an MBA in international business and formerly held a career as a financial analyst before turning his talent to crafting chilling stories and unforgettable characters. His novels have received global attention and have been translated into more than half a dozen languages. Originally from Tennessee, he currently lives in California with his spouse, Rich. Visit www.JDHornAuthor.com.